AGASHA:

MASTER OF WISDOM

AGASHA:
MASTER OF WISDOM

His Philosophy and Teachings

By
WILLIAM EISEN

Foreword by James Crenshaw

Teachings Received through the Instrumentality of
Reverend Richard Zenor, Trance Intermediary

DeVORSS & COMPANY
P.O. Box 550, Marina del Rey, Ca. 90291

Agasha: Master of Wisdom

ISBN: 0-87516-241-X
Library of Congress Catalog Card Number: 77-85423
Second Printing, 2001

DeVorss & Company, Publisher
P.O. Box 550
Marina del Rey, CA 90294-0550

w w w . d e v o r s s . c o m

Printed in The United States of America

This book is respectfully dedicated to all of the Teachers of the Agashan Organization and especially that Illumined One known to the author as Rhebaumaus Tate, without whose assistance this work could never have been written.

Appreciation is also extended to Manzaholla, and to his disciple Walter Anderson who is now in spirit, for leaving us with much of the material that we have incorporated in Chapter One of this work.

TABLE OF CONTENTS

FOREWORD

By James Crenshaw[1]

ONE OF THE stumbling blocks to an understanding or acceptance of the concept of life beyond the earthly plane of existence has been the constant reference in mediumistic communications to realms of substance and form in a non-subjective reality. What do the supposed communicators mean when they talk about places and things, buildings, homes, gardens, animals—all sorts of *things*—in their dimensions? Is it only a kind of mystical imagery? Or is everything, everywhere, including the earth world, only imagery?

Whole books with descriptions of living people engaging in real activities in objective environments have been "dictated" by personalities who represent themselves as existing in the so-called afterlife planes. They persist in claiming *things*—the whole panorama of after-death existence—are as solid and real to them as our world is to us.

Faced with such seemingly nonsensical representations, the average sophisticate and even the average person both tend to recoil. The abode of the "dead" is regarded, if anything, as a misty never-never land in which the shades of those presumably dead either flutter around aimlessly (except when they choose to haunt a desolate farmhouse or murder scene) or gravitate to a wonder-filled "glory" kingdom that becomes their heritage forever by reason of past virtues.

It is clear then that the obstacle of an apparent physical reality in the afterlife must first be overcome if we are to comprehend, with any feeling of integrity, books of the type mentioned. The same likewise applies to the present book for which this is a foreword. Otherwise, there will be an overwhelming urge to dismiss the whole idea of a post-mortem existence as so much myth and fantasy.

The late Dr. Gustaf Strömberg, for many years a noted astronomer on the staff of the Mt. Wilson Observatory in California, sought to solve the dilemma by positing a system of non-physical structures, a scientifically comprehensible archetypal pattern, behind all biological and inanimate matter. Both in his book, *The Soul of the Universe*,[2] and in a foreword to my own book, *Telephone Between Worlds*,[3] he contended there was enough scientific evidence in support of the theory to conclude that the non-physical structures remain intact after biological death. Memories therefore persist, he theorized, and the soul or carrier of these memories is immortal.

After taking this giant metaphysical leap into the unknown (though he was primarily a physicist), he was able to conclude in the conservatively written foreword to my book:

"It is clear that, if souls survive at death without any loss of memory and if our mind is able to communicate with a non-physical world in which it is rooted, it should, at least in principle, be possible to contact the minds of departed persons."

Yet Dr. Strömberg seemed unable to go as far as the communicators themselves who would describe a kind of supra-physical or quasi-physical world of people, places and things. I remember joining with him and author-philosopher Aldous Huxley in a three-way discussion of the subject during a Los Angeles radio broadcast many years ago. But neither Dr. Strömberg nor Huxley could seem to fit their own notions of continuing consciousness into a concept of life, form and tangible activity in a mental or non-physical world.

In the above-mentioned book, I tried to put across the concept of the "reality" of these non-physical worlds, along with some of the other basic principles of life, the afterlife and rebirth, as taught by those speaking through the channelship of Richard Zenor who, incidentally, was also the subject of my own book.

These points were stressed because then as well as now, the purported messages from those who had "gone on" continued to insist that progress in the supernal realms had its definite physical aspects—not, however, without a point of termination. When the cycles of physical experience here and hereafter were thoroughly explored, the communicators said the progressing soul would then be emancipated and graduated into a domain of such vastness and splendor that no measure of form could be ascribed to it. Agasha calls this domain the "Consciousness of Immensity" and refers to some of the great spiritual beings to be found in the far reaches of its cosmic vastness as "Pillars of Light."

The communicators through Richard Zenor, as through many another psychic "instrument," are quite explicit about the reality of form in the afterlife. The word itself—afterlife—turns out to be a misnomer, for the constant emphasis is upon teaching that there is neither a *before* nor an *after* life; rather, life is continuous—cyclic, to be sure, and with combinations and permutations of an incredible variety—but never terminal. Therefore, life was and is eternal, they say, within the inconceivable, all-embracing Oneness we call God.

But if, as Dr. Strömberg conceived it, the earthly world is supported by a non-physical matrix, then what are the communicators talking about when they describe their active, often busy form-filled lives? How can you have a tree or a flower or a physical body in a non-physical world? The answer appeared to be at the time: you can't.

Or how, for example, could they speak of "spiritual architecture" (a term I have heard) or schools, colleges and libraries, music and concerts, unless there were the equivalent? In fact, they would often speak of entire communities in an order of ascending planes—"etheric" levels where people live according to the development of their consciousness and awareness. But how could these communities exist without a suitable atomic structure?

Therefore, unless these questions were answered, the obstacle to understanding would remain.

The issues were brought up and discussed many times by the communicators during the earlier years of the Zenor classes, and perhaps it would be in order to now share with the reader how these questions came to be eventually resolved. But it did not happen overnight. The gradual explanation went through almost an evolutionary process with each succeeding year bringing it more and more into focus.

In the beginning, it is only fair to say that many minds, especially those that were steeped in the mechanics of the material world, were quite naturally turned off by the very materialism, incomprehensible on its face, of the picture presented by these putative souls of the dead. But the basic answers to the questions, as they developed, were relatively simple, with complications arising only as to details such as the nature of time, or the effect of mind on substance in our own and the other worlds. The truth is, the communicators made plain, you don't drop the physical aspects of life simply because you drop the body.

For the time being then, you keep a body—in fact, a series of bodies, both subtle and solid, according to the "vibration" to which you are drawn in the after-earth worlds.

The word *vibration* is the key. It is a word repeatedly used by clairvoyants and trance communicators in referring to conditions, places and things, even people, in earthly or other environments. One could be said to live in a "vibration" or an occurrence might be described as a "vibration."

"Everything is vibration," the communicators would emphasize. They would also say: "Everything is a manifestation of consciousness for everything *is* consciousness." In the realms of personal experience then, it can be construed that consciousness manifests itself as vibration.

"The only difference between you and us is that we *go* at a faster rate than you do," they would often explain; except that the explanation did not seem to be too clear until it was translated into: "The only difference is that we vibrate at a faster rate than you do."

It was also not unusual for the communicators to compare the varying rates of vibration to a fan or a wheel. Then as the fan or the wheel rotates faster and faster, the blades or the spokes become invisible to the observer, and are only perceptible to one more finely attuned to the higher rates of vibration.

Then as these earlier classes progressed, some of the communicators began to use a few of the terminologies of electronics. It seems that the reason we were unable to perceive the forms and "vibrations" of what had erroneously been thought to be strictly non-physical realms, was that these were vibrating at higher *frequency* levels. Thus the wave nature of all creation then made it possible to visualize a model in which there were planes, levels and degrees of frequencies suitable to not only the mental, but also the bodily states in which individuals found themselves.

Therefore, it turned out that the communicators were talking about a kind of sublimated matter—a sublimated substance, if you will. Actually, however, they were careful to insist that the material substance in the ascending planes was *precisely* the same as that which constitutes the earth level, the only difference being the vibrational patterns or ranges of frequency.

So we found in these early classes that terms such as "astral body," "etheric body" and "astral plane" began to take on acceptable meanings—meanings vitally necessary for a proper understanding of the nature of communication between the world of matter and mechanics and other worlds where life appears to go on with a credible continuity.

As it was said in *Telephone Between Worlds*:

"All matter, in essence, is a complex of wave patterns; and these strata or layers of vibrational grouping surround the lowest level, the earth plane, in a rising order of increased frequencies." It could be said then that forms and bodies gravitate to the "plane" or "degree" appropriate to the state of consciousness that prevails. The individual personality is therefore drawn to the appropriate level by what is called the "law of attraction," this law being a basic fundamental in the teachings of Agasha and the others associated with him.

Of course, there is much more to it than this somewhat simplistic statement of principle; the Zenor teachers have also attempted to explain the mystery in terms of atomic physics. Not only are there the "worlds within worlds" which constitute the environments of developing and creative consciousness, but the very building blocks of matter itself are made up of these ascending orders of vibration—wave patterns which in the ultimate sense are expressions of consciousness.

The teacher Agasha (he always pronounces it: a-guy-sha, with emphasis on the second syllable) uses the word *anim*. Just as the physical body has a replica or matrix called the *astral* or *etheric* body (as well as replicas in the higher frequencies), so too does the atom itself. Normally it is undetected by ordinary laboratory instruments, but Agasha says each atom has its counterpart or complex of counterparts—namely, the *anim*.

The *anim* might be called the "ghost" of the atom, except that "ghost" somehow implies a kind of non-substantial entity inconsistent with the idea of degrees of tangible vibration or frequency patterns. The etheric worlds, as described by Agasha, are made up of the attenuated residue of atoms—anims as he calls them—with vibrational levels or planes equivalent to the environments of which they are a part. These are the sublimated degrees of "spiritual matter" that are perceptible only to those who have become attuned to the appropriate frequencies.

Just as the frequency range of a radio or television broadcast is limited, so too are the various levels and degrees of this "spiritual matter." The distinction between the various kinds of matter thus becomes one of degree, a word the communicators themselves so often use, rather than kind: a quantitative rather than a qualitative difference.

With this in mind, it becomes apparent that Dr. Strömberg's tentative acceptance of possible communication between the here-and-now world and the various degrees of the hereafter is comprehensible. The non-physical structure is not, strictly speaking, without physical attributes after all. All that remained to complete this theory of communication was a plausible identification of an "instrument"—or, as the electronics experts would say, a *transducer*—to convert the frequencies transmitted from the so-called "higher" planes into the lower frequencies consistent with the levels of the earth plane.

Therefore, it is not merely as a metaphor that the communicators speak of mediums like Richard Zenor as "instruments," or in other words, biological transducers capable of relaying and translating the etheric wave patterns so that we may perceive them. Exactly how human sensitives accomplish this, either voluntarily or involuntarily, is both a matter of mechanics and consciousness, but the evidence that the instrument works can be obtained by observation and recordation.

So much for the mechanics of spiritual communication and the interrelationship between these worlds of consciousness. Some of the evidence was described in my book, along with my newsman's report of other transmissions through the instrument named Richard Zenor. I sometimes refer to this as the *who, what, when, where* and *why* of life in the other worlds. However, it was quite beyond the capacity of the present writer to do other than bring into focus a sampling of the broad sweep of the transmitted material.

The greater task, therefore, was taken over by a few very dedicated workers who started transcribing this material, word for word, directly from the tapes of the Agashan classes. One of these individuals was William Eisen, the author of this present work. He became convinced that the accumulation of the material not only should be compiled, but that it should also be edited and correlated into systematic classifications. But the sheer magnitude of the material that has been given over the years is enormous; and this volume, I understand, represents only the first of three books which when complete will be an in-depth study of the entire Agashan material in total.

Consequently, he saw his task as one of up-dating this ancient knowledge and wisdom in order that it might be understandable for the modern reader. But his intention, however, was not to promote a new philosophy, much less a theology, or to elevate any guide or guru to the rank of demi-god (as has happened so often to philosophers and teachers in the past) but to present the Agashan teachings with a coherence and accuracy relevant to modern times.

The tremendous amount of labor required to accomplish this goal is obvious. Years of concentrated effort have been required. The result as reflected herein will lead, I am sure, to a rewarding experience for any reader who truly seeks some answers to the absorbing and puzzling questions: *Who* are we? *What* are we doing here? *Where* are we going when we leave here? *When*, if ever, will we return? And *why* does it all seem so difficult at times?

James Crenshaw
Los Angeles, Calif.
December 5, 1976

NOTES FOR FOREWORD

1. James Crenshaw is a well-known Los Angeles newspaper reporter and free-lance writer with more than 40 years experience. He has been a member of the staffs of daily newspapers in both San Diego and Los Angeles, where he became a specialist in court cases. This training then enabled him to apply the "rules of evidence" when he gathered his facts for his first book, *Telephone Between Worlds*, which is considered by some to be a minor classic in metaphysical literature. This work has also received considerable acclaim in Japan since being published there in the Japanese language. Being married to still another well-known medium, Brenda Rowland Crenshaw, Mr. Crenshaw has become somewhat of an authority on psychic subjects, and he is a regular contributor to magazines and periodicals such as *Fate, National Enquirer*, and others.
2. Gustaf Strömberg, *The Soul of the Universe* (Philadelphia, David McKay Co., 1940)
3. James Crenshaw, *Telephone Between Worlds* (Los Angeles, DeVorss & Co., 1950)

NOTES FOR INTRODUCTION

1. Mark Probert, *The Magic Bag* (San Diego, The Inner Circle Kethra E'Da Fdn., 1963, c/o Borderland Sciences Research Fdn., Vista, Calif.)
2. Jane Roberts, *Seth Speaks* (New Jersey, Prentice-Hall, Inc., 1972) p. 45, 46
3. Hal Lindsey, *The Late Great Planet Earth* (New York, Bantam Books, 1973)
4. Édouard Schuré, *The Great Initiates* (Blauvelt, N.Y., Steinerbooks, 1961, 1976)
5. Ibid.

INTRODUCTION

At the end of every age must come the clarification of all that had been misinterpreted before. This is the law. Otherwise man, in his unfoldment, would never be able to extricate himself from the net of illusion and false teaching that had heretofore held him in bondage. And we see signs indeed that we are now at the end of the age. They are all around and about us. Some of these signs showing us that we are now in the "latter days" are the vast amount of New Age teachings that are currently being expounded through the lips and writings of philosophers, mediums, psychics, and thinkers. And the young are refusing to accept the outmoded religious concepts of their elders and are beginning to study occultism and the hidden mysteries of life at a tremendously increased pace. Even Science is now embarking deep within the realms of the unknown in its constant search to discover the laws that govern time and space. Yes indeed, the walls of materialism are coming tumbling down—and fast!

But occultism is on the increase, and mediumship is as old as life itself. Ever since the beginning of time man has used his extrasensory powers to communicate with those in a higher consciousness, and it is not the purpose of this volume to either prove or disprove this statement. There are many other books going into the subject at great length, and so for all practical purposes this present volume is based upon the premise that communication with discarnate entities in the spirit realms is a well established fact. We are especially in reference to trance mediumship. This type of mediumship enables a discarnate entity to control the vocal cords of another individual who is in a deep state of trance (completely unconscious and in a deep sleep) and thus speak unto those present in much the same way that you would use your telephone.

Now if a medium is able to raise his rate of vibration to a sufficiently high state whereby those in the higher realms of spirit expression are able to take control—and I do not mean communicating with Father, Mother, Sister, or Brother in the astral world—the communications thus received can sometimes be quite profound. This present volume is a report on just that. It is basically a report on the information received through the channelship of an extremely sensitive and well-known medium in Los Angeles, the Reverend Richard Zenor of the Agasha Temple of Wisdom. But it is not limited entirely to this particular channel. Occasionally, we will refer from time to time to information obtained through other sources, but this is done only to substantiate and verify the information received through the Zenor mediumship. For if there is any one thing that becomes apparent above all others to the student of the occult, it is that the teachings now being taught through the higher channels of the earth plane are basically the same. True, there may be minor differences, but the higher, more profound teachings only restate in our modern language and reestablish that which has always been known as the Ancient Wisdom.

For instance: a student of Theosophy, the Rosicrucians, or any of the other modern Mystery Schools cannot really argue with the basic tenets of the philosophy expressed through another famous medium, Mark Probert in San Diego. Through this channel, a group of teachers identifying themselves as members of the Inner Circle gave (up until 1969 at the death of Mr. Probert) some truly remarkable discourses. One that comes to mind is given by the control, Lao-Tse, in the Introduction to a book written by Probert, *The Magic Bag.*[1] This is the same Lao-Tse who is accredited with founding Taoism in China in the sixth century B.C., incidentally.

"The Magic Bag—what do we mean by this?" he begins. "What is the 'bag'? The bag is *consciousness*—and in this bag is *all.* Now, a bag appears to have two sides, an inner and an outer, but it does not really. For if there were an *actual* outer and inner, the bag could not be turned inside out because there would be no interrelationship between them, which means they would be two separate things. When we enter into the physical-chemical world, we are turning the bag inside out; and when we return to other states of consciousness apart from the physical, we are turning it back again. However the belief of going in and out of consciousness is but *maya,* illusion, for in truth we *are* the bag and all that is in it!"

Other quite profound discourses have been given by the teacher Seth through the mediumship of Jane Roberts in New York. His statements on reincarnation, clairvoyance, and the universe beyond the five senses are sometimes mind boggling because of the tremendous new concepts expressed, but nevertheless they are still compatible with other New Age teachings. For instance, in a volume dictated by Seth himself, titled *Seth Speaks,*[2] Seth discusses the influence of mind over matter.

"Your scientists are finally learning what philosophers have known for centuries—that mind can influence matter," he starts out. But then he finishes that statement with rather a profound thought: "They still have to discover the fact that mind *creates* and forms matter.

"Now your closest environment, physically speaking, is your body. It is not like some manikin-shape in which you are imprisoned, that exists apart from you like a casing. Your body is not beautiful or ugly, healthy or deformed, swift or slow simply because this is the kind of body that was thrust upon you indiscriminately at birth. Instead your physical form, your corporeal personal environment, is the physical materialization of your own thoughts, emotions, and interpretations.

"Quite literally," he continues, "the 'inner self' forms the body by magically transforming thoughts and emotions into physical counterparts. You *grow* the body. Its condition perfectly mirrors your subjective state at any given time. Using atoms and molecules, you build your body, forming basic elements into a form that you call your own."

These two illustrations, taken at random from two very different sources, illustrate quite vividly that the bringing forth of New Age wisdom or philosophy is not limited or unique to any one particular channel on the earth plane today. Indeed Agasha, that great Master of Wisdom whose teachings are the subject of this present work, has stated over and over again that no one, absolutely no one, has a monopoly on truth. But at the end of every age there still must come that clarification. Therefore he has come to clarify and rectify many of the misconceptions embraced by the average individual of today so that the golden thread of truth may weave back and forth and eventually sew all philosophies into the grand philosophy of the Oneness.

Agasha states that many of the students of the mysteries are today being inspired by the soul. This is the time when the correct information relative to life is now coming to the surface, and much that was hidden before is today being brought out into the sunlight of understanding. This is so because many seekers of truth are now experiencing what Agasha terms the "soul awakening." In fact, this is the fundamental and basic reason that he has returned here in the 20th century. Aside from explaining the simple A, B, C's of life, Agasha has also returned to introduce you, the reader, to your Higher Self and to awaken mankind to that which it already knows. Once you are introduced to your Higher Self you will have that soul awakening, for he says that you are in truth infinitely intelligent.

There is an inscription on the walls of the Temple of Delphi, and it reads: "Man, know thyself—and then thou wilt know the Universe and the Gods." This saying, more than any other, reflects the basic tenets of the philosophy set forth within this present volume. It has been said over and over again in the Agashan classes, "You are your own Avatar, and the knowledge of this truth will set you free." And in reality, the Second Coming of the true Jesus occurs when you have discovered Him living in you—in your own soul. But this subject will be covered at length in a later chapter.

Now this is not to imply that the historical Jesus of Nazareth will not also manifest to many souls here in the "latter days" of our present cycle. In truth, He has never really been away, as this great Adept has remained on the inner planes working within the hierarchy of the planet and assisting mankind down through the years. And here again is a misconception embraced by millions of orthodox Christians that fairly cries out for clarification and understanding relative to His return and the Apocalypse in general.

On the one hand, the Fundamentalists are vividly portraying the imminent beginning of a seven-year tribulation period whereby millions of "true Christians" will vanish suddenly as they are taken up into Heaven in a disappearing act called the "Rapture" and which is followed in turn by the appearance of the Antichrist and his aid, the False Prophet. Then after this seven-year period of holocaust, the final Battle of Armageddon will bring about the actual physical Second Coming of Jesus the Christ, and this will all then be followed by the Millennium. This is roughly the script of this forthcoming drama as believed by millions of souls throughout the world today, a point in fact being such books as Hal Lindsey's *The Late Great Planet Earth*[3] and others which portray more or less a literal interpretation of Biblical Scripture. This book alone has become immensely popular and has now sold over 10 million copies.

But on the other hand, the bulk of Christianity avoids

obsession with these subjects. They allude simply to the New Testament verses which indicate that Jesus will return "like a thief in the night"—unexpectedly—and that no one will know beforehand the exact hour or day. Thus we have a great discrepancy between the Fundamentalists and the vast bulk of orthodox Christianity. Where is the truth in all of this? Agasha tells us that in one sense they both are true, although they must be taken more symbolically than literally.

Therefore we need a clarification and this present volume is an attempt to do just that. The teachers manifesting in the Agashan classes state that it never was the intention of the original Scriptures to imply that the historical Jesus of Nazareth would make a final *physical* reappearance in the latter days. For that great Adept arose and had his ascendency at that time, and now he has no need for further physical embodiments. But he most certainly has fulfilled his promise to return *spiritually* by manifesting many times through the great channels of the earth plane and communicating through the means of mediumship.

In fact, he has spoken to the Agashan class on a number of occasions, and he has discussed quite frankly and openly incidents that occurred during his last physical incarnation as Jesus of Nazareth in Palestine. Today, he is known as Kraio. His voice is soft, and low, and filled with great love and compassion as he tells many stories about his life, his birth, and the mission he had to perform. Those who have had the privilege of hearing him speak through the Zenor mediumship have stated time and again that the quality of the voice itself seems to offer the greatest proof of its validity. It just seems to be the way it ought to be.

Why should the return of this Master Teacher be so unusual here in these latter days? Kraio is only one of the many Master Teachers who have selected this particular instrument as a means for their manifestation in what Agasha calls "The Grand Finale" of the present cycle or age. These are the days when the Masters make themselves known unto mankind once more. These are the days when the clarification of the many misstatements made by mankind in the past must come to the surface. It is the law, and they are only fulfilling the law.

But this clarification does not only relate to Christianity; no, not by any means. It is the Universal Religion that has been taught by all of the great Masters of the past in all of the great religions that needs to be clarified. But this Universal Religion is nothing more than that which has always been known as the Ancient Wisdom. It has been taught in all of the great Mystery Schools of the past, and it shall be taught in all of the great Mystery Schools of the future for it is forever and always—One.

Édouard Schuré, the 19th century French historian and philosopher, makes this doubly clear in the Introduction to the first edition in 1889 of his classic work, *The Great Initiates.*[4] He chose as his motto the following quotation from Claude Bernard: "I am convinced that the day will come when psychologists, poets, and philosophers will speak the same language, and will understand one another." And this is precisely what Schuré went on to prove insofar as the leaders of the various religions of mankind are concerned. In this volume he traces the lives of Rama, and the Aryan Cycle; Krishna, and India and Brahmanic Initiation; Hermes, and the Mysteries of Egypt; Moses, and the Mission of Israel; Orpheus, and the Mysteries of Dionysus; Pythagoras, and the Mysteries of Delphi; Plato, and the Mysteries of Eleusis; and lastly Jesus, and the Mission of Christ.

This work which covers the lives of eight famous Initiates also tends to indicate that we are now in the clarification period because of the book's tremendous popularity even today. Since its first publication in Paris in 1889, it has gone through 220 new editions, and it is estimated that it has been read by somewhere between three and four million people. But the reason that we have this continued interest today is that it is still another one of the great clarifying factors in our present Grand Finale.

"All religions, in the final analysis, are as one," Agasha

explains, "and each great teacher had to bring forth that particular aspect of truth that was necessary according to the state of consciousness of the people of the period. Yet they all come together in the Grand Finale."

This inner truth that binds all religions together was burned forever into Schuré's consciousness one day when he was in the Uffizi library at Florence, and the psychic experience that came upon him at that time is well worth repeating here because it emphasizes that which Agasha has been trying to explain for these many, many years. Schuré had been asking himself, "What is mankind's origin? What is humanity's destination? From what abyss has humanity escaped, only to plunge into what annihilation, or into what Eternity? What relation does mankind bear to the cosmic powers working behind the apparent chaos of the universe, in order to produce so marvelous a harmony?"

Are not these the same questions that you and I are asking today? Of course they are. And to answer them is precisely why Agasha has returned in the 20th century, and the purpose for this present work. In one sense, Agasha could rightfully be called the first great Initiate inasmuch as having lived approximately 5000 B.C., he predates the eight Initiates that Schuré refers to.

But be that as it may, Schuré then went on to try to reconstruct a living chain of the various religions and thus restore to Hellenism and Christianity their original unity. In this effort he did a magnificent job, but only because of a psychic experience that was not only to answer his questions, but was also to change his destiny for the rest of his life and give him proof, once and for all, of the Oneness of all religions.

In his own words, he says, "At that instant, as in a flash I saw the light that flows from one mighty founder of religion to another, from the Himalayas to the plateau of Iran, from Sinai to Tabor, from the crypts of Egypt to the sanctuary of Eleusis. Those great prophets, those powerful figures whom we call Rama, Krishna, Hermes, Moses, Orpheus, Pythagoras, Plato, and Jesus, appeared before me in a homogeneous group. How diverse in form, appearance, and color! Nevertheless, through them all moved the impulse of the eternal Word. To be in harmony with them is to hear the Word which was in the Beginning. It is to know and experience the continuity of inspiration in history as an historical fact."[5]

Now this psychic experience of Schuré's is not a unique experience. No indeed. It has been experienced by all of the great Initiates since the beginning of time itself, and even the student of today who has had the privilege of seeing the great All-Seeing Eye of God loom before him while in a state of meditation must at least be vaguely aware of this great truth. For the symbol is always the same in much the same manner that the Word of God, although diverse in its many and varied aspects, is likewise always the same.

"Basically, truth is very simple," Agasha tells us, "for it all stems from the Oneness." And perhaps this can best be expressed by restating that which all of the Initiates both before and after him have so taught: "Evolution is the law of Life, Number is the law of the Universe, and Unity is the law of God. Therefore, in Unity all things and all truth will be as One and speak as one voice."

But, unfortunately, it has also been pointed out in the Agashan classes that the vast bulk of humanity never has and never shall embrace that which could be termed to be a "Universal Religion." Why is this? We must remember that the higher understanding of life only comes to an individual after many lifetimes of seeking, striving, and personal unfoldment. All are not on the same rung of the ladder towards spiritual attainment, so to speak. Therefore, each individual must out of necessity embrace only those facets of truth which he is capable of understanding. A child, for example, is not in a position to understand the higher calculus, but this is not to imply that in time he will not embrace it completely. To the contrary, he may even surpass the teacher! Such is the way of life.

Yet the Agashan teachers state that an advanced intellect

is not a necessary prerequisite towards understanding the simple A, B, C's of life and what life is all about. For that reason Agasha's teachings are basically simple, and he uses words and phraseologies so devised that even a child can understand concepts that sometimes are quite abstruse. In other words, he takes your hand and guides you into a philosophy of life so profound and so beautiful, that if it were not true, you would want to believe it anyway.

It is well to remember that the open release of the higher esoteric teachings to the public at large has not always been the case. It is only now that we are in the final days of the Piscean age and the opening days of the new age of Aquarius, that this becomes possible. And the Aquarian age is the age of Man. Prior to this time it was only the advanced disciples of the ancient Mystery Schools that were taught the esoteric or inner teachings. The public at large was given the exoteric or outer teachings because that was all it was ready for at the time. And it is more or less these exoteric or outer teachings, unfortunately, which the average student of religion embraces today.

One of the reasons for this is that much of the inner teachings were only given orally and never set down by the written word lest they fall into the hands of the profane. Another reason is that the general karma (the law of cause and effect) of mankind forced him to remain in ignorance down through the years until certain lessons were learned and obstacles overcome. But today there is no longer any need for secrecy. The doors of the Temple are open wide to all those who would seek entry and who desire to embark upon the path of initiation which ultimately can only lead to illumination or perhaps adeptship. And the Temple that we speak of is the Temple of your own Being.

This present volume then could act as a stimulus towards unlocking the doors of memory to the things that you, the reader, already know. Why do we say this? We can make that statement because we are only repeating Agasha when we state that in truth you are infinitely intelligent. You are also more than likely the return of an Atlantean. Therefore many seemingly ordinary people who have returned here in the 20th century—and please include yourself here also—are in reality far more advanced in spirit than you make yourselves out to be here on the physical plane. For this reason Agasha has returned not necessarily to bring forth new teachings, but rather to stimulate your thinking so that you who are about to embark upon a journey into consciousness, as you absorb the truths contained within these pages, may then draw your own conclusions relative to your life and your place in the scheme of things. For it is as Agasha has stated so many times in the past, "You have only to go within yourself to find the answer to all."

All of the above now begins to explain why we have gone to such great length in this Introduction to speak of another volume, by another author, in another time. We have referred to eight great Initiates from Rama to Jesus and the light of truth that flows from the one to the other. We have also referred to Agasha, Master of Wisdom, as being the first and therefore preceding these eight other Initiates. In essence then they make up the numbers one to nine. Who then is the tenth great Initiate? All who have studied number realize that ten is only the remanifestation once again of the number one; the ten always reverts back to the one. But who then is the tenth great Initiate? The answer is that he is none other than you, the reader of this book, once you have taken the initiative to open the door and step through its portals into the Temple of your own Being. For in truth, you are the Temple of the Living God.

Agasha has stated many times that he comes to introduce you to your Higher Self. Who then is your Higher Self? If you be the number ten, your Higher Self could then be represented as being the number one, the great Unity from which you sprang. It is the greater *You* of which the lesser you is but a part. It is the Master within your own Being. It is your own personal Avatar, the Living Master that directs you from the Center of your Consciousness—from within your very soul. But this Living Master is not just a symbol; it is a reality—a living, conscious Being, another aspect of yourself that has trod the same road in ages past that you are now treading today. It is your own individual Master Self, the one that guides you along the way, the one who is ever by your side, and the one who is with you always unto the end of time.

But let us not confuse Agasha, or any of the other Ascended Master Teachers within the Agashan organization, with this Master that is you. They are only other Illumined Ones who are on a higher rung of the great ladder of life, and thus have returned to show you the way and introduce you to your Higher Self. But there is a very definite spiritual tie between a soul teacher, one who is destined to make this introduction, and the disciple. In one sense, it has been said that the disciple is the teacher's masterpiece, for the great inspiration of the teacher only comes into manifestation through the works of his disciples. But this interesting teacher-disciple relationship will be covered at length in later chapters.

Perhaps a few words would now be in order regarding the subject matter of this present volume. Basically, it might very well be called the great saga of Agasha. The word *saga* means a modern heroic narrative of an historic or almost legendary hero or sage. The word *sage* refers to one who has become wise through reflection and experience. And the use of both of these terms seems most appropriate in referring to the life and teachings of this great Master of Wisdom and their hidden influences on Western civilization and thought down through the centuries.

Therefore this work is a biography, but more than that, it is the history of an age. We have traced this great saga from its inception approximately 7,000 years ago in Egypt, or Austa as it was known then, and we then follow the influences of the life of this sage down through the centuries right up to and including his final appearance here in the

20th century in Chapter 10 which we have called "The Grand Finale."

As he takes this spiritual journey back into the past, the reader will be introduced to such things as the essence and basic teachings of the Agashan philosophy, some new concepts as it relates to the laws governing time and space, and the true history and meaning of the Great Pyramid. He will also be taken right into some of the great Spiritual Centers that now exist on the earth, and he will meet a few of these great Ascended Adepts who are still living in the flesh today. Yes, it promises to be a new and exciting journey into consciousness.

For indeed this volume is just that. It is the story of *your* life, what it has been, and what it shall be. It is also the saga of a great sage, true, but you will find that that great sage or wise man is likewise none other than you, once you have opened the door and entered the Temple of your own Being. Therefore you, too, embark upon this very same journey. Indeed, the key to the entire volume is discovered when you, the reader, identify yourself with your Greater Self who is symbolically represented as the great Adept Agasha, Master of Wisdom.

Many people have asked who painted the picture of Agasha that appears on the frontispiece. They have also asked whether or not it is a true likeness of this great teacher. The answer to the first question is relatively easy inasmuch as it was painted by a disciple who had attended the class a few years prior to the writer's time; his name was Graham Keene and he had claimed to have seen Agasha clairvoyantly. The writer can also bear witness to the fact that it is an excellent likeness as he too had the privilege of seeing Agasha one night in class shortly after he had begun work on this book.

It was January 5, 1970, and Agasha had just finished speaking. He then said that he was going to step down and be with the members of the class for a few moments, and it was at this precise time that his face appeared to me as a portrait within a beautiful golden frame. It was a three-quarter view, and there was no doubt but that it was Agasha as I immediately recognized him from the Keene picture. At least one other disciple can also verify the likeness, although she states that in reality no earthly picture can portray adequately his magnificent features in much the same manner that the picture of the Mona Lisa undoubtedly does not portray the full magnificence of the true Mona Lisa. And in all probability still others will also see him in time. But in the final analysis, the true answer to the second question relative to his actual appearance will have to remain within your individual concept of him. For after all, seeing a picture of a teacher of the magnitude of Agasha is indeed a spiritual experience, and unfortunately it does not happen too frequently.

All of the above now brings us to the end of this somewhat lengthy Introduction, but the writer feels that all of the points brought out are absolutely necessary in order for the reader to gain a proper understanding of what this book is really all about. For as we have just said, besides being the story of a great Master Teacher, it is also the story of *your* life, what it has been, and what it shall be. Try then to identify yourself with the disciples, the teachers, and the others as they appear from time to time in this present work; for in truth, these very same individuals reflect only different and varying aspects of your own Being. So therefore, come with us as we embark upon a new and exciting journey into consciousness, and then travel with us through the past 7,000 years of *your* lives. May a pleasant journey be had by all.

Los Angeles, California, August, 1976
William Eisen

CHAPTER ONE

MANZAHOLLA

If you ever meet a man of wisdom,
Let your footsteps wear out his threshold.
—Anonymous

CAN YOU for a few moments accept the theory that some great teacher of wisdom, one who had lived many thousands of years ago, can help you *now* in your material life, in your spiritual life? Can you stretch your imagination to the point that it will allow you to believe that someone walks with you throughout the day—to help you, to guide you, to protect you? If you can accept this supposition as a premise, and if you have the courage to investigate it, your life, regardless of your position, could very well move forward and upward. You will be able to find peace, happiness, opulence and a most glorious way of living.

Most of us proceed throughout our days as though a certain truth cannot exist until it has been established as such by "our own" method of observation. Then is it not rather strange that many, without any qualms whatsoever, accept as factual the statement that Jesus, after the crucifixion, appeared unto his disciples? They have no proof of this, but they have the *faith* to believe that it was so. Why then is it so difficult to accept another theory, equally as valid in its philosophical assumptions, which states that in the dimensions from which Jesus stepped to manifest there are yet other Master Teachers, Illumined Ones?

There is no problem here for the enlightened individual. The only problem lies with the average person on the earth plane who would rather leave all things of a spiritual nature strictly up to the church; he feels that he does not have the time to think these things out for himself. So therefore he merely accepts that which he had been taught in order to avoid arguments. Is he spiritually lazy? No, not necessarily. He may be ever such a fine individual and do many wonderful things for humanity, but he is so preoccupied with the material things that are necessary for him to earn a living and survive in society that he neglects his spiritual unfoldment. In other words, he has grown too materialistic.

Yet the child knows. The child understands these things because he has not yet become contaminated with materialism. For an example: Most of us remember that as children we were told that we must watch our actions for there was one that would always be with us. We must never do anything wrong, for in so doing we would hurt the one that walked beside us. We were probably told that it was our Guardian Angel, or perhaps that it was Jesus. Then through the years we felt someone near, and believing that it was He, we liked that. I am sure that this belief that He was there restrained us in many things.

But then as we became adults, we found ourselves caught up in other factors of life. The striving for success, the grasping for material things, the struggle in the arena—all of these things usually took possession of our lives, and such things as Guardian Angels soon became a very dim picture and in fact one that was quite forgotten.

Therefore the average person becomes rather materialistic, but he may walk his path for many years with assurance and confidence. He may even feel that he alone is master of his destiny if he has stooped so low as to lose belief in any force outside of himself. Successful years then mean only that he is smart; failure is brushed off as an incident of bad luck. His days are just like that—success and failure, success and failure, success and failure. However, if we are here to learn, as many great voices have so proclaimed, life has at times a dramatic way of awakening us.

Perhaps it was during one of the times when you appeared to be doing so well that tragedy came into your life with the loss of a loved one. She had been so very much alive, and then suddenly the curtain came crashing down leaving only death—and silence. Everything then seemed so useless, the plans that you had made, the trips that you would make . . . and then suddenly you found yourself asking, "Why, oh Lord? Why?" But there was no answer in your loneliness.

It is tragic moments like this that force us to become quiet, to sit, to think, to seek for answers within ourselves. It is that unbearable loneliness, that great sense of loss, that behooves us to read and to try to move our thoughts into a place of peace. However, this could be that great moment of awakening, whereby through our reaching out for help, we unknowingly touch the unseen hand of one whose greatest desire is to provide just the help we need.

This is the teacher. This is the very same one who had walked with you since you were a child—helping, guiding, and protecting. Your great sorrow has enabled him to come and help you much more fully; he had been waiting for you to reach the proper frame of mind so that you would be receptive to the spiritual. You have had to go through that experience for a spiritual cleansing, and it would seem that your tears have now washed away your sins. Through suffering and sorrow you have come in tune with the God-Self, and being in tune with the God-Self now makes it possible to be also in tune with the teacher. You have become that little child again, and you are now ready to learn; you have awakened the still-small-voice that lies within, and you are now ready to follow its guidance. You have asked and so you have received, but you have asked from the very depths of your being, and not just superficially. This is most important.

After such an awakening by the disciple, the teacher is in a position to bring the needed help and guide his disciple accordingly, for it is as the old adage states: "When the disciple is ready, the teacher appears." He will guide him in the form of mental impressions, and the disciple may suddenly be impressed to go to the library in search of a book, or walk down a certain street, or do this, or do that. In any event, it should not be long before he finds himself in the presence of the proper earthly teacher or a member of some church, school, society, order, or group to best suit his spiritual needs. All are not on the same rung of the spiritual ladder, so to speak, and each disciple of the many teachers is treated differently. But if the disciple is to enter upon the Path of Initiation, he will probably be directed to one of the many schools on the earth plane which teach the Ancient Wisdom. These schools are scattered around the earth in various locations in both the East and the West.

The Agasha Temple of Wisdom

Such a school is the Agasha Temple of Wisdom in Los Angeles. The founder and pastor of this temple, this spiritual fountainhead of light and wisdom, is Reverend Richard Zenor, internationally known trance intermediary. Richard Zenor has the amazing ability of self-inducing, at will, the hypnotic trance state while simply relaxing in a chair in front of a large audience, or in a private session with only the sitter present. No one who has ever witnessed any of his demonstrations can fail to be impressed.

The procedure of entering into the trance state is quite simple. After a few moments of concentration his body suddenly becomes limp, apparently in an extremely deep state of sleep. His body is now in the position where it can be animated by a new and completely different entity, and with the suddenness of an electric shock, the body jerks back to life. The first one who always appears is the doorkeeper whose function is to open and close the doors of the physical mechanism known as Richard Zenor. The doorkeeper is usually Dr. Navajo (on Sunday evening church services it is Dr. Adams), and he then allows the communicating loved one, guide, or teacher to manifest and express his or her completely different mannerisms, voice, and personality.

The elation brought about by this almost unbelievable discovery will carry one on for some time. The seeker quickly discovers that the activity at "The Temple," the name most often used by the average disciple, is not antagonistic to any spiritual group that is dedicated to helping humanity. The teachers continuously indicate that the doors of the temple swing both ways and permit perfect freedom for all. One is free to come and go as he pleases; in fact there is no formal membership of any kind. The Agasha Temple of Wisdom simply seeks to help all to understand the workings of the great basic law of love, so that each in his own particular manner may express his life in a better way. The philosophical lectures given by the teachers through the instrumentality of Reverend Zenor are dramatic, inspirational and beautiful, comparing favorably with those of the great thinkers of the world.

However, the very fact of trance mediumship, which permits a discarnate entity who had lived thousands of years before to speak through the vocal cords and lips of a living human being, is sometimes difficult for the average mortal, conscious mind to accept. It appears to be the general rule for those who seek in this direction. The first step into the world of mediums invariably brings to the seeker some incident of evidential verification whereby he is convinced beyond a shadow of a doubt. The manifesting entity sometimes appears to be almost frantic in his or her efforts to convince the seeker that he is who he claims to be—that he is alive, well and happy, and that he wants you to seek further in this direction. Quite often the proof is astounding.

It may be something that only you and the spirit entity were aware of, and perhaps you hadn't even thought of it for years.

But after a period of time the mortal mind, which the Agashan philosophy states is the only devil any of us will ever have to face, will begin to doubt and then ask such questions as, "What am I doing here? Am I out of my mind? Some of these lectures are repetitious, and all I do is fall asleep." This is the moment when the seeker must be master of himself, or the mortal mind will take him out of the temple and send him forth to attract the expression most needed at that particular time.

Until recently, only a small number of people have understood mediumship. Sir Arthur Keith, a former president of the British Association for the Advancement of Science, in telling of his "strange reluctance" to reveal his unorthodox opinion concerning religious issues, frankly states, "The real explanation is fear—cowardice, if you will. By nature I am of the common herd. I fear ostracism." Fortunately, however, public opinion has now changed, and men and women of science and others in positions of high standing are openly discussing communication with the "other world" without fear of reprisal.

But in bringing forth spirit communication, mediums evidently differ in their potential. Singers quite obviously differ in theirs. Some singers are born great while others must practice and work for many years in order to gain any degree of efficiency. Yet even though they can never bring forth the glorious tones of one born to sing, they can still bring into being beautiful music. Can this not also be true with mediums? Can they not attract different forces, all good, yet possibly some that are greater than others? Cannot even their physical mechanisms differ in the same fashion as a Stradivarius violin differs from a modern practice violin?

This appears logical, and it is very likely that Richard Zenor is demonstrating a very rare phase of mediumship that is particularly significant today. Teachers of an unusually high consciousness—Master Teachers who are still in the flesh, other teachers long since ascended from the flesh, teachers from the dawn of history, ascended teachers from Atlantis—all of these make use of his instrumentality. It is not uncommon for as many as a dozen different entities to manifest during a single two-hour class session. Also one of the most impressive features of Richard Zenor's channelship is the astonishing range of sounds capable of being produced through his vocal cords. Voices in the rich, deep, sonorous tones of the baritone will sometimes be followed with a seductively beautiful feminine voice from the Celestial. Add this to the dozens of foreign tongues, both known and unknown that have flowed through his lips, and you have a truly remarkable medium, or trance intermediary as he prefers to be called.

Who Are the Teachers?

It should be remembered that these Illumined Ones who communicate through the Zenor vehicle are human, even as you and I. They have walked this earth in the same manner that you and I are now walking this earth, but through repeated experiences and determined effort in many earth lives, they have cleansed and purified the mind to such an extent that they have gained mastery over the gross appetites and desires of the personal mortal self. In this achievement, they have become One with the source of all wisdom—the impersonal God-Self. It could be said that they and the Father are One.

They arose from all of the great civilizations of the past, from the lands of Egypt, Palestine, Persia, Greece, China, and many others. They were the prophets of old, and the list, just to name a few, includes such famous names known down in recorded history as Zoroaster, Confucius, Moses, Jeremiah, Elijah, and Jesus. These great souls—and even more in a far larger number both known and unknown to us—arose and ascended into that mighty consciousness known as the Consciousness of Immensity, and there they became the great Teachers of Light who return to us today to help struggling humanity. Yet, strangely enough, they are all interrelated. They had all lived together in a still earlier period, working for the same cause, and then they returned individually several times again later in the periods that we read about in history.

However, the great Teachers of Light are divided into many categories, and being so divided, they are thus able to cover all needs of mankind in the different stages of evolution—from the very lowest stage on through the extreme, highest point of attainment. But each Master Teacher, in whatever category he is functioning, is always working for the betterment of mankind and never for his own personal gain.

Now a person on the Path of Initiation is supposed to make contact with these teachers. It is part of the Divine Plan that the teachers descend and work with their disciples on the earth plane, and the idea expressed in some occult circles that we must go to them and that these arisen ones will never descend to us is a mistaken idea. For each student on the Path of Initiation can and does make contact with these teachers in one way or another, and in all probability he is not even consciously aware of it, that is, in the beginning.

A Teacher of Light then is a teacher of wisdom. He is a Master. We might say he has a master's degree in the great Consciousness of God—the Consciousness of Immensity. But these teachers are divided into several categories insofar as they relate to you as an individual student on the path. They are known as assigned teachers, overseers, and soul teachers.

All on the earth plane are helped by their so-called "invisible friends." These are the teachers and guides from the many states of consciousness running from the astral all the way up to the divine. But the teachers that we now will refer to are individual teachers who have worked with you through many lives and through many generations of earthly living. Your teacher has seen you succeed and he has seen you fail, and he knows you better than you know yourself. He knows your soul pattern. He knows when you are about to return to the earth plane, and he has been able to work with you directly down through the generations. He may become oblivious of you at times, but he still knows his connection with you.

This teacher is called the *soul teacher,* and he has been your teacher for many thousands of years. His relationship with you is unique; it is not at all like your relationship with any other teacher. He comes into your presence because of a great spiritual tie—a truly human as well as divine relationship. This is the reason that many feel so near and dear to their teachers, and yet in all probability they do not even consciously know them. They usually think it is Jesus. There is that harmonious blending force that is quite unexplainable. And it does not need to be explained, it only needs to be experienced and felt. You hold on to the teacher because you blend with that force.

However, the average disciple does not usually meet up with his soul teacher in the beginning of his journey along the Path of Initiation, no, not necessarily. Ordinarily he will become acquainted with what is known as an *assigned teacher* when he first starts to embrace the higher teachings. An assigned teacher is then one who is attracted to a particular disciple in this embodiment, or one who knew him in the lifetime just previous to this one.

An assigned teacher will then work with you temporarily for a time to see how you can round out your experiences. But he makes you work for yourself. He works along with you, but he is going to hold you back to a certain extent because he knows that your mortal mind is dangerous. He knows that it is dangerous to you as well as an obstacle to him. But he goes along with you to see how you are going to shape up—to see how you respond to his call and shape up your affairs on the earth plane.

Then when he sees that you are not going to fail—as you

had failed so miserably in the past in either this lifetime or others—he will step aside and provide a way for the second type of teacher to take over. This is called the *overseer.* The overseer will automatically take over at this point in time and will become your intermediary for the next cycle of your probationary period. But Agasha says that it is possible for the soul teacher to sometimes play the role of the overseer as well. This would be so in the case of an advanced disciple who had fallen off the path in one lifetime and then had to get back on it again in another. In this situation it would be the soul teacher who would be the overseer, but he would not reveal it to the outer mind of his disciple.

It should be pointed out that the average advanced student of the occult undoubtedly has been on the Path of Initiation for many previous lifetimes. And even though he has momentarily lost consciousness of this fact, he is in reality well along the road in this particular embodiment. This is the reason that the average teacher that a student first encounters at the Agasha Temple of Wisdom is more than likely the soul teacher. In fact, in all probability it was the soul teacher who had brought him to the temple in the first place.

The Why and Wherefore of Prophecy

In the Agasha Temple of Wisdom, the teachers offer a simple, satisfactory explanation of their functions. Along with teaching, a teacher will use suggestion to alert the student of a wrong action that could very well, in its reaction, bring about a future problem. A soul teacher can do this because he can very easily see the result of your actions. He knows what you will do even before you do it because you have created that action. You are drawn into it. In other words, it was your fate and it was preordained because you had not taken the steps to avert it. Therefore, this ability to help the student is simply an action of prophecy. This is a very important feature and Agasha, the principal teacher of the Agashan organization, has given the class accurate evidence that the teachers do just that—see ahead into the future.

All of the classes since 1949 have been recorded for posterity. Before the advent of the modern tape recorder, which was about 1949, we have to refer to some handwritten notes and a few disk and wire recordings. But since that date, every word spoken in every class—two nights a week in the earlier years and every Monday night thereafter—has been faithfully recorded, and from these recordings one can find the most startling and amazing prophecies.

There was the period of World War II, and the records are filled with prophecies regarding Hitler, Goering, Mussolini, and the war in general. The later verifications were amazing and correct. Of course, these earlier prophecies are only recorded by means of longhand notes. But words of evidence of the ability to see into the future have continued throughout the years, and these later words are all recorded on tape.

The frightening and disastrous earthquake in Anchorage, Alaska, was foretold days before. The assassination of President Kennedy was clearly foreseen in 1962 and 1963. From a tape dated September 8, 1966, appear the words: "Tragic fire indicated for Chicago." A few days later, headlines from the *Los Angeles Times* told of the holocaust in the Chicago Exhibition Center. On September 12, 1966, Agasha told of an impending flood in Italy, one, he said, "that would be the worst in its history." The papers headlined it on November 6, 1966: "Eighty-seven bodies counted in wake of floods in Italy. Florence, historical cradle of the Renaissance where Michelangelo worked for a 16th century pope, is deep in mud and sluggish water. The Museum of the History of Science is badly damaged, great works of art are destroyed, and . . ." The account goes on and on to tell of Italy and its worst flood. These are only samples taken at random. A complete analysis of the numerous prophecies that have been given down through the years, along with their consequent fulfillment or lack of fulfillment—yes, there have been a few that were stayed off, as the teachers say—would fill an entire volume in itself. We are only listing these examples to point out that the future is sometimes, though not always, clearly seen in advance.

This use of the powers of prophecy is considered by the teachers at the Agasha Temple to be one of the most important functions in relation to their work. They point out that in dealing with prophecy they are working in a field where there is no past, no present, and no future. It is all merely a continuation of Being. If a teacher were to see clairvoyantly an incident of the past, he would see it as though it were now transpiring. This continuation of the past through the present and into the future is a movement of causation moving from cause to effect. Because cause and effect will exist at all points during the sequence, the teacher will clairvoyantly see the final action even before the final effort has taken place. This is what constitutes the average spirit of prophecy, for prophecy is nothing more than the reading of subjective tendencies and then seeing them as already accomplished facts. Thus the use of prophecy continues on in the classes throughout the years, and its action proves quite significant in helping the students.

One might think that the action of prophecy, working through the law of cause and effect, might appear on the surface to be fatalistic, but this is not necessarily so. On the contrary, it tends to do just the reverse; it tends to temper the law of cause and effect. Let us use a simplified example that will illustrate the general rule.

A teacher, upon seeing some action by the student that could bring about a negative reaction, will immediately alert him to refute it and even might suggest a means for doing so. This procedure is ofttimes simple, almost childlike, with a suggestion posing as a question such as, "Do you think that is good for you? Do you really want that?" If the student is alert to hear aright the teacher's words—and not misinterpret them in his desire to hear what he wants—he will realize that the situation is not one in which he should become involved, for if he were to continue in that direction the end result could prove quite disastrous. If the action had been desirous, and one in which the teacher was in agreement, his phrasing would have been something like this: "Fine, we can go ahead with that." Thus through the use of prophecy, one can be forewarned of the impending result and take positive alter-nate actions which sometimes will change the picture entirely. Therefore prophecy can indeed prove to be a valuable tool towards regulating life on the earth plane.

Another law which is considered by the teachers to be of the utmost importance is the law of karma, which simply means cause and effect. They understand that karma will guide the mortal into those conditions where the individual will meet the challenges he needs in order that he may learn the higher lessons. Whereas many situations under the law of karma cannot be changed, the condition can, however, through the help of the teacher and from constructive effort put forth by the student, be modified.

These modifications can be achieved because negation usually exists in the realm of subjective causation. The subjective mind will act upon a command; it has no power of initiative or self choice. It is compelled by its very nature to act upon the suggestion it receives. It does not argue nor does it deny, but it goes right to work to create the new idea presented, and it will, in this new action, negate the preceding thought. This is the basis for the teacher's help. In his promptings, the teacher will make an effort to straighten out the thinking of the student and try to get him to release the confusion or the condition. In other words, he will help the student to rearrange his thinking into a more constructive manner. When this is accomplished, the teacher can then add his own force and understanding to the student's inherent wisdom of the "Oneness" and thus place him back once again onto the path of harmony. Karma, no matter how powerful, can through constructive and painstaking effort always be modified and lessened to some degree.

The casual way in which the average student accepts the

teachers at the Agasha Temple does not in any way detract from the dignity of their advanced state. It is always a respectful, trusting, and harmonious relationship, especially when we are speaking of that which exists between the student and his own individual personal teacher from the higher states of consciousness. Both realize that no one, no matter how high he may be, can give spiritual development—only the soul can earn it. Yet it is truly a magnificent experience and one that can certainly not be forgotten in this lifetime, the first time the lonely and spiritually empty seeker makes contact with a Teacher of Light.

The *modus operandi* for this introduction varies considerably in many of the Schools of the Ancient Wisdom. But at the Agasha Temple of Wisdom, it is the privacy of the contact room along with the vocal cords of the entranced medium that makes this experience a reality.

The Teacher Manzaholla

The writer is indebted for much of the material that is given in this chapter to a very dedicated student who entered the Agashan class in 1953 and remained active for fifteen years until his passing into spirit in 1968. His name was Walter V. Anderson, but he was known to most of us simply as "Andy." The reason that we are making a point about all of this is that the teacher that he personally contacted proved to be a very significant teacher unto the Agashan organization. The name that he gave was Manzaholla, and for reasons set forth in Chapter Four, the name *Manzaholla* has come to mean down through the centuries "until we meet again." Even today in the 20th century, Agasha begins and ends every Monday night class with the word *Manzaholla*, and it is an excellent title for the first chapter of this book since the members of the Agashan class all use this word again today as a form of greeting and good-bye.

Through many conversations Walter learned a bit about him. Manzaholla was born about 7,000 years ago near the location of the small town of Abydos in the land that is now known as Egypt. It was called Austa then. His father, Massu, was well educated and a scribe in government service. His mother, Tekahut, was a small and gentle woman of honesty and sincerity who knew very little of the ways of the world. She told the boy that the name they had given him, Manzaholla, was a word that meant goodness and love, but he had no way of knowing then that this word would cross the barriers of time to become, 7,000 years later, an important symbol of a new philosophy, in a new era, in a new land.

At the age of six, Manzaholla's father placed him in a school where an old pedagogue taught him the rudiments of reading and writing. But even as a student, his questioning mind was asking, "Who am I? Why am I here? Where am I going?" However, time moved quickly and soon Manzaholla grew into a young man. Yet in working with his father, he found that his interest was not in government. His meditative moments were always concerned with the philosophy of life, with the great god Ammon, and with the meaning of it all in connection with himself.

It came to pass that through his searching Manzaholla heard rumors of another voice in the land, a voice speaking of a new philosophy telling of a Universal God of Oneness and that each individual was a part of this Oneness. These words which were ringing throughout the land were being spoken by one who was destined to lead the two kingdoms along the Nile, the upper and the lower, into a new era of peace and religious harmony that would last for 2,000 years. This was the same voice that is now, 7,000 years later, speaking in a new land across the sea, America, and telling once again of this Oneness. This was the Master Teacher of the Agashan philosophy. This was Agasha. These words of Agasha rang out as a note of truth to the young Manzaholla, and from that moment on he followed in his footsteps. Indeed, to walk with Agasha and learn more of the Universal Consciousness of God became the very keynote of his life.

Therefore Manzaholla spent many years teaching along

the Nile. He completely dedicated his life to this new philosophy, but his path was far from easy. He wore out many sandals as he would walk through the desert sands, and he had to make new ones with his own hands. But in spite of these minor hardships, what is important is that he learned to walk in the light and thus come to the realization that he and the Father *are* truly One.

He also learned that both dynasties and men pass on, with each leaving its own particular mark upon history and civilization. But he knew that there the similarity ends. While dynasties and temples pass on to mingle with the dust of the land, Man, the individual spirit, evolves upwards and onwards through many earth lives only to eventually gain a more glorious understanding of himself and the Universe. He thus becomes a "teacher."

The Function of a Teacher

As such a one, Manzaholla, now a Master Teacher from the Consciousness of Immensity, describes in his own words the function of a teacher: "The purpose of the teacher," he begins, "is to give forth light, and the word *light* means wisdom. Therefore, clarification in the lives of men must come.

"If I were to go among the masses and say, 'That which I do, you can do also, and that which I do now has been done before and greater things yet will be done,' I would be received with ridicule in many places. To one seeking, however, these words would have meaning. The reason that he would recognize these truths is that, by having previously gone through the cycles of life, the essence of what he had learned had filtered down into his outer consciousness. A Teacher of Light could not have arisen, he could not have gone on, he could not now be in this wonderful state had he not first been persistent and attained while still in the flesh.

"Having attained this wonderful consciousness, if I should say something to a mortal that would give an indication of impatience, or be dictatorial in some statement so made or be belligerent, or be a part of that which would mean conniving, or be insidious in any way—then I would not be a teacher. For a teacher has become so attuned to the Infinite State that he cannot be a part of that which is wrong. He will work with a person who is striving to improve, but should that person in his striving happen to fail or fall, then the teacher will be immediately at his side to help him to his feet and try to get him back on the path once more.

"The only time that he cannot reach a disciple is when the disciple, knowing better, deliberately makes a move to achieve some desired end which is in direct opposition to accepted laws. And it makes no difference whether this is in the accumulation of worldly goods or whatever else it might be. A teacher cannot have a part of that. He does not condone nor does he condemn; he can only send forth the light. It would seem that he says, 'Forgive them, for they know not what they do or say.'

"The important thing to keep in mind is the fact that the teachers are not dictatorial, they only suggest. They can work out many things for the disciple that he could not possibly by himself accomplish. But this does not take away his responsibility. The teacher merely blends and adapts himself to the student in such a manner so as to assist him and bring on good conditions or good vibrations. This action is always in order because the teacher is attuned to the God Presence of the entity whom he is desirous of helping and keeping on the path.

"Words are the expressions of thoughts, and ofttimes we find that words are inadequate to describe accurately that which is or that which the teacher wants to bring out unto the disciple. Words never can do justice in their entirety to the beauty that be in Immensity. Therefore we depend, in the final analysis, on the soul awakening, and in that way the student may then have the experience and grasp more readily that which we intended to communicate verbally.

"The teacher cannot go along with anything that is contrary to the laws of the land, and most certainly this is also the same with reference to the laws of Nature. That which is and that which shall be are the result of the working out of God's laws which are immutable. Mankind can, out of necessity, amend or correct the laws of the land, but he cannot do so with God's laws. They are immutable.

"Therefore, Man must earn every step of the way. And if a teacher has come to bring light and peace unto a disciple, it is only because the disciple had opened the doors. However, this is no promise—or perhaps we should say no guarantee—that the student is going to be consistent. Most certainly, we find that it takes a strong individual to stay on the path and be consistent. This is where, as I said before, we depend on the awakening of the soul.

"We do not employ what you people on the earth plane refer to as a gimmick. The only thing that we do employ is proof that we see ahead. We plan ahead, and as long as the disciple walks in that light, regardless of his characteristics or temperament or whatever it might be, he should succeed. The teacher knows the reason for these particular characteristics in the makeup of the disciple, and with this understanding he exercises tolerance and patience. Intellect, which is of the mortal mind, is not exercised by the teacher. Yet there will be ways to employ words in such a manner so that the student may see more clearly, or grasp more readily, the suggestion that is being presented.

"A teacher from the Kingdom of Immensity is free from all encumbrances; yet he is not removed from the mundane affairs that concern the disciple who is searching. Therefore he is always working towards balancing the disciple's life materially. This is accomplished through the disciple's staying on the path and working with the teacher. But in the broader sense of the meaning, this means that the disciple must also accept the bitter with the sweet. Whatever this amounts to, the action is gainful.

"Agasha has said, 'Oh, it is so sad to see mortals denying and depriving themselves of things that they do not need to deny themselves.' And this is quite true. It is sad for us to observe the wrong actions of men, for these actions only tend to rob them of things that could have otherwise been there for their enjoyment, for their pleasure. It is said, in the final analysis, that we are to enjoy the fruits of our actions; but if our actions be wrong, the fruit will be bitter and we cannot enjoy it.

"Therefore we realize that the behavior of the mortal on various occasions is highly questionable. I know this and you know this. But there is no condemnation; we are not hypercritical. We only try to indicate that there could have been a better way. We respect every phase of life and what it has to offer. In the final analysis, we say that each one is here for the time being because this is where he has placed himself. He is in his rightful life category, whatever it be, and you are where you are because you have earned the right to be there, be it bad or be it good.

"The criminal mind needs to be pitied and the sensual man is in a similar category. We can only forgive him for he knows not what he does or says, but he will still have to pay the penalty for his deeds. However, the soul will deal out a far harsher penalty for action taken when it is known to be wrong than for wrong action performed simply in ignorance. As Teachers of Light, we realize that the things he has done usually have come about because he had not yet come into the awakening. His concepts were far removed from the truth. He may appease himself for what he has done or is about to do by the reasoning of his mortal mind; yet he does not foresee the price he must pay.

"Let us take an example. There are two bottles before us, each giving the appearance of containing pure water. We take one and drink from it; our thirst is quenched and we think no more about it. The other bottle, which contains a fluid of instant death, is later tasted by another individual, and what is the result? The individual leaves the body and he is pronounced dead. Now just because he did not know any better does not change the picture. He is still denied the right to finish his mortal life and derive from it whatever experiences were to be gained. This is where the teachers come in. We try to prevent and change the conditions whereby the disciple will not taste the contents of the second bottle. In this way, many tragedies are averted and accidents prevented. There may be minor accidents, true, but the major problems that could be very serious are avoided.

"Mankind does not have to seek very far in this particular field until he finds out that there are messengers and helpers of a great variety, all unseen by his mortal senses, that are always trying to help and assist their loved ones. Because of this help and guidance, many problems of the earth plane are modified. Of course, many are not aware that their help has come from a source other than through their own efforts, and should they recognize it as such, they have a word for it—luck. However, a helper or teacher of the higher order is not concerned in the slightest whether the mortal was conscious of the source of the help or not. His reward lies in the knowledge that good was accomplished, that disaster was averted, and that wrong action was corrected. But this is not to say that giving credit to your Indian or loved ones is not helpful. Indeed, the contrary is sometimes true because your thoughts enable your helpers to become even more attuned to your physical vibrations. We appreciate your thoughts in this direction, indeed we do.

"Another very important point to be brought out is that the one who comes to help, the one who has your interest at heart, does not come because you are you. He comes because you have enabled him to come by opening the door. It is written that if you seek, the door will open, and in your seeking you will commune with God. By your seeking, you are then going directly to the source that enabled you to become the entity that you are. And that source is the 'I' within. It is that inner 'I' that then opens the door so that help may be forthcoming from the spiritual realms.

"So then always remember, my son, that the 'I' goes before us to prepare a place in the consciousness that lies just beyond the present one. And that consciousness will be the direct result of our actions and our deeds in the many lives up to where we find ourself to be at the moment. This is the law that I cannot change and you cannot change. It is immutable. Bless you, my son, for affording me the opportunity to say these few words tonight. Manzaholla."

The Path of Initiation

Through these words, spoken by Manzaholla, we begin to have an awareness of the wonderful help given us by these teachers as we walk down that path known as *The Path of Initiation.* We begin to understand that the lessons that we must learn become increasingly easier as the voice of intuition substitutes for the more difficult experience of trial and error. There is no way for the writer to vouch for the authenticity of the many unusual incidents that have been reported in the lives of the different disciples of the Agasha Temple. There have been, however, changes so remarkable in the lives of some that the evidence for betterment is discernible to even the least objective viewer.

These changes automatically occur with the awakening of the soul. But the changes are not so much material changes as they are spiritual changes—changes in one's spiritual attitude toward life. The teachers state that each one of us, from the lowest reprobate to the highest saint, is within ourselves a part of the Oneness. This means that we are each a spark of Divine Consciousness growing toward a state of individual realization and personal responsibility. Therefore it is possible for us to awaken the soul, this Divine Consciousness that dwells within, and thus attain.

But this is accomplished only through individual effort. It is through my effort, your effort, all of our efforts, that we attain. It is our attitude towards life that sets up the character of our life, and then with the proper attitude it is possible for us to place ourselves in conscious touch with the Master. But it depends on no one but yourself.

As to making such a contact, there are no explicit directions that anyone can give. One must wait in silent meditation until his own intuition speaks. Books and earthly teachers can give the soul all it needs up to a certain stage in growth, but when the moment comes that there is no longer inspiration there, the soul will cry out and try to move one on to greater heights of grandeur. This is the time that one must go within, and in this meditation will come the still-small-voice. Through careful, kindly promptings this gentle inner voice will then begin to help you to gradually chip away the corrosion that has been accumulating through misuse of the mortal mind, and consequently eating away at the finer, grander instincts of the soul. But as you listen, and follow the leads you receive, you will be directed to that which will make your days more wonderful in every sense of the word. And when this occurs, you will find yourself in the presence of one you can love and trust, for it is written that when you are ready, the Master will appear.

In this seeking or attaining, it is important for us to remember that a thing that costs you nothing is valued at nothing. If we intensely desire some material thing such as a new car, a new home, or whatever else it might be that we feel will make our life better or bring more happiness into it, the very intensity of the desire will cause us to put forth every effort in order to attain it. The same can be said for things of a spiritual nature. If your greatest desire is for spiritual growth, then you are at the point of unfolding the highest aspects of your nature. But before you can attract unto yourself the fruits of spirit, love, peace, or humility, you must first plant their seeds and then let them grow into your life. This also takes effort, but eventually these things, too, shall be added unto you.

Therefore the student, as he stays on the path and tries to live the truth as he knows it, will gradually evolve upwards and onwards. He will take many definite steps and he will reach points where the old values, which in other days seemed to be so satisfying, will be seen in the light of a new perspective and cast aside. In that moment, he will with much happiness welcome the new order with its greater understanding, greater vision, and greater life.

But it takes courage to listen, obey, and stay on the path. The Path of Initiation has many obstacles along the way. But if you overcome them, and walk in the light which is sent forth from your own soul, the glory that comes with achievement is so wonderful and beautiful that there seem to be no words to adequately describe it.

The great lesson then is for us to learn to follow the dictates of our Higher Self. And if we do this, the teachers promise that we will never again be left to wander aimlessly, or left in doubt as to what is right and what is wrong. We will always know the proper thing to do, for both the still-small-voice as well as the teacher are always near to guide and suggest. The answer is to be still and listen with all your heart, and then you will know the way.

But first you must seek for guidance, and it is only through your own individual effort, thoughts, and desires that you will be able to place yourself in personal, conscious touch with a teacher—whoever he may be. Eventually you shall find him, and when you do, it will be because you will have opened the door and allowed him to enter. But this is only the beginning; the ending is still concealed. There is an even more wondrous discovery yet to be made. Then one day you will know. It will happen during a great flash of illumination when you will find yourself face to face with still another teacher. And in this great moment, the Illumined One assigned to guide you will most certainly be joyous, for he will know that you have finally removed the veil from Isis and learned the great truth—that the ultimate teacher is YOU.

CHAPTER TWO

THE AGASHAN PHILOSOPHY

Ours is a practical philosophy, with no special rules or rituals except the ritual of living harmoniously and naturally, having our experiences, and developing the beauty of our expressions until we and all about us are in tune with the Infinite Consciousness, the Divine Light.

—Agasha

If there is an absolute center to that great sprawling metropolis of Los Angeles, it could very well be the spot where stands the old but beautiful, two-storied, double-winged home of the Agasha Temple of Wisdom. And it is in order that it should be so located, because from every point in this great area come people to drink from this fountain of wisdom.

If you were to stand some evening at the temple entrance before the lecture, you would see entering its portals youth and maturity, the great, the average, the humble, the meek. You would see parents accompanied by their children, business and professional people, students, tradesmen, clerks, secretaries, housewives, the aged, the retired. You would see, basically, humble and likeable people of all ages and from all walks of life. But down through the years many prominent people representing many diversified professions have also attended the Agashan classes. Among them have been men of science greatly respected in their particular field (including one who was awarded an "oscar" by the Academy of Motion Picture Arts and Sciences), one of America's most highly regarded band leaders, prominent names associated with television and motion pictures of the present day, featured players of the theater and screen of other days, respected teachers of philosophy, doctors of medicine, religious leaders, lawyers, singers of renown, writers, and many more. Why do they come? They come because they are seekers of truth. They come because, like most of us, they are seeking a higher understanding of life.

What Are Its Principles?

One of the questions most frequently asked by the average seeker is, "What are the basic principles of the Agashan philosophy? What does it teach?" I think we can best answer this by restating what the Agashan teachers have always stated in answer to this question: "The Agashan philosophy is the clarification, the verification, and the rectification of the overall picture of life on the earth plane. It is presented in an effort to correct many things that are misinterpreted by the human mind. It respects all organized religions, modern as well as ancient. It respects other teachers, other philosophers of the past, and teachers of all denominations in the ministry on the earth plane today."

However, this does not necessarily mean to imply that the Agashan philosophy embraces and accepts all of the dogmas so taught. No, it definitely does not, and in many cases some of the dogmas are even at the opposite end of the spectrum. But there is still truth in that same dogma or doctrine; it only needs to be clarified and presented in a different light. There has never been a book written by mortal, no matter how learned the author, that is completely true to every last dot of the "i." Unfortunately, error sometimes creeps in through the misunderstanding of the channel receiving the message, and the net result is then that there are some misinterpretations of truth mixed in with the message being given.

But just because there is some error in a philosophy as stated in a book, this does not necessarily mean that we should discard the entire philosophy contained therein. If we were to do this, it would be much like throwing out the baby with the bath water and thus losing and denying to ourselves all of the many other invaluable truths and wisdom given in the balance of the volume. We must remember that everything in life is neither black nor white; no philosophy is either all true or all false. Like the "gray matter" of the brain, all earthly philosophies expressed by mortal will usually fall somewhere within that vast gray spectrum of thought between light and darkness. Agasha states that there is truth in all philosophies and all religions of the earth plane, for truth in the end result is simply where you find it.

Thus the teachers are constantly stressing that it is not the purpose of the Agashsn philosophy to take individuals from their religious affiliation, but rather it is to help them to see more clearly this picture of life, whatever the picture may be. The philosophy endeavors to enhance and broaden their present understanding to a more overall concept that seems, at times, to tax to the limit an individual's mental capacity for understanding.

Let us get down to basic principles. There comes a time in the life evolution of mankind when man wants to know. He becomes tired and weary of old outworn ideas, fairy tales, and superstition; he wants truth, knowledge, and wisdom. Yet as he seeks for this knowledge and understanding, he must first embrace many other things that are necessary at the time in order to later understand other aspects and facets during his lifetime of learning. The Agashan teachers do not condemn that which we previously embraced, but rather they recognize it as a step upward on the higher ladder of life.

The philosophy states that all things are related to their causes and no cause is without purpose. It also indicates that there is no new way to truth—no exclusive approach to wisdom. But the Agashan teachers are constantly stressing that there is one way that *is* universal; that is the way of individual responsibility.

Language Has Been the Confusing Factor

The teachers have said time and again that the trouble with many of the things that have been taught in the past, and that are being taught today by the various religious organizations of the physical plane, is in their misinterpretation and consequent deviation from the original teachings. The original written manuscripts, scrolls, or hieroglyphic tablets which stated the simple teachings given by men of wisdom have been frequently misinterpreted and mistranslated down through the ages. Error seems to be compounded upon error as each new translation is made. Language changes, words change—even the meaning of words within the same language changes over a period of time. Try reading a book written in early English, or even one in modern English published just 200 years ago. Add all this to the fact that because the original teachings were so simple, men complicated them—possibly in an effort to make them sound more mystifying and beyond the comprehension of the average lay mind. Some translators edited and even purposely omitted certain paragraphs if the thought that was expressed did not conform to the accepted religion of the day. Then, too, much of the teachings of the past has been handed down orally because large segments of the population, until recently, could neither read nor write. It would seem then that language has been the confusing factor. Language is invariably the barrier as the simple words of truth are often lost in a maze of perplexing terminologies which only tend to confuse.

Agasha tells us that the things he brings out, as he communicates with us, are given through the usage of words, of course. Yet he stresses that words alone will usually not bring out the facets that he wants us to see at the moment.

"How is one to word it to touch the minds of men, to awaken them to their Divine State?" he asked on at least one occasion. But he answered his own question by stating that the words themselves are not so all important. What is important is that the soul, as we unfold, will eventually give us the true picture in the way we should see it. Then there will be fewer blunders in our lives.

Therefore, intellect without wisdom is rather empty, for words alone do not give the answer. For that reason the various usages of words, phraseologies, and terminologies are usually somewhat confusing to the average student of life. Agasha speaks in very simple terms. In this manner, he endeavors to teach that it is through the application of a practical philosophy that people will derive more out of their life; for religion is simply, in its broader sense, a way of living. It should be an everyday experience.

Reincarnation and Karma

Agasha states that each one of us, being a spark of Divine Consciousness from the Core of Life, is growing toward a state of individual realization and personal responsibility. This action is taking place either consciously or unconsciously in everyone. Therefore each of us, as this Divine Spark, is a part of and an expression of the Oneness—the Universal Consciousness that men call God.

In the beginning the soul, this Divine Spark from the Oneness, seeking an objective expression, moved from the perfect Consciousness of Immensity into the difficult, imperfect forms of the material world. Through a period of eons, through countless cycles of physical expressions, we have evolved and unfolded to where we find ourselves today, well on the roadway toward self-realization.

This advancement is achieved through the principle of *reincarnation*—the continual reembodiment of the soul in a physical body. Though one will go through the change called death, the individual will be born again after a sojourn in the astral world of approximately 100 to 300 years on the average. There is no fixed time for this period. The new embodiment will then offer him the opportunity to correct the mistakes of the past and thus learn the new lessons that life has to offer. But the principle of reincarnation does not go on forever. Once man has perfected himself in every lesson the world has to teach, he then ascends into the higher Consciousness of Immensity, never to return again unto the physical plane of life.

This principle of reincarnation applies to all life, incidentally. The cat returns to be a better cat, the flower becomes another flower, and the butterfly returns to be a caterpillar once more. Thus all life is perfecting itself through countless cycles of physical reembodiments.

In these periods of learning, the thoughts and actions of an individual will produce reactions called *karma,* a law which decrees that no one may do harm to another or to himself without returning a like harm or some other adverse reaction back to himself. This is the same as in physics—for every action, there is an equal and opposite reaction. This is the great law of compensation, the law of retribution, whereby each soul is its own judge and administrator. Thus the soul attracts unto itself the proper punishment or reward to best suit a previous action.

These actions in our daily lives are registered in the soul itself, in what is known as the *Akashic Record,* and there they remain as a permanent record which, in the final analysis, must be rectified or balanced as we seek to attain Universal Wisdom. "We earn every step of the way," says Agasha, "and we learn by the quality of our expressions. Nothing is added unto us but that which we have already earned."

The "I" Within

Agasha is always stating that the God that moves the reprobate, the lowly, the unlearned, is the same God that moves the arisen teacher. This is reasonable to believe as there is only one God Presence. Thus we must come to the divine realization of the God Presence within us, the "I" within, and we must strive to understand that we are pulsating with this God Presence. The overall picture of life then is simply all there is, and the supremacy of all of this is the Absolute—the Oneness that we refer to as God, the Supreme Force, the Supreme Being.

To reinforce this thought, Agasha gave us an affirmation many years ago, and it is always repeated at the beginning of every class. It goes as follows:

I am master of myself.
I am all powerful,
And nothing can come to me
Of an inferior nature.
I am peace.
I am power.
I am all there is.

Now who is the "I am"? The "I am" is yourself, the Spark of Divinity that is your true self. It may be compared to a drop of water, and the God Consciousness to the entire ocean. Yet it is all water. The same analogy holds true when we compare a spark from the fire to the fire itself. The spark has the same potential as the fire.

This *Spark of Divinity* is as minute as a tiny atom. But it clothes itself with the etheric substance of the consciousness that it is in. Therefore, the Spark of Divinity when taken together with its outer garment is what is termed the *soul.* It is an egg-shaped form and basically it is white. This is the soul.

The soul is located at the very center of the human anatomy, the solar plexus. Thus we find that this egg-shaped form—following the example set by the Spark of Divinity—has now clothed itself in turn with a far larger amount of matter from the mental, astral, and physical planes. This is your physical, outer body which you call yourself. Yet your true self is that minute Spark of Divinity which is at the very core of the soul. That is the real you.

But as we said earlier, this Divine Spark is also a part of and an expression of the Oneness. Therefore, the amazing thought that must now be brought out is that the "I" within you, your true self, is in fact, God.

The Worlds to Come

Agasha has often said that since the "I" within records everything we had ever experienced, down through eons of time, it is well that we are oblivious to those things done in the flesh while we were evolving to become the human that we are today, and the human that we will be in the worlds to come. The phrase "worlds to come" refers to the kingdoms we shall find ourselves in, not only in the astral world immediately after our release from the physical body, but also in the higher realms of the Consciousness of Immensity after our ultimate ascension from the physical plane altogether.

These will be worlds created by minds of the collective group of the same caliber; as like attracts like, so shall we be among our own kind. The atmosphere and the environment will indicate the thinking of the group, and this then will constitute its own particular world. These worlds will be for all intents and purposes the equivalent of our "world here," but the etheric worlds will be in a state of consciousness where we will not have to contend with the things that obstruct us while we are living in, and dealing with, gross material matter.

Do you have to be freed from the physical garment in order to enter one of these worlds to come? No, not necessarily. As a matter of fact, you can come into the heavenly state right here on the earth plane, which is proof that it is all a state of mind. Then on the other hand, you can live in a castle, have all of its beauty and refinement, and yet still be in hell at the same time. It is quite how you think. Thoughts are things and things were thoughts before they became manifest. All material things on the earth plane were first thoughts of men before they were brought into manifestation. Even our world of today was only in the mental stage, and consequently a "world to come," at the time that we were living through our last previous incarnation.

Therefore, the Agashan philosophy asserts that heaven or hell is only a state of mind. We take it with us. Why should the "I" within permit me, as a mortal leaving the physical body, to find myself in a heaven that is beautiful if I did nothing to create heaven on the earth plane? Let us say that I was a despicable individual. I was everything but good, and yet I find myself in heaven? How could I? I did not take heaven with me, but I took hell. So I will have to work out of hell to come into a heavenly state.

Jesus, according to one of the many translations, said, "In the great galaxie, in the great cosmos of light, which is wisdom, I go before you to prepare a place." Now what does he mean by that? Agasha interprets this by explaining that in the use of the word "I," Jesus was referring to the universal "I" within. The term "great galaxie and cosmos of light" means in the Agashan terminology the Consciousness of Immensity and all of the many worlds to come. Therefore, the phrase "I go before you to prepare a place" means simply that the "I" within goes before us to prepare our heavenly state in the next phase of our existence. This will be in accordance with our just deserts.

Or we may look at it in another way. The "I go before you to prepare a place" also means that the actions which we are now performing will ultimately bring about a result that will be either good or bad. We know that if we think wrong we are not going to attract good things unto us, because as we *think* wrong our actions invariably are also going to *be* wrong. Then as we are freed from our earthly garment, we take the real "I," or I take the real "me" (it can be said both ways), and we go into the kingdom we have thus created for ourselves by our behavior, by our actions, and by our accumulation of knowledge.

The Infinite State

We find then that life on the earth plane is highly temporal, but life itself is eternal. We must realize that we are living in eternity now; this present life is but the dense phase of spirit expression. So let us now understand the Infinite State, but first we must define the meaning of this term. Agasha tells us that the *Infinite State* is that state of consciousness where the "I" within resides. Therefore, we must come to understand that basically we are infinitely intelligent, that it is possible for us to call upon that Infinite State and thus receive valuable information (Agasha's words) and other help while we are here on the earth plane.

This is where the teachers who preceded us come in. This is where they can help us to awaken to that which they know, help us to attain that which they have attained, and help to introduce us to that same Infinite State.

Jesus and many other teachers, both before and after him, have said, "That which I attained, you can attain the same; and this that I do, you can do also." However, Agasha qualifies this by adding, "but only if you unfold your reasoning faculties and come into the knowing. This is accomplished by becoming attuned to the Infinite State within; but you cannot do this in any one lifetime without first earning the right to do so by your previous actions."

This then is the answer, when mortal asks why he has not progressed or unfolded in a particular life in the way he would like. He had simply not earned the right to do so. "You have to first work in the light and know that it comes from the God Kingdom," Agasha says, "for that which I know you know already, that is, in reality you know it. I have only come to awaken you from your slumber."

Therefore, it follows that we are in truth infinitely intelligent, but we can never realize this in its entirety within the span of one lifetime. But we can, however, and many individuals do, learn to call upon the Infinite State to give forth unto us that which is needed. Jesus said, "Whatsoever ye shall ask the Father in my name, he will give it to you. Hitherto have ye asked nothing in my name; ask, and ye shall receive, that your joy may be full." He is plainly referring to God, the Father. And the Father that he speaks of is the Infinite State that lies within.

We will thus be able to answer our own questions once we have learned how to call upon that Infinite State. But first we must become so still in mind, become ever so relaxed, and put our outer mind into a quiescent state. Then, as our outer mind becomes quiescent and inactive, we can hear a voice within us say, "Be still, my child, and it will be revealed unto you." This will not be audible, perhaps, but it will still be a voice, a presence, a something through which God speaks to us.

At various times in life, some individuals will display something that is far beyond the average in the fields of art, literature, music, and so on. These persons will work for the betterment of humanity, excel in their endeavors, and receive great recognition—and much will be left to posterity. We are aware of this through the great works of art, music, and philosophy that had seemingly flowed from the minds of great men and women who at one time had lived upon the earth plane. Their works have lived down in the history of mankind and are equally as inspiring today.

Great artists, great writers, great philosophers—all called upon the Infinite State. They earned the right to give forth that which they presented in the light, and mankind should be ever grateful for their efforts. But at the same time, if we were to study them as mortal, we would find that most of them would be lacking in some other department of their life. Though they were clear channels in their main field, undoubtedly there were other areas of their life that became what Agasha terms the "challenging factor." Thus we find that the entirety of the Infinite State is never displayed in any one life.

God Versus the Devil

It was said earlier that for every action there is always an equal and opposite reaction. Therefore, the devil is the *challenging factor*, the opposition, and always in a lifetime it has to do with the mortal mind. Now the divine mind is the God mind; and one of them, the divine mind or the mortal mind, has to yield to the other. But they both are creators—the divine mind that creates the positive and spiritual thought forms, versus the mortal mind which only creates negative or mortal thought forms. Each is simply the reverse of the other. One is the positive side of the coin, and the other is the negative side of the coin; one lifts you up, and the other pulls you down.

Even language itself tells us the same story. Much can be learned from semantics, which is the study of the true meaning of words. For example: Spell the word *live* backwards, and we have *evil.* Since they both are composed of the same letters only in reverse order, one can readily see then that the word *evil* simply means to "live" life in the wrong direction and contrary to God's laws. Now add a "d" to *evil,* and we have *devil.* Subtract an "o" from *good,* and we have *God.* The words themselves would then also imply that the devil is generated from evil, and that God is generated from good. But the truth is that both good and evil are again merely opposite sides of the same coin and coexist with each other. One is a positive force and the other is a negative force—the God mind versus the mortal mind.

We might refer to Jesus. He allowed the God mind to take over, and he brought forth great light and wisdom as he taught the simple truths of life. Yet in the final analysis he was crucified on the cross by those with little understanding. Those unfortunate souls had allowed the mortal mind to take over, and they brought forth darkness and ignorance along with their own destruction.

We might also mention Mahatma Gandhi, a man of great understanding and spiritual insight. He worked to bring good into the lives of his people, even though his teachings seemed at the time to be rather strange to many who lived in the Western world. Yet he walked in the light of truth as he saw it. Here again, he allowed the God mind to take over; but he was of the flesh, and the flesh was destroyed.

We are using these examples to demonstrate the action of a universal principle. It would seem that when one individual stands out as a great beacon of light as he gives expression to the thoughts of the divine mind, there is always some fanatic, some crank with little understanding, to come along to ambush, to destroy, to crucify. This is what is happening today, and this has been going on down through the ages. This is the mortal devil in manifestation.

All of the above then leads us up to a very interesting paradox, for it would appear on the surface that evil is generated from good. An extreme positive action seems to generate an extreme negative reaction. This is contrary to what we just pointed out a moment ago, but it is only apparently so. Agasha tells us that nothing is ever accomplished without duress, for man must have opposition in order to overcome. This too is the law. Opposition only strengthens one's spiritual power, and if a man dies a martyr, that which he taught will invariably live on down in the histories of mankind.

On the one hand then, we have the God Presence. This is the God mind within us. This is the God force that moves us inasmuch as we are also an integral part of the overall picture of the Universal Spirit God—the Absolute, the Oneness. We have learned that we are all-knowing because God is ever present in each of us. Therefore, to become acquainted with this God Presence is our great mission in life.

But on the other hand, we have the opposition, the devil, the mortal mind. All that is contrary to the divine or God mind is the mortal mind. This is the mortal devil that creates evil. The evil that we do then is the action and the result of the mortal mind and not the God mind. Agasha has said many times that the only devil that will ever be brought into manifestation is the devil that men create through their evil actions. But it is mankind itself that becomes that devil.

However, both the God Presence and the mortal mind are necessary unto life. The purpose of life here on the physical plane is for us to do battle with the mortal self, which in its ignorance would seek to destroy us. It can be easily seen then that we must first defeat this demon self, or rather educate it, before we can come into the God Presence within. This will take learning, growing, and considerable effort and patience on our part.

Therefore, when one takes the initiative and says unto his own kingdom, the God Kingdom within, "I, being master of myself, give my mortal self completely over to the divine kingdom, and I shall obey the divine dictates," then the "I" within will take over and envelop him in a beautiful illumination of light. Agasha says that this light is wisdom, and as it is shown upon his path, the disciple will henceforth walk in that light. The path could then be said to be the path of *righteousness.*

Many times Agasha has said, "Having eyes we see not, having ears we hear not; yet through striving and seeking we shall eventually move into the light." Then with the proper effort we can gain the power and courage to subdue the mortal self and purify and transmute the baser qualities of ourselves into spiritual gold. But it is only through the help of the God Kingdom that we will be able to climb our particular mountain, the pyramid of our own Being, and then restore the fallen golden apex to its original position. For we ourselves are that apex.

Then, as we stand there on the summit that we so valiantly struggled to reach, we shall look down into the valley of the shadow of death and see all that was hidden before. We shall have eyes that see life from a vantage point never before experienced. This is our future. This is our heritage when we say unto ourselves, "I walk in the light. I walk in the light because I know it is brought into manifestation only through the understanding and application of wisdom—wisdom that comes from the Infinite State, the integral part of God."

Living in the Light

How does one go about applying the philosophy? Are there any general rules for day-to-day living? Has Agasha ever discussed the effect on one's life as he endeavors to walk down the spiritual path? Agasha has given many talks on these subjects on numerous occasions, and the specific answer seems to be that it is always an individual experience. This is so because all of our lives are different. There is one little talk, however, that he gave way back in 1952, and because it expresses so beautifully his thoughts on the application of the philosophy, it is well worth repeating here. Agasha is speaking:

"Philosophy and understanding is of little value unless you apply it. We know that, disciples, but we sometimes fall short in the application. That is why you must be constantly on guard to protect yourself from inferior vibrations emanating from the minds of men. You should say to yourself, 'I am the way, I am the light, and I am on my way to a greater understanding. I must learn now because I am preparing and building my home in the next phase of my existence.'

"You should take inventory of your thoughts and emotions and endeavor to correct any of your shortcomings. You should strive to do better in your everyday life. That is the only way for the disciple to try to go. I cannot live your life for you; nor can your teacher live your life for you. I can only try to teach you and try to direct your life, for each one is individually responsible for his own acts.

"You must be conscious of your illumination. You must be conscious of the power that illuminates from your soul. Magnetically speaking it can be of therapeutic value to those with whom you come in contact. Then if you live in the illumination at all times and become conscious of this power, it will be felt by all those around you.

"If you live in a beautiful consciousness, your problems will be fewer. You will not have the trials that you have today, or make the errors, or bear the crosses that you have to bear. I say this because you have learned in this class that each of you has a cross to bear and a responsibility, whether it be physical or mental. Whatever it is, you have some particular cross to bear. No one is exempt, whoever it be, but it becomes lighter as you grow in the light. Then you diminish whatever the burden is, but you must consciously live in that beautiful illumination at all times.

"This is not an imaginary light, and you must walk in that illumination. You instinctively know that the light is ever present, emanating from your soul, because you have created that wonderful light and you keep it aglow by working in harmony with the law. When you do this, you can see the difference in your life. You become an inspirer, and you draw people to you in such a blessed way that even those that have no understanding of the occult feel wonderful in your presence. You want to radiate this wonderful power and force. Then they can draw from you, and you have plenty to give because you can always replenish it by seeing yourself in this blessed light. So then visualize yourself living in that consciousness; but if you are in a state of negation, you cannot have illumination. You cannot have the illumination if you have anything negative on your mind, and you must diminish it immediately. You must cleanse your thinking process and get everything in order before you visualize the great illumination.

"Then as you send forth the light, a great force begins to generate. It is a burning force that seems to consume you as it envelops you. When this point is reached, you can then soar out into space and be with the blessed teacher. You can go to the temples or wherever it might be. It is the great illumination that enables you to do this, and it will always see you through on the physical plane as you grow in the Divine Light.

"We must have stability of purpose to know the truth. We are pursuing the truth in order to grow, to live among men harmoniously, and to have that which is right for us. We must never ask for anything but that which is right for our mental and physical growth. We want to arise, but not for a selfish purpose; we want to arise to be of service to mankind.

"Therefore, we become selfless as we grow. And by becoming selfless, disciples, we become pure and we are able to live in harmony with the physical and spiritual laws. We know that we are now working in the light of the Masters, and that our illumination blends so beautifully with theirs. Then, when we have earned that right, we may arise and say, 'Farewell to the flesh; farewell to the earth for I have arisen!'

"We do not condemn. You must realize that the very thing that you are going to condemn is the very same thing you may have to do yourself. Therefore, we have no condemnation in our hearts. Each individual is responsible for his own acts, the same as you are for yours. Each one is evolving out of whatever condition he is in, and if you can give someone assistance, it is your duty, provided it is wanted and accepted by the individual. God, the Universal Spirit, certainly does not expect you to thrust yourself upon an individual and force him to do things he doesn't want to do.

"Remember, we can learn from the errors of others. In this way we can avoid pitfalls which the average man must face because of his lack of understanding.

"No man is perfect on the physical plane. Every man has something to learn. No matter what great heights he may reach in a lifetime, he still has something to learn.

"So then arise with a smile and say, 'I love life and life loves me, for I love people.' Go out into the world and say, 'I want to serve and give forth light; and I know that I will always be wise when I give that light with the same joy and happiness as when I receive it.'

"Remember, you will only derive out of life what you put into it. So be happy, be up and doing, and be mentally alert. Manzaholla."

The Temple of the Living God

All of the above now brings us to the crux of the whole matter—the vital, basic, and essential aspect of the Agashan philosophy—and that is that man is a spiritual Being, a spirit living in a body. His soul is his inner consciousness, and his body is his outer consciousness. But this is not entirely correct, as we should say that the body is only the vessel that *contains* his outer consciousness. Therefore it is, in fact, the *Temple of the Living God.* And that god who lives in that temple is you.

We can say this because that is exactly what man is: a veritable god in the becoming. He is literally a "fallen angel" trying to regain his original estate. Agasha tells us that man does this by going through the wheel of life, through innumerable incarnations, as he makes amends for his previous sins and errors in order to regain his lost kingdom.

Since you are primarily a spirit living in this "temple"—your physical body that contains your outer consciousness—your spirit will therefore fill up all the "space" of your body or temple at one and the same time. For it cannot be said that you exist any more in your toe, or your finger, or even in your head than you do in any other part of your body. You just seem to exist simultaneously within every atom of your body at one and the same time. Thus your consciousness is *one.*

This can be compared with a God that also exists everywhere in the Universe at one and the same time. The Agashan teachers state that this is the Universal Consciousness, or simply God. And since Man is the microcosm of God which is the macrocosm, it follows then that God is in the same manner also *one* consciousness. The Ancient Wisdom has taught this truth for several thousand years, and it is the crux or essential part of not only the Agashan philosophy, but also of every other religion or philosophy that teaches the Oneness of God.

Now the Temple of the Living God is not always a physical temple. It is the house you live in wherever that may be; and after the change called death, the soul leaves the physical temple and moves into the astral body which then becomes the equivalent of an astral or spiritual temple. This is a little more ethereal, perhaps, when compared to the dense, physical temple, but it is just as "solid" to the astral touch as the physical temple is to your physical touch. But no matter what body you may be living in—be it a mental body, a physical body, or a spiritual body—that body is still the Temple of the Living God.

Therefore man cannot die. He has to exist someplace or somewhere because he will always find himself living in the equivalent body or temple of the consciousness of the plane in which he awakens. This, too, is the same as in physics. There is a law which states: Energy can neither be created nor destroyed, but it can only be transmuted into another state. The Agashan teachers refer to the normal transmutation process as *spiritual chemistry* or *alchemy*. However, the transmutation of the soul might better be referred to as *spiritual* alchemy.

It is for this reason then that the teachers teach that one does not necessarily have to go to a church for his spiritual unfoldment; a great edifice is not required for this purpose. Beautiful buildings are a wonderful place to assemble, indeed so, but they are not a prerequisite either to receive light or to bring it into manifestation. This action should be an everyday experience, and it should not happen only on one day a week on Sundays. On the other hand though, in referring to the expression of truth, one must be ever so careful to know when to speak and when not to speak. Sometimes much more can be accomplished in the silence. A clear understanding of these principles is somehow difficult for many people to comprehend. Yet the Agashan explanation that God or Christ dwells within us, and that we are the temple in which He lives, seems more meaningful than the teachings of some orthodox sects which seem to imply that the church itself is the only doorway to Heaven.

Another important point to be brought up before we leave this subject is that *balance* is the very keynote of our lives. Daily life in our "physical temple" should always be balanced mentally, physically, and spiritually. One should devote 50 percent of his time to spiritual affairs and the other 50 percent to material affairs. In this way then you can be your natural, everyday self and enjoy life materially as you unfold spiritually. Otherwise, you would become an unbalanced individual and this is not good. Too much effort spent in trying to unfold spiritually is just as bad as becoming too materialistic. This is why the teachers are always alert to nurture one's material dreams or desires, if by so doing they can bring balance and harmony into one's life. Therefore your material efforts are just as necessary for your overall growth as your spiritual efforts.

This then brings to a close this little chapter on Agasha's philosophy. But perhaps we should let the great Master Teacher himself summarize it in his own words as he asks us to remember: "In your philosophy everything is in order acccording to the actions of men. So always know that your mind is working with you for your good as long as it works in harmony with your soul; but your mortal mind will rebel at the soul. The soul will always respond to the higher; the soul will never respond to the lower. The soul will work only in harmony with the Universal Spirit God. Mortal imperfections will be the temptation. Conquer the mortal: you have conquered all your trials. Conquer the mortal: you will make no more mistakes. Conquer the mortal: you have conquered the earth. Conquer the mortal: you thus become master of your kingdom and know that eventually the soul must prevail."

Such is the essence of the Agashan approach to wisdom.

CHAPTER THREE

RICHARD ZENOR: THE INSTRUMENT

We are but as the instrument of Heaven.
Our work is not design, but destiny.
—Owen Meredith
Clytemnestra

THIS present work would certainly not be complete without devoting at least a portion of it to the man who made Agasha's manifestation in our present era possible—the "instrument" of his manifestation—the trance intermediary who literally brings Agasha, that great Master of Wisdom, back into the 20th century once again. For we can no more divorce Richard Zenor from Agasha than we can divorce the outer shell of an atom from its nucleus, inasmuch as the life of the Master Teacher is always irrevocably linked with the life of his disciple. Jesus once said that when you see the son you see the father, but that it is the *Father* within that doeth the work. Perhaps this can then explain the strange and unusual life of one of the most remarkable mediums of our time—a literal instrument of destiny. And the story of this remarkable life will be the subject of the present chapter.

Richard Zenor Slocum was born at exactly 12:50 P.M. in

the early afternoon of August 25, 1911. He had a very unusual birth as he was born with a double veil, completely covered from head to foot, and the psychic manifestations that were to occur within his lifetime were even more remarkable. But the site of his birth, a little mining town in Western Indiana called Bunson, and his relatively large family were as typical and unpretentious as apple pie.

His father, John Thomas Slocum, was in business as the owner of a confectionary store. He was also a Justice of the Peace, and on Sundays he would preach at the United Brethren Church. His mother, Nancy Ann Bell Zenor, was very psychic and quite a healer in her own right when free from the chores of looking after her husband and raising a family of three daughters and three sons. There were really seven children in all as there was another daughter who lived for only a few hours. Richard, who was the sixth child of the seven, was also the first male child to be born in Bunson, incidentally. He was actually given the name of Richard Thomas Slocum at birth, but in his teens when appearing before large audiences he adopted the use of his mother's maiden name as it sounded more euphonious, and he has used the name of Richard Zenor ever since. His legal name now is Richard Zenor Slocum.

The Child Medium

Richard Zenor's mediumship began very early in childhood, and Richard himself can very vividly remember an incident that occurred to him when he was but two years and eight months of age. It seems that the family had by that time moved to a little town near Terre Haute called New Goshen, Indiana. They lived on a small plot of land containing a house and a barn, and the child would love to spend many an hour playing with the horse down in the barn. But one evening as he left the barn and walked up toward the house, he heard a voice speaking to him. It was getting dark and the light was subdued, but he heard the voice very audibly and very clearly. It told him what he was to do in life, it told him of his life's work in helping others, and it told him that he would eventually be "universal." Yet, it was just as though he had expected to hear that voice, and it did not surprise him in the slightest. It is interesting to note that today the town of his birth, Bunson, Indiana, has likewise been renamed in the same fashion. It, too, is now called Universal, Indiana.

Then he began to see clairvoyantly and to have visions. He recalls another incident that also occurred before the age of three. His mother had been weeping because of the death of her own mother, and he told her in his childish way, "Don't cry, Mommy; Grandma is here beside you and she says not to feel sad. Don't cry, for she is now with other members of the family."

He continued seeing into the other world, and he told his family about the things that he saw. His mother in later years was able to verify much of this. Then by the time he was four years old he wanted to go to school, but they did not have a kindergarten, and so they put him in the first grade.

Gradually others became aware of his psychic powers. Neighbors and friends would ask him questions about what would happen, and he would answer them and tell them what he psychically saw. He became extremely clairvoyant and he could see the spirit entities all around and about him. Yet in his childish way, he simply could not understand why everybody else could not also see them.

But all the while he was growing up, he was conscious of a sort of protective force that was always by his side. It would speak to him as an inner voice, and it would warn him of danger. Then one day the Voice said, "Don't get up on the wagon or you will break your arm." But he disobeyed, and he fell off from the tongue where the ledge of the wagon was, and he did break his arm. His older brother then carried him to the country doctor, and just before the chloroform was administered those present recalled his asking intently, "Doctor, am I going to live? I have so much to do to help people!" Thus even at that tender age, we find that this talented child was ever so much aware of his future destiny.

After a short stay in New Goshen, the Slocum family then moved to nearby Terre Haute where his father could better look after his newly expanded chain of confectionery stores. He also had concessions at the various amusement parks in the neighboring towns, and he simply loved to show his young son off. "Want to see what my boy can do?" he would say to his customers. And then young Richard would get up on the stool and punch the prize winning number. Of course, he wasn't given the prizes, but both father and son loved every moment of it.

In Terre Haute, Richard's mother had a friend who asked her one day if she would like to attend a direct voice or a materialization seance. Now Mrs. Slocum had had no previous experience with these types of phenomena, as the family had heretofore only been attending orthodox church services. Yet the psychic powers that her young son had been displaying intrigued her greatly, and quite naturally she was desirous of learning as much as she could of things of a psychic nature, if only to better explain the strange phenomena that enabled him to see and hear that which was imperceptible to others. So therefore she attended a seance given by a well-known medium from Evansville, Indiana, whose name was Reverend Stuckey. This particular seance was a materialization seance, and she was absolutely flabbergasted when three or four of her very dear relatives came out in full form and conversed as intelligently as if they were still living here in the physical body. Never again would she ever doubt, not only the continuity of life, but the actual "physical" reality of the afterlife. And not only that, she also realized that mediumship such as this was the answer behind her young son's strange powers.

After the seance given by the visiting medium, she then spoke with the regular minister of the church saying, "I think I have a son with these same powers, for he sees visions and also loved ones around people whom he describes quite accurately." The Reverend then told Mrs. Slocum to bring her little boy to the next seance she was to hold, which would be a trumpet seance where the entities would speak by direct voice. Needless to say, young Richard not only attended this seance, but he also ended up by being the star of the show. He saw visions of the future and he correctly told many of the sitters what was going to take place in their lives. And his age at this time was only five!

Perhaps at this point we should explain what is meant by a trumpet seance. Firstly, a trumpet is a small, cone-shaped aluminum tube, anywhere from 24 inches to 48 inches in length, with a luminous band around its larger end. Secondly, due to the nature of the levitating power that is built up in the room, all trumpet seances out of necessity are held in absolute darkness, or if the power is strong enough, sometimes in a very dim red light. And thirdly, they are usually attended by only a small group of people—the medium, the one whose body chemistry furnishes the necessary etheric power, and perhaps a dozen or so sitters or observers. With these requirements met, the spirit chemists are usually able to construct etheric voice boxes within the trumpets themselves, and in this manner the various spirit entities can speak through the trumpets unto those gathered to witness the demonstration. When the trumpets are in operation, they are always levitated into the air and move about the room as if they had a life all of their own. Sometimes four or five trumpets will all be in the air at once, each one being controlled by a different spirit entity, and each one producing a different sound or voice. The luminous bands can always reveal where each trumpet is at any given time. This type of seance is also sometimes referred to as a direct voice seance.

After this first experience, Mrs. Slocum then proceeded to bring Richard to many, many more seances during his early life in Indiana, and her persistent efforts in this direction eventually enabled young Richard to fully develop at one time or another practically every known phase of mediumship. But in those early years it was the direct voice type of phenomena that became his forte. He found that he was able to go into trance, build up the power, and then awaken to see and hear the very wonderful manifestations that then occurred. This phase he enjoyed tremendously, as he was then able to participate consciously and actively in the phenomena that had been produced through his own power. This was quite unusual because most direct voice mediums ordinarily remain in the trance state while the voices that are built up within the trumpets speak unto those present.

However, his early years while growing up and going to school in Terre Haute were not always a bed of roses. He felt self-conscious while with others in his school, for his classmates would sometimes look upon him as being "different." Sometimes he would slip into trance and then out again. This embarrassed him. He also baffled his teachers as he never seemed to study, but when it came time for him to answer questions he was never at a moment's loss for the correct answer. This greatly puzzled his playmates as well as his teachers, for they had not seen him do any preparation work whatsoever. He just seemed to know things he could not possibly have known.

Margie, one of his spirit guides, tells us that on one occasion a teacher kept him after school and asked him why it was he didn't seem to study, yet he could always write down his arithmetic answers and they were always right. Richard just simply shrugged his shoulders and said, "I don't know." How could he possibly explain it to her?

For this reason as well as many others, he became known in Terre Haute as the "Miracle Boy." Several years ago an article about his manifestations was written by a person who recalled going to the same school, the Hook School in Terre Haute. He verified in the article that this astonishing young medium was indeed called "Richard, the Miracle Boy."

Richard always felt that going to school was a waste of time because it seemed to him that his work was far more important. He was far more interested in thinking about what was going on on the other side of life than he was in his mundane studies. Even to this day he tells us that he never reads a book in its entirety, but he has used his psychic powers on numerous occasions to find the essence of what is contained within any particular book. Therefore his life today is really not that much different from what it was then. He developed into a full-fledged medium by the time he had reached the age of nine, and ever since then his life has been completely dedicated to going into trance to help others.

He would come home from school usually to find a house full of neighbors and visitors waiting for him to give a seance. Like all boys, he wanted to go out and play, but he stayed home and went into trance for them. This then is a general idea of what his school days were like: one continuous cycle of going to school, coming home, going into trance for a house full of people, doing his chores, and then going back to school again the next day. I think one would have to agree that this is not exactly the normal climate for a youngster to mature in while he is not yet even in his teens.

Strange Happenings

But it was not only in seances that the phenomena were produced. Even before the time that Richard was conducting seances, he was beginning to develop a good deal of power inasmuch as he was coming into the physical phenomena stage more and more all the time.

Richard tells us of an incident that occurred in 1918 when he was but seven years of age. The family were seated at the breakfast table and they had just said grace. But then at the precise moment that Mary, their maid, was bringing in a large platter of eggs, a nearby pedestal suddenly decided to live a life of its own. It was a heavy pedestal, about four feet high, and without any warning whatsoever it bowed down clear to the floor—one time, two times, and then even three times. I am sure we can all picture in our minds the look of astonishment on all of the faces in the room. They were simply speechless. It evidently was a very funny sight and it provided Richard's father, who had a delightful sense of humor, with a marvelous opportunity to take command of the situation as he said, "Do that again; that's funny!"

But this incident was only one of many which were to occur over an extended period of time. Sometimes members of the family would close the doors, and then these very same doors would open again at once without any human aid. At other times the piano would start playing in the daytime when there was no one even near the piano. And many, many times there would be a thump, thump, thump down the stairs and the walk would be very heavy. It was just as if someone on the second floor of the house would first pound with a poker to announce its presence, and then clunk down the stairs as if to annoy them.

The family finally became so disturbed, for these things kept repeating themselves, that Richard's mother decided to ask their next door neighbor if she had ever heard the previous tenants speak of strange noises or other unusual things occurring in the house in which they then lived. The neighbor's reply was not entirely unexpected. "The house is haunted," she replied. "No one ever lives there long. They have all moved out, and I was just waiting for someone in your family to speak to me about the house." The neighbor then proceeded to inform Mrs. Slocum that a very mean, very miserly old lady had once lived there and that she had made a vow that if anyone ever again lived in her house she would make it miserable for them.

The reason that I say that the neighbor's answer was not entirely unexpected was that young Richard had been telling the family all along what was occurring and who was causing the disturbance. He had described this elderly lady's appearance to his family, and he had even seen her fingers on the piano as it would play. And the ultimate proof of all of this was finally verified when his mother spoke with the neighbor next door.

Here we have an excellent demonstration of poltergeist activity caused from an earthbound spirit. Agasha tells us that any poltergeist or "ghost" needs a suitable channel or medium from which it may draw the power in order to produce the phenomena. Whenever this type of activity occurs there is usually, although not always, a child present; and the inherent powers within young Richard evidently were ideally suited to bring all this about.

His Preteen Years: A Period for Phenomena

Yet the physical phenomena stage of Richard Zenor's mediumship was only just beginning. His preteen years would see him demonstrate practically every known phase of physical mediumship. But be that as it may, the time came for the family to move on further west. Richard's uncle, Frank McCrocklin, owned many of the coal mines in Southern Indiana at the time, and his father had become interested in coal mining. He also had heard of the rich coal mines in Colorado, and being of an adventurous spirit, he decided to seek his fortune in that state. Richard was about nine years old at this time.

Just before leaving Indiana, a seance was held where Richard's sister, Nadine, came in to speak by direct voice through the trumpet. Nadine, incidentally, was the firstborn of the family and she had lived only twenty-four hours before she passed on to the other side. But she remained very close in spirit with the family, and she often manifested through her younger brother's mediumship. Therefore, it was not unusual when Nadine came through and announced that the family would have a safe trip on the train to Colorado, but she could also see it going off the track. She said that they would not know anything about the accident at the time for they would all be asleep. Needless to say, it happened just that way. The train actually did go off the track, but no one was injured.

Once in Colorado, the family lived for a while in Trinidad where Richard went to school and then returned home to go into trance for individuals waiting to see him. He and his mother also held group seances which were always conducted in the evenings, but he did help many people in the afternoons on an individual basis. Later they moved to Aguilar, a little mining town about nineteen miles from Trinidad, and it was here the family would remain until Richard would reach his early teens.

But unfortunately this little town was populated mostly by Mexicans and Italians, and many of them could not even speak English. The evening seances might have become a problem except for the fact that a neighbor, Mrs. Rich, could speak these languages fluently and could act as interpreter. Therefore, they invited many of their Mexican and Italian neighbors into their home for the seances, and young Richard, who incidentally wore knee pants at the time, would then sit in a chair and go into trance. After he had produced the power, he would then awaken and sometimes observe as many as four or five trumpets going through the air at once—and all speaking in either Spanish or Italian or both. Richard recalls telling his mother, "All they speak is either Mexican or Italian," and this was quite true for a good part of the time.

But even though neither Richard nor his mother could understand a word of what was being said, the sitters would seem quite satisfied that they had indeed made contact with their friends in spirit. After the seances were over, they would each in their own way tell Richard and his mother what had been said, and of course, Mrs. Rich's presence was indispensable.

On one particular occasion, however, Mrs. Rich was not there, and when Richard came out of trance there were four or five Mexicans on one side of the circle and a like number of Italians on the other side—all listening to a spirit voice in the trumpet which appeared to be in a severe state of agitation. One of the sitters in particular would then speak to the spirit, and the conversation went on for some time. "Mom, what are they talking about?" Richard asked. But all his mother could do was to shake her head in uncomprehension.

Now the conclusion to this little story reads like the ending of a television mystery drama, but Richard Zenor declares to this day that every word of it is true. It seems that right in the middle of the seance and at the very height of the discussion, a knock was heard at the door. It was Dick Smith, the sheriff of Aguilar, and a very good friend of Richard's father. He had just dropped by while making his rounds of the town, but the timing was most appropriate inasmuch as the sheriff could speak all three languages quite fluently. It was not very long before he gained an understanding of the situation, after listening for a few moments to the spirit voice who was cursing and swearing and carrying on in a frightful manner. The sitter the spirit was talking to was his brother, and in Spanish he was telling him, "Get my body out of the creek in Walsenburg; you will see my arm is still sticking out of the water!" He had been murdered, and his brother was first hearing about it in this seance.

Therefore, on the following morning Richard's father, the sheriff, and a few others took it upon themselves to pay a visit to the place where the voice had said his body would be found. Walsenburg, incidentally, is a town some 19 or 20 miles north of Aguilar, and they knew that there was a creek that ran through the town. The journey itself was without incident, but what they found seemed almost incredible at the time. They could hardly believe their eyes for there under the bridge and covered with brush was the body. It was lying half in the water and half out, and more than that, it had one arm sticking out in plain sight, just as the Mexican had said it would be.

Another incident of an equally spectacular nature occurred a short time later. One day a man from Walsenburg was waiting to see Richard when he arrived home from school. The man had heard of the young medium's very unusual powers, and he wanted him to go into trance and attempt to contact a Chinese friend who had just died. Richard's mother complied with the request and sat with her son as he went into trance. This she always did because he was so young. Sure enough, the Chinaman came through and spoke to his friend in Chinese and very broken English. It seems that he had owned a restaurant in Walsenburg called the Blue Bird Cafe and had sold it just before his death. But he told his friend that he had buried the $10,000 that he had received from the sale in a dutch oven in the hills just above the city of Walsenburg.

After the seance, the visitor then said to Richard's mother, "I know that man and he told me about the sale at the time that he buried the money. Would you let your little boy go up the hill with me and go into trance so that my friend can direct him to where it is hidden?" She hesitated, but the man had a good reputation and so she consented to have Richard go with him. The next morning Richard went with the man up into the hills and while in trance walked to right where the money had been buried. But Richard recalls the man telling him that, since other people were looking for the money too, he did not want others to see Richard with him and so Richard was taken back to his parents before the digging began. But the story has a happy ending. The man eventually dug up the treasure and used it in the way the so-called dead Chinaman had wanted.

There were also many other phases of the young medium's psychic powers that became fully developed during this period of time. Prior to any physical knowledge of them, Richard was able to see events and conditions clairvoyantly that surrounded persons who came to him. He was able to do this out of trance and while in his normal, conscious state. He made predictions and was later to learn that they had been correct. He located missing persons. He found missing articles and many other things of great sentimental as well as material value. In his seances he continued to be very strong as a direct voice medium; however, full form materializations quite frequently took place. Sometimes entities from the spirit world would wind up the victrola, and it would play without being touched by human hands. Once the auto harp, seemingly by itself, rose into the air and was played by invisible fingers. The mandolin was also similarly played, and numerous demonstrations of levitation were most convincing to those privileged to witness them.

On one occasion, for instance, a doctor from Kansas City, who had learned of the levitation powers of this remarkable young medium, drove to Colorado to see one of these seances for himself. The spirit entities had said that they would levitate young Richard to the ceiling, and the doctor was chosen to be the witness for this demonstration. He was a huge man and he sat beside the boy all during the seance. He even placed one of his legs over Richard's little body to hold him down when it was announced that the levitation would begin. But the "Force" came, and even though the doctor tried to hold on to him, the body of the young boy floated up to the ceiling. Then this perfectly safe "Force" gradually lowered him ever so gently to the floor. The doctor was flabbergasted.

Yes indeed, the phenomena that this young medium brought into manifestation during his preteens can only be described as fantastic. While in the darkened room his mother would sometimes ask for a particular passage of Scripture in the Bible, and then they would all hear the rippling of the pages as they would be turned by unseen hands to the desired Scripture. And then on another occasion in the private home of a family in Florence, Colorado, the "dead" brother of one of the sitters who lived in the house came through. He called his sister by name and stated that he would accompany her on the violin while she played on the piano. They had done this together many times before he had gone away to war (World War I). He then took possession of Richard's entranced body, picked up the violin, and accompanied her as proficiently as he had ever been able to do in the physical body.

But the full form materializations were possibly the most profound of all. For instance, at one of his seances held in Canon City, Colorado, Richard's sister Ynema was to have a great surprise. Her boyfriend had just recently entered the spirit world as a result of a losing bout with pneumonia, and she was feeling quite depressed. But he was able to materialize in full form, and when he walked out of the cabinet (a small enclosure used by the medium to build up the power) he even appeared in shirtsleeves, the same as he had always appeared in the drug store where he had worked. These materializations were not filmy or ectoplasmic forms. But on the other hand, the spirit entities who were able to materialize at that time were not teachers clothed in robes either. They were simply loved ones and relatives, and they endeavored to appear exactly as they had appeared while in the physical body on earth.

Physical phenomena were not the only powers that he demonstrated. Indeed not! The young medium's clairvoyant, or rather precognitive, ability was at times beyond compare. Even the life of Richard's own father was once saved as the result of heeding the warnings coming from his young son who saw visions. Mr. Slocum was a mine inspector, and Richard recalls one day when he said to his mother, "Mom, don't let Dad go into the mine today for I see it blowing up, and I see many bodies that are being brought out and they are all lying around dead." Richard was very insistent about this, and so his father heeded the warning and stayed at home. But unfortunately it was too late to pass the warning unto the others, and the explosion that occurred a short time later was devastating. Carbide lamps were used and the gas pockets blew up killing a number of workmen. Even Richard himself heard the "boom" as he was playing in his back yard.

On still another occasion, however, the family was not so quick to heed the child's warnings and barely escaped with their lives. Richard had said one day, "Mom, I see water coming down and taking our house away." Their house was located on the side of an arroyo, and two weeks after this prediction rain started coming down rather heavily. Again the lad said, "Mom, this is the night the rain will take our house away." But the storm did not appear to be too bad, and the family took the warning rather lightly. At nine o'clock he again pleaded with his mother, and again they did not feel the urgency of leaving. But by two o'clock in the morning it became apparent that perhaps there was some validity in the child's warnings, and they left barely in the nick of time. An avalanche of water soon roared down the arroyo sweeping everything in its path, and Richard regretted for a long time afterwards that they had not left sooner. Aside from the damage to their house, a pet coyote that had been chained to the barn was drowned. It was a pet that he dearly loved, and he was the only one who could do anything with it because it was so vicious to the others.

A New and Broader Phase of Activity

We must remember that all of Richard's demonstrations in his preteen years were performed only before small groups and usually in the darkened seance room. This was necessary because of the nature of physical mediumship as opposed to mental mediumship. Somewhere around the age of twelve, however, Richard began a new and somewhat different phase from what had been demonstrated previously. The change happened suddenly with no other warning than the boy's own statement that he felt something different was about to happen to him. And it did. Instead of speaking through the trumpet, voices now began coming through his own lips—but only after he had lapsed into the familiar trance. This phase then facilitated his appearances before larger and greater audiences in the nearby cities because darkness or the red light was no longer a requirement for his demonstrations.

Yet this new phase was in one sense a disappointment to the boy medium. Previously it had been possible for him to be conscious of all the phenomena that appeared around and about him. He himself had been able to converse with the spirits, and he had enjoyed it immensely. But with this new phase, he was outwardly unconscious during the time his body was being used as a literal "telephone between worlds." Be that as it may, many hundreds of individuals were now able to listen to the communications, as opposed to only a mere dozen or so that had heretofore attended the darkened seances.

As the mining at Aguilar played out, the family then moved on to Canon City where Mr. Slocum opened up a chili factory. And from there they moved to Pueblo, Colorado, where he entered the pizza business. Richard's father had the amazing versatility to go into business wherever he travelled and in whatever town he found himself living. It was this extremely flexible capability of his father, as he would move from place to place, that enabled the young medium to demonstrate his powers all the way across the country from Indiana to California, where he was destined to eventually enter the highest phase of his work.

In Pueblo, Colorado, Richard came to be called the "Wonder Boy" as he appeared before large audiences giving psychic and test demonstrations. He was about fourteen at the time. Then in Douglas, Arizona, the place where they moved next, he gave ESP demonstrations at the Kiwanis Club and various other clubs while being blindfolded.

But people also continued to consult him in his home. Inasmuch as Douglas was quite close to the Mexican border, his fame spread across the border into Mexico, and those that could not cross the line into this country then sent questions by means of friends. Richard would always answer every question, even of those who were in the most humble circumstances. In Douglas, he was known as the "Mystery Boy."

On numerous occasions, both public as well as private, he was able to quite effectively demonstrate various phases of precognition and clairvoyance. If the conditions were just right, incidents would appear before him as clearly as a motion picture. He has envisioned in an instant: names, places, things, events—and in all cases he immediately told exactly what he saw. Then later, he would usually find out that the scene had occurred precisely in the way he had seen it. In this manner, he was able to assist in the return of many lost articles, a phase of mediumship that became quite a specialty of his at the time. And he still does it to this day.

For instance: A beautiful girl once came to see him in Douglas and she was quite distraught. "You want to know who stole your coat," he told her. "That's right," she replied. Then the scene came before him in exact detail, and he said, "Tomorrow evening, at exactly four o'clock, a Mexican woman will come out of a building at such and such address in the little town of Bisbee, and she will be wearing your coat." Needless to say, the next day at the appointed hour the rather upset girl was in Bisbee, ready and waiting. Then two days later, Richard found out that the girl had indeed found her coat, exactly as predicted, and she got it back.

But this little story is not over yet. It has an interesting sequel. Years later, Richard was driving down Wilshire Boulevard in Los Angeles when he was asked to assist in pushing a car which was stalled. He got out of his car after giving the push and made light conversation with the man and his wife who were the occupants of the other car. But the girl kept looking at him and finally said, "Excuse me for staring at you, but aren't you the 'Mystery Boy' from Douglas, Arizona?" Taken aback a bit, Richard nodded. "My goodness," she went on. "I came to you and you found my coat."

California and an Assignment with Destiny

Ultimately the family left Arizona and traveled across the desert and up the California coast to the city of Santa Clara. Here, his father entered into still another new business, but by now his life was becoming more and more involved in the activities of his gifted son. He made arrangements for Richard's first California seance to be held in the famous Winchester Mystery House in nearby San Jose, but somehow this fell through. Instead, it was held in a residence in Santa Clara. The year was 1928 and Richard was only sixteen.

Then they moved on to Los Angeles and lived for a while on the east side of town. Richard continued with his seances and psychic demonstrations, but now he was also becoming quite proficient in the field of psychometry. This is the ability to hold an object, such as a watch, in one's hands, and then receive information about its owner or other events connected with the object. Through this technique, Richard found that he was able to enhance his ability in locating missing objects to a considerable degree. On various occasions he has even located missing persons. Down through the years he has found, among other things, missing rings, missing cars, and once even a lost airplane.

One of his first followers in Southern California was a black butler by the name of John Robinson. Now Robinson was employed in Beverly Hills, and Beverly Hills was the home of many who were quite active in the motion picture industry at that time as well as now. Therefore, it was inevitable that through Robinson's contacts many motion picture people also came to see the young medium. It was only a question of time then before the family moved closer to this environment and set up residence on Hudson Avenue in the very heart of Hollywood.

But Hollywood at that time was a mecca for the charlatan, the fortune teller, and the con artist. And the great numbers of people who were now coming to the Hudson Avenue address soon attracted the attention of the Los Angeles Police Department. On one occasion an undercover police woman, acting under the disguise of a woman who was in deep trouble and needing help, came to the door and practically forced her way in. Richard told her, "You have a watch there that George gave you. May I touch it?" The woman handed him the watch. But then with the watch in his hand, Richard was able to sense the true reason for her visit. "You are not in any trouble," he said rather candidly. "In fact, you even have $2.00 in marked money in your purse to give to me."

Flabbergasted, the woman gave him the money saying, "You're the best I ever came to. You know, you have a lot of enemies—fortune tellers who are jealous of you. But I'll have to take you in anyway." She then arrested him on the spot for fortune telling, and he was taken right then and there to court. It seems that justice was a lot quicker in those days than it is today. He went before a lady judge, and his father, who had followed behind in his sports car, testified in his behalf. And the verdict? Richard was acquitted, of course.

But this experience only demonstrated quite emphatically the need for working under the auspices of a duly recognized church. Richard's mother had become a medium in her own right, and she was fully aware that her son was gradually being trained to become a channel for great spiritual teachings. His seances were more and more taking on the air of classes in spiritual instruction rather than just being used for the purpose of communication with loved ones who had passed on in spirit. And more than that, Richard's work was divine in origin, and protection from any further harassment from the authorities was an absolute necessity. Therefore, with the assistance of some friends in the material world as well as those in spirit, the Church of Divine Knowledge was duly established and Richard Zenor was ordained its minister.

They began a search for a suitable place to assemble and soon found one in a building near the corner of Sunset Boulevard and Western Avenue. The building was in an excellent location and it contained a hall that was available for meetings. Therefore the hall was leased, and for several months literally hundreds and hundreds witnessed various demonstrations of mediumship which included talks by the spirit controls, direct communications with loved ones, and here and there some phenomena as well.

But this was only the beginning. As fate would have it, a reputable medical doctor, an Oxford graduate incidentally, also had an office in this very same building. Thus he painstakingly studied every movement and reaction of the entranced medium while he was giving his demonstrations; and eventually the doctor became so impressed that life in the spirit world was now a provable reality that he offered to give up his entire medical practice for a year or so and accompany the young medium on a tour acting as his manager. This was in early 1930, and Richard was still only in his teens—eighteen, to be precise.

Tours, Demonstrations, and Public Acclaim

The tour proved to be a great success, and it marked the beginning of a decade of frequent demonstrations before both large and small audiences in various cities of the West. This particular tour took them as far away as Florida, but it primarily centered along the West Coast. They traveled to many cities and towns including San Diego, San Jose, San Francisco, Oakland, Sacramento, Portland, Seattle, and cities as far north as Vancouver and Victoria in Canada.

Return engagements were frequent, and wherever they traveled large audiences awaited. Richard recalls that in some of the cities such as Portland and Vancouver, people would sometimes form long lines down the street waiting to get into the auditorium.

These meetings were not without quite spectacular manifestations at times. For instance, an interesting incident occurred when they appeared in Victoria, British Columbia, for the first time. They arrived there by boat, and as it was docking they learned that a little boy had recently drowned in the harbor. They docked on a Saturday, and a local organization had scheduled a demonstration of spirit communication to be held on the following Tuesday. It so happened that the drowned boy's mother was also present at this meeting, and sure enough, the lad was able to communicate with his mother through the Zenor channelship. All present heard him tearfully relate the details of his passing, and the mother was absolutely convinced by things that were said that she had indeed talked with her son.

On still another occasion, this time during a public demonstration in San Diego, a goiter completely disappeared in full view of the audience. Upon seeing this demonstration of instantaneous healing, Richard's manager could only say,

"Here I am, an Oxford graduate with a degree in medicine, and one who has spent many years practicing medicine, and I cannot even attempt to do what you just did. You just raise your hands while in trance, and the healing takes place automatically."

At the conclusion of the tour, the medium returned once again to Los Angeles, and this city has remained his headquarters ever since. But the die was cast, and he continued in this cycle all through the 1930's, making frequent appearances before both large and small gatherings of clubs, church groups, and other organizations in not only Los Angeles, but also in many other cities of the Western States. These public appearances were in addition to his private classes or seances which were usually conducted, when he was not traveling, every Friday night in his home, wherever that was at the time.

At first it was hard for many to accept as valid the demonstrations that he performed, but time and again they continued to be amazed. For instance: In the early 1930's he made an appearance before an organization of hotel owners called the Greeters Club. And on this particular occasion, a man came up to him and rather scornfully said, "If you are this so-called 'miracle boy,' then pick out the winning number for the watch that is being raffled off." Without hesitation, Richard answered, "Number 42 will win." Now many heard him make this statement, and there were quite a few rather prominent people present including the Governor of California, James Rolph Jr., as well as other well-known personalities. Consequently, when Number 42 proved to be the actual winning number a few moments later, this demonstration received considerable publicity in the newspapers and other media.

The 1930's then can be categorized as being a decade for demonstrations, a period whereby his spirit controls attempted to prove the continuity of life to as many as would listen. And some orthodox churches, strangely enough, were in those years not as adverse to demonstrating mediumship as they are today. For instance, around 1935 Richard appeared for a full week's engagement at the United Brethren Church then near Hoover and Alvarado. Sheldon Shepherd, the pastor of the church at the time, was his sponsor. It was a very large church, three balconies high, and it was packed each night by the many hundreds desiring to see his psychic demonstrations. The reaction by the church-going public was basically quite positive. Newspaperman James Crenshaw, incidentally, was also among those who were quite favorably impressed, it being his first experience into the world of mediumship.

For a short time Richard even appeared in the Theater—in Los Angeles, Tucson, and elsewhere. On the marquee were the words "Zenor the Great," but he just did not care for showmanship of this type because basically Richard Zenor is a very humble person, and having to perform in a tight tuxedo and under the glare of spotlights simply was not his forte. Besides, it was too time-consuming, and he felt he could be more helpful to people in other ways. But he did perform, and he did prove survival, and he did find lost articles. Once he even did a radio broadcast before a theater audience in Tucson where people would phone in directly and ask questions. Before going off the air he had found a lot of things, including a diamond ring that had been lost for eight months.

Now we must remember that these types of psychic demonstrations were not the only phases of mediumship that Richard Zenor was demonstrating all through these years. His ability to locate lost articles and his trance-voice demonstrations were possibly the most important phases, yes, but they most certainly were not the only phases. Occasionally he would give a dark seance and thus permit other types of physical phenomena to come into manifestation and take place. It was for these reasons that a former member of the British Psychical Research Society once stated that Richard Zenor was one of the most versatile mediums in his field—much like a one man band.

In the early 1930's, for an example, he was asked to demonstrate spirit photography under strict test conditions. Richard agreed, and a special committee in the field of psychic research arranged for him to appear in the Public Library in Los Angeles. They set up a special room, they brought their own cameras and film, and they took every possible precaution to preclude even any question of fraud. Yet spirit photographs were obtained; the likenesses of spirit entities actually appeared on the film.

Then on another occasion, this time in Seattle, he gave a dark seance for the purpose of producing apports. But it turned out to be not only an apport seance, but also an excellent demonstration of independent voice as well. Independent voice, incidentally, is that phase of mediumship whereby the voice is produced right in the air without either the aid of a trumpet or the medium's vocal cords. The night was cold and it was snowing outside, but the results were spectacular. Richard awoke from his trance and Chief Waterfall (one of the spirit entities who spoke through him at the time) was speaking independently. He asked him what he would like. Richard answered, "Go and get me a white rose." And in a few moments a white rose, fresh and fragrant, was dropped into his lap.

Now we must remember that there were other sitters at this seance, and they were all in evidence of the phenomena that were produced that evening. Richard then said, "This is wonderful, Chief Waterfall, but now can you go and get me a flower not common to this part of the country?" The Indian replied, "Me go get." Then a second flower was apported into the room. After the seance, it was taken to a botanist to find out what kind of flower it was. "Where did you get this?" he asked. "This flower has never been known to grow in this country. It is only found in India." The investigators were dumbfounded, and besides, it had been snowing in Seattle at the time that it was apported. The flower lasted about 21 days, and it was shown to other audiences as well as spoken about on the radio.

On another occasion, also in Seattle, a feminine voice from spirit who called herself Nadine (not necessarily Richard's sister) spoke independently and said, "I will now bring you a present from Heaven, and it will never be lost." Then in what seemed to be no time at all, a small piece of parchment, perhaps only six inches across, dropped into Richard's lap. A closer examination revealed that it was a very beautiful etching portraying three angels, all elegantly imprinted into the parchment-like material. Nadine said that it was symbolical of the Trinity. Two of the angels were holding calla lilies in their arms, and the third angel in the center was blowing a trumpet. During his travels it very nearly was lost, but Richard has it to this day and many in the temple have seen it.

The Hollywood Years

Becoming so widely known, word of Richard's psychic ability eventually reached the ears of Louella Parsons, the motion picture gossip columnist. Sensing his potential, she took him under her wing and gave him the use of one of the rooms in her house for his consultations. Here, he helped scores of movie celebrities in their individual fields of endeavor, and many returned again and again and again. And, of course, Louella was always looking for a new "scoop."

A few tidbits: Richard recalls once telling Joan Blondell that her marriage to Dick Powell would not last, and that eventually Dick would remarry and pass away at the age of 58. All this came to pass. On another occasion, this time at one of the large parties that were so frequently given by the movie crowd in those days, Jean Harlow came up to Richard in the presence of Louella, William Powell, and Marian Davies and wanted to know if she would marry the man she was living with. She was very inebriated and not responsible for her actions. But Richard could only see death around her, and so he politely told her that she would not. He told the others, however, that she would be dead in three days. This, too, came to pass. Louella just never could get over the accuracy of his predictions, especially those pertaining to death. When she was speaking about it one day to others, Richard told her, "In your case you have nothing to worry about; you will live into your eighties." And this is precisely what she did.

He also gave readings to many other stars including Judy Garland, Mae West, Mary Martin—just to name a few. He remembers Eva Tangway, the one who became famous as the "I don't care girl," telling him once that she really did care since she had found out that she was going blind. But he helped her as much as he could. Yes, tragedy and unhappiness as well as romance and success filled the lives of the movie greats in those days. But Richard did not care for the constant party life, the drinking and the like that went on at the parties, and so he eventually broke away and severed his relationship with the gossip columnist.

Occasionally he would give private seances in individual homes. Once during a rather routine trance session in a private home in Beverly Hills, a most amazing precognitive demonstration came about rather inadvertently. The year was 1933 and several motion picture stars and producers were present including Charles Ray, Chick Sales, and others. But most important, a large contraption with over a mile or so of silver wire was also present. It was the first prototype of the just recently invented wire recorder, and it was brought along to make a test recording before it was put on the market.

The recorder was turned on and the medium went into trance. Soon an entity by the name of Marshall was speaking through his lips. Now this was the same Marshall who had previously appeared on the stage as the "Question Mark," and he was well-known by some of those present. After some introductory remarks, Marshall went on to give a prediction saying, "There will be an earthquake in Long Beach in three days." Then he told exactly how it was going to happen and to what extent the damage would be. The prediction proved fantastically accurate, for exactly three days later, on March 10, 1933, California experienced its first major earthquake in over 25 years. And not only was its center in the city of Long Beach, but through a strange coincidence the prediction was also recorded.

Now for a bit of nostalgia. Later, while living in the Carthay Circle area, silent screen star Ruth Roland began coming to the seances that Richard held each Friday night in his home. On one particular occasion, just before the seance, Richard recalls walking over to the fireplace and telling her, "You know, when I was a little boy living in Colorado, back in the flicker days, I just had to go see your serials. I remember it would cost six cents, but I would see the cowboy pictures over and over for the same price. I would usually have either a penny or a nickel, and when I would finally get the six cents together, I would go and stay in the movie until my father came and got me." He also told her that even as a little boy, while listening to the voices speak through the trumpet, he had been told that some day Ruth Roland as well as many others would be in his home to consult with him. "Isn't that strange?" he said to her, "and here you are tonight fulfilling that very prophecy."

But tragedy was just around the corner. One day shortly afterwards, Ruth Roland said that she would bring Thelma Todd to the next seance that was to be held the following week. However, in the interim, Miss Todd met up with a mishap which ended in her death. But it was all under mysterious circumstances. She had apparently driven her car into the garage and was then asphyxiated by the fumes; yet there was no motive for this action, and some thought that she had been murdered. But the mystery was not to remain a mystery for long. In the very next seance, Thelma Todd herself revealed what had really happened. She came in and spoke with her friend Ruth Roland, and it seems that she had just come home from a party on that fateful evening of her death. She had been drinking more than she should have, and she became so sleepy that she stayed in the car and didn't have the presence of mind to turn off the motor. It was just as simple as that. One moment of carelessness, and there she was on the other side.

His Great Work Begins

Gradually the phenomenal phase of Richard Zenor's mediumship drew to a close giving rise to a brand new phase, completely different from all of the other phases, and a phase which was destined to become his life's work. This is the highest phase of mediumship known to mortal man—the lending of one's body for the use of the great Masters of Light. But first the body had to be cleansed so that it could become a clearer channel for their higher vibrations. This was the reason for the many years of preparatory work in the other phases. Thus the physical mechanism of Richard Zenor, the practice violin so to speak, eventually became the equivalent of the Stradivarius, and because of its extremely high rate of vibration it was now capable of being used for the first time by the great Teachers from Immensity.

By his own admission, Agasha first spoke through the channel in the year 1933, but this was only for a few words and he probably did not even give his name. Then a year or so later he tested it once more, and by the year 1939 he was manifesting occasionally and giving a little talk now and then. It was about this time that Richard suddenly found himself jerked out of a cycle of psychic manifestations and test demonstrations and thrown into what he terms "a cracker box."

He had come home from his travels and was resting. But one day while visiting with Dr. Henry Duncan McFarland, then President of the National Spiritualist Association, a suggestion was made that Richard take over the available portion of a building on Western Avenue to use for his meetings. The space was small, quite unpretentious, and had few conveniences. But the "Forces," which were always his manager, literally directed him to take the space; and so in the rather inconspicuous premises of this somewhat worn building at 353 North Western Avenue, in the very heart of

Los Angeles, the arisen Teachers of Light began to bring forth their message.

Soon Agasha was manifesting quite frequently, but it had taken several years before his instrument was ready to receive the full impact of the force of his vibrations, not only for an hour or two at a time, but also on a regular basis. And even so, Agasha tells us, he must greatly reduce his frequency or it would severely damage the medium's solar plexus. Then by the year 1943, a full ten years after he had first manifested through his instrument, all was in order and the Agasha Temple of Wisdom was duly founded and organized. It was formally incorporated in the State of California on May 5, 1943.

It should be pointed out at this point that Richard had never been told in his younger years the particulars about his ultimate future work. The knowledge of Agasha and the other Master Teachers had been withheld from him, and the coming of these Illumined Ones came as a complete surprise. He had always known that he had some destiny to fulfill, but as to how it was to be brought about was a complete mystery. Now at last he knew. With the formal establishing of the Agasha Temple of Wisdom in 1943, he realized that his life from that point on (he was then 31) would be completely different; the phenomena stage was over, and now his life would be devoted entirely to enabling the many Master Teachers and other Adepts to take over his body and speak through him, and in so doing accomplish their great work.

With the passing of the years newer and larger quarters were required, and almost by Divine Providence the perfect building became available just a block up the street. It was spacious and provided ample facilities for all of the functions of the growing organization. This new home, at 460 North Western Avenue, was formally dedicated on Sunday evening, October 25, 1953.

Now just what type of an individual is Richard Zenor, really? Most of his friends who have come to know him regard his instrumentality as being entirely separate from his normally easy-going, good-humored, every-day self. And this also includes his quite personable wife, Thelma Turner, whom he married in 1940. They have no children, incidentally. But what do these people say about him? Some have come to know him quite well after a stay for a weekend or so at his house in the desert, or a swim in the pool at his home in Tarzana, or perhaps a summer vacation in his motor home along the highways and byways of America. And it is the unanimous opinion of them all that Richard Zenor is a perfect example of one who has learned true humility. Never once have they heard him complain or speak an unkind word about anyone. And even when he does not agree, his disagreements are always intuitive, kind, and forgiving.

His life over the years has also been one of tremendous activity, but his work week is not the same as yours or mine. There was a time when he would spend a good part of the day and all night long almost every night of the week at work with only a few hours off near breakfast time for sleep. Now he has cut it down to three nights a week, but his work day usually starts shortly after noon and continues uninterrupted until the early hours of the following morning except for a brief break between each trance session. This might be anywhere from just a few minutes up to half an hour or so, depending on the circumstances.

Yes indeed, dedication and service such as this inevitably must end in success, both spiritually and otherwise, and one would certainly have to agree that it has been earned. For Richard Zenor Slocum demonstrates daily how to live a life in a manner befitting the love and understanding that is expressed by the Master Teachers who speak through him.

CHAPTER FOUR

AGASHA: MASTER OF WISDOM

The wise man is ever humble and preserves a willingness to be humble in the eyes of the great or the small. The farther we advance the humbler we become. But as we evolve and learn and grow, we become shining lights to assist ourselves and to guide others. Be ever conscious of the light and of life and of the privilege of having experiences which unfold the light.

—Agasha

JUST who is the Master Teacher Agasha who has returned once more in the 20th century? Just who is this "voice" that manifests and lectures through the entranced Richard Zenor? The words and the philosophy and the wisdom so taught are truly eloquent, but one might ask who he is as an individual and from where has he come. From what fountain of knowledge did he receive his wisdom, and how did he attain it? "What are his credentials?" one might ask, "and how has he the authority to know the truth?" He has always claimed that he will eventually prove every statement that he makes, but how is this to be accomplished? If it is the truth, how can we know that it is so? He states that he returns to us from a consciousness of "knowing," where he no longer has to believe; but where is this consciousness, and how is it different from ours? These are the types of questions an inquiring mind is liable to ask, and an attempt to answer them will occupy our attention now.

In the first place, we must remember that the true story of Agasha is the saga of a great sage. This great saga which comprises his struggles, his trials, his tribulations, and his achievements down through the centuries would make a truly amazing narrative if it were told in its entirety, and it would fill an entire volume in itself. Unfortunately, however, we can only cover the highlights and piece together the bits of information that have been given to the class from time to time. Yet even though this that follows is only a partial story, it should still shed a little more light on the past and consequently on the last earthly incarnation of this great teacher.

9,000 Years Ago in Persia

As every story must have a beginning, so to speak, let us now travel backwards through the centuries and approach a country that until only recently was known as Persia. It is called Iran today. Let us travel far back to a time before recorded history; let us move through a span of time covering 9,000 years. Now let us focus our attention on the era of 7000 B.C. There, in that part of the world, we gaze out on a civilization that was destined not to last long for it perished comparatively soon, that is, as far as civilizations in general are concerned. Eventually the sands of time covered up those cities, and then the civilizations that they represented became extinct.

But for the moment, let us try to understand a little bit about this particular civilization and let us resurrect it, so to speak, from the fragments of information given us from time to time in the classes. It was evidently a very important period, inasmuch as Agasha is always referring to this 9,000 year period as being of the utmost importance as it was the forebearer of the later great Austa civilization. It was in manifestation some 2,000 years before Austa was to give forth its light upon the world and some 4,000 years before this very same Austa was to be renamed Egypt. The teacher of the period refers to it as the "element" of Austa. So then let us listen to him as he gives us some information on this early period in a class in October, 1950.

"During that time," he starts out, "it was a great struggle to bring our people not only into spiritual realization, but also to bring them into life and for them to sustain themselves. We had not the same conditions that later developed in Austa. We tried to help them to recall the existence of their prior lives, and it was also very difficult for me to bring unto my people the understanding of what would transpire. When I told them about life on the great continent of Atlantis, they were not in a position to understand it because my people during the time of my stay upon the earth plane lived in a very primitive way. I lived and I struggled with those who had not the understanding on the surface, but inwardly I knew that they knew. I knew that they would eventually come unto the correct understanding.

"Now Agasha also lived during my period. In fact, he reembodied himself many times over this 2,000-year preparatory period in order to perfect himself and prepare himself for his greater destiny to come later in Austa. It was my privilege to make contact with Agasha many times, and I witnessed his demonstrations and the things that he did for the people."

Then the teacher started talking about the future as he knew it at the time. He went on to say, "I would often gaze out over the desert land and picture clearly the world that I knew would eventually come into manifestation there. For during the time that I had lived, I was able to see so clearly the great, great temples that would be erected there in the desert in time, and along the great river which represents the Nile of today. Yes, I knew of what was to be."

This teacher then told the class that even though their land in the area of Persia was quite beautiful, although rather primitive, many of the people became disgruntled. They were not having the peace that they should have had, and the cooperation among the native population was very poor. As a consequence, many then left that part of the world and migrated into the adjoining countries. Eventually a great number established their kingdom along the Nile, and this later came to be known as Austa. Others established their kingdoms elsewhere.

But in Austa, a far greater peace began to prevail than had ever been known in the earlier country. Messengers were sent back to inform the friends and relatives of the immigrants that here indeed was the promised land. They told them of the great new country that they had found, a place where peace prevailed, and even more then migrated into Austa. Eventually, the few that remained in the mother country then passed out of the physical body and the earlier civilization was no more.

Austa: The Promised Land

Agasha states that the Austa civilization did not come into manifestation all of a sudden. It took many hundreds of years for it to become established. Earlier, the travelers of the period had traversed all over that part of the known world seeking for a kingdom that would be not exactly a retreat, but a place where a kingdom of peace could be established. Agasha tells us that the neighboring countries were always warring among themselves and that there was much confusion, the same as there is today. But he says that the kingdom that these pioneers eventually established along the Nile, through many, many incarnations, came to be almost a paradise when compared with the adjoining countries.

The Nile was very beautiful, particularly so when the sun would set and cast its rays upon the waters. And the morning sunrise was truly superb as the sun would peek above the horizon and then reflect the glory of that which was to be the promised land—the land that those early pioneers had so chosen at the time. Of course, Austa was very different then and nothing like the Egypt of today. They also knew that they would be able to erect great temples in time, if they were patient.

So it came to pass that eventually practically every individual who had lived in the 9,000 year period in Persia reembodied himself into Austa, or into the neighboring countries that were called by various names during that time. This then covers a span of over 2,000 years from the 9,000 year period up to the 7,000 year period. Even many who had first migrated into one of the neighboring countries eventually ended up in Austa during the 2,000-year Peace Period to follow, dating from 5000 B.C. to 3000 B.C. Thus we find that there are a great number of people on the earth today who have had lives at one time or another in Austa—and this could run into the millions! There is a very good chance that you, the reader of this book, may have participated in the 2,000-year period of peace.

However, in the early years of Austa, the people migrating there realized that they had to have organization. They had to have leaders before the great Austa consciousness could become what it was destined to become. Thus various groups were formed and leaders emerged from within the groups. These leaders then became the instructors, the inspired ones, the healers, the workers. They became all of these things to the many followers that they were able to attract unto themselves.

The Beginnings of the 37 Sects

We find then the sects beginning to form. Perhaps there were many in one sect and few in another. Some of the sects expanded to the point where they contained well over 100,000 members, others perhaps reached only 50,000, and still others never contained more than a few thousand. The size of the sect depended only upon the desire of the people following that particular leader. Of course, all of the members of each sect always worked under the auspices of the sect leader. But having more members in his congregation did not mean that one leader was any greater or any more powerful than any other leader. Agasha says that the size of the sect was determined not only by the popularity of its leadership, but also by how far the individual members had gone in their spiritual attainment. Some of the sects limited their membership to only those who could qualify and pass into the various degrees, thus attracting only the serious-minded students.

This building of the sects went on over a long period of time as Austa was being established, until 37 different sects were ultimately formed and recognized. The procedure was much the same as the state system in America today whereby the 13 original states gradually increased to the present number of 50 over a period of time.

Thus we see that from the initial, courageous efforts of the few brave souls who originally pioneered this land, a great new kingdom was eventually established. Or perhaps we should call it the state of Austa as there were no kings in the sense of the word. However, the leaders felt perfectly free to direct and control their individual subjects in such a way so that each sect member would have the maximum opportunity for spiritual growth. In this way, many were able to unfold and become attuned to the God within.

Therefore, by the time the 2,000-year preparatory period had run its course (5000 B.C.), Austa had become a truly enlightened state. This was so because the people of Austa, apart from all of the other surrounding countries, well recognized their significance unto mankind, unto the world, and unto the universe. Of course, each of the sects had differences of opinion, indeed they did, but at least they all recognized their relationship unto the Universal God Consciousness. Consequently, Austa was well established by the time the man called Agasha had his great incarnation of destiny and that which was to be his last physical life.

We can readily see then that Agasha personally had nothing to do with the eventual establishment of the 37 different sects—that is not outwardly, not unto his outer consciousness. Yet this is certainly not to imply that he did not aid in their growth. He was very active in many incarnations during the 2,000-year preparatory period as he strove to prove his competency, his capability, his healing ability, and his general leadership. Thus it is only natural that we find him as the leader of his own sect in this, his final incarnation. He had many followers and he could speak on various subjects, always inspiring the ones who were listening.

However, even in this last life he was not the leader of his sect in the early days of his career. He had to earn that position by striving every step of the way. We do not know too much of his youth, but he did tell the class one evening of an incident that happened to him once while he was crossing the desert country on foot. This is a very interesting story, not only because it tells us of his first meeting with his teacher, Coman Coban, but also because of the lesson that it teaches. Therefore it is worth repeating here.

An Encounter on the Desert

Agasha had begun a journey across the burning sands to a destination that was some distance away. As there was no other means of transportation in those days he had to walk—and to walk he had to have sandals, and he had to have food to eat, and he had to have water to drink. All well and good. But there came a time in this journey when he had none of these things. His few worldly resources were eventually used up and, worse yet, he had only the merest of garments, and these were badly worn and patched. Soon even his sandals that he had repaired so often became absolutely beyond repair and were quite useless to him. When this time finally did come, it was in the very worst period that it could have happened, on what seemed to him to be the hottest day of the year.

He had to walk in the heat of the sun on the hot sands,

with no sandals, and with no way to cool his feet. There was no shade for miles, and all he could do was jump up and down because his feet were very tender. Tears came to his eyes because his feet were extremely painful and he had neither food nor water with which to slack his hunger or quench his thirst.

In his agony, he heard a voice speaking. It was as though it came from no particular place, yet he heard it distinctly. It spoke and said, "Be still, my son. Be still within your own kingdom." He looked around to see if he could see from whence it came, but he could not. He saw no one; he only heard the voice. His feet were still burning, the same as before, so he kept on hopping. The voice came again, and again it bade him to be still. But it was very difficult to be still.

Then there appeared before him, not in the flesh of the material sense, but there was the faint outline of a man, and a very wonderful man he was. He was dressed in robes that were beautiful and colorful. In his hands he held the food that they ate in those days and the equivalent of a canteen of water. There it was, that which he needed so badly, for Agasha knew full well that anyone who had not a supply of food and water soon would perish. Then as he looked at the one who had appeared there before him, he also knew that he had come from nowhere on this earth for indeed there was nowhere for the stranger to have concealed himself. Nothing but barren sands could be seen as far as the eye could reach, and yet he saw him not until he had appeared there before him with his soulful eyes and fine, expressive face. He even found that as he looked upon him, he had ceased hopping from one foot to another almost without knowing it, and somehow the fears of losing his life had gone away.

Agasha reached out, thinking of course that the stranger was going to give him the water. He was not unkind or forbidding, but neither did he offer it. Then with his left hand he reached out for the food, but somehow, although the stranger did not move, he was not able to reach that which he desired so much. He tried to seize some of the cloth from the ample robe that he wore, but as he did this he realized that it was not real to the touch and that he could not grasp it. Then he began to think that he was losing his mind. But this fear did not last long as gradually he came to the realization that this was a Master Teacher who had appeared before him, and at a time when he was in great distress and in the last stages of physical suffering.

As the voice had spoken to him before, it then spoke again: "The food take not, nor drink from the water. If I saved your life, then you would be very grateful that I had appeared unto you. But I have not come for that reason. I have appeared instead to teach you a very valuable lesson." There was silence for a moment, and then he continued saying, "First of all, you must know that you are as much a part of the Universal Spirit God as I am."

Agasha listened to what he was saying, but he asked no questions as to who he really was. What really mattered to Agasha was that this stranger had the food that he wanted, and he also had the water. He was past caring whether he was spirit or flesh; the food looked tangible and he wanted it because he wanted to survive. And a philosophical discourse was probably the last thing that he desired at that particular moment. But he again looked down at his feet, and he noticed that he was no longer hopping from one foot to another. The sand was just as hot as it had been before, but the pain had gone. So Agasha listened and tried to absorb what was being said.

"The food that I hold here in my hand is within you," the teacher continued, "and the water that I have has already quenched your thirst. But you do not yet realize that this has happened. As soon as you come to the divine realization within yourself that you have the food and the water and the other things you need, and as soon as you become peaceful and right within yourself, then these things will permit me to lead you to a village that is only a short distance away where you can obtain everything that you need."

Agasha then became ever so peaceful within himself, and as he did this he found that he had renewed strength and vigor. He then followed the teacher faithfully for what seemed to be several miles, and eventually they reached a little community. It seemed to appear out of nowhere for it had been hidden from Agasha previously; he had been blind to that which was in reality so very, very close. Then when he was not looking, and when he did not expect it, the teacher disappeared taking with him the sandals and the food and the water that he had so desired. But Agasha knew that even though he had taken these material things away with him, the teacher had left him on the *path that leads to understanding*. He then quenched his thirst at the well in the center of the village and was ever so thankful as he drank the pure cool water from the gourd.

It was not until many years later, many years even after he had become the leader of his own sect, that Agasha learned the identity of the teacher that had appeared before him on that lonely day in the early period of his career. Eventually he was told by his own Master Teacher, Coman Coban, that this experience had indeed been a test for him, that he had actually seen what he had wanted to see, and that Coman Coban had produced it. He had appeared to Agasha at that time because all he had been thinking of was his own comfort, and it was necessary for the teacher to prod the disciple to search within his inner self and thus begin learning the laws of life.

Agasha's Early Years

Agasha evidently took this "prod" quite well because, as we said earlier, he went on to become the leader of his sect. But we still might say that in that particular incarnation he had it comparatively easy when we compare it to the many, many previous lifetimes of struggle and strife. We must remember that he lived in a country where they were not contaminated by the material as we are contaminated today. He did not have so many material things to contend with.

Yet, basically, men were the same then as they are today, for they would fight if they were not inclined to accept or believe the things that were imposed upon them. And they would most certainly argue with new religious concepts that were not in agreement with their own thinking. However, as most teachers at that time had had the awakening and were attuned to the Atlantean consciousness, there were not the tremendous religious conflicts there in the land of Austa that exist in the world today. While the neighboring countries were still in a state of stress, confusion, and misunderstanding, the people of Austa had it comparatively easy because they were destined to come into the higher understanding and reestablish the kingdom. It was these conditions that later enabled Agasha to put across his thoughts unto the various other sects without too much opposition, and this was especially true when we consider that the others were also in a position to come into the same understanding of the laws that he unveiled.

We can say this because the leaders of the various sects were channels, and they received their messages and their information from teachers of the most high. Thus these leaders or channels—mediums, if you want to use the term—were deeply engrossed in bringing forth much from that vast Atlantean consciousness. Yet at the same time, their interpretations of what they had received seemed to vary. The single thread that would tie it all together was missing. But all during the first century of the Peace Period, these great souls were still directly attuned to that great reservoir of information which dated back to the Atlantean consciousness.

Now the various sects of the time, although not necessarily disagreeing as there was not that disagreement, seemed to want to go off by themselves in various groups to try to find their own interpretation of God. They were wondering about God, they were wondering about life, and they were speculating as to the teachings that were originally given during the time of Atlantis. They were not too far removed from the past, nor from the truth, but they needed organization. It was not that they needed a single individual to be in control over all of the sects; no indeed, it was only that they needed guidance in the right direction so that each one could then unfold in the proper manner and thus bring back the true memory of the past. Perhaps this is the same situation that exists today, who knows? But in any event, Agasha says that all of their interpretations at the time varied to one degree or another.

However, this condition offered no particular problem. What was important was that the great Atlantean teachings of the past were once more brought forth into the present through the channelship of the many great souls of the period. Atlantis became the textbook, and many great truths were read from these pages of the past. For instance, the great numerical force that controls each and every individual was unveiled and understood. Thus they became very conscious of numerals. The numerical meanings of names and words were also revealed, as well as were the symbols that were associated with them. The very name *Austa* itself, incidentally, is an Atlantean word meaning land of beauty, land of peace. Likewise the origins of many of the words in the languages of today are pure Atlantean. Even the names of almost all of the teachers in the Agashan organization are no exception to this rule. These examples will suffice for the moment, but down through the years Agasha has given us a considerable amount of material relative to the Atlantean teachings that were brought forth there in Austa.

Now Agasha has never set himself up as an authority on this point, but needless to say we can surmise that he was one of the major instruments or channels of the period. But earning this channelship did not come easy. It was not until after ceaseless efforts that Agasha was eventually able to draw the great power from the great Cosmic Force. He learned to draw the anims (spiritual thought atoms) unto himself, and through his meditations he came to know their power as they relate to mankind. He never ceased with his daily efforts in going into meditation in order to receive more and more information pertaining to things he desired to know, and during the course of his meditations and through his mediumship many teachers were able to visit him frequently. Eventually Agasha and the others who were on the same path contacted higher and higher degrees of consciousness until ultimately they broke through into the great consciousness of Atlantis. But Agasha's crowning achievement occurred when he made contact once again with his own individual, beloved Atlantean teacher whom the many Agashans now know as Coman Coban.

Contact with the Atlanteans

The story of Agasha's second contact with Coman Coban during the early days of his last incarnation in Austa is a fascinating one. And it came at the precise moment when he finally achieved that inner experience known as the "Great Awakening." Agasha had struggled for a long period of time to have this ultimate experience, and finally the great moment arrived. Finally it was to be given unto him. But when it did occur, he realized that it had been coming to him all the while, ever so gradually, but that he had not been aware of the significance. In the earlier stages of his growth it seemed as though he could vaguely remember things of the past, but he could not describe them. He could not tell others because he was not too sure himself what he had remembered. It was like having a dream, and even though the dream itself was so very, very clear, upon awakening most of the pertinent details vanished from his consciousness. All that was left to him was that a few moments before, a very beautiful experience was occurring. He waited for more impressions. Gradually he had the impression of a voice—a voice far away in the distance. He had heard the voice many times before down through the years, but he had never realized its significance.

Then one day it happened. There was the voice again in the distance, and it came closer, and closer, and closer. What was happening to him? Where was he? This time the answer was soon forthcoming as a great dam was about to burst from within his own being. Then as the waters of consciousness finally flooded in upon him, he awakened into the consciousness of Coman Coban. It was the Great Awakening! And more than that, here he was in the presence of the very same teacher who had appeared before him in the desert a number of years earlier and who had started him on that *path that leads to understanding.*

It turned out that Coman Coban had been directing Agasha's movements down through the ages. He had been watching him pay karma upon the earth plane for a time too long to remember. And during the prior 2,000 years especially, it had been quite stressful for the average person upon the earth plane in that part of the world. Agasha's karma was no exception. He had been struggling the same as we in our present generation have been struggling for the past 2,000 years. The situation was the same; only the time element was different. But Agasha's great awakening came through a great teacher, one of the Intermediaries of Intermediaries, and one who had known him in the consciousness of Atlantis. He had even known him prior to Atlantis; indeed, it seemed that he had always known him. Agasha immediately felt this great closeness, even though he outwardly did not then understand its significance.

Through the power of this great Ascended Master, Agasha was able to learn many things. Or perhaps we should say it was through the powers of his own soul, as the teacher appears, basically, to introduce the disciple to his own Higher Self. And once the Great Awakening has occurred, the disciple is left pretty much to his own resources although always under the watchful guidance of the teacher. Thus each day that Agasha now went into meditation, many wonderful things were given and on a larger scale than before. At times he did not know what he was going to receive, but he was willing to receive whatever he could—whatever his soul wanted to reveal unto him. And he did have many things revealed because he had learned to open the door, to arouse the soul, and thus to awaken the Divine Consciousness from within.

Agasha would usually go into meditation in a special chamber in the temple which was provided for that purpose. These were called chambers of purification or chambers of cleansing. In a class in April, 1950, he recalled so clearly the time he had entered one of these great chambers and remained therein for a period of seven days. Through the application of certain principles of yoga he was able to obtain such a complete state of relaxation that the body had no further need for either food or water. It simply drew the prana out of the atmosphere for its sustenance. Thus the body was cleansed as the impurities were expended—literally consumed by the cosmic fire contained within the soul.

On this particular occasion he was able to reexperience many events that took place on the great continent of Atlantis. He saw himself as he had appeared there; he recalled many incarnations of the Atlantean period. Then he recalled his lives in Persia as well as in Austa during the 2,000-year preparatory period. And these visions of the past were presented so clearly unto his consciousness that it was just as if he were living there at that particular time. Then other experiences of an even more incredible nature were also given to him. It was like a journey into the universe of his own Being, and there are no words to adequately describe it. He went on to say that after awakening in the chamber and returning once more to the sunlight of the outer world, he quite naturally spoke to his disciples and the others of his experiences and what he had learned. He found that the majority of them had had quite similar experiences which only went to prove that the souls living in Austa at that time were directly related to one another during the Atlantean period.

But then a strange mystery seemed to develop. He found

out through his teacher, Coman Coban, that the Atlantean lives dated back more than 165,000 years (172,000 years from the present date), and of course he realized that the more recent lives in Persia dated back only 2,000 years. But what of the intervening period? There was a time lapse here. He seemed to have become oblivious to that great gap in time and, try as he might, he could receive no information on any lives whatsoever during the intervening period from Atlantis to Persia. The curtain remained closed for this tremendous lapse in time. He asked his teacher about it, but Coman Coban's answer was equally as mysterious. The answer was simply that it was the soul's desire not to reveal this desired information at that particular time. He was not to question why it was not given unto him. His soul had desired for him to recall his Atlantean experiences and had replayed the tape, so to speak. But the door was closed on the intervening period. This satisfied Agasha, but at the same time he realized that there was much more to life than what appeared on the surface.

As he continued with his meditations, he also realized that he had been given the power to step out into the sunlight, contact individuals, and then recognize them not so much from their physiognomy or physical features, but recognize them on a soul level. He could feel the drawing power connecting his soul with their soul, and there was an inner recognition over and above that of the outer personality. Agasha tells us that there is still that same connection that connects us all together today, but it was a very strange experience for him at that time and he asked Coman Coban about it: "Is it possible for all on the earth plane to have this experience and gain this knowledge of the connection with all other souls?" he asked. "Can all receive the same validation?" Agasha was rather astounded inasmuch as he had not only learned, but he had actually realized the Oneness that connects all souls together.

Coman Coban replied, "Yes, that which you have learned

and attained shall likewise be attained by others. It eventually shall be attained by all children of the earth plane; no matter how many lives they live, they shall all attain the same—the knowledge and the realization that all is One." Agasha thought this answer was quite wonderful, for he says that this experience of the Oneness simply cannot be described.

Then Coman Coban proceeded to inform Agasha that he had a great mission to perform. He would have much work to do upon the earth plane, and after this had been accomplished, he then would have an even greater awakening. He was to obey certain commands made of him by the soul as well as by other teachers who were to manifest to him from time to time. He told him that this was the period when the Teachers of Light would bring forth the Universal Consciousness of God unto those living within the Land of Austa once again, and then eventually, thousands of years into the future, to all of mankind. It was through destiny that they had come together, he went on to explain, and it had been so ordained that Agasha would become the channel through which this Universal God Consciousness of the Oneness could be reestablished.

Coman Coban acknowledged the fact that the various sect leaders differed in their opinions as to the ultimate nature of the God Consciousness. This was only natural because they lacked the golden thread that would unite their beliefs into one composite whole. He also had the knowledge that Agasha would be given the understanding in such a way that he would be able to prove unto the other sects, without a question of a doubt, the ultimate nature of the Oneness. Thus Agasha was then to prepare himself to become more sensitive to the higher vibrations, and in this way be able to bring forth these revelations to the 37 different sects whereby they could then merge and become a single Grand Unit of the Great White Way.

Agasha was informed that Austa was a chosen land,

chosen by the Atlanteans back in a time when Atlantis was in full swing and in full power. This was indeed the promised land. Coman Coban then went on to explain that this enlightened consciousness of God would only prevail in the small land of Austa for a period of 2,000 years, after which there would ensue a 5,000-year period of darkness. Eventually though, in the distant tomorrows, a new Atlantis would be established once more in a land across the sea.

Perhaps we can best understand the mission of Agasha—a mission to bring back the Atlantean consciousness through his channelship under the direction of the Atlantean Masters—by quoting that great Atlantean directly. Even in the days of Austa, some 7,000 years ago, Coman Coban would be a favored one to bring forth the message from Atlantis. Many times he would speak through Agasha to the assembled congregation in much the same manner as Agasha manifests to his disciples in the present-day class through Richard Zenor. In fact, they often called Coman Coban the "Voice of Atlantis." Therefore, let us now hear from the old maestro himself as he speaks so humbly, and so unpretentiously, to the people of the 20th century—or to the return of the Atlanteans, as he so often says. Coman Coban's voice is deep and charming. The date is November 19, 1951.

Coman Coban: The Voice of Atlantis

"Well," he pauses, and then continues, "how do you do, blessed disciples of Agasha? How are you? Are you happy tonight? I know that when I first came unto Agasha, many years before he called the 37 sects into one group under one heading, he was certainly happy. For happiness is a way of life. Then when the time came for me to inform him on the inner planes that it would be necessary for us to discuss the great message that was to be given to his people, why, he was overjoyed. For this was the same great message that was given to the Atlanteans during my day and to other civilizations even before that. I said unto Agasha that it must be revived, and that he would be in a position to bring this message unto his people, for it would be generally accepted by those who had sought in this direction.

"And so it was done. That which did exist many thousands of years ago was again given unto mankind. It was shown unto mankind once more because I was desirous of letting mankind realize his position in the physical expression. I wanted to let him know of his life which was to come and to remind him that he must not live in despair, nor think that he is being deprived of special things in his existence upon the physical plane, indeed not.

"How well I can recall the great city of Atlantis! How well I can recall that great civilization, but it is a myth to some today. Many that roam the earth do not believe it existed, but it did exist as truly as I am manifesting unto you tonight. It was in existence, and many children of the earth today took an active part during that great civilization. It is my desire then to bring unto your attention tonight that I came forth during that time, and that I brought forth light and peace unto the many whom I was able to contact there in that great consciousness.

"Then I appeared again 7,000 years ago when I realized that my son, who had come back many times, had made the call for the Great Awakening. But long before I appeared, I was preparing and conditioning him to receive my message. I wanted every word, absolutely every word, to be understood so that my meaning could never be misconstrued simply because I was on this side and he was on the physical plane. Nor did I want the mortal mind to misunderstand; I wanted it to respond most heartily unto the consciousness that I had found myself in. Thus it was made possible for me to come and to be able to say unto my son of the earth, 'Go and touch the people, reach them, reach their hearts, and bring them unto one common cause. In this way then the Understanding of God can be established so that it may be perpetuated down through the years.' And he went, and he taught, and he gave forth light. He sought this one out, he sought that one out, and he conversed. When he conversed he won their confidence, and they in turn cooperated. In time then, that which was to last for 2,000 years was finally established.

"Yet tonight we realize that men have suffered unmercifully down through the generations because of a lack of understanding. But only seemingly had they become oblivious to the things that were given to them in the beginning. Yes, we are definitely trying to renew; we are trying once more to bring forth light and power and peace unto mankind.

"I will bring unto your attention tonight that Agasha has fulfilled my wish. He has fulfilled his soul's wish and he has fulfilled the Universal Consciousness God's wish. The wish is for you to know the purpose of life. We who descend upon the physical plane wish to help you to arise and become the same as we are. Agasha is giving it to you now. He is taking you back thousands of years and millions of years, explaining life to you and explaining your life and your life to come. There could be no better way for you to find happiness upon the earth than through the method that Agasha is employing. Indeed, he is fulfilling the wish of the Great White Way as well as—reverting back again—fulfilling my wish, his soul's wish, and the Universal Consciousness God's wish. And so it is being given again today.

"In those early days I told my son that there would be many to come and that there would be many to go, but to be not dismayed, for I told him that there would be other teachers who would come upon the earth plane, generations hence, who would also have their message. There would come Moses, and there would come Kraio—the one whom the Christian minds refer to as Jesus but who is known as Kraio to you. Then other great souls would come as they were given unto mankind including the great prophets: Jeremiah, for one, and then Zoroaster when we come into the lesser period of time. We come to all these souls who brought forth light and peace during their particular period. All had had to revert back to Atlantis. All had had to revert back to the consciousness of Agasha. The modern era began when Agasha established the great Peace Period, which was our desire from the great Consciousness of Immensity. So he obeyed, the same as Kraio obeyed, and thus fulfilled his mission.

"Agasha and I know full well that the Masters had returned onto the earth *after* they had earned their great mastership. They then returned onto the earth to serve in their own humble way, so as to finish up their karma or whatever it might be at the time. The word *master* means teacher to us, and the teacher has to earn every step of the way.

"Agasha, however, instead of having to go through the toils and torments of hell as he had gone through before, was then able to arise after he had finished his period upon the physical plane. He went then into the Consciousness and ascended, only to wait patiently for the other souls, the disciples, and the remaining ones upon the earth plane to return and finish up their karma. Thus the many souls connected with him in the past have returned onto the earth plane to live various lives in different races and in different parts of the world. This brings you right up to where you are today, to where you stand in the light still striving to understand and still paying your karma in order to prepare yourself for better things.

"We realize then that we have been striving to establish the great kingdom whereby the higher learning could be given unto mankind. Now this was not appreciated in the earlier days by some who had returned onto the earth, of course not. But I told Agasha that in time, although many men would fail in some embodiments, they would always eventually return and thus be able to pick up that which we desired to give and what is being given today. So when Agasha speaks on this subject again, I want you to realize that if we are to learn, we must get to the origin of all things in order to understand the true meaning of life.

"So I am grateful to come in behalf of Agasha, bringing forth light and peace as I did in his earlier day. I also knew of his work when he was a young man, how he went forth, and how he tried to bring forth light in his earlier days even before he knew about the great powers of Immensity. He was oblivious to it, children of the earth, the same as many were down through the ages, and the same as you are today. Now we have come to revive and to renew the strength so that all of you who were members at some time or other of the various sects may realize the significance of same. It is very vital to know about them and to realize your connection in the future with the Agashan movement. You see, we realized that all of these things would come about, and they have turned out just exactly as we saw them some 7,000 years in the past. Now we realize what the future holds for all disciples and what we shall be able to accomplish. I am grateful then to speak in behalf of my son, Agasha, who brings forth light and peace. This is his teacher, Coman Coban, fulfilling the wish of the Great White Way. God bless you, and good night."

Good night, Coman Coban, and thank you. Agasha has said that the higher you are the more humble you become, and Coman Coban is no exception. The simple love that is expressed between father and son, guru and chela, teacher and disciple, is beyond compare. Likewise, whenever Agasha speaks of his teacher, Coman Coban, the mutual love and admiration of the one for the other seems to shine forth and back up the words that are expressed. Consequently, a true understanding of the Master Teacher Agasha, this Master of Wisdom, cannot be adequately obtained without likewise bringing in the Teacher, or the force behind the Master.

Realization of the Oneness

Thus it came to pass that after Agasha had had the Great Awakening—that awakening into the consciousness of the Master Teacher and likewise into the consciousness of Atlantis—he received instruction over a period of several years. He became what is known as a "clear channel," an instrument, a medium to bring forth the ancient Atlantean teachings of the Universal Consciousness God—the Consciousness of the great Oneness, of which all that is in existence is a part.

Then during this period he was also able to observe the activity among the members of the various other religious sects which made up Austa at the time. He visited the different regions along the Nile; he covered the Lower Nile and he covered the Upper Nile. He visited with the people, and he conversed with the teachers and the leaders of the various sects. But the important thing was that he listened intently to what was said by these teachers, and then he compared the viewpoints expressed by the sect leaders with the message as set forth by his own teacher, Coman Coban. There were discrepancies, true, but there were not overwhelming discrepancies. Each sect seemed to be convinced that the answer that they each had received individually was the correct truth. The situation was fairly crying out for clarification and enlightenment—a simple, provable statement of ultimate truth which would bind the teachings of all of the sects into one, true, undisputable, ultimate reality. In back of his mind he always remembered those words that Coman Coban had once said unto him, "You shall go and clear the way. You shall be *One* and you shall act as an instrument upon the physical plane to prove unto mankind that all men, in the ultimate reality, are also *One.*"

Now just what did Coman Coban really mean by this? How could Agasha prove that all men were One? He had never doubted Coman Coban before because to Agasha this great teacher was *The* Intermediary of the Intermediaries. An Intermediary, incidentally, is a high teacher who acts as a channel or medium between two different states of consciousness. And, of course, Agasha also knew that to others Coman Coban was only *One* of the Intermediaries of the Intermediaries. But be this as it may, what was Coman Coban really trying to tell him? What was the real significance behind these words?

Agasha pondered over this question for many hours, and

then suddenly one day he knew. Of course—why didn't he think of it before? The answer was basically very simple, but more than that, it could quite easily be proved mathematically. What was this mathematical solution? For the answer to this question, the reader will have to wait for the third volume of this series titled *The English Cabalah*; in this book, Agasha's mathematics are elucidated in considerable detail. But for the moment, let us just say that Agasha readily understood that there simply could not be any other solution. Yes, it was true; all men in the ultimate reality *are* One. And that One is God.

The Unification of the 37 Sects

Soon after this tremendous realization, Coman Coban came unto Agasha one day in his meditations and said, "Agasha, now that you have come unto the realization of the Oneness, it is time for us to make an attempt to call the 37 sects together into *One Grand Unit.* In this way we can establish once again that which had been given unto them in the past, but which they are oblivious of today. This realization should now be given unto these people in such a manner so that they will be able to accept it. This you can now do. Then after the kingdom is thus established, we can have even more harmony and peace among the sects; and this harmony and peace shall then be perpetuated down through the years."

So Agasha, having implicit faith in the philosophy of the Oneness as set forth by his teacher, Coman Coban, set out to do just that. He had no particular opposition because these simple truths of life became so obvious once they were presented in the light of his understanding. Agasha had evidently become quite learned in the laws of mathematics because he was able to demonstrate, quite forcefully, the truths of the philosophy so taught. He also visualized everyone in a state of perfection and saw them coming unto the understanding. This power of visualization was a tool that he used as he prepared the way and as he sent out the call, and then they all responded most beautifully to the call. Agasha tells us that as he conversed with them, one by one, he showed them that what they had previously understood was not false, but that this new understanding was only a higher truth that embraced all of the teachings and tied them all together, most beautifully, into one, single, grand philosophy of life. Thus by unification they could then establish this great movement.

The first sect leader that Agasha contacted was a man of great repute and also one of great wealth. His name was Mamon. He was wealthy not so much in the sense that we refer to wealth today, but he was wealthy insofar that he was privileged, through his own efforts, to have the cooperation, the backing, and the power necessary to accomplish many things and bring forth much unto his people. He helped them to grow mentally, physically, and spiritually and to have many psychic presentations. Mamon was also a great leader, and Agasha always pays him the highest tribute, for it was through Mamon's efforts, to a large extent, that eventually Agasha was enabled to bring the entire 37 sects to one understanding and under one heading. Mamon has returned in the 20th century, incidentally, as the personal teacher of James Crenshaw, the author of the first book about Agasha, *Telephone Between Worlds.*[1]

Thus it was because of Mamon's great influence, that Agasha called upon him first. He spoke to him about this great truth of the Oneness, about how he was endeavoring to establish the Universal Consciousness of God, the same as it had once before been established during the great consciousness of Atlantis. Mamon was impressed with the depth of the understanding brought forth by Coman Coban, and he believed with Agasha that all of the sects would cooperate. Thus a great bond of friendship was established that was to endure down through the years. Mamon could see the value in the unification of the sects, and he then visited the other sect leaders in much the same manner that Agasha had been doing over the years, only now a definite program was presented for their acceptance. Therefore, it was not long before they both realized that they were well on their way toward accomplishing that which they had set out to accomplish, and through the combined efforts of these two great leaders the sects were gradually brought into the fold.

As the various sects were admitted into the group, they were numbered in the order of their acceptance—from one to 37. This seemingly arbitrary numbering system lasted for almost 2,000 years, and even to this day, each sect in the Agashan organization is known by the particular number it was given at the time of its acceptance into the kingdom. Agasha's sect is naturally known as Number One inasmuch as his was the original sect to embrace the Universal Consciousness of God, to embrace not a person, but the Universal Consciousness of which you, and I, and all of the infinite life throughout the entire universe are a part. Mamon's sect then came to be known as Sect Number Two, which in turn was followed by Sect Number Three, and so forth up to Sect Number 37.

Now the individuals within these sects ranged into the thousands, and eventually into the hundreds of thousands, and Agasha says that after acceptance into the group a great blessing was bestowed upon all of the people through the great power of *unification with one united cause and purpose.* All were most harmonious in their relationship with one another, and peace prevailed for 2,000 years.

The Great Convention

As a climactic event to the sects being absorbed into one movement, a great convention was called and held in order to cement together the bonds between the 37 different sects which were now united into one Grand Unit of the Great White Way, a Universal Brotherhood of the Masters. This grand meeting was convened with representatives from all of the sects coming together from afar, traveling across the desert sands from the farthest reaches of the land of Austa, and assembling by the thousands along the banks of the River Nile, and not too far, incidentally, from the site of the Great Pyramid which had not yet come into manifestation. The date of this grand convention was exactly 7,000 years prior to the year 1965 according to our present calendar.

Not only did Agasha speak, but all the leaders of the other sects also participated to a remarkable extent. First one would speak, and then another, as the various speakers gave out their thoughts as they began to debate. They eliminated, they corrected, they adjusted. And eventually they established a mutual bond of understanding which was to endure for the next 2,000 years. It must have been a truly magnificent sight to observe the thousands who were present, people from all over the land, as they moved and mingled about with their garments all blending so harmoniously. Agasha says that the people in that day garbed themselves very colorfully, and all this was enhanced in the bright sunlight of the desert sky.

But perhaps the most beautiful thing of all was the simple fact that people could come together in a small country which was surrounded by warring factions, and in the midst of this confusion, not only agree upon but actually establish the peace and harmony that did prevail. They knew intuitively that it could not prevail forever, but they also knew that it would prevail in that chosen land for many generations to come. Actually, it went on to last for 2,000 years until the powers of darkness would once again settle over the land, but for that period of time Austa was truly blessed with the sunlight of God.

The system of sound amplification was quite naturally very different than it is today. Without the electronics of our present era, one would think that it would present a problem, but never underestimate the powers of necessity. They were able to perfect a system where one group of people would relay the message unto the adjoining group, and so on and on from one group to another. This was done in perfect rhythm and unison so that none of the words were garbled, and with this system in operation every man, woman, and child in the entire mass meeting could then very easily hear the words and understand what was spoken in a most beautiful way. It really was beautiful and melodious because the native tongue of that time in Austa was a most expressive language, far more expressive in its sound quality than the English language is today.

Then at the conclusion of the convention, and during a quiet moment while Agasha gazed out over that vast audience, Agasha suddenly received a mental call from his teacher, Coman Coban, who said, "Son, it has become a success. Now we are going to perpetuate the message and establish the kingdom. Ask all to now join in with the understanding that peace shall prevail for 2,000 years in this land of ours." So Agasha did just that.

He spoke out unto the multitude and told them that this was just the beginning of a great, great friendship among the sects. But he also warned them that this would not last forever. He expressed the thought that eventually the future generations would encounter much opposition as millions of souls that needed further understanding gradually embodied themselves in their land. These souls would come from unenlightened countries a great distance away. Then, as these young souls would become absorbed in their midst, much toil and suffering would be encountered. But for the next 2,000 years a great future was assured.

But before they adjourned and traveled back over the desert sands to their respective kingdoms or states, the various sect leaders fully realized that a great deal had been accomplished. Firstly, they were thankful for the united understanding of the nature of the Universal God Consciousness and also for the illumination that this understanding necessarily brought forth. Secondly, plans were made to assemble again, and again, and again, and they knew that their new understanding of the God Consciousness would enable them to erect great temples and other structures so that meeting places for the various sects to assemble could be provided. In fact, it was at this convention that the nucleus of the idea to erect that great monument of spirituality known as the Great Pyramid was actually born. But more will be given about this in the following chapter. And then thirdly, a large plaque with a central pyramidal design and which in turn carried the symbols of each of the 37 different sects—but now united into one grand unit—was prepared and carried out to symbolize the occasion. Agasha even states that this plaque will eventually be rediscovered, and when the hieroglyphics are deciphered correctly, it will prove to mankind the existence of this convention and verify other details pertaining to the unification of the sects.

All of these things, and many others, were then discussed and either accepted or rejected within the committees or subcommittees of the various groups so assembled. But eventually, with so much accomplished, that final moment came when it was time to adjourn. However, one final climax was yet to occur which would forever tie and unify the 37 sects into one grand whole. It started out rather insignificantly, but its ramifications have lasted until the present day.

Out of the huge crowd a figure arose to speak. It was Manzaholla. He suggested that there should be some one word, some symbol, that could be used to express their association with one another. Agasha, remembering the very same word his own teacher had once used as a blessing, replied, "Manzaholla has suggested it and it is good, so henceforth let the name *Manzaholla* be used in our greeting and in our good-bye."

Then he raised his hand as a benediction and closed the convention with these words: "Manzaholla, and until we meet again. The pact we make this day is good. Down through the ages we may not meet, we may not cross one another's path in some of our lives, but we know that eventually we will all come together and meet again in some other consciousness after our work on this plane is over. But for now, I bid all farewell until our next meeting. Manzaholla."

After these words were spoken all who had assembled, including the many who had come so far, then thoughtfully packed up their gear and departed. Much had been accomplished; much had been gained. In a short time the convention site was empty as the last caravan receded into the distance. Nightfall then descended over the land and all became silent. A new era had been born. Austa had come into maturity, but Egypt slept on.

NOTES

1. James Crenshaw, *Telephone Between Worlds* (Los Angeles, DeVorss & Co., 1950)

CHAPTER FIVE

THE GREAT PYRAMID

Does the Great Pyramid of Cheops enshrine a lost science? Was this last remaining of the Seven Wonders of the World, often described as the most sublime landmark in history, designed by mysterious architects who had a deeper knowledge of the secrets of this universe than those who followed them?

—Peter Tompkins
Secrets of the Great Pyramid

PERHAPS the most mysterious, the most awesome, of the ancient monuments that still exist in the world today is the Great Pyramid at Giza in the land of Egypt. The inquiring mind can very easily ask from whence came this great monument in stone which is sometimes referred to as the miracle of the ages. Its very size itself is mind boggling. Peter Tompkins states in his most informative book[1] that it is comprised of over two-and-a-half *million* blocks of limestone and granite, each weighing from two to 70 tons apiece. Think of it! From its 13 acre base these two-and-a-half million (2,500,000) stone blocks soar into the desert sky in 201 stepped tiers to the height of a modern 40-story office building. If such a structure were to be constructed today, even with the aid of all our "advanced" technologies, mechanized equipment, and engineering skills, it would tax our ingenuity to the utmost. The original casing stones were cut with such precision that when fitted together, without the aid of cement, a razor blade could not be slipped between the joints. Compare this with the sloppy tolerances accepted in the construction of our modern structures.

Even the mathematical and astronomical knowledge demonstrated by the geometry of its construction—from both a study of its outer dimensions as well as from a study of the dimensions and proportions of its inner passageways and chambers—expresses an intelligence far beyond that of our modern day. The very existence of this awesome structure, which modern science would just as soon forget, seems to taunt mankind by saying, "Man, harken unto me. I exist. And even though the sands of time and the destructiveness of mankind have defaced my outer appearance, I still am. I dare thee to find out why I am." Its companion the Sphinx, half man and half beast, seems to echo the same question.

Where were these enormous stones that were used in its construction quarried? A cursory study reveals that the nearest possible site was many miles away, and yet this, too, is under some disagreement. Some think that the actual site was even further away. Were they floated upon rafts down the Nile? Perhaps—but then the rafts would have had to be constructed as ships, as no raft could have supported the weight of the stones. Were they dragged over the sands from quarries hundreds of miles away at Thebes? Perhaps—but transportation from such a distance without some appropriate vehicle seems to present an engineering impossibility even to our modern standards.

Then we come to the question of how they were raised into position. Imagine constructing a 40-story skyscraper without the use of modern equipment. Imagine it—if you can. Elevate two-and-a-half million blocks of granite and limestone, each weighing from two to 70 tons apiece, into position in a building 40 stories high. And let us also not forget the precise manner in which they were placed. Slave labor, you say? Perhaps—but just imagine thousands and thousands of Egyptian slaves, all pulling on ropes and cables of considerable strength and dragging these monumental stones up some tremendous ramp into their final position. The picture staggers the imagination. We realize that in the dark ages of Egypt under the pharaohs, this undoubtedly was the process. But those structures, temples, obelisks, and the like were relatively small when compared with the enormous pyramids at Giza. Even though tremendous feats of strength and endurance were required to construct those structures of a relatively smaller size, it was still technically possible. However, when we attempt to study and uncover the actual method used in the construction of these larger and more incredible structures, simple intelligence fairly demands that we search for an alternate solution.

Austa in 5000 B.C.

To find an alternate solution, let us return once more to the Egypt of 7,000 years ago. From the Agashan classes we have learned that it was then called Austa; Egypt was yet to be born. It was a simple land, relatively primitive as far as its civilization was concerned. Its population consisted basically of souls from the adjoining lands who had been attracted to that part of the country in search of peace and inner spiritual understanding. The leaders of the various sects, ever striving to unfold in a spiritual manner, had learned the art of meditation, of going within, and they taught these procedures to their subjects or followers.

But somewhere around this date the situation changed. Suddenly the barriers were broken as the leaders made contact with the consciousness of the Ascended Masters—great Adepts who had arisen from a yet earlier civilization on the ancient continent of Atlantis, 172,000 years back in the sands of time from the present day. These Egyptian initiates had become mediums, channels, whereby they could actually communicate with a much higher spiritual consciousness which they call today, using the over-all term, the Consciousness of Immensity.

The veil was lifted; the doors were opened. Light and understanding pierced the veil of darkness that ordinarily surrounds this physical plane. These high, ascended Atlantean Masters could now freely converse with the people of the land through the channelship of those leaders who had so cleansed themselves, and so purified themselves, that the contact could be established and the communication made possible. Thus a new age of enlightenment was born in the land of Austa that was destined to last for 2,000 years, up to the date known by modern historians as 3000 B.C. Then, at the conclusion of this period or cycle, this age was also destined to vanish from the physical plane as suddenly as it had first arrived.

The Grand Idea

"What has all this to do with the Great Pyramid?" you might ask. The answer is that it has a great deal to do with the Great Pyramid—that great Monument of Spirituality as it is so reverently called by the Agashan teachers. For it was in the beginning of this great period of enlightenment that the idea to bring it back into manifestation once again on the physical plane was born.

"Once again to be brought back into manifestation?" I hear you question. Yes, that is what the Agashan teachers so state, and the full story, when it is finally revealed in its entirety, promises to be one of the most exciting stories of the present era. All has not yet been revealed, much has been withheld, and much more remains to be discovered. That which follows is only a summary of the material that has already been given on this subject, and much more will be forthcoming as the years go by.

It seems that during the first generation of this period of peace, about the time that Agasha was endeavoring to unite the 37 sects into one grand unit of consciousness and understanding, some of the leaders became so attuned to the

Infinite State that they could vividly recall the ancient Atlantean civilization. And several of these souls recalled a great monument of spirituality that was constructed in the form of a pyramid. This pyramid had been erected many thousands of years earlier in the great city of Atlantis that submerged so long ago. It had housed every record of that great Atlantean civilization, some of which dated back for thousands of years. It also contained information on the great cultures of the future and other prophecies of the tomorrows to come. It came to be called the great Monument of Spirituality because it stored the entire history of that great Atlantean civilization, not only of its past, but its future as well.

It was constructed with a dazzling white exterior and a golden apex that reflected the sunlight of the day in a most glorious manner. These leaders who could recall so clearly this ancient structure came to the realization that the crowning achievement for this newly born civilization of Austa would be to build a replica of this ancient monument of the past. Thus the idea was born. But the ability to construct such an awesome structure, even with their newly awakened powers, was not to be had so easily. Even though they could see it so clearly and distinctly in their meditations, the actual physical construction of such a structure was quite another matter, indeed.

When It Was Built

Therefore, long before the Great Pyramid was finally erected, we see that it was planned. Agasha says that it was "drawn on the sands of time" and that it took many years to plan it ever so carefully. In answer to the question as to when it was built, let me quote Agasha from the class of October 8, 1951:

"The 37 sects were established long before the Great Pyramid was brought into manifestation. We have history today of many things relative to the life of long ago, and much of the history is distorted. That is neither here nor there. The fact remains that there are many, many thousands of ways that people have described the pyramid, what it stands for, when it was erected, who built it, and for what purpose. Yes, there have been thousands of statements made in that direction, and it is not my desire to come and dispute any of those statements, not at all. I merely give it to you the way I know it to be, as many of you in the class tonight were present both before and after this great erection. You see, it was during the great convention that we brought forth the message to erect the Great Pyramid, and then it was brought into manifestation a few years later. Now I realize that historians go back about 5,000—some even say 6,000—years on the pyramid, but the truth in the inner circles is that it is 7,000 years old."

It was also learned in November, 1952, that the actual length of time for its construction was surprisingly not long. In the short period of only seven years, all was complete, and the great Monument of Spirituality was born again and lived once more upon the physical plane.

Who Were the Builders?

We must remember that during the first century of this 2,000-year period of peace, it was the Atlantean Masters who taught and assisted these newly awakened peoples. These first hundred years were an era of immense building activity. Beautiful temples were constructed, music was brought into manifestation, and other great works of art, sculpture, and painting were likewise brought unto the land. But the inspiration relative to all of this activity was brought forth from the higher planes. It was the Teachers from Atlantis, those great Atlanteans, who gave the necessary information unto the prophets of the period.

But who was basically responsible for the construction of the Great Pyramid? Who then were its builders? To answer this we can only point out that pure faith and effort ofttimes bring about their own reward. Perhaps it was through the striving and efforts of those inspired leaders, or then again, perhaps it was through the laws of destiny. Who can say? In any event, that which transpired in the first golden years of the newly born son, Austa, was certainly blessed by the father, Egypt, for seven Universal Masters—seven Teachers about whom we know but very little—took it upon themselves to render their assistance and thus bring once again unto the physical expression of the planet a new Monument of Spirituality. We can say then that it was these seven Universal Teachers who were basically responsible.

Agasha has not given us much pertaining to how this was actually accomplished. It has been difficult to find a great deal of information on this subject from the Agashan tapes. But we do know the following facts: First, it was designed and brought into manifestation largely through the efforts of these seven Universal Teachers; and secondly, these Universal Teachers worked through the channelship of seven particular individuals who had been gifted with extraordinary powers, powers far and above those of even the average sect leader.

This point is clarified a bit when we study the tape of the class of September 1, 1952. Agasha is speaking: "We have had channelship down through the ages, disciples, and all during the time of Atlantis we had some very wonderful things manifested by the channels of that time. The seven who were responsible for the erection of the Great Pyramid were all channels for the Spirit to work through. These seven men had the necessary power which enabled them to help erect our great Monument of Spirituality which remains there today representing wisdom and the mysteries of life. They also helped establish some of the other temples of our period."

When questioned further about the actual construction of the Great Pyramid, the Agashan teachers will usually reply that all who lived in the sects at that particular time had a part to play in its being brought into manifestation. It was a tremendous community effort shared by all. Much had to be placed on the scrolls recording the data as it was needed.

Much had to be chiseled out in hieroglyphic form upon the tablets of time. It took tremendous planning and actual hard work by all. The pyramid most certainly did not erect itself. But all who were there at the time blended their efforts in a most skillful manner, with each performing that function that he was best able to do.

How It Was Built

How was the pyramid actually erected? The Agashan teachers state that this was all accomplished through learning the higher laws of alchemy as taught by the ascended Atlantean Teachers, and this then enabled them not only to bring into manifestation the Great Pyramid, but also to erect other temples, buildings, and works of art of great beauty. Thus these great structures were constructed not only through hard effort, but also through the higher laws of alchemy, through the anims and the forces of the other world, in order to assist and supplement the physical effort.

In the classes of November 18, 1949, and August 14, 1950, Agasha states: "I don't care how many things had been given by others to mankind, or how many books had been written on Egypt, but I am only telling you children that the Great Pyramid was erected spiritually, and most reverently was it erected. It was all brought forth through the great powers of the Inner Circle.

"It has always been a great mystery to mankind today as to how the ancient civilizations of the past were able to transport those huge blocks of stone in order to erect such a great temple as it stands there so nobly and high. Yet I have so informed you on the inner planes that these great stones, as you would say, were levitated into position and many of them were apported from various parts of the country through the powers of the instruments who possessed great mediumistic powers. Much of the material was also precipitated, the same as they do right there in the land of Cocoda. It is only through precipitation, incidentally, that things are brought into Cocoda and the other Spiritual

Centers. We then precipitated by degrees, ounce by ounce and pound by pound as you would say, and we erected our temples in that way. Yes, blessed ones, much of the material—not all of it but much of it—was obtained through precipitation.

"Therefore, many of the people of today think it so strange and they speculate as to how the materials were brought into that part of the world. "Where did they mine them? Where did they get the materials to erect such structures?" they will ask. But the answer is as I have just said. And many will also say that it was the slaves who had built the Great Pyramid. In the case of the lesser pyramids that go back to approximately 5,000 years ago, perhaps so, but as far as the Great Pyramid is concerned, it is not true."

Thus the mysteries pertaining to the erection of these ancient monuments begin to unravel, and the answer to the question proposed by Peter Tompkins at the beginning of this chapter seems to be in the affirmitive. Many of the great stones were evidently first quarried in other parts of the country and then either apported or levitated to the pyramid site. And it becomes apparent that the gold that was used in the great golden apex that originally capped this great monument was either transmuted from baser metals or precipitated out of the atmosphere. We can see in our mind's eye these great stones of enormous weight being levitated into position as easily as if they had only the weight of a feather. And then, too, the polishing and the cutting of the casing stones were most probably accomplished through occult efforts. Once the mortal mind can accept the reality of these spiritual and superphysical forces and powers, the erection of these ancient monuments becomes no longer a mystery.

Why It Was Built

Besides the actual method of construction of these monuments, another very important fact seems to become apparent. That is that the purpose behind their being brought into manifestation is also of a spiritual nature. The design of the

Great Pyramid, for instance, is such that it represents in stone the true history of mankind and the laws of the Universe. It also represents the God Consciousness as well as man's relationship to God.

"It was all carried out symbolically," Agasha goes on to state, "and there is where *your* connection comes in. Just talk to anyone who has but the slightest interest in occultism, and mention the Great Pyramid, and always they will be drawn to it. They don't necessarily know why they are so attracted, but nevertheless they are drawn to it. You cannot escape it, disciples, if you are a true occultist today. You cannot escape it because it is a part of your training and your heritage.

"When we speak of the Great Pyramid, I am literally handing you the key to the greater unfoldment of the Higher Self. I am handing you the key to introduce you to your Higher Self, and when I speak of 'I,' I am referring to the 'I' within you, of course. The pyramid is a symbol to the greater awakening, which means then that by first unlocking the consciousness within, we are then able to awaken the soul. And in the same manner we may say that by unlocking the soul of mankind in general, we are then able to unlock that great land of Egypt—that land which had claimed so many great souls of the past and who in turn had left so many records to be found."

Agasha also says that the designs of the other pyramids, temples, and monuments of the Peace Period likewise portray some great spiritual theme or motive. The great Sphinx that stands guard by the Great Pyramid is certainly no exception and undoubtedly has a most interesting story to tell.

All of the above further tends to emphasize the importance that symbology plays in the life of mankind. If this point has been stressed once, it has been expressed hundreds of other times during the many years that Agasha has been conducting his classes in the 20th century. Symbolically speaking then, it could very well be said that Man himself is a living symbol, and that the Great Pyramid is the totality of all of this.

Agasha tells us that when Higher Masonry had been first brought unto mankind in its original state, it was all taken from the consciousness of the Peace Period, and this in turn was brought forth from Atlantis. He also states that eventually he intends to give the true meaning of the Great Pyramid, in its entirety, and that that will then become the main part of his message to be left to the world.

Let us now hear from Coman Coban as he discusses the same subject in a class in August, 1952: "You and I, disciples of Agasha, must ever strive to understand symbolism and the importance of symbolism. Indeed, it was through the great symbols of God that we were enabled to erect the Great Pyramid in the first place. The great golden apex that stood there so nobly and high, shining in the sunlight of God for such a long period of time, was a magnificent symbol. It had been handed down by the great powers most spiritually. Then, eventually, it toppled over into the sands nearby where it lies buried and waits to be found once again at the right and proper time. The symbolic interpretation of the fall of the golden apex (some say it never existed) varies considerably with the different dynasties or periods of time in which men lived. This is because the language so employed often describes things quite differently. However, the things that existed then and the things that exist today are appreciably the same, and this is found to be true once man has aroused his inner consciousness."

Now let us turn to the inner chambers and the passages within the Great Pyramid itself. Why were they constructed in the manner that they were, and for what purpose did they function? These questions have been answered partially, but a great deal remains yet to be revealed. We do know, for instance, that the Pyramid was in reality a great Temple of Initiation. It was here where the disciples or those taking the various degrees had to traverse along the labyrinth of passages and then probably meet up with all sorts of obstacles on the way. But with these overcome, they would eventually find themselves within one of the upper chambers, and in so doing come into a greater awareness.

We also know that what today is known as the King's Chamber was really used for the purpose of purification and enlightenment. The powers generated within this chamber, which is located at the very heart of the pyramid, would enable the adept or one who was ready for the higher initiation to go into deep meditation and thus be able to raise his or her consciousness to an extremely high state. The other chambers or passageways likewise had their own individual function and symbology. Yet, the ultimate function of all was for one unqualified purpose—the raising of the consciousness of Man to the realization of his own Divine State.

The Subterranean

In addition to the halls, chambers, and passages located within the main or central part of the Pyramid, occult tradition has long had it that there are still other underground passageways connecting it with the Sphinx, and quite possibly with the two adjacent pyramids of Cephren and Mycerinus. The Agashan teachers state that this is true, at least as far as the passageway between the Sphinx and the Great Pyramid is concerned. The knowledge of the existence of these subterranean halls and passages has been lost by the outer world for many thousands of years, but it has still been preserved on secret scrolls and manuscripts possessed by the archivists of some of the mystery schools of the West as well as Tibet.

It seems that shortly after the Great Pyramid was constructed, the great Sphinx, along with its underground reception chamber, temple, and passageways, was also brought into manifestation. One of the underground corridors leads directly to the main chamber within the Great Pyramid itself, and the others form one grand interlocking complex—all dedicated to the preservation of truth and knowledge. This, taken as a whole, is what Agasha terms the subterranean.

And it is destined to be rediscovered by the outer world once more.

Agasha goes on to tell us that on the walls of that particular subterranean passageway that extends from the Great Pyramid to the Sphinx, there are many niches which contain a great deal of information on Atlantis. Signs and symbols in the form of hieroglyphics have been placed upon plaques, and the inscriptions will give the true knowledge of that great continent. They will be recorded in a way that they can be clearly understood by the Egyptologists of today. There will also be much information on their own day, the 7,000 year period, and the niches will contain jewelry and the like of that period.

But the truly surprising thing about all of this is that these niches will also contain records of *our* day, the present 20th century, for America is the reincarnation of the Atlantean civilization. And not only that, they will also contain a good deal of information of our past during the last few thousand years. They will cover much that is in the Bible and tell of the past wars and of the conflicts here in the 20th century.

"How is this possible," you might ask, "that records of a civilization yet to come into manifestation can be placed within a tomb within the earth 7,000 years prior to its manifestation?" The answer to this question is not as complicated as it might appear to be on the surface. We must remember that these adepts, teachers, sect leaders—call them what we will—who had lived at that time became most proficient in the art of meditation. And they simply had the ability to go within themselves and extract the desired information and knowledge. They had seen the ancient civilization of Atlantis. They had peered into the future and they had seen the America of the present day. Thus they were able to bring back the memory of the things they had seen, things of the past as well as the future, and then record this information and place it in the niches for the sole purpose of its discovery in the 20th century. Thus they could prove once and for all to a civilization that they knew would be steeped in materiality the reality of the Spirit and man's true relationship with God.

The records will tell of what Agasha terms the latter days of the seven cycle (our present era). They will tell of the strange things that would be seen in the skies in the form of our present UFO or unidentified flying objects, and they will give other items of interest pertaining to our present civilization. They will show that all that was to be in the future was only a takeoff of that which had been known before. Inasmuch as all of this was given for the sole purpose of proving unto mankind that the ancients truly had the ability to peer into the future, a great effort was made to present the information in a way that it would be understood.

Yes, indeed, Agasha promises that these chambers and passageways known as the subterranean will reveal a great deal.

The Upper Chamber

Have all of the halls and chambers within the body of the Great Pyramid itself now been discovered? This is the question that is usually asked by the average researcher in this field. It has long been believed by some that a special chamber yet remains unopened. Agasha verifies that this is so. He has stated on many occasions that the greatest and truly most wondrous discovery of all is yet to come. Even though the modern world is convinced that all of these passages and rooms have now been discovered, they have not.

There is a secret passageway that leads up to the main chamber of the Pyramid, which Agasha prefers to call the Upper Chamber. This chamber is well concealed inasmuch as it has been sealed off for thousands of years. Agasha states that it was sealed on purpose because nothing contained within this chamber was supposed to be revealed unto the nations of the world until the end of the 7,000-year cycle, or the latter part of the 20th century. Then, at the right and proper time, it will be opened up when a certain group of individuals seek in this direction. They will be able to go right to it; they will be led by the Divine Hand, so to speak. It can happen any time, and when it is finally opened much will be revealed. The Agashan teachers say that then the true history of Egypt, which is a takeoff from Agasha's message, will once more be known to the outer world.

Even though it has been said in the classes that the main function of the Upper Chamber was for the purposes of spiritual unfoldment, it is also a tomb, strangely enough. "But whose tomb?" one might ask. The answer has not been given. All we know is that within this Upper Chamber lies at least one particular sarcophagus that is most beautiful. It will at first appear to be of solid gold, but on further inspection we will find that this pertains only to the head. The balance will just be trimmed in gold, but it will be very beautiful. There will be several others that also will be brought to the surface, although it is not clear whether or not they are in this particular chamber.

Within this Upper Chamber will also be found additional records and prophecies that will enhance and supplement those contained within the niches of the subterranean passageway. They, too, will have been placed therein in the 7,000 year period, and they will date back to the time of Atlantis.

One of the prophecies will foretell the return of the Atlanteans. This prophecy will go on to state that the land that would be chosen by the Masters of Light for the return of the Atlanteans would be called "The Land of Freedom," and that there would be a way that men would be led to pioneer that great land. This is America today. This was the prophecy that was given to the teachers and prophets of the day, and this same prophecy was then placed there within the chamber.

These prophecies will be clearly understood and interpreted through the discovery within the Upper Chamber itself of a set of hieroglyphics that will lead the scholars to more correctly translate the Egyptian language. Then much that has previously been mistranslated may be translated into a more correct understanding. Agasha states that some of the hieroglyphics pertaining to the earlier dynasties especially have not been deciphered properly. In fact, the interpretation that is generally accepted today is way off and far from the truth in some cases. A good example is the cartouche that historians attribute to Khufu, the second Pharaoh of the Fourth Dynasty. It seems more than likely that this symbol originally belonged to the early Peace Period in that it is found among the quarry marks on some of the courses behind the casing stones of the Great Pyramid. The Pharaoh Khufu or Cheops evidently used this same symbol as a cartouche some two thousand years later.

The finding of the Upper Chamber will then clarify all of this. But there is still a mystery related to this chamber. Agasha says that its real purpose or function is directly related to its physical location within the mass of the pyramid. One may assume that it undoubtedly is located above the King's Chamber, although Agasha has not directly intimated this. He stated on December 23, 1974 (for the first time to the writer's knowledge) that its location enabled a circle of magnetic force of great magnitude to be created, and this in turn gave forth an inner illumination. It was here that the disciples went to receive revelations from the soul while in a state of twilight sleep. Here much was revealed unto the average disciple of the period.

Yes, we may truly say that the Great Pyramid at Giza, the Seventh Wonder of the World as some writers call it, will once more become the height of discussion among the peoples of the world. It is called the Great Pyramid of Cheops by some, and in other circles it is known as the Great Pyramid of Khufu. But in the light of what we have said here, I would prefer to call it the Great Pyramid of Agasha.

NOTES

1. Peter Tompkins, *Secrets of the Great Pyramid* (New York, Harper & Row, 1971), p. 1

CHAPTER SIX

2,000 YEARS OF PEACE

For a thousand years in thy sight are but as yesterday when it is past, and as a watch in the night.
—Psalms. XC. 4

AMERICA is often referred to in the Agashan classes as being the second Atlantis—a reincarnation, so to speak, of an entire civilization. However, in between any two civilizations there is always an intervening step, a zero point from which the returned consciousness springs forth. Thus even in the life cycle of an entire civilization, we again see the Holy Trinity being brought once more into manifestation. As Agasha has stated so many times in his classes, everything seems to be brought into manifestation in threes. First we have Atlantis, a vast civilization equally as great as America is today. Then we have the intervening period, that mysterious land called Austa or that which is known as Egypt today. And finally we come up to the present and we have America, the land of Freedom, the second Atlantis.

Agasha states that we, as Americans today, are in reality the Atlanteans of the past. And many that are currently living in America likewise had several lives during that

2,000-year period of peace and harmony in the land of Austa. According to our modern-day calendar, this covers the period of time from 5000 B.C. to 3000 B.C. Others undoubtedly lived during the following 3,000-year dark period of Egypt while the pharaohs ruled by the iron hand. It was all preordained. The teachers of the past could see what people were building up in their consciousness and what would be the result in the next phase of their existence. And all this has turned out precisely as it was predicted during the peaceful, enlightened period of Austa.

What was it like during those 2,000 years of peace? Indeed, with the world in such a chaotic state today, it seems hard to realize a land where all was peaceful, harmonious, and beautiful. It would seem that for 2,000 years the Universal Spirit God had embraced this consciousness into its bosom. Yet 2,000 years is a long time. Just think how many lives one would have had during that period—perhaps ten, fifteen? The period lasted for a length of time that is equivalent to the time span between the manifestation of Jesus in Palestine and the present day. Just think of it—2,000 years of peace, harmony, and love, and when learning, understanding, and enlightenment were the keynote of the day. Yet it did exist, and a description of life as it was lived during that period will be the subject of this chapter.

Agasha has said that our stay in the astral world during those early years was not so long when compared with the time that we stay over there now. In other words, the average person today lives in the astral world between 100 to 300 years before returning again to the physical plane. This is the ordinary individual; there always are exceptions. However, during our period in Austa our time in the astral world was shorter. There were even times when those that were freed from the physical body returned within ten years, 15 years, or perhaps 50 years. They often recalled their previous life and became reacquainted once more with their relatives who were still living in the flesh. They knew and recognized their kind. Of course, it went in cycles; all lives were not that frequent. Perhaps one would have two or three lives quite close together at the beginning of the period, we will say, and then not return again for several hundred years. In any event, there were quite a few lives that were lived during that 2,000-year period for the average individual who was part of that consciousness.

Now through the occult system that Agasha is striving to unravel, as it were, the average disciple endeavors to dig deeper, and then as he does this, memory often returns all so clearly. To dig deeper is Agasha's method as taught today, and it was his method that was taught then. That is why many things that are said today in the Agashan class seem so familiar to the disciples who are present. The same can be said to have been true during the 2,000-year Peace Period. But in those days each disciple in the various sects was capable of recalling his previous life quite clearly. This is the difference between the present period and the previous period. In the earlier age they would return after a generation or so, recognize the teachers, and then continue on almost where they had left off. Quite often the scholars of the day would be in a position whereby they could read the hieroglyphics on the tablets within the tombs or temples, and then after reading them, sometimes even recall quite clearly having placed those very same hieroglyphics on the tablet of sand that they were now reading once again. Yes indeed, Agasha tells us that the people in that land were very sensitive for it was a psychic period, a clairvoyant period, a period in which men were very much attuned to the Infinite State.

Life in the Sects

Now let us take a brief look into the way life was lived in the average sect. In the beginning, of course, each particular sect was originally formed by a teacher. It could have been formed by a single teacher, or it might have been formed through the cooperation or the collaboration of two or more teachers. In any event, each of the 37 sects had its own teacher or group leader. He would serve over his own particular group for a time, and then another teacher would take over after he had ascended from the flesh. Each teacher acted in his own capacity of serving, and he was always followed by his successor who took over and kept on with the work in the same manner as the original teacher. Thus the same message was brought forth unto the oncoming generations. Each teacher lived his span and then arose into the Consciousness of Immensity after living some 30 or 40 years in the flesh, and even less time than that for some. Consequently there were many teachers within each individual sect during this 2,000-year period of peace.

Another point that should not be overlooked is that the sects were made up of both men and women. The importance of both sexes, the male and the female, the positive and the negative, was thoroughly understood and gloriously expressed. If we think we are approaching women's lib today, it is nothing when compared to the equality given the sexes during that period. In fact, it has never been expressed on the earth plane in the same manner since. The female principle was embraced most reverently and beautifully inasmuch as it was thoroughly understood that the higher soul consciousness was a union of both the male and the female principles.

Life as it was lived during that period was vastly different from the life that the average individual lives today. Then they had more time for meditation, and far less time was spent in the mundane affairs that today seem to control our lives. Their soul could speak to them in their quiet moments and reveal firsthand the inner mysteries of the Cosmos, and everyday living was a most beautiful experience. Of course, this was not so for all, but it was there for the disciple who strove and honestly endeavored to know. Agasha says that it was given unto them then in the way that it should be given unto us today, but unfortunately today we are prone to so many material things that we have to spend almost all of our available time simply striving to overcome the effects of 20th century living. However, the teachers state that this is all in order as the present strenuous experiences are necessary for our soul growth and attainment that we need at this time.

The disciple was trained at a very early age how to breathe properly, how to partake of food, and how to conserve his strength. He was taught how to conserve that great power that lies within so that over a period of time he could become attuned to the Infinite State. And as we just stated, this all occurred at a very early age. Then following these preliminary periods of instruction, he was taught about the other life and of the Consciousness of Immensity. He was told about that land that had seemingly been forgotten for so many generations—the land of Atlantis. He was told of the great leaders that had arisen during the time of Atlantis, and he was told of those who were yet to come. But aside from learning the histories of the past and the prophecies for the future, he was also taught how to live in the present. He was taught how to exercise and how to keep the physical body in good health at all times. He was taught handicrafts, art, and many other things of interest, and all this kept him busy throughout the day.

Economics and Art

Being a less complicated society, the principles of economics were also vastly different in the early years of Austa. Later years were to see changes, of course. There were no coins of the realm; money was an unknown and quite unnecessary commodity. Each individual created his own garments, or he exchanged them with others for other desired materials. Barter was the means of exchange during the Peace Period, but it was not the same type of barter that is in use by the primitive societies of today. In Austa, materials were exchanged simply for the needs of the individual, and no particular attention was given to the value of the materials. There is a vast difference between these two principles. There was plenty for all, and no one was in want. A "dollar value" was not placed upon any article of clothing, food, or jewelry, for the exchange was based purely upon the need, and not upon the value of the goods exchanged.

An illustration seems to be in order. For instance: I would create and you would create. I might create a beautiful piece of jewelry, and you might grow some vegetables or produce some dried fruits or nuts. Or perhaps you had sewn together a garment, sandals, or whatever. Then there was the market-place. I would exchange and you would exchange. There, you would take what you wanted, within reason, and you would leave in its place perhaps something that was far more valuable than what you took. But you took what you needed, and it would make no difference whether it was fruit, garments, salt, or this or that. You then left in its place whatever you so desired, and the next one who would come along would then pick up what you had left. Perhaps it was the raw material for a garment that he was desirous of making, or another piece of jewelry for that matter. Agasha tells us that this was the system that was used then, but in that uncomplicated society it worked most beautifully.

Could that same system be used today? Of course not. Today mankind has not only advanced himself mechanically with his outer technology of mass production to the point whereby a medium of exchange becomes an absolute necessity, but he has also seemingly retrogressed spiritually to the point whereby a medium of exchange becomes not only necessary but mandatory. Why do we say this? We must remember that in those days there was a supply for all and no one was in want. Furthermore, with the higher understanding of life taught to children in their early years, crime was nonexistent. People *knew better* than to steal from others that which they had not earned the right to have for themselves. They *knew* of the laws of cause and effect, of the principle that life would eventually punish them for wrong-doing. We must remember that those enlightened individuals—many of them—were in communication with the soul! Crime or dishonesty was unthinkable. Fairness and honesty was the keynote of the day, and beauty, love, and harmony prevailed.

Besides being an age of great spiritual attainment, this 2,000-year period also produced works of art comparable to the finest ever known on the physical plane. Some of these master craftsmen in working with the various metals were able to weave intricate patterns of such exquisite beauty that visitors from the neighboring lands would gasp in wonderment as they gazed at the perfection expressed therein. Cloisonné of the very finest caliber was produced out of materials that were extremely durable and lasting. The colors were fast. Even the common clay pottery at the peak of the period was superior to that which was later produced under the pharaohs. Some of the jewelry was of such magnificence that it could only be compared with the "crown jewels" of today and not with that of the ordinary variety. These jewels were so intricate, so beautiful, and so precise in their manifestation that in gazing at them one could only say, "Well, there were certainly wonderful artists during that period." This, the world will soon have a chance to say, as the Agashan teachers state that soon—and this could happen almost any time—these beautiful works of art, these great masterpieces of the 2,000-year Peace Period, will be rediscovered and brought to the surface once again.

It would seem that life was very beautiful and harmonious during this period, but this was not always the case. Sandstorms of the most frightful variety would ofttimes sweep across the face of the land, and as they would approach, funnel-shaped like a tornado and whirling with devastating fury, they would pick up sand and then destroy everything lying in their path. Even the massive temples, which were built in a very solid manner, would sometimes be lifted causing great damage. At other times the sand would completely bury them until such time that they could again be restored. However, as the teachers of the period were very highly attuned to the soul, they would always know when a sandstorm would be approaching and a great loss of life would usually be averted. Being forewarned, the populace could then seek a suitable shelter. But they still had to go through these cataclysms of nature, for once nature goes on the rampage, Agasha says that even the Adept has to take a back seat and wait for the storm to subside. However, this can sometimes be modified through using the higher laws of alchemy—but this is for a later chapter. In any event, these sandstorms gradually faded away, and by the latter part of the 2,000-year Peace Period they no longer had to contend with them.

Another very important feature that dominated this 2,000-year period of peace was the tremendous building activity. Thousands of structures were brought into manifestation expressing magnificent architectural beauty and great splendor. The construction of the Great Pyramid marked only the beginning of this fantastic era, and before too many years had elapsed a great many other temples had been so constructed. Yes, occult forces were used quite extensively in the early years, and through these powers they were able to levitate and do many other spectacular things. Some of the temples were designed to accommodate thousands of individuals at one time, and this activity went on for almost 2,000 years.

Just think of it—2,000 years of peace, harmony, enlightenment, and spiritual understanding. And this all came about through the laws of higher occultism, through the ability of those enlightened individuals to receive and bring forth the message from the great Atlantean consciousness. This was all very vital unto man. There was no such thing as a man living on the earth plane in the land of Austa who had a misunderstanding as to God. All were able to recall the things of the past after they had gone through the procedure, taken their initiation and cleansed themselves mentally and physically. Once this had been accomplished, they were then able to establish communication and become so infinitely attuned.

The Temple of Mamon: The First Great Temple

One of the first of the new order of temples to be erected after the great convention at the start of the 2,000-year Peace Period was the new Temple of Mamon. The original temple had been constructed many years previously, but this new temple surpassed it in beauty many times over. Much color was expressed and it became a very important temple, indeed. Agasha tells us that it was one of the most significant temples because it was here that the leaders of the new order of the 37 sects held their meetings over an extended period of time. Being along the Nile, and very near the location of the Great Pyramid, it was a most beautiful sight to behold. It was erected largely through the powers of Mamon himself, and an excellent description of the temple was given by Agasha in a class back in November, 1951.

"Tonight," Agasha begins, "let us once again enter the Temple of Mamon. I can recall so clearly when Mamon in his own right, through his own efforts and through his own desire, came to erect that great temple along the Nile whereby there would be many who would come to have their ascension in this wonderful temple. To me, it was one of the most beautiful structures that I could point out in comparison with other structures on the earth today. During the time that it was being erected, great ceremonies were held and the teachers came from far and wide to pay their tributes and to offer their suggestions. It was with great reverence that they assembled there for the erection of this great temple. And it was then and there that we were in a position to understand the beauty that was expressed from the souls of men, for men were ever so creative in that day, and having that creative art in their soul they were then able to bring back the consciousness of Atlantis. Yes indeed, the Temple of Mamon was a temple that could be compared very easily with the temples that existed during the Atlantean period.

"It was in this temple where Mamon brought forth light and peace unto so many souls. It was in this temple where the teachers congregated on various occasions to carry out their plans in furthering the movement that was established at the convention. We point out the Temple of Mamon because it was so very significant. There were other temples, true; there were other great centers, indeed there were, but the Temple of Mamon stood out. It was designated as the complete whole of the organization, as you would say. It was established so that the Universal Consciousness of God could be carried down through the ages in the hearts of men, or perhaps we should say in the soul.

"I see the Temple of Mamon ever so clearly as it arises once more before my sight. As I gaze upon this magnificent temple, I see great architectural beauty, indeed I do. The colors are so beautifully blended. I see people entering and leaving through the great archway. I see smiles upon their faces and I see them so very joyful. I see them radiantly happy. How very beautiful and noble it is as it stands beside the Nile! Let us observe and absorb its colorful beauty. Let us enter it and go into the great sanctuary where the disciples went to receive the many blessings that would be bestowed upon them by the soul and by the great teachers who had ascended. How colorful it is, and how quiet and peaceful and still it can be. Its floor is of alabaster, polished to a very high degree. There is much stone employed, and it likewise is highly polished. The stone is very beautiful and quite similar to marble or agate of today. A great deal of gold is also employed in the form of decoration, and it all blends together most beautifully. Yes, the Temple of Mamon is very picturesque, indeed."

The Chambers of Initiation

A further study of the tapes of the Agashan classes during the early 1950's especially gives us a good deal of other information relative to the Temple of Mamon. It seems that this particular temple was a temple where the disciples would go on certain occasions in order to adjust their life and become attuned to the Infinite State. They would go into meditation and thus receive their message and their purification from the soul. The respective rooms or chambers enabled those who had attained a high rate of vibration to sit in meditation for a long period of time, and after a prescribed course of instruction, they were able to enter the chambers and do just that. However, prior to their stay in the chamber, the disciples had to go through a preliminary stage of preparation. They were not permitted to be with others and they had to remain very quiet and very peaceful. They had to have plenty of rest and not too much exercise. They had to fast moderately, and they could only partake of certain limited foods for a period of days prior to entering the chamber. In this manner they would become quite sensitized and very sensitive to the higher vibrations. Thus, after this preliminary stage of purification, it would then be possible for them to become ever so holy and attuned to the Divine State.

At the appointed hour, they would then enter the chamber. After putting on a robe which, incidentally, was extremely significant during that time, they would then go into meditation. This could be done alone or it could be done with others present. Agasha tells us that each one, in his own respective kingdom, would then go into meditation by sitting in the same yoga position that Agasha always uses while lecturing to our present-day classes. This is known as the lotus posture and it appears quite tiring to most of us today, but the disciples of that age had learned to relax every nerve of the body after having become proficient in certain mental and physical exercises. They would then dim the mind of thoughts and give up all thoughts of the earth. They would breathe rhythmically and thus draw forth the anims (spiritual atoms) unto themselves. In this way then they were able to relax the physical body completely, and after both the mental and the physical had reached a certain relaxed state, they would then enter a state of twilight sleep. This would be the equivalent of the trance state. The coma state was not reached at this stage of their development as it was reserved for the more advanced initiates.

While in this complete state of relaxation, the disciples needed neither food nor water to sustain themselves. It was the essence of life that sustained them; they were fed by the great prana or the life force. While they were out of the body, or while their body was going through a stage of purification, the prana in the atmosphere was drawn into the body for its sustenance. Many would be gone from the physical body for many hours at a time, and sometimes they would remain in the chamber for days. Agasha has said that those who were taking advanced initiations sometimes remained in that chamber and state of consciousness for as long as seven days and seven nights. Usually they would leave the body intermittently, soar out into space, and then bring back the memory of the experience and record it on a tablet that was put before them. The disciple was able to bring back the memory because it was retained by the subjective and transferred to the objective consciousness. Then after recording the experience, he would automatically go out again. He would travel once more out into space and into the Consciousness of Immensity for more information which he was desirous of receiving. Then he would return again to the physical body and record this new information. This procedure would be repeated several times until the disciple had received what he was supposed to receive, and until he had gone through the necessary process of elimination.

In this state of consciousness, past lives would come before the average disciple to a remarkable degree. He was often able to recall quite clearly things that had transpired back many thousands of years into the past. He saw how he had lived, what he had learned, whom he had met. He saw these past karmic relations and the effects that they would have on his future karmic relations with others many years into the future. Yes, he could even peer into the future and see some of the lives that he was destined to live on the earth plane in generations yet to come. Thus these people were well aware of future lives whereby they would apparently lose the great wisdom and understanding that they then possessed.

The future of the land of Austa was also seen quite clearly. They could see it rise and blossom out like a beautiful flower in the years to come; they could also see its inevitable downfall. They could see the pharaohs ruling with their awesome might and power their beloved land which would then be known as Egypt. They also knew that eventually the people of the land would have to go through great periods of trials and tribulations in still other lands. And last but not least, they could even see the rise of a civilization in the far distant tomorrows—a vast and mighty civilization on a continent across the sea which would be called the *Land of Freedom.* These are the things that were given unto the disciples who had taken the initiative of going through the procedures, passing the initiations, and embracing the activity provided by the powers of Mamon.

We must remember that these people were in the position whereby they could receive this valuable information from the soul because they had prepared themselves through a long period of prior training. No disciple was ever allowed to enter the great sanctuary for meditative purposes until he had first earned the right to do so by passing various initiations and by reaching certain pinnacles of unfoldment. Furthermore, they were not in meditation for selfish reasons, but they were in meditation for the world. They desired to learn how to prepare the way for the many, many millions who were to be reembodied in different parts of the earth. Thus the powers of clairvoyance and clear and extended vision were granted to those who were in the sanctuary. These are the reasons for the many blessings that were bestowed upon the disciples during those periods of communion with the soul and with the great teachers who had ascended.

After the disciple had adjourned from the chamber, he would then make a full report to the teachers at the Mamon Temple. This would consist of the information on the original tablets containing his notes after each out-of-the-body experience as well as a complete summary of what had transpired during the entire meditation. The teachers would then go over the material in detail and give the disciple further explanations if it were of a symbolic nature or if the scenes were unclear. They would also study his aura to determine what he had accomplished spiritually during the meditation as well as in that particular embodiment. This became most interesting for the disciples, as in this way they were able to understand their stage of growth at the time.

These periods of time spent in the sanctuary were called earthly initiations. Agasha says that today we have them in spirit while out of the body during the sleep state. The physical initiation is not needed at this time inasmuch as today the average student on the path must devote most of his time to mundane affairs. But in the days of Austa, the initiations were earthly. Some of the teachers of other occult schools have stated that artificial means were used by the ancients to contact the soul. However, Agasha states that in Austa the only artificiality was the chambers that were so provided. No mechanical or chemical means were used whatsoever; nor did they necessarily have to resort to ritualistic activity to receive their inspiration. But they did have the chambers of wisdom, the chambers of cleansing.

Austa: The Light of the World

Now let us leave the Temple of Mamon for the moment and travel a little further into the period. What do we find? We find generation after generation of peace, harmony, and enlightenment. Oh how many wonderful things were created and brought into manifestation by the peoples of that land! And going into the period even further, we find more of the same. Thus it came to pass that for generation after generation the peoples of this great land of Austa reembodied themselves and enjoyed the splendor of these 2,000 years of peace.

The rest of the world, however, was going through many

trials and tribulations. Wars were taking place all over the world, perhaps not wars in the sense of the word, at least not everywhere on earth, but people were combatting among themselves, fighting a good part of the time, trying to conquer this, trying to conquer that. Now the people of Austa were quite conscious of this, and in their silent moments they prayed and sent forth light and peace unto those struggling countries. But on the whole, for these same 2,000 years that the people of Austa were enjoying peace and understanding, the suffering humanity of the rest of the world remained bogged down in the mire of ignorance.

However, for the same reason that darkness seeks the light, light also seeks the darkness. And not too many years had passed before news of this land of peace had spread afar into the neighboring countries and even to the peoples of distant lands. Thus the light from Austa broke through the clouds of darkness as a brilliant sun on a cloudy day. Many did not understand, but they soon heard about this strange land where there was peace, where there was comfort, where there was joy.

Many were also helped through the aid of the teachers who upon leaving their physical body would then go and inspire. And through that inspiration, the souls of the higher order were able to descend and assist and gradually help those mortals to evolve out of that negative state. But this 2,000-year period was really no different from any other 2,000-year period as far as that is concerned, for the Great White Brotherhood is always endeavoring to send out light and inspiration unto mortal mind wherever it might be.

"Free the people in the lands where they are suffering," was the cry among those who had learned. "Leave Austa and go into the other lands of suffering humanity, and as you go into those lands, then educate and enlighten the hearts of those who will listen." Thus for generation after generation many disciples as well as teachers went into those neighboring countries in much the same manner as missionaries do today. They gave forth the message to those who would listen, and they told them of the land of plenty, the land of peace. People would look at them rather oddly, saying, "Is there such a land as you speak of? Could it be true that such does exist?" But there were some who would believe, and there were some who would listen. These, they encouraged. They told them about the Universal Consciousness of God, and they told them of all of the things that could be accomplished once they had become awakened. Then they taught them how to partake of food properly, and they brought dried fruits and the like into the other countries, food that would help to sustain the body for a long period of time. And finally they told them that they must now put aside their dumb idols, their false gods, and listen to the Inner Consciousness of the God within. Many of the inspired ones did, but the vast majority did not.

However the seed was planted, and in the course of time many of the people from the other countries, those who were free to leave their communities, gradually made their way to this land of Austa. But we are told by Agasha that the journey was rough because they had but very little in some of those countries. And these brave souls suffered through great torment, torture, and very often even starvation as they would make their way in their pilgrimage to the promised land. Many had not learned how to partake of the proper foods that would sustain themselves over a long period of time, and thus they perished along the way. But the many still came. Hundreds and hundreds and hundreds, after traveling for months through great hardship and toil, migrated to that land to establish their kingdom. They came from the neighboring countries which were later to be called Palestine, Persia, Syria, and the like. They also came across the water from Greece, and they even came from afar, from various other countries in other parts of the world. But they were all provided for, cared for, and given shelter and clothing. They had come to the promised land.

After becoming acclimated to their new-found conditions, these pilgrims from the other lands then joined in with the community life. They were taught the arts, handicrafts, and spiritual day-to-day living. They joined the various sects, and they blended in most beautifully. They even saw visions when they attended the meetings, and they had other psychic presentations, for it was as true then as it is true today that only those who were ready would be attracted to help establish the kingdom and lay the foundation for the future. Thus eventually they all became an integrated part of the movement—a member and a citizen of the Land of Austa.

Thus we find that many generations had come and gone. These enlightened souls had reembodied themselves again and again in order to carry on and to perpetuate the message of peace. They continued to bring forth the great message from the Atlanteans, which was the same message that Agasha and the other Master Teachers had given so many, many years earlier. Agasha had long since departed from the physical plane and ascended into the great Consciousness of Immensity—that spiritual consciousness that had been created by all of the Ascended Masters who had gone on before. In the interim, many of the other teachers and sect leaders had likewise ascended as their work was finished and there was no further need for them to return unto the flesh.

Let us now go forward in time to a point a little over 1,900 years after the beginning—after that great convention had first initiated the start of this great movement. We are now approaching the close of this great era. We are in the last days and the peaceful period is now tapering off. The peoples of the land are now called Egyptians, and the Land of Austa has now become known as the Land of Egypt. The political situation had changed all of this a few years earlier with the inauguration of the first Egyptian dynasty in 3100 B.C.[1]. King Menes, whom archaeologists identify with King Narmer, had then politically united the upper and lower kingdoms of the land that had been known as Austa. Yet all is still peaceful. The foreboding clouds of darkness have not yet appeared upon the horizon.

The Temple of Kayanon: The Last Great Temple

As we gaze out over this beautiful land, let us focus our attention on one particular temple, a temple where light, love, and understanding is the keynote of the day. This is the Temple of Kayanon. It is a very wonderful temple and a temple which was most beautifully erected. The architectural design had been carried out in a manner very similar to the temples of the past. But many of the older temples had by now withered away with the sands of time, and because of the sandstorms they had crumbled and were never rebuilt. This is a relatively new temple, and it has been in manifestation for only a little over 200 years. Yet, as we gaze into the Akashic Records, we find its life to be almost over. It is destined to fall in its 213th year, after having served its purpose most beautifully.

The Kayanons were a very wonderful group of people. They were people who taught the Universal Brotherhood of Mankind; they also taught the Universal Understanding of God. They lived, moved, and had their being in this understanding. Kayanon, himself, was a Master Teacher who had brought the message down through the generations. He had reembodied himself purposely, many times, to live in that consciousness and to bring forth light and peace. However, he knew that the fall would come. He knew that too much evil was being created in the minds of the new unlearned souls that were now incarnating in the land. Many of the older and wiser souls had either ascended into the Consciousness of Immensity or they had incarnated into other lands for newer and different types of experience. Egypt was now attracting a younger type of soul, souls that needed to be ruled by the iron hand before they could evolve into higher states of consciousness. However, the fall had not yet come. There was still peace in the land.

The Atlantean Jewels

Agasha tells us that great reverence for the physical body was taught in the Kayanon Temple. They taught that the physical body actually was the Temple of the Living God. They also taught that each gland of the physical body could in turn be represented by a corresponding jewel of the mineral kingdom; each jewel then would have its corresponding counterpart in the physical body. Thus the physical body of Man could in turn be represented by assembling together a large number of jewels, carefully placed in juxtaposition, side by side, so as to accurately correspond with the correct location of each and every gland in the human body. If this were done, so they taught, it would then create a very powerful force. This would represent the "holy body" of Man.

The Atlanteans were also very much aware of this principle. In fact, at one time a group of Atlanteans had taken great pains to assemble together a replica of the human form in jewels. Now this in itself is not so outstanding, but the amazing and almost unbelievable thing is that many of these jewels, these very same jewels that had existed at one time on the continent of Atlantis, had actually survived the submergence and had been handed down for thousands and thousands of years until they eventually ended up at the Temple of Kayanon for safekeeping. Agasha gives us this information on good authority and goes on to state that these particular jewels are only part of a number of Atlantean jewels that still survive someplace—somewhere.

Thus we find that the Kayanons had the good fortune to possess many of these jewels. And the particular jewels that were on display in the Temple of Kayanon were not only very beautiful, but the Kayanons also considered them to be extremely valuable. However to the Kayanons, they were valuable not so much in the physical sense, but they were valuable because of the principle that they represented. They always taught that it is the significance that is attached to a thing that makes it important, and not the thing itself. This principle was thoroughly understood by the Kayanons, and therefore they held these magnificent gems in great reverence.

Intrigue from Greece

Now let us change the scene, for the moment, and travel across the water to the land now known as Greece. The date, according to our modern calendar, is approximately 3100 B.C. This corresponds with the 1,900th year of the Agashan Peace Period. We find these ancient Grecians to be a very powerful people, but at the same time they loved beauty. Agasha tells us that even at this early age in their civilization they had their philosophers, although they have not lived down in recorded history. But even so, many of the philosophers were very well known among the Masters of that particular period. However, these ancient Grecians knew very well that there was something missing in their country at that time. Quite naturally, they had heard about Austa, but they simply could not understand what secrets the people of Austa, and then later the Egyptians, possessed that would enable them to have such peace and harmony for such a long period of time.

Consequently many had ventured into the land of Egypt and had returned with as much information as they could to enhance their kingdom. They copied the Egyptian architecture and the various other items of beauty, and there was a fairly close association between the Grecian consciousness of this period and the consciousness of Egypt. This accounts for the similarity of the architectural designs that were carried out at the time, although the records of same have long since vanished into the sands of time. However, Agasha states that there was that similarity. But the Grecian philosophers still realized that the Egyptians possessed a certain power that they did not. They had learned of the Egyptian religion that taught the "Oneness" of the Universal Spirit, or simply God. They knew that it was a "takeoff" from that which had been taught during the great Atlantean period so many thousands of years earlier. They knew all this, but they did not understand it. We must remember that the Grecians were a very powerful and a very proud people at this time. But they lacked the simple humility that is so necessary for true spiritual understanding. Thus with all of their power, they simply could not understand the "magical force" that had protected the land of Austa or Egypt, with all of its wealth and beauty, from outside intervention for such a long period of time.

Thus it came to pass that on a bright summer day, and on a day that was such a long time ago, we find two Grecian travelers approaching the Temple of Kayanon. They were not unanticipated. The teacher, Kayanon, had known that they would come because he had watched them, clairvoyantly, approach the land. He knew what was in their thoughts. They had heard of the jewels that were in his safekeeping, and they wanted to see them and find out the secret of their power. Their mortal mind had come to the conclusion that the protective power that seemed to surround all of Egypt, that power that enabled the people to live so peacefully, was somehow connected with these Atlantean jewels. They wanted to first find out their "magical secrets" and then to possess them any way that they possibly could. What heroes they would be when they brought them back to their own land! Just think of the ovation they would receive when Greece, and no longer Egypt, had become invincible to all of its enemies.

However, the Master Teacher Kayanon, being ever so gracious to all who would visit the temple, greeted them with love, friendship, and understanding. He spoke softly unto the two travelers as he told them that he had known that they would come. He said unto them, "Greetings my sons, the doors to the Temple of Kayanon are always open to those who seek spiritual gifts, spiritual power, and spiritual relations. May your stay here be filled with spiritual realization."

After they had rested, he then took them into the chamber

where these Atlantean jewels were on display. The two Grecians gazed at them absolutely spellbound. Never had they witnessed such magnificent and dazzling beauty! Then Kayanon explained to them that the value of the jewels lay not in the jewels themselves, but in that which they represented. He said that the jewels were merely symbols of spiritual power, and that the jewels in themselves had really nothing to do with the power. But even the greatest spiritual wisdom only falls on deaf ears when those who are being taught are not ready to learn. The only thing that these two men could understand was that the jewels were very, very valuable, and that they absolutely must bring them back to Greece no matter what the cost. But alas, Kayanon only smiled as they endeavored to trade, bargain, and barter in all possible ways. Thievery was out of the question; the jewels were very secure. There seemed to be absolutely no way to obtain them, on this trip at least, and so with sad hearts they returned empty-handed back to their homeland.

Once back in their native land, our two Grecian travelers lost no time at all in spreading the word of what they had seen. It was not only the jewels that had impressed them, the dazzling magnificence of the Atlantean jewels, but they also were impressed with the beauty, the splendor, and the grandeur of this beautiful temple. They told of the finery of its décor, and they also told of the peace that they had felt while in its environment. They tried to visualize it, and they made architectural drawings of it from their memory. In fact, other similar temples were eventually to be erected from these very drawings. Unfortunately, however, not a trace of these temples remains today. All have long since vanished into the sands of time.

The Downfall

However, as far as Egypt was concerned the die was cast. Over a period of time, all of this activity in Greece only acted to encourage others to also seek out the Temple of Kayanon. But unfortunately, it was not for spiritual understanding or enlightenment that they sought it. The motive was greed—greed to possess those valuable jewels. And Agasha states, in relating this most interesting story, that it was right then and there that the powers of evil began to take over the land of Egypt.

We must keep in mind that for almost 2,000 years, from the period of 5000 B.C. to 3100 B.C., Egypt had enjoyed an unprecedented era whereby *all* of the populace were allowed full freedom of expression in the arts, literature, music, and the pursuit of spiritual understanding. It was a perfectly glorious time in which to live and unfold in a spiritual manner.

But now we move into a different era. We find that many had fallen into a negative state. They had placed themselves in this state of negation through violations of God's laws, and therefore their soul had brought them back into that part of the world which was now to become the complete opposite of that which it had been before. The oncoming generations were now striving to take over and rule by the iron hand—the upper hand of power and authority. This then brought about the downfall. The previously benevolent priest-kings were now to become mighty rulers of absolute authority over the rights and privileges of others. Pharaoh had become God. Pharaoh's law was absolute, whether it be for good or whether it be for bad.

It was in the First Dynasty of the Archaic Period, from 3100 B.C. to 2890 B.C., when this change became noticeable. And then later on other men went into the kingdom thinking that they could rule the people—and they did. Not all of the pharaohs were of Egyptian extraction, incidentally, not all of the Dynasties. Thus we have 3,000 years of hell in Egypt under the Pharaohs, which in turn has been followed by 2,000 years of hell in some of the other countries of the world, until we come up to the present day. But these were not periods of hell for all. To the contrary, some of the periods, such as the Egyptian era, were truly magnificent periods of wealth, prosperity, freedom, and happiness—but this was only for the few! For the many they were painful periods of lack, privation, slavery, and suffering. However, we might add that those souls who were to go through these painful experiences had brought it all on themselves. They had done this by their prior disobedience of God's laws.

Were the Grecians who had sought to steal the Atlantean jewels from the Temple of Kayanon among those who had returned to pay for their crimes? Probably so. But were they ever successful in their endeavors? And if they were, what ever became of those magnificent jewels? These last two questions are good questions, and in answer to them Agasha has given us a positively incredible postscript to this little story. The full details are not clear, but we do know one thing: The Master Kayanon was not to be outwitted at the very end. Even when the temple was to fall, those who had attempted to bring about its destruction were destined once more to walk away empty-handed.

The Tomb of Kayanon

Near or at the site of the original Temple of Kayanon is a tomb. And by the great fate of the Gods—as souls on the earth plane would say—that tomb is still intact at the present day, having been protected for 5,000 years from the sight of men. Upon this tomb several dwellings were later erected only to eventually fall victim to the sands of time. Over the debris from these dwellings, still other buildings were erected, and these too have long since fallen into ruin and decay. Also near the location of this tomb lie the ruins of an old temple that was unearthed a few years ago (prior to 1950), parts of which have since been removed to a museum. In fact, archaeologists have been excavating in this area for a long time. But the time is not far off, Agasha says, when this tomb shall once again see the light of day.

It will be a great find! It will become an outstanding landmark among the annals of archaeological discovery. However, this tomb will be very simple and plain and not comparable at all with other tombs that have been discovered in the past. It will be devoid of the usual furnishings and will express a simple elegance in its simplicity. Over there, within a niche, resplendent in their exquisite beauty, lie the jewels of the Temple of Kayanon—the very same jewels that had been handed down for thousands and thousands of years from the continent of Atlantis. Over here, alongside of the niche, is a sarcophagus. And there within the sarcophagus, looking as peaceful and serene as the day he arose from the physical body, is the great teacher. The body of the Master Teacher Kayanon will be in an almost perfect state of preservation!

"How is it possible," one might ask, "that without the freezing technology and equipment of today this ancient race was able to arrest and stop the normal process of decay for so many thousands of years?" True, the Egyptians of the dark period of Egypt had perfected the art of mummification to a remarkable degree, but the Masters in this earlier age of light had stopped deterioration altogether! Agasha states that the answer is that the peoples of this earlier period were very knowledgeable in the higher laws of alchemy. He says that through the use of certain chemicals they were able to so purify organic matter, that the point where decay would normally begin could be put off indefinitely. It is only natural to try to compare the two processes, but there is no comparison.

Why is it that the ancients took so much pain to preserve the physical body? It would seem that they were more interested in death than in life. In a way this is true. Even in the dark ages of Egypt, they were well aware that the real life lay in spirit. But in the latter period, they had lost the real meaning. They were doing all their religious rituals by rote. They had substituted the symbol for the reality. The dark force that had descended over Egypt had contaminated their thinking, and they could then no longer think in the pure, clear manner that they were so capable of doing in the earlier period. Thus, what had only been symbolical in the earlier period, now became the reality in the latter period. Hence the preservation of the physical body, which is actually only a replica or a *symbol* of the spiritual body, became the dominant force in the latter period. In the earlier period, however, the sole purpose of the preservation of the body was to demonstrate to those in the 20th century, those who would be in reality the return of the Atlanteans, not only the continuity of life or the indestructibility of life, but the actual physical appearance of certain great souls who had lived, moved, and had their being in this great land.

Thus we come to the end of an age, the end of an era. It was an age of great spiritual growth, and it was an age of great enlightenment as well. It was all these things and many more. But is this age now to be forgotten and relegated forevermore to the lost histories of mankind? No, that is not its destiny. Agasha states that the records of this great age will be preserved for posterity in a new and larger museum that will eventually be erected in the city of Cairo. This museum will house all of the records of the Agashan era that are still buried within the earth and that have not yet been brought to the surface. It will house the records of the 37 sects. It will house the records of the great convention. It will house many other records extending from the period of the first great temple, the Temple of Mamon, to the time of the last great temple, the Temple of Kayanon. It will also house the records of Cara Boga Coty, which will be the subject of the following chapter. Thus the true history of these 2,000 years of peace will once more be known by man.

NOTES

1. Cyril Aldred, *Tutankhamun's Egypt* (London, British Broadcasting Corp., 1972), p. 6

CHAPTER SEVEN

CARA BOGA COTY

To have and to hold from this day forward, for better, for worse, for richer, for poorer, in sickness, and in health, to love and to cherish, till death us do part.

—Book of Common Prayer

THE saga of Agasha would never be complete without also embracing his counterpart, his twin soul, the feminine half of his being known to the Agashan class as Donna, the Light. This beautiful Being, equal to Agasha in every sense of the word, descends and communicates in the present-day class in a very soft and quiet manner. Whereas the masculine entity, Agasha, brings forth his teachings in a voice filled with authority, and in oratory comparable to the great speakers of the past, his feminine counterpart always manifests in a soft-spoken manner, in a voice filled with the compassion and love so gracefully expressed by the feminine nature. The two complement each other in a most beautiful manner. Where Agasha is strong and forceful, Donna is gentle and compassionate. Where Agasha expounds forth in rich, sonorous tones that fairly captivate the class with the force of their utterance, Donna speaks softly, in a low, quite feminine voice that soothes and comforts as it brings forth solace and peace. However, the basic teachings are brought forth by Agasha as he uses up the larger part of the average class. Donna usually comes in with only a few words to complement and balance Agasha's strong masculine force.

Donna's base of operations, so to speak, at the present time is from a beautiful feminine consciousness in the higher planes of spiritual awareness known as the Celestial Consciousness. Here, she administers over vast legions of arisen feminine souls known as "Angels of Light." These beautiful Beings are constantly helping those in the physical plane of our planet Earth with errands of mercy and compassion. Excursions with Donna on some of these errands of mercy are a nightly occurrence for many of the enlightened helpers of the earth plane while out of their physical bodies during the so-called sleep state. They administer help and assistance wherever the need arises, and in this way many souls have been helped who otherwise would not have been helped. A few in the Agashan class have even brought back memory of assisting in this spiritual way, although, as in the case with most of our out-of-the-body experiences, actually but very little usually filters back to the mortal mind as memory. However, the teachers say that these experiences are always retained by the soul and that they can be reexperienced at some future date when the disciple has arisen to that higher state of consciousness.

Soul Mates

All of the above now brings us to a discussion as to the meaning of the term "soul mates" in general. This principle of the twin soul concept is not new, and it has long been believed to be true by many seekers of the higher truths in the various occult schools of the earth plane. Indeed, it becomes the very essence of the entire Agashan philosophy. It composes the element of every romantic story down through the ages, and the story of Agasha and Donna is no exception. Neither is the story of your life an exception, as this great principle is a universal principle and it applies equally as well unto all.

It is taught in the Agashan classes that in the beginning, going back to the very dawn of time, you and I and every other individual that had ever lived upon any earth plane whatsoever had first been sent forth from the great Core of Life as a light—a Spark of Divinity, one so minute as to be absolutely undetected by the physical eye. This Spark of Divinity then split into two distinct entities, one positive and one negative, one male and one female, and thus the very essence of the twin-soul principle was brought into manifestation. Each of these twin souls then clothed itself in a body of the spiritual plane most appropriate to its stage of development, and thus we have the male and the female of the species. Therefore, the fact remains that there is a part of every one of us that is missing. This is called the counterpart.

These parts then became separated at the time that we first came into life, and ever since that time each soul has been searching, seeking, and yearning for that which is lacking—for the other half of itself which is needed in order to make up the complete whole. Symbolically speaking, the united souls may be considered a circle, a perfect circle. Separated, the individual soul may then be represented by a semi-circle. Thus the ultimate purpose in life is to unite these two halves, the positive and the negative, once again into the complete whole that it had been prior to the separation. However, this does not mean that one loses his or her individuality; it is more like a spiritual marriage where the two become united and yet separate individuals throughout eternity.

Before this ultimate "marriage," and all through the course of their many lives in the various earth planes, these twin souls are actually never really far apart for any extended period of time. One particular life might find both on the earth plane, living together, and working out their karma together. Another lifetime might find one in the spirit realm while the other is struggling in the physical arena of life. Then in the next life the situation might be reversed. But on the whole they are never really far apart, spiritually, and there always is that inner communion. However, in the earlier stages of our development and progress, this was not always the case. There was a time when the two were quite oblivious to each other, perhaps for eons, but that is not the case with the advanced individual on the earth plane today. The one in the higher spiritual consciousness is sometimes quite conscious of its counterpart in the dense physical body, and it sends forth light and love whenever possible.

We find then that each particular soul is basically either male or female. However, the teachers also stress that each one of us has been both male and female in countless lives. We have been men in some lives and we have been women in others. We have had to experience the two lives in order to have compassion for our fellows while they are suffering through their trials both in the male as well as in the female of the species. But basically we are either male or female. This is not to deny the fact, however, that in any one life each soul has both the positive (male) as well as the negative (female) vibrations. Both of these vibrations are pronounced to a certain extent, and it does not make any real difference whether one is in a masculine or feminine body. But, in whichever body it finds itself functioning at the moment, the true self will always endeavor to express itself. This is the reason that a feminine soul who has come back in a masculine body will sometimes act in just the opposite manner, and vice versa.

Cara Boga Coty[1]

With the foregoing as a background, we are now in a position to attempt to embrace that most beautiful and wondrous story of Cara Boga Coty. "Cara Boga Coty? What strange words are these?" you will ask. Yet, if there were one single phrase that would tell the story of the Agashan philosophy more than any other, it would be these three words. Down through the years Agasha has referred to them many, many times, and it is always in a most reverent manner. For instance, at the conclusion of a lecture he will sometimes ask the class, "Let us all at this time now say the familiar words." And the class will then respond with all voices in unison, "Cara Boga Coty." "Say it again, children," he will say, and the class will once more bring forth a loud "Cara Boga Coty." Then he might give us a clue to this great mystery with something like, "Bear in mind now the importance of these words. They are leading up to a great thing which will be most outstanding and most interesting, and eventually you will find that I am right." Then he will usually dismiss the subject as abruptly as he had brought it up, and leave us dangling, as it were, as he proceeds on to other topics.

And this strange chain of events has been going on for over 25 years! If ever there were a mystery woven into any one class on the earth plane, and covering such a long period of time, it would be indeed the mystery of "Cara Boga Coty." He has asked the class to meditate on these words on numerous occasions, and on still other occasions he has asked us to repeat them silently to ourselves before retiring. "These are very powerful words, disciples," he goes on to say as he endeavors to give us a clue to the great mystery, "and they can aid a meditation to a great extent." But on the whole, the average disciple of the Agashan organization does not fully understand their entire meaning.

A few years ago the class was asked to try to bring forth from the subjective consciousness a certain symbol. Agasha said that this particular symbol that he had in mind was most important, and he was desirous that at least one individual in the class could bring it forth. Over a period of a year or so, many of the disciples told about what they had received, but none apparently tuned in on the correct answer. Agasha would thank them for voicing their impressions, but it was not the symbol that he had in mind. The writer even thought that he had it at one time, but this too was incorrect. However, in thinking back on the answer, I am quite surprised that no one had seen it, in view of all that had been given previously. But hindsight is better than foresight, and as all things must eventually come to an end, the symbol was finally revealed.

"Picture three circles, slightly separated, in a row," Agasha said one evening. "Inside the first circle is a sarcophagus. Inside the second circle is a sarcophagus. Inside the third circle is a sarcophagus. Now underneath the first circle write the word *Cara*. Underneath the second circle write the word *Boga*. Underneath the third circle write the word *Coty*." This then was the symbol that Agasha had endeavored for the class to pick up from the subjective consciousness over the past many months. But it was all so simple. Of course, it was the symbol for Cara Boga Coty. Why didn't we think of it? Surely, that was the main thing that Agasha had been talking about for years and years and years, but somehow no one had connected the words *Cara Boga Coty* with the particular symbol that we were trying to bring forth. But now we had a partial answer, at least, as to the meaning of those strange words. However, it would seem that the answer only uncovered more questions and left the class as deeply mystified as before.

Then Agasha went on to explain that the word *Cara* means the mental aspect of our being, the word *Boga* means the physical aspect, and the word *Coty* means the spiritual aspect. Each individual represents the Holy Trinity; that is, each soul has three modes of expression. One body manifests on the mental planes, one in the physical plane, and a third body in the spiritual realms. Each soul is a trinity with three facets of its own being. "Be aware of Being," Agasha is constantly saying. "Only by being aware of Being will you know thy true self." These are the words that Agasha had said many times in the past, but on that particular evening he also went on to say, "You are Cara Boga Coty. That is you."

Again he reiterated that these words represent the mental, the physical, and the spiritual aspects of every soul ever to walk on any earth plane.

Yet the implications contained within this symbol are most disturbing. "What," one might ask, "are we doing in a sarcophagus, in a coffin? Are we dead? We seem to be very much alive, but on the other hand . . . ?" If one were to seriously meditate on the true meaning of this most extraordinary symbol, he could come to some very interesting conclusions. In fact, one is usually drawn to the conclusion that the above statement is undoubtedly true. Our real selves are asleep while our outer, mortal self blunders through this physical earthly plane of illusion. "The real life is yet to be lived," the teachers are constantly reminding us, "and when you awaken to the Kingdom of Reality, your physical plane lives could be likened as to a dream."

Our purpose in life then seems to be to awaken the soul from its slumber. It is then, and only then, that we really begin to live. Agasha has said many times that once the soul is awake it then guides our life and directs our life in a most amazing manner. That is precisely the teacher's duty—to awaken our soul and introduce us to our Higher Self. Therefore, awakening and arousing the genie that sleeps within then becomes our most important act while still living in an earthly body. To the person who is only "motivating" (Agasha's term for being driven by external forces) on the physical plane, Cara Boga Coty sleeps on. But to the enlightened individual, that individual who has been introduced to his higher self, Cara Boga Coty becomes very much awake.

It is at this point that we can then move forward and accomplish our real purpose in life, whatever that purpose is to be. Yes, it would seem that Cara, Boga, and Coty—we are now referring to them as three separate entities or forces—are literally in chains while imprisoned within the physical jail, the physical earthly body. But this, as we have just pointed out, is true only in the case of the gross, unenlightened individual. The enlightened individual, one who has through his learning and spiritual understanding released the chains that had heretofore enslaved his higher selves, has then complete mastery over his life. His higher bodies, Cara, Boga, and Coty, are then free—free to soar out into space and explore the vastness of life, that not only lies within our own being but on other planes of consciousness as well. Thus out-of-the-body experiences may then become as natural and as easily accomplished as willing oneself to walk into the next room. This is what an Adept does; this is the secret of his powers. He only releases the power that lies within so that it may do its work and he may be about the Father's business, whatever that work may be.

There are still other aspects to Cara Boga Coty. The symbology contained therein seems endless when we consider the many varied ways of attempting to solve the apparent mysteries of life or Being. For instance, let us refer once more to the Holy Trinity—the Father, the Son, and the Holy Ghost, or simply Cara Boga Coty. In this analogy Cara, which represents the mind of God, becomes the Father, the powerhouse, the creator, the activator of all things. It is the great mind of God through which everything that was, is, or ever shall be was brought into manifestation. For it is through the power of mind and mind alone that all things were created. Boga then, representing the physical, becomes Jesus Christ, the Son, the incarnation of the Father. He is the doer, the Avatar, our own individual Savior who resides within the innermost depths of our own being and who is in turn crucified upon the cross of matter. And then finally we have Coty, representing the spiritual, who becomes the Virgin Mother, the Madonna, the Holy Spirit.

Thus we find that Cara, Boga, and Coty, when combined into a unity, become the equivalent or the reflection of God. For if we be Cara Boga Coty, one being, with these three aspects or powers fully expressed and unfolded to the "nth" degree, then we could be said to be the equivalent of everything that is, was, or ever shall be. Of course, this point would only be reached when man had once more evolved back to the high status that he had in the beginning, and before he had been sent forth from the great Core of Life to descend into matter.

Another beautiful way of expressing Cara Boga Coty is to bring the counterpart, or the soul mate, into consideration. Here, Coty, being the spiritual aspect of life, would now represent the Spark of Divinity that was originally sent forth from the great Core of Life prior to its split into two different entities. Boga and Cara then become the male and female counterparts respectively after the split. Boga is the masculine force, the male, the positive force. It is this force that fights all the battles. It is this force that can be likened unto the knights of old who went forth in the crusades to return with the Holy Grail. We venture forth in the physical realms of expression as mortal, only to be tried and proven in the fiery crucibles of life. This is the masculine force, the Boga force. The Cara force then is the feminine counterpart, the negative half of its positive counterpart, that beautiful feminine force that brings forth light and peace and love and harmony unto its mate. It is the still waters within the mind of Cara that reflect the thoughts and the aspirations of Man. Cara is uncomparable beauty, the likes of which the eyes of mortal man are yet to behold.

We could go on and on with our comparisons and with our analogies. We can make a Cara Boga Coty analogy with every situation that could possibly occur on any plane whatsoever. We can use it to study every event that has ever taken place or ever shall take place. For instance: every possible happening has both a negative as well as a positive aspect. Where there is a cause, there is always a result. A coin always has two sides: a heads and a tails. This Yin and Yang principle is applicable throughout all of nature. The Yin or Cara force is negative, dark, and feminine; the Yang or Boga force is positive, bright, and masculine. And then, of course, we also have Coty or the neutral force, the complete whole. In Coty, the positive and negative are united into one. It is the great spiritual force that is the neutral force, the complete circle which unites its two component parts. Thus the God Consciousness can see and understand both sides of the question; It loves all with equal love and affection.

However, an interesting point is brought out when we find that as mortals; we cannot help one thing without apparently hindering the progress of something else. True, the thing that we act in opposition to may be out of the realm of our experience, but it is still there none the less. We may do great good unto our fellows by ridding the city of pestilence which has brought a plague unto our kingdom, but on the other hand, we will appear unto the consciousness of the pestilence as a negative force that is annihilating its very species and its "God given" right to exist. From the one point of view we are positive; from the other point of view we are negative. But to the spiritual point of view, all is in order.

The Tomb

Let us now retrace our steps backwards, if we may, through the sands of time (words often used by Agasha) and return once more to the land of Egypt. Let us also turn the clock backwards and once again pierce through the previous 5,000 years of darkness. We find ourselves once more in that 2,000-year period of peace, harmony, and understanding. In our mind's eye, let us now travel northward along the Nile until the Great Pyramid, that great monument of spirituality, comes into view. We feel very comfortable and uplifted as its golden apex appears like a giant eye as it reflects the sunlight across the desert sands. The contrast between the golden apex and the highly polished white limestone of its four triangular faces is spectacular. The time is the 1,800th year of the Agashan Peace Period. The date is approximately 3200 B.C.

A short distance away from the Great Pyramid a ceremony is in progress. A grand and massive tomb is being readied and prepared so that it too may fulfill its destiny. Its great door has not yet fallen shut, but from what we can gather from the ritualistic activities that are being carried out, the time is only a few minutes away. Peering inside, we are awed with its spaciousness; its galleries are grand and mighty. Ordinarily, tombs are very small. But this one is massive! Everywhere the eye can see, in every corner of every chamber, are records of this beautiful period. Beautiful works of art decorate the walls in brilliant and fast colors; fine furnishings are abundantly displayed. Jewelry beyond compare, articles of clothing, beautiful cloth, parchment, tablets—absolutely everything that could possibly be used to show the exact activity and the customs of these beautiful people are placed therein. Over there are symbols of Atlantis. Over here is the story of something else, and each article is displayed in much the same manner as in the museum of today. The story of how the women of the day conducted their life, how they took care of themselves as far as hygiene is concerned, is most beautifully portrayed. We gaze enthralled, as we can see so clearly that women then were basically the same as women are today.

But wait! The door is about to be closed and we have not yet seen the central chamber of this magnificent tomb. There it is, and our eyes open wide in wonder as we gaze at three of the most beautiful sarcophagi ever to be seen by mortal man. Each one of the three is of solid gold! Each one of the three is most beautifully displayed in its own unique style and manner. And there within each of the three golden sarcophagi, a body lies in repose as if in sleep. We withdraw. The massive stone door drops with an enormous, resounding thud. Silence prevails. The earthly remains of that which once housed the spirits of still another Cara, Boga, and Coty are laid to eternal rest.

So they have remained, intact, down through the centuries sealed from the sight of mortal man. This tomb of Cara Boga Coty, the same as with the tomb of Kayanon and the many others, has been protected by the seal of Divine Providence. For 5,200 years, Agasha tells us, this tomb has remained intact, sealed for all this time from the sight of grave robbers and the many who would desecrate the tombs of the ancients in order to enrich themselves with earthly treasures.

But the magical spells, the curses of the ancient priests of the dark period of Egypt, did little to prevent the tombs of the pharaohs from being desecrated. The greed of mortal man proved to be far more powerful than the incantations of the magicians of the dark period. Yet when we attempt to learn a little more of the enlightened period before the dawn of modern history, we find the situation to be entirely different. Here Divine Providence comes into play. Those ancient priests were Adepts—Masters in their own right. They knew the laws of God, and they knew that the records would be protected by the laws of destiny during the intervening period until the Atlanteans of the 20th century would once again bring them into the light of day. Yes, they knew that they would be safe for they had peered into the future and they had seen that this was so.

Just who were these souls who bore the titles of Cara, Boga, and Coty in that particular earthly incarnation? Why were they important unto mankind? Just why would the Universal Spirit God see to it that their earthly likenesses would be preserved in an almost perfect state of preservation down through the centuries and for such a long period of time? These are very good questions, and their answers as of the date of this writing are still a mystery. Of course, as we had learned in the previous chapter, the basic answer was that these ancient peoples endeavored to preserve for posterity, for the new Atlanteans yet to arise, the records of their civilization during those 2,000 years of peace. But is there an underlying higher mystery that does not seem to be apparent on the surface? The writer feels that this is so.

Agasha, who excels in the art of story telling and who loves to keep us dangling (his own words), will not help. In fact, one of the secrets of the success of the Agashan classes, the one thing that keeps the many coming down through the years, is this element of the mysterious, the element of suspense on the pathway of learning. The answers to many things have been gradually revealed, sometimes ever so slowly, down through the years. But then the answers to many other things are still concealed, waiting, as the teachers so often say, for the right and proper time when they can be once again revealed unto mankind. There is a time for sowing and there is a time for reaping. Everything has its time. And the same principle applies to the time when this particular tomb can be "found" and once more brought to the surface.

Three Strange Voices

Have we now exhausted the subject of Cara Boga Coty? Or have we at least touched upon most of the basic concepts that have gradually been revealed down through the years? The answer is definitely no. Perhaps the most beautiful and by far the most romantic aspect of Cara Boga Coty was given in two particular classes in the latter part of 1950 and, to the writer's knowledge, has not been repeated since except briefly in the class of January 12, 1959. Therefore, some of the following material will be entirely new even to the many disciples who have followed Agasha for the past twenty some odd years or so.

The date was October 2, 1950. Agasha had been speaking and had just concluded the first part of his lecture. There was the usual pause. Suddenly three distinct voices broke the silence and spoke through the instrument almost simultaneously. The language was soft and melodious and beautiful. First one would speak, and then another, with scarcely a pause in between. It was not like the usual communication to the class in some unknown tongue, but it was more like an intimate conversation between two men and a woman. In listening to the tape for the full five minutes of this almost musical conversation, one has the distinct impression that the speakers are not speaking to the class but are speaking to themselves. Then Agasha returned and had the class repeat the three familiar words. Did he then explain the meaning of the conversation? Of course not. Here again, we see how the elements of suspense and intrigue are constantly being woven into the Agashan classes. It would not be until ten classes later that the answer would be forthcoming. However, I am sure that the class realized that it had just had the privilege of listening to Cara, Boga, and Coty.

The class of Monday evening, November 6, 1950, was probably one of the most dramatic classes ever given to the Agashan disciples. We can say this because it revealed and explained many things relevant to the Agashan philosophy. It was also a very important class as it marked the conclusion of the first phase of Agasha's manifestation here in the 20th century. Much of this material will be given here as well as later in the chapter titled *The Grand Finale*; however, only that portion of the class which pertains to Cara Boga Coty is included herein. It was in this particular class that Agasha, being the masterful storyteller that he is, recreated in English that same conversation that had previously been given to the class just five weeks earlier in the ancient Egyptian language. Practically all of the material that follows is presented more or less as Agasha gave it to the class. It is his story, and with the exception of the background material, the words and descriptions are his. We have only changed it into the third person for clarity.

A Romantic Interlude

So therefore let us once again retrace our steps backwards in time, and let us return once more to the land of Austa, Egypt. Only this time, instead of stopping off at the year 3200 B.C., let us continue back for the full 7,000 years. The date is approximately 5000 B.C., or possibly a few years earlier. We are once more near the site of the Great Pyramid, the only difference being that we have gone back to a time before it was even erected. But instead, let us observe in the distance a very beautiful temple adjacent to the River Nile. This is the original Temple of Mamon, the temple that was in existence prior to the construction of the later, more magnificent structure. It is evening time, and the moon is full. We project ourselves to the bank of the river, to a particular location not so very far from this beautiful temple. A lone figure is silently strolling along the bank obviously lost in thought. It is Agasha.

He is contemplating a vision that had been presented to him while in meditation a few hours earlier. He had been meditating upon the world, and he had seen the 20th century as clearly as one could see it today. He had seen the nations at war, and he had seen the many children (a term he uses to describe you and me) going through our numerous trials and difficulties. And peering into the future as if in retrospect, so to speak, he could clearly see that these very same trials and tribulations were the direct result of the actions of Man going in the wrong direction. It seemed such a pity, especially since it could have so easily been otherwise. All that hustle and bustle, all of that which should have brought magnificent results, would only bring forth frustration. Yet, he could see that in those great cities of the future—those cities with their magnificent skyscrapers, technologies, and other inventions to come—there would also be a tremendous advancement in the arts, literature, and music. And he knew that these things would at times bring forth great joy. How interesting it was to compare that civilization of the tomorrows to come with the Atlantean civilization of the past!

Agasha had often gone down to the Nile. He loved to go by and walk near it as he was always inspired with its beauty. On many, many previous occasions he had observed the moon as it would reflect its light so beautifully in the Nile, and this night was no exception. It was a night of the full moon and the multitude of stars sparkled in the cloudless sky. These were the stars that he loved so much and that he understood so thoroughly, philosophically speaking, that is. But as he gazed upon the moon and onto the stars on this particular summer evening, a great feeling of expectation suddenly arose from within his very being. It was a feeling that is very difficult to describe. It was not only a feeling of expectancy, but it was also a feeling of great calmness as well. It seemed as if he were once again about to cross the threshold of eternity, that his life was about to change; but at the moment it had come to a pause, suspended somewhere between the past and the future. It is no wonder that he felt this way, for it was right then and there that he was to receive not only his great inspiration, but also his greatest romance. A love story as tender as the most fragile flower, and as enduring as eternity itself, was about to begin. Yes indeed, this night was to become the night of all nights, and for Agasha, the first step on that great stairway to the stars.

And so on this night we find Agasha quite lost in thought and contemplating the wonder of it all. But the silence will not last for long, for out of the moonlight now steps a very beautiful figure. She is truly beautiful. Her long flowing hair is loosely draped about herself, and it partially conceals a garment of the palest blue. It also seems to shimmer quite delightfully in the moonlight as we observe her approaching Agasha. He turns towards her. He is spellbound. We are also, as we gaze upon this beautiful picture. In a few moments she reaches him and then stands so very nobly by his side. Her eyes are now focused upon Agasha's, and she gives him a beautiful smile. It is a smile that goes through; it penetrates. It seems to reach the very depth of his soul. Indeed, it is a smile which would seem to send forth light and peace unto all who would be in her presence, but now it is concentrated upon Agasha. He quite naturally returns the smile as he feels her great radiance and warmth.

"Is it not a beautiful evening?" she inquires softly.

Agasha answers that it is indeed a most beautiful evening, and that tonight he is greatly inspired. "I do not recall having met you before," he adds.

We watch fascinated as she replies, "No, not in the way that we usually meet, but having met you on the inner planes I have come to bring you my blessings this very evening." The language that they are speaking is soft and melodious, and they stand there quietly for several moments. Then Agasha glances out into space and she does likewise.

Now her gaze turns thoughtful as we hear her remark, "If we could only bring an understanding unto mankind that would last down through the ages!" She seems greatly inspired as she continues, "I don't mean this so much for today, because today will be provided for; today, men either have the true understanding of life or they will shortly come into this understanding. I mean, wouldn't it be grand if this message could be perpetuated? If this could happen, then down through the ages men would understand the ways of the world, the significance of their coming into manifestation, and their direct relationship with one another. Then men of the earth would always have the key of life, and they would always know how to use it for their greater unfoldment."

It is interesting to watch Agasha's expression as this beautiful soul, this soul who only moments before had been apparently only a perfect stranger, now expounds so knowledgeably and so beautifully on a subject so dear to Agasha's heart. He seems astonished at her great understanding and wisdom. He gazes at her thoughtfully, but he speaks unto her saying only, "Yes, yes, that is very true." Then we observe them walk slowly, hand in hand, back to the Temple of Mamon. We have the distinct impression that one of Cupid's arrows has found its mark.

They are now speaking of themselves. "What part of Austa are you from," Agasha inquires.

"I have come from quite a distance, from the lower portion of the Nile where it joins the sea. I came to the Temple of Mamon tonight and I inquired where you were. They told me that you were near the Nile, that you often walked there in the moonlight."

Agasha replies, "Yes, I do." We can see that he is puzzled. Why should this beautiful stranger seek him out? We can practically read his thoughts as he mentally questions her for a further explanation.

"I have learned of your mission," she continues, "and I have heard of what you are doing in this part of the world. I have received the message that you are endeavoring to establish the Universal Consciousness of God now that you have become so divinely inspired. I have also heard that you are in direct attunement with your teacher from the higher Consciousness of Immensity."

A look of astonishment appears on Agasha's face. He had obviously not been aware that his ideas and the knowledge of his spiritual contacts had traveled so far. We must remember that we have projected ourselves back in time to a point very early in Agasha's career. He had not yet shared his private thoughts with any great number of individuals, and he had really not even formulated his plan to any great extent. To Agasha, it was then more of a dream than a reality. We can consequently understand his puzzlement as to how this beautiful stranger had come unto her information.

"Yes, it is my intention," he replies. "It is my desire to point out unto the world, to point out unto the children of the Nile, the correct interpretation of the universal understanding of God. It is also my desire that in time it shall be perpetuated because I have seen the generations come and go and I have seen many things that shall transpire."

Now Donna is talking. Yes, dear reader, you have guessed it. This beautiful soul who is so knowledgeable of Agasha is none other than our blessed Donna—Donna the Light, the counterpart, the soul mate, of our unfolding Master of Wisdom. Of course, at this first meeting Agasha is completely unaware, on the surface that is, of what Donna would eventually come to mean unto him. But her name in those days was not Donna. Therefore, we can only refer to her as the beautiful stranger who appeared out of the moonlight. She continues, talking at great length, telling Agasha what she too is able to see. Agasha is listening, absorbing every word, totally enraptured with her presence.

Perhaps I should point out that by now the two have gradually made their way back to the Temple of Mamon. They are standing within one of its spacious galleries and they now are alone. The hour is getting late and the others have departed. As the eye of our camera slowly pans around the room, our attention is focused upon the numerous works of art that adorn the niches within this ancient temple. It is so peaceful here. Heavenly music, as if from a choir of angels, seems to issue forth from the soul to strike the inner ear. But wait! Did I say that Agasha and Donna are alone? I must have been in error because standing there in the corner is one of the most handsome, stately, and distinguished individuals that the observer, as a mortal, has ever had the privilege to know. He is a large man and he is clothed most beautifully. A twinkle is in his eye. Donna is observing him as she is speaking. Agasha, perhaps sensing his presence, now suddenly turns around and directs his attention toward the object of Donna's gaze. He too seems taken aback a bit at the sight of this very imposing and august personality.

The stranger, now that he has been recognized, greets them in a most joyful and pleasant manner. "It *is* a beautiful evening!" His words which are filled with affection fairly resound against the marble walls as there is a very definite resonant quality to his voice. He swiftly walks toward them as the two, obviously inspired with his presence, return the greeting. A light seems to surround the group, and the observer has the distinct impression that there is a very great attunement to the Infinite State on this particular occasion.

Agasha is saying, "I do not recall having seen you before." He seems to be searching his mind for a clue as to the stranger's identity. He knows that he knows him, but he does not know from where or when. There are many coming from the different parts of Austa to the Temple of Mamon at this particular time, and there is certainly nothing unusual in a stranger showing up at the temple. But this stranger is different!

Agasha seems to be a little perplexed because of the strange things that seem to be happening to him now in the flesh. First, there was the arrival of Donna, this angelic being who seems to know his innermost thoughts. And now he is in the presence of still another mysterious being. In the past, he had never thought it particularly strange when mysterious events had taken place in a psychic manner or while out of the body in the inner planes. To the contrary, it seemed to be the norm for those planes of consciousness, and he had always accepted everything that had ever come unto him, knowing it all to be good. But now strange things were happening to him in the flesh! Heretofore this had been unheard of, at least as far as his own awareness was concerned.

And not only that, he now had the distinct suspicion that even stranger things yet were about to happen. This wondrous evening, which had started out so very romantically in the beginning, now seemed to have the potential for an even greater spiritual experience. Yes, as we observe Agasha, it becomes apparent that he is aware that some great spiritual truth, something that had previously been concealed from his mortal consciousness by the soul, is now about to be unveiled.

His mouth opens as if to speak, but before he can utter a word the stranger beats him to it. "You made the remark a moment ago that you had not seen me before," the stranger begins. "Now look at me again and see if you can recognize me. See if you can discern anything about me that is familiar."

"I shall try," Agasha replies, "but my soul is not giving me a thing at this very moment." But now he observes the stranger a bit more carefully than he had before, and as he does this one can tell that Agasha is beginning to feel very invigorated. He seems to be feeling very happy and grateful to be alive in the flesh. Perhaps he is thinking that now he might be able to carry out his plan to bring forth the correct understanding of the Universal God Consciousness. He turns to talk to Donna with the thought that she might know this stranger. Perhaps he has come from one of the sects not very far from the Mamon sect, or then again, perhaps he has come from Donna's own sect.

He looks at Donna and is about to ask what be the name of her sect. Funny, he had not thought to ask that before. He stiffens. He utters not a word. He has the distinct impression that something strange has taken place behind him. And indeed there has, for as he turns around to speak to the stranger his mouth opens wide in astonishment. This very wonderful person, this person who only a moment ago had stood within inches of his body, is now nowhere to be seen. He has simply vanished into the nothingness!

Agasha turns back to Donna, now completely perplexed. "That man, that soul, whoever he was, has disappeared!" The words flow from his mouth as fast as he can utter them. Donna merely smiles and makes no comment. Apparently she does not think it even strange. Agasha, however, is simply astounded! His very expression conveys his thoughts. "How is this possible?" he seems to be thinking, "This is the physical plane, and we are in the flesh." We, as observers, likewise share his amazement. There is absolutely no doubt in any of our minds but that only a moment before a very commanding and majestic individual, a presence who was as real as anything can be real, had simply vanished from our sight.

Agasha's eyes continue to search the gallery, as if still not believing what he had seen. Donna is now smiling and is almost laughing at his amazement. Then her attention is drawn to something occurring behind him. It seems to her to be even more amusing. Agasha, now apparently beginning to realize that he has just been made the object of only some good-natured humor, begins to smile also. In fact, his smile now turns to laughter as soon as he turns around and beholds once more the imposing presence of our magnificent stranger. Now they all burst out laughing, one with the other, as tears of joy moisten the cheeks of three very happy individuals.

"Now as I appear unto you, your soul will tell you who I am," the stranger begins. He walks forward to Agasha and stands beside him. The laughter has now erased all reserve that may or may not have existed before, and a great camaraderie seems to exist between the three. And more than that, a great light of recognition suddenly lights up the face of Agasha which completely erases any puzzlement that might previously have been expressed, and the two embrace each other as long lost friends.

"My soul has given it, my soul has given it!" Agasha exclaims, as full memory as to the identity of this enlightened being floods into his consciousness. It is none other than Coman Coban, his great Atlantean teacher from the Consciousness of Immensity, who has materialized all so solidly and so clearly unto the presence of Donna and himself. There he is, once again, this great teacher whom he had learned to love and to know on the inner planes of life; only this time the action is taking place on the physical plane, for standing before him, in the flesh, is this great teacher from Immensity.

We must go back several years in time in order to fully understand the significance of this moment insofar as it relates to Agasha's outer mortal consciousness. In the beginning he had only seen his teacher as a light. We are not referring to the etheric experience while in the desert during his youth. We will come to that later. But as he began unfolding his psychic powers, his teacher would appear to him as a light. Then, as the years went by, he had become aware of his voice through the principle of mediumship known today as "direct voice." Sometimes the teacher would entrance him and speak through him. On other occasions Agasha would listen to the voice independently. In any event, he had gradually become conscious of Coman Coban as an individual, and he looked forward to his contacts with great anticipation.

However, it was a long period of time before Agasha had any direct knowledge of the teacher's appearance or even his personality. He had known that his teacher was from Atlantis, but other than that he had known but very little. It was not until he had had his momentous "breakthrough"—that inner plane contact with Coman Coban which we covered in an earlier chapter—that he was able to know him, to love him, and to respect him as the individual that he is. And ever since that time, Agasha had been able to bring back memory of Coman Coban guiding him and informing him of many things.

But this had all occurred on the inner planes—out-of-the-body experiences on the inner, spiritual realms of consciousness. Even his first contact on the desert during his youth was not a physical experience. And at that time he was practically delirious from lack of food and water. Therefore, all of his prior experiences had been on the inner planes of life, and it had simply never occurred to him that he would *ever* be able to converse with this teacher on the physical plane. It is quite understandable then as to why his mortal mind had not at first equated the identity of this remarkable stranger with the teacher on the inner planes. The two levels of experience were simply out of context with each other. Then too, in the beginning the soul had not aided the outer mind with the recall. In fact, it would almost seem that it had deliberately blocked off the memory of the appearance of Coman Coban in such a way so that the mortal mind had become oblivious to his actual features, etc., until this remarkable meeting in the flesh. Then, in one brilliant flash of realization, the complete memory of how Coman Coban had appeared on the inner planes suddenly flooded back into his outer consciousness.

Donna, on the other hand, had apparently been aware of the identity of Coman Coban all along. She is now smiling and laughing and actively participating in the conversation. Sometimes it would appear that they are all talking at once in their eagerness to express their innermost thoughts. It is indeed a joyful reunion. We also share in their happiness as we observe them now walking through the portals of the temple and out into the open air, only this time instead of the two there are the three. There they are. They are now standing outside the Temple of Mamon and continuing their discussion in the soft glow of the beautiful moonlight. The language of the ancient Egyptians is very expressive, and if we could fully understand it, we would know that the main course of the discussion relates to the fulfillment of the plan—the carrying out of the establishing in that part of the world the Universal Consciousness of God.

Coman Coban is now speaking. The others are listening. "It is going to be a very difficult task, but you are to be patient," he tells Agasha. "And then we three, acting as the Trinity at this moment, can draw the 37 sects into one grand unit. Then all the teachers and all the scholars who are later to become teachers will be intermingled, and we will thus create the spiritual pattern. Now this spiritual pattern, having once been created, will then enable us all to be interwoven into that pattern. Although we shall go far and wide, and perhaps be sprinkled all over the universe as we are living our many lives, please know that we will always invariably come together in the different lives and have our experiences. Then finally, in what will be known as the 20th century, we will meet again."

There is a pause as both Agasha and Donna thoughtfully absorb the words that this great teacher has just uttered. He gazes unto them with compassion as he speaks one final word as a blessing and a benediction. The word is, "Manzaholla!" Perhaps the reader will think it strange that Coman Coban used this word as a blessing many years prior to the date of the great convention. But there is nothing particularly strange in that inasmuch as the word meant "goodness and love" in the language of the day.

Overcome with emotion, Agasha now turns to Donna, and if I were to say that he is now not only shocked but speechless as well, it would be a masterpiece of understatement. Why do I say this? Take a look yourself. If you had been watching the scene carefully, you would have seen her disappear and vanish at the precise moment that Agasha turned around to face her. How could this be possible? Agasha is simply flabbergasted. And I might add that we are also. We see a tear fall from his eye as he turns back to face Coman Coban. The single tear now turns into two, and then into three, for Coman Coban also is not there. In the same manner as Donna, he has likewise disappeared and vanished into the night, and Agasha now stands alone.

He gazes out into space, very thoughtfully now, obviously pondering over the fantastic events of the evening. You saw it, I saw it, and Agasha saw it. Two human beings, very much alive and in the flesh, had simply vanished from sight in much the same manner as one would turn off a light. How could this be possible? And more than that, something even more wondrous had occurred. Almost simultaneously he had been brought into physical contact with not only his teacher from the Consciousness of Immensity, but also with a strangely familiar feminine soul who had aroused such a yearning within himself that it seemed to stem from the very core of his being. And all this had happened on an evening which at first had started out as any other evening with a simple stroll along the Nile. We can feel his feelings and read his thoughts as he contemplates the wonderment of it all. Then, after a few moments, he seems to absorb the initial shock and now he is beginning to plan many things.

He is thinking about this great plan, one that he had originally not planned himself, but one that had been so beautifully presented by the Teacher. He is thinking of all of the scholars, those in the physical body like himself, going through their many lives in the physical plane until they would eventually ascend to become Teachers of Light. And he is also thinking of these very same Teachers of Light, those Arisen Beings who could travel to the far reaches of the universe, likewise living through their own lives and experiences in the spiritual realms at one and the same time. But the beautiful thing of it all was that once this great spiritual pattern was established, the teachers then would be in a position to never lose sight of those still in the physical plane for any extended period of time. They would always be watching and assisting the disciples in the flesh. "Yes indeed," we can hear him say to himself, "this meeting tonight has truly been a great meeting."

The full moon is now gradually descending upon the horizon. It seems to be accompanying the curtain which is also descending, and quite rapidly now, and in a few moments our consciousness will be separated from this amazing scene from the past. We return once more to the 20th century.

Acting a bit startled, in much the same manner as when one returns to consciousness after having experienced a very vivid and most beautiful dream, we are aware once more of the Agasha Temple. It is still Monday evening, November 6, 1950, although it seems an eternity since we had first dozed off and had seemingly become a part of the story that Agasha had just finished relating. How beautiful it was! His voice, at times, has the ability of putting one into a deep meditative state, and this evening was no exception. It seemed as if we were floating on a cloud as Agasha's voice built the mental pictures within our consciousness, but tonight, as is not always the case, we can remember every word.

The Mystery Unravels

"And so we have reenacted," Agasha is saying, "a conversation that was held many centuries ago. The other evening, a few classes ago, it was given to you in the ancient Egyptian language. Tonight it was given to you in English. We had trained ourselves to go back into the great memory in order to carry out the plan and try to keep you not in ignorance. Thus we were able, once again, to carry on the conversation that was held on that occasion between Cara, Boga, and Coty.

"You see, blessed children," Agasha continues, "when you become a part of the Inner Circle, you are going to learn far more and you are going to understand far more than anything that has ever before been brought unto your attention upon earth. Now *Cara Boga Coty* meant a great deal unto our consciousness during that period. Those were names, children; those were names like your names today. *Coty*, dating back into the great consciousness of Atlantis, meant the 'Learned One.' *Boga* means 'One to Obey.' *Cara* means

'Light and Inspiration.' Those words meant that. We had those names like you would name yourself today. They had a great meaning and so it was then that we were Cara, Boga, and Coty.

"Now mind you," Agasha goes on, "the Temple of Mamon was flourishing then. The city of Mamon was beautiful. There was no disease; disease did not exist in our part of the world of Austa, Egypt. This was the time when we were laying the foundation and when we were establishing the great Universal Consciousness of God that was later to be carried down through the oncoming generations for nearly 2,000 years. All this time we were in the temples bringing forth light and peace unto men. We were also arranging and making preparations so that everything could be recorded—by that I mean the history of Man since the beginning of time on earth. We had been in contact with the teachers from Atlantis and we had learned much. Therefore, we were endeavoring to write upon the tablets of time and place there, in the great tomb, within the niches that still remain intact today, the full records of our consciousness of Atlantis. That is why that particular evening becomes so all important, for it marked the beginning of the establishment of that great pattern that we all find ourselves interwoven in today. Many a teacher of the occult who is sensitive to the land of Egypt is interlocked in this pattern. Therefore, we are now all dovetailing into the pattern that was first set up that evening so long ago when Cara Boga Coty had come together to establish the great Universal Consciousness of God."

What an impressive thought! It seems fantastic at times when we realize that the voice that is coming through the entranced medium, a voice that expounds so beautifully on so many varied and intricate subjects, is actually the voice of a great Master Teacher who had once lived, moved, and had his being so many thousands of years ago in the past. But there he is: there he sits on the platform in front of the class with his feet tucked under him in the typical yoga posture, his body swaying to and fro, and his hands gesturing so expressively with every word.

Agasha is now giving out more material about the Adepts who have once more, as they had in the past, returned onto the earth. It would seem that all of the great souls who had returned back to the earth at different time periods are in reality souls who had lived in Egypt during the 2,000-year Peace Period. This includes the ancient Hebrews as they brought forth what is known as the *Old Testament*. It also includes those who participated in the creation of the *New Testament* as well as the more modern schools of western occult thought. He states that all of these souls are interlocked and interwoven in this great pattern.

He further goes on to say that there is far more to *Cara Boga Coty* than what was given tonight. They are also the spiritual names of three Mystery Schools, three in particular, which have been in existence from the time of the Peace Period until the present day. There are the Bogas, the Cotys, and the Caras; but they are not known by these names in the modern world today. We learn that it has been a part of Donna's mission to work for the continuance of these schools down through the years.

Agasha now brings the first portion of the class to a close as he asks us to sound the "Aum" after the familiar, "One . . . two . . . three . . ." The silence that prevails after the resounding vibrations of this beautiful tone have dissipated themselves is quite profound. We lose ourselves in the stillness of the moment as we endeavor to bring forth some additional impressions from the soul. All is peaceful and quiet. A beautifully soft, feminine voice now returns us once more to the consciousness of the class. It is Donna.

A Message from Donna

"Oh blessed souls," she begins, "it is my desire to come in tonight to give you my blessings and to bless all of you who have worked so diligently and sincerely in the consciousness of Agasha during these past months. May we never now turn aside; may we always go on. I repeat this tonight because Agasha once said unto me these very same words. He said that there was no turning back now that we had made our plans for we had created that which we knew was right. We had consulted the Higher Self, and once the Higher Self had been consulted the move most assuredly would be in the right direction.

"Agasha desires now to go deeper and deeper with you as he becomes even more attuned to his Infinite State. I am with Agasha much of the time, and I have seen him go into deep meditation and ponder over just one thought in order to see how best he could express it and put it across to you disciples. I offer assistance, as you would your neighbor, and we together go over a subject many times before he brings it unto you. He is giving you the opportunity now to follow him, and things that he is about to learn you may now learn with him, and perhaps for the first time. Thus as you grow, so shall Agasha grow; and as you expand, so shall he expand. It can be said unto you that we are all growing together.

"And so tonight as we have come together," Donna continues, "we now know the significance of Agasha's work and of his message. This includes my work also as I am in the presence, always there in the background. I am on the right side of Agasha and I am the negative contact, not as a negative individual, but as the negative or feminine part of Agasha. He being the positive or masculine aspect, I therefore fulfill the negative aspect in order to continue on with our great activity. Agasha has served beautifully down through the ages, how well I know. He is an individual the same as you, the same as I. He has his work to do and you have your work to do, the same as I have my own work to do. We are all individuals and we never lose our individuality.

"Therefore when Agasha ascended into the Consciousness of Immensity, it was my desire that I would have my own division, and I went into the Celestial. There in the Celestial

Consciousness I was able to carry out my work among those who had also earned the right to be in that consciousness, and you have termed them the Angels of Light. They work with the many disciples upon the earth plane by bringing forth the inspired word, and they thus help you on your way. They work with your teacher, perhaps in the silence, and they may even knowingly make themselves known unto you. Of course, this is not the only work that we do. The work that we are carrying out from the Celestial Consciousness also includes helping so much all over the world. We have carried out this program of bringing forth light and peace unto struggling humanity for oh so many generations, even going on for thousands of years for some. This is my program and this is my work."

Just to hear this beautiful soul speak so charmingly and so softly is an experience in itself. It is always a delight to hear the words of tenderness and affection expressed by either Agasha or Donna for each other, for they tend to inspire one with a glimpse of that which is eventually destined for all. Donna, by the way, is the supervisory head of a division of this feminine consciousness. However, she has not always been the head of the Celestial Division for she has had to return to the earth plane several times in physical incarnations since the ascension of Agasha some 7,000 years ago. These were for particular assignments by the soul to accomplish a specific purpose. Thus she too had become oblivious to many things during the interim period, for one of the penalties for incarnation into the physical plane is loss of memory by the outer consciousness. However, this is all in the past now as she has long since ascended into the higher consciousness, and she is equal to Agasha in every sense of the word.

There has always been some mystery as to Donna's relationship with the blessed soul who manifests quite frequently in the Agashan classes under the name of *Kraio.* Kraio (phonetically pronounced Krai-o) is one of the Universal

Teachers currently holding office within the spiritual hierarchy of the planet. It was also Kraio who returned to Palestine and Egypt a little less than 2,000 years ago as Jesus of Nazareth, the great Master Teacher whose original teachings dovetailed so beautifully with the philosophy as taught by Agasha. This particular life completed his own earth cycle after he had manifested several times during the Austa Peace Period. His soft-spoken manner fairly rings with authenticity as he recites some anecdote relative to his life as Jesus. He always speaks very humbly and with a voice filled with compassion, and there is seldom a class in which Kraio will manifest without Donna either preceding or immediately following him. Some clue as to this relationship may be gleaned by the discerning reader as we return once more to our little talk by Donna the Light, although the full story has not yet been completely told.

"Someday I want to come and tell you about Kraio," Donna continues, "Kraio, whom I know very well, or I most certainly should. I will tell you about Kraio someday, and perhaps the story that I will tell will give you a better understanding as to that individual who was blessed unto the Universal Spirit God. But that one who lived, who served, and who went through torture and then ascended was no more so blessed than either you or I. I have gone through that stage after having gone through many trials myself, and remember this: We all at some time or another have either gone through it in the past or we shall go through it in the future. Agasha has also paid much karma upon the earth plane, but he has not had to return to the earth for nearly 7,000 years.

"So then there is no turning back now, children; we must all go on and realize our works that we are to do. When Agasha and I realized the male and the female principle—the positive and negative contact in everything upon earth—then we saw and understood the harmonizing force. We saw how important it was for this harmonizing force to continue, and we knew that it would continue for a long time. But we also knew that there would be friction down through the ages. And because of this friction there would be much confusion, but we knew that in the midst of confusion we would always endeavor to be present—to be in the presence of those whom we knew and with whom we had had direct relations in the past.

"I hope that some of you will then be able to see me, and I will do my very best to become visible. You will know it is I when I appear. I know that Agasha is doing this as well as helping others to be seen, and I know that some of you have either seen your teacher or felt his presence and thus know that he is very near. Please understand that your teachers and I are always working for you, and of course this includes your wonderful Agasha.

"I would like you then tonight to visualize Agasha and I walking down our single path, and there in the view ahead is the great sunlight of God, which represents the Core of Life. There we go, hand in hand, and as we are walking forward we then see you in back of us, following us as though it were our children that we were taking back home to the Core of Life. If you would visualize this as a mental picture, you would then be gazing at a living symbol of the great harmonizing force of God."

What a beautiful thought! It would seem that this particular class could be likened unto a spiritual bath—a class where all negativity had been washed away in the sunlight of understanding. It is a class where the true meaning of the words *Cara Boga Coty* seems to be becoming clearer and clearer. It would almost seem that these three little words contain within themselves the very essence of spiritual harmony. The teachers have always said that they come to introduce us to our Higher Self, and one has the distinct feeling that Cara Boga Coty may be symbolical of just that.

"We must always know about who we are and what our thoughts are at the moment," Donna is saying, "and as we go within, we shall also receive. Many things shall then be given unto you which you had never expected. This can be much the same as what had happened to Agasha outside the Temple of Mamon during that evening so many thousands of years ago. I don't mean that your experience would necessarily be in the physical sense as it was with Agasha, but it would in all probability be as a spiritual, out-of-the-body experience.

"You see, I knew at the time our relationship in Atlantis. I knew that Agasha and I had returned to the land of Austa to carry out our great program. However, Agasha, being in the physical body at the time, had become temporarily oblivious to much of this. Then, on that particular evening, he had had the awakening as the higher powers enabled us to materialize unto his consciousness. His soul likewise revealed the memory unto his outer mind and it was then that we were able to say, 'It shall be done.'

"Today we are renewing it," she continues "You children who are following Agasha are now to carry on, perhaps for the rest of your life, and then eventually into the spiritual consciousness that you will find yourself in. You see, blessed ones, we have become so inspired tonight because we have become so attuned to the Holy Light. We know that the Holy Light is shining upon you at all times because this class of Agasha's has become one of the great groups of the exalted ones. They in turn appreciate you as an individual working with them as you have earned the way, every step of the way. You have not only listened to, but you have also lived the Agashan philosophy.

"So as Agasha brings forth these tremendous subjects, and as he tries to gradually lead you up to the higher understanding of life, please be patient with yourself. I know that you will all eventually have many things revealed unto you that you had never dreamed were possible—things that you had never thought could ever possibly come unto you. It will be given to you now and you will understand. So try, try, try to become attuned to all things that are right. Work with Agasha and soon the Angels of Light will be with you. God bless you and this is Donna and good night."

A silence now falls over the room as we wait for Agasha to again control the channel, the medium or instrument, once more. He did have us guessing, he admits, as he answers a few questions put forth by the disciples. Much of the remainder of the class relates to the material which will be covered in the chapter titled *The Grand Finale*, and so we will not discuss it here. We do know, however, that we have gained a very valuable insight into the saga of that great Master of Wisdom, Agasha, and his beloved counterpart known to the Agashans as Donna the Light. We have also been initiated, to a certain extent at least, into the inner meaning of those powerful words—*Cara Boga Coty*.

NOTES

1. The Words *Cara Boga Coty* rhyme with "had a yoga body."

CHAPTER EIGHT

THE SPIRITUAL CENTERS

Shangri-La—Valley of Enchantment: There, amid the towering peaks of the Himalayas, lay Shangri-La, the place where time stood still. Conway could think only of his crashed plane, of the home he might never see again. He little realized that he was soon to enter a world of love, peace, and eternal life such as no Westerner had known before.

—James Hilton
Lost Horizon[1]

SHANGRI-LA—its very name seems to bring such things as mystery, glamour, wonderment, and inspiration into the mind of the average man in the world today. Ever since James Hilton first wrote of this enchanted valley hidden away deep within the heights of the Himalayas,[2] man has speculated, wondered, and reflected within the fantasies of his daydreams on the possibility, the very remote possibility, that such a place as this might actually exist—perhaps somewhere, at sometime?

Do we really and truly know this earth that we are living on? Can we honestly say that now in the last quarter of the 20th century, this fantastic century that has brought forth so much in scientific achievement, a century that has even enabled man to walk on the moon and return safely to earth, that we now have explored every nook and cranny of the earth's surface? Can we state forcibly and with conviction that there definitely are no "lost civilizations" either within or on the surface of the earth? Modern science would have us to believe that this is so. Other than the possibility of a few more primitive Indian tribes, such as the ones recently discovered in the jungles of Brazil or the Philippines, it would have us believe that we are now aware of, or at least conscious of, all of the peoples of the earth. However, to the contrary, and even though the statement may appear quite fantastic on the surface, the Agashan teachers unequivocally state that our discoveries in this direction have only just begun.

Before we shed more light on this most interesting subject, let us first center our attention on the actual structure of the earth itself. If we were to lay bare its interior by a slice from pole to pole, its cross section would reveal a structure much like that of some titanic fruit. The deep core of the earth would be a gigantic ball of molten iron, some 4,000 miles in diameter, or about the size of the planet Mars. The stupendous pressures created within this core then crush the iron molecules into a strange dense liquid, yet unlike any liquid known to exist on the surface. Its temperature would be about 8,000 degrees, or about that of the surface of the sun. Thus we can say that the inner core of our planet is a veritable "sun" in a constant state of agitation, churning over and over, and containing within itself forces of gigantic magnitude. Surrounding and containing this molten core, and reaching almost to the surface, is the earth's great inner shell, some 2,000 miles thick, and called "the mantle." Its temperature is roughly at the melting point of rocks (2,200 degrees), and it is from the mantle that the lavas of volcanoes are formed, working upward through cracks in the solid layers above.

It would seem that the Greek philosopher Heraclitus might be right when he said, "This world was ever, is now, and ever shall be an ever-living Fire." Yet this is not exactly true as science has since determined, and the Agashan teachers agree, that the earth did not always exist. It was born a few billion years ago when the thin crust of man's world, a thin layer comparable to the skin of an apple to the fruit, finally cooled to the point where it solidified.

It is this outer crust of some 30 miles in thickness which will concern us now and become the subject of this chapter. Its basement layer appears to be a shell of basaltic rock, 10 to 20 miles thick, and this shell lines the ocean basins and supports the great land masses of granite continents which seem to "float" upon its surface. Then, as the earth's interior continued to cool, it contracted and shrank away from its outer crust in much the same manner as a dried apple shrinks within its skin. Thus the earth's crust wrinkled and the wrinkles became mountains. In fact, all of the high mountains of the modern world were created just within the last 60 million years or so, and it was only one million years ago when the youngest of all, the Cascade Mountains which line America's west coast, arose out of the sea amidst a great outburst of volcanic activity. Thus mountains as well as entire continents either arise or submerge as the great forces contained within the earth itself are unleashed in gigantic cataclysmic eruptions. This is the conclusion of Science after several hundred years of exhaustive scientific research.[3]

What is not so generally known, however, is that thousands and thousands of great caverns that stretch for miles and miles at great depth were also created and brought into manifestation through these same earthquakes and great upheavals of the physical plane. The teachers of the Agashan class state that it sometimes takes only a period of just a fraction of time for the great earth itself to open up and then reclose once again. Thus in that fraction of time, great caverns were created in the outer shell from the forces set forth from the great bowels of the earth. We are all well aware of the caverns and caves that we know to exist in the different parts of the United States as well as other portions of the world, and these have been explored to a small extent. But these are in a modified form and are just samples. Then multiply these caverns that we know of by a thousand times and it becomes very interesting. Now multiply this in turn many, many thousands of times again, and we have miles and miles of caverns not even dreamed of by the average individual. Thus the teachers say that we have to go back many hundreds of thousands and even millions of years to get to the beginning of these great caverns, and they still exist today, honeycombing the great outer crust of this spaceship that men call Earth.

Some of these caverns are enormous in size, being many miles long and many miles wide. Others are much smaller. In any event, it is here in some of these caverns that we will find life—all types of life, both animal and sub-human, gradually evolving to become greater than what it is today. Some of these creatures could not see a thing if they were to venture forth into the sunlight, but they can see quite well in the darkness of the caverns. Other forms of life venture forth only occasionally, but they have been observed here and there and have been given such names as Bigfoot, Yeti, and Sasquatch.

But this evolutionary form of life that exists in many of these caverns is not the subject of this chapter. Instead, let us direct our gaze to some of the caverns that be not in darkness, but are filled with light, power, and spiritual energy. These are the abode of great Arisen Adepts, Ascended Masters from many of the great civilizations of the past, who utilize these caverns today so that they may isolate themselves for the sole purpose of the benefit of humanity. It seems that these Masters are gradually, bit by bit, making themselves known to the outer world at large, and publishing a little more information relative to their work is the purpose for this chapter.

The Great Brotherhoods of the Ascended Masters

Some of these great Brotherhoods of the Ascended Masters relate way back to the dawn of time. Others are more recent. In any event, these great Arisen Adepts remain connected with the earth and still live in the flesh in various spiritual retreats scattered throughout the world. However, inasmuch as their physical bodies are ascended and not strictly mortal as yours or mine, they must out of necessity remain in isolation, protected from the earthly vibrations. Some of these Brotherhoods have many members; some even number into the thousands. Other Brotherhoods contain only a few, the number of Adepts in any one Center of Light being limited only by the desire of that particular group of Adepts.

The teachers manifesting in the Agashan classes call these great earthly vortexes of light "Spiritual Centers." It is said that the world would be in a far worse state than it is in today, far worse than even the present chaotic state, were it not for the great efforts put forth by these powerful Arisen Beings. Indeed, human expression would have long ago ceased to exist, having annihilated itself through the negativity constantly being created by the power of the mortal mind. Therefore, these Adepts in the great Spiritual Centers are most important unto the life of mankind, having worked diligently and constantly for the advancement of not only the present and previous generations, but also for the generations to come.

Yet it must be pointed out that these advanced Adepts had existed at one time on the earth plane in an outer mortal body, the same as you or I. They have simply arisen in the flesh, but they remain connected to the earth plane even after having ascended into the higher Consciousness of Immensity. They have been able to adapt themselves to the atmosphere of the great caverns, some of which extend quite a way into the depths of the earth, solely through the powers of alchemy. Each individual Adept is most proficient and learned in this ancient art, and therefore he is able to live seemingly in two worlds at the same time—the spiritual as well as the physical. We might say then that they are in the consciousness of the physical world but not of it.

The author realizes that the subject matter of this particular chapter is going to tax the credulity of the average reader to the utmost. Perhaps it is because we do not have a proper concept of time. Perhaps it is because the mortal mind is simply just too materialistic—somehow being unable to comprehend the true spiritual inner nature of things. We must remember that the world that we see with our eyes, and sense with our physical senses, is only a fragment of the spiritual world that interpenetrates and coexists with the physical world. Therefore if we can allow ourselves the luxury, if only for a moment, of expanding our consciousness and trying to *believe* what is given in this chapter, we will have advanced a great deal towards breaking down the barriers that have been set up by the mortal mind. Agasha has always stated that he tries to deal with our intelligence and not our intellect. The use of our basic intelligence in thinking a problem through to its conclusion will usually lead to truth; it is the use of our intellect that sometimes leads to illusion.

For instance, let us try to believe for the moment that through proper diet and mental attitude the human body is capable of remaining healthy and youthful for, let us say, a hundred years. Our simple intelligence will tell us that perhaps, just maybe, this might be so. Our intellect will tell us that this would be impossible, that the body has to go through the aging process. But who is to say that the intellect is correct? Perhaps there are laws not yet discovered by modern man, but known by the ancient Adepts, that would enable the physical body to remain in a state of perfection for not only a hundred years or more, but perhaps even indefinitely!

It is a common belief among the scholars of today that some of the Alchemists or Hermetic Philosophers of the past millennium did indeed do just that—discover the secret Elixir of Life that enabled them to remain ageless for an extended period of time. Basic intelligence will tell us that once the aging process has been conquered, then the element of time does not enter into the equation. Once the aging process is brought to the zero point, to the absolute zero point, then it would be actually *impossible* for the body *ever* to get old as long as it remained in the proper environment and safe from destruction. A hundred years, a thousand years, and even hundreds of thousands of years—all would be as one.

Therefore, when we are told in the Agashan classes that some of the ancients—a few Ascended Masters from many of the great civilizations of the past, even as far back as Lemuria some 300,000 years ago—knew of these laws of alchemy and sought out places of isolation in order that they could remain in the physical body, we have to admit that it just could be possible and not just pass it off as a fantasy of imagination, as the intellect is so often prone to do. After all, when we realize that once we break away from the cycle of reincarnation we then live for *millions* of years in our spiritual body in the Consciousness of Immensity, why then is it so impossible for an Arisen Adept to do the same thing in a quasi-physical or supra-physical body on the planet Earth? That is, of course, if he were able to protect it from destruction, purify it from contamination, and free his consciousness so that he could travel in a duplicate etheric body to any location of his choosing.

Therefore, in this chapter we will learn of the great Masters of the Far East—Adepts who not only lived before the time of Christ, but who are still living today! It was the Spiritual Retreats of these very same Adepts that the great Master Teacher Jesus, as well as the others before him, visited in their etheric bodies during their life span on earth—that is, they would project their consciousness to these Centers while out of the body during the so-called sleep or trance state. We will also learn of still other great Masters, great Adepts who have lived on the earth for many thousands and thousands of years, and some not even known to any of the occult schools of the outer world today.

Agasha tells us that it is not that these schools are not privileged to make contact with these great Teachers of Light, but that these particular Spiritual Centers have simply not been brought to their attention. Many of the great Centers that we will hear about for the first time in this chapter are now just beginning to make their presence known unto the outer world. These great Masters have worked in absolute secrecy down through the ages assisting in the course of human affairs—the secrecy being necessary for their protection—for had their Centers been violated and destroyed, our present civilization in all probability would have long since vanished from the face of the earth. It is only now that man is entering the new Golden Age of Peace and Understanding, an age known to some as the age of the Holy Spirit, that they can begin to make their presence known.

Not all of these Adepts are from the ancient civilizations of antiquity. Some have been born as mortal in our own time, even as you or I, and after reaching a certain pinnacle of unfoldment had attained their great mastership while living in the flesh in our present era. Then, having finished their work on earth and through a personal desire, they had sought out a particular cave, cavern, retreat, or other place of isolation and thus secluded themselves in their selected retreat. In this manner they were able to attain the higher consciousness because in isolation they were not contaminated by earthly affairs. If they had remained living in the outer world of negativity for any extended period of time, the contamination alone would have eventually forced them out of the physical body.

Therefore it is doubly difficult for the average individual in the Western world today to attain the same consciousness as the Adept, simply because of the fact that he has to put up with so much more negativity than the man in isolation. But these Adepts sometimes venture forth into the outside world, and the worthy one can meet them occasionally in India, China, Tibet, or various other parts of the world. Incidentally, they are not limited by the political situation because they are very knowledgeable of the laws of alchemy; these laws then enable them to intermingle freely with the populace, blend with the crowd, and go unnoticed if they so desire.

But the Agashan teachers stress that many students of the occult in the Western world today, those that are on the spiritual path and who are dedicating their lives toward some spiritual goal, are indeed accomplishing and achieving results in the same manner as the Adept of the East. In other words, these seekers of truth in the Western world are actually on a par with the Adept insofar as they have the same privileges extended unto them that are extended unto the Adept. They are given a challenge and an opportunity to attain, even though the opportunity is sometimes offered under the most trying conditions. Many of these students on the path are not outwardly conscious of this insofar as their spiritual instruction is usually given on the inner planes while out of the body in the so-called sleep state. And the memory of these experiences does not usually filter back into the outer mind.

Therefore, it can be said that many students in the outer world assist unknowingly the real directors of the planet, the Ascended Masters within the Spiritual Centers of the earth. These Adepts direct life on the earth in the same manner that the Pillars of Light direct life in the Universe. As above: so below. Mankind is not just automatically unfolding. Mankind's unfoldment comes about only through hard, conscious effort by these great Adepts and their assistants in the outer world.

Speaking broadly then, we can define a Spiritual Center as being any cave, cavern, or other place of isolation where an arisen Adept, group of Adepts, or sometimes even an entire community of Adepts have established a spiritual retreat. There is no other particular secret or mystery pertaining to these Centers of Light.

For an example, let us say that a particular group of five or six higher Initiates had earned the right to ascend in the flesh and still retain their earthly bodies indefinitely. But this would be impossible unless they were in utter isolation whereby their physical bodies could remain pure and uncontaminated by the earthly vibrations of the outer world. Therefore with this goal in mind, they would then use their higher occult powers to seek out and find some remote spot, a modern-day Shangri-La, and isolate themselves so that they could start another Center. We have all heard of great Adepts of the East retiring to some cave and remaining there for an indefinite period of time. They may stay there for only a few years and then return again to the outer world. But if they are to become "Ascended Adepts," they will raise the frequency of the atoms that make up their physical body, and thereby sustain it entirely through the powers of alchemy. Then while it remains there safe within the cave, it is completely free from the aging process. And the Adept's consciousness is free to travel anywhere in the universe.

The writer heard a lecture a short time ago where the speaker (a noted religious leader and a disciple of one of the Masters of the Far East) told of his experience when he was invited to visit the cave where a particular Master had secluded himself for many years. After days of travel on foot through the jungles of India, their small group finally arrived at the cave of the Master. The speaker was at first a little apprehensive about coming into the presence of one who had been in isolation for so long, but the apprehension vanished as soon as they entered the cave. An immense feeling of great love and compassion seemed to envelop the entire chamber, but all that could be seen was only a brilliant white light. Then, gradually, the light dimmed and the physical body of the Adept, or the Mahatma as he so chose to call him, came into view and materialized. But the amazing thing about all of this, the speaker went on to say, was that this great Adept, instead of appearing very aged and wasted from his long period of isolation, actually appeared as youthful, and as presentable, and as well-groomed as anyone ever could be. His eyes sparkled as he spoke, and there was absolutely no sign of any debility of the body whatsoever. He did, however, respectfully decline to partake of some cake that his followers had brought with them. This, incidentally, seems to bear out the point that gross feeding is unnecessary for the Ascended Adept.

This episode, if one will think about it, should tend to alleviate some of the confusion that exists relative to the state or condition of the physical body of the Ascended Master who elects to remain in the flesh. To the observer, the body of the Adept at first only appeared as a "light." But then, as he reduced his vibration or frequency, the atoms of his body returned again to the physical level and he became visible. Yet to the Adept, his body of "light" was evidently just as solid and real to his higher consciousness as our physical body is to our mortal consciousness.

But it is still only natural to think that inasmuch as these are "ascended" Masters, their bodies should also be ascended. In one sense this is true; in another sense it is not. Agasha states that the body of the Adept in a Spiritual Center, although giving evidence of being physical, is almost the equivalent of the sublimated bodies that exist in the Seventh Degree or the various other planes of the Consciousness of Immensity. Therefore he affirms that there is no gross feeding necessary to the inhabitants of these Spiritual Centers. They automatically breathe into their bodies the substances that are needed to sustain themselves; this is done entirely through spiritual chemistry and through the great laws of alchemy.

Let us hear from the great Adept Earshin as he describes his own body. The Earshin Valley, incidentally, is one of the leading Spiritual Centers in America today, and we will be hearing more about it a little later on in the chapter. Earshin is speaking:

"You see, we here in the Earshin Valley are in the flesh. You disciples living in the outer world are also in the flesh. Therefore, you are in the flesh and I am in the flesh; however my flesh is far more sensitive than your flesh. My rate of vibration is higher. My body is composed of flesh and bone just the same as yours, only I am on a different frequency with my flesh and bone than the frequency that you are on out there in the outside world. You understand that, don't you? I still have my flesh, bone, blood, et cetera—in fact, I have everything the same as you—but remember, my body is attuned to the higher rate of vibration of the Consciousness of Immensity. Therefore, we here in the Earshin Valley are actually living in two worlds at the same time. We are living in spirit and we are in the higher spiritual consciousness; yet at the same time we have the outer body, the dense body. We do live in the flesh, but we do not have a dense body in the sense of the word. We have a physical body, but we are more ethereal than you would understand us to be. Yet the only difference between my body and your body is that my body is finer than yours; it is of a different texture as well as being in a different rate of vibration."

The teachings brought out in the study of *Theosophy*[4] dovetail completely with this explanation as given by Earshin. For instance, Theosophy asserts that the nature of physical matter exists in seven different planes or states. These states vary from an extremely dense or solid state at one end of the scale to an extremely ethereal or etheric state at the opposite end. Each state of matter can thus pass through the higher states as easily as a fish can swim in the water or a satellite can travel through space. But it can also be said that matter in the higher rates of vibration, matter in the etheric state, can likewise pass through the dense or slower frequencies of matter in much the same fashion as the wind blows through a screen of wire mesh, or a spirit passes through the "solid" walls of a house, or a gnome passes through a rock. The three denser states of the physical plane are of course the solid, the liquid, and the gaseous states. But Theosophy says that there are also four finer or etheric states of physical matter, each one being in a successively higher rate of vibration.

Theosophy also teaches that besides the different *states* of matter, there are also seven different *planes* of matter, varying from the dense physical plane to the extremely etheric Divine plane of manifestation. But this is also the Agashan philosophy, only with slightly different terminologies. Therefore, following the ancient dictum: "As above: so below," we find then that each of these seven planes contains matter divided into seven distinct substates. Each plane of life has its own individual spectrum of density—seven states of matter from the dense to the ethereal. The total of all this then is 49 different states of matter, of which man with his physical senses is aware of but three.

The physical body of the Ascended Adept could then very easily be functioning in the three higher etheric states of physical plane matter in much the same way our own physical bodies function in the three lower, denser states—the solid, the liquid, and the gaseous. The middle state, which is sometimes called the Fire or Chemical Ether, would then separate the two potential bodies of Man on the physical plane of life. The subtle body would then be made up of the three higher etheric states which are called in Theosophical terms the Life Ether, the Light Ether, and the Reflecting Ether in the order of increasing frequencies. This would be the body of the Arisen Adept. Of course, his physical body would then be invisible to normal physical eyesight unless he so chose to reduce his rate of vibration, in which case his body would then come into visibility and appear as any other body on the physical plane.

And of course we could go up and down the scale with the same analogy—two potential bodies for *each* of the seven planes of spirit expression, from the physical to the Divine.

This makes fourteen in all, one for each of the doors in the Temple of the Initiate, of which more will be said in Chapter Ten. We might also further classify the denser body as being the *outer* body as opposed to the etheric body being related to the *inner* body. This, of course, then brings us right back to the basic tenets of the Agashan philosophy—the atom or outer state versus its counterpart, the anim or inner state. And yet each body contains the equivalent of the solid, the liquid, and the gaseous states of matter.

Another bit of confusion that clouds the mind of the average student of the occult, in reference to these Ascended Masters in the flesh, is whether they have the ability to travel and move about freely in the outer world. For an answer to this perplexing question, let us return once again to the Ascended Master Earshin who answers it in the following manner:

"Here in the Earshin Valley, if we are desirous to traverse out of the cavern and go elsewhere, we have to leave our physical body and project ourself in the same manner that I am projecting my spirit to control this channel and speak unto you tonight. If we desired to take the physical body, we would have to arise to the surface and come down into the different parts of the country in our physical body and be like ordinary people. But we have no necessity for that sort of thing, and so our physical body remains in our own kingdom. We do all of our activity, carry out our entire program, and perform all of our functions on the inner planes by spiritual contact or projection to wherever we so desire.

"However, we also have the ability to, let us say, materialize the etheric body and produce a replica of the physical body at any location we so desire. Thus in appearing on the various scenes, my body would appear no different from anyone else. I can appear in any garment that I so desire, and I can appear in a way that could never be detected. I thus can change my rate of vibration so that it would not be noticeable by any one individual. You understand that, don't you? But that body that is so provided is also protected from harm by a certain vibratorial ray. If an emergency should arise, it would simply disappear from view.

"We are not interested in your phenomena work. Our manifestations go on all the time and they are not phenomenal to us. It is the natural law that we operate, and it is not through the laws of mediumship that we appear. It is the natural law that we use in order for us to produce the power to project ourselves and become visible at intervals and at various locations throughout the world. However, in the main we move about invisible to your physical eyesight. We can appear on the scene immediately in answer to your call, but we will be invisible. Yet we can and do lower our rates of vibration at times and become visible if we so desire. But we never make spectacles of ourselves; we never produce the body to satisfy anyone's curiosity. There is always a definite purpose in our manifestations.

"You have probably heard of cases where people are seen walking down the street, and then they suddenly disappear. Now we are working the same law, but the people that you see disappear are usually from the astral world. In certain cases the anims and the animatical forces can build up and then produce the ectoplasmic force which enables the astral entity to become momentarily visible. Moreover as I am in the flesh, I have to produce a replica of the flesh. I am not producing a replica of myself tonight as I speak to you for that would be phenomena, and we are not interested in proving phenomena. Therefore, as I said earlier, my body is put aside for the time being as I project myself through this channel in the same manner as anyone else would come in and speak from the astral or the higher planes. Bless you, this is Earshin, and good night."

Thus we find that the Ascended Masters from the Spiritual Centers do have the ability, if they wish, to materialize themselves and walk the streets as anyone else in the physical body. Now this statement may sound quite incredible at first, especially to those of us in the Western world who have become so steeped in materialism that we believe such things just cannot be. It even shocked Agasha 7,000 years ago when both Coman Coban and Donna materialized in his presence in the Temple of Mamon. This we learned in the previous chapter. But are these things really so strange? We must remember that those Adepts in the Spiritual Centers are not like you or me. They are obviously not bound by the laws of time and space in the same way that we are; and being isolated and away from material forces, they are then free to move about as needed. Moreover, they are constantly assisting mankind in their efforts to bring light and understanding to a world which at times can only be described as chaotic.

Do we have any other verification that they are able to do this? That is, do we have any recorded cases in history where they have obviously assisted? An astute researcher will find many incidents that seem to bear this out. One that comes to mind is an incident that occurred in our own Continental Congress just prior to the actual signing of the Declaration of Independence. Now this incident is not widely known, but the noted philosopher Manly Palmer Hall tells us about it in his work titled *The Secret Destiny of America.*[5] The source of his story is a rare old volume of early American political speeches of a date earlier than those preserved in the first volumes of the *Congressional Record.* The date was July 4, 1776, and I am quoting the words of Mr. Hall directly:

"Faced with the death penalty for high treason, courageous men debated long before they picked up the quill pen to sign the parchment that declared the independence of the colonies from the mother country. For many hours they had debated in the State House at Philadelphia, with the lower chamber doors locked and a guard posted—when suddenly a voice rang out from the balcony. A burst of eloquence to the keynote, 'God has given America to be free!' ended with the delegates rushing forward to sign. . . . The American patriots then turned to express their gratitude to the unknown speaker. The speaker was not in the balcony; he was not to be found anywhere. How he entered and left the locked and guarded room is not known. No one knows to this day who he was."

We might very well ask ourselves as to the real identity of this unknown speaker who suddenly appeared on the balcony and whose eloquent words tilted the scale in the direction of signing. Was he an Ascended Master from one of the Spiritual Centers? It could very well be so. It would certainly be typical of one of their actions. For how else can we explain the facts of his sudden "appearance" and then just as sudden "disappearance." Mr. Hall voices the same question a little later in the volume, and I quote:

"Who was this strange man, who seemed to speak with a divine authority, whose solemn words gave courage to the doubters and sealed the destiny of the new nation? Unfortunately, no one knows. His name is not recorded; none of those present knew him; or if they did, not one acknowledged the acquaintance. How he had entered into the locked and guarded room is not told, nor is there any record of the manner of his departure. No one claimed to have seen him before, and there is no mention of him after this single episode. Only his imperishable speech bears witness to his presence.

"There are many interesting implications in his words. He speaks of the 'rights of man,' although Thomas Paine's book by that name was not published until thirteen years later. He mentions the all-seeing eye of God which was afterwards to appear on the reverse of the Great Seal of the new nation. In all, there is much to indicate that the unknown speaker was one of the agents of the secret Order, guarding and directing the destiny of America." Thus we find that even Mr. Hall, himself, acknowledges some divine manifestation at work on this particular occasion.

Before we leave the subject of the Ascended Masters in general, let us cover one other somewhat controversial point. This relates to the possible materialization of the teachers from the various degrees of the Consciousness of Immensity.

Agasha, as we have learned from the classes, had long ago given up his physical body and now manifests in his spiritual body which is built up of anims (spiritual atoms) vibrating at the frequency of the higher Consciousness of Immensity. But by lowering his rate of vibration, he can also manifest on any other plane of consciousness that he so desires; yet, if he were to do this, he would need a "channel" to project through.

Let us say that Agasha is desirous of visiting one of the major Spiritual Centers of the earth plane. This he has done on many occasions. But to manifest there, the Masters in that particular Center must become a channel and produce a ray, a visibility force, which when directed on his spiritual body will immediately materialize it and bring it into visibility. Yet the teachers say that it is difficult to produce that same ray within the atmospheric vibrations of the outer world. In the pure atmosphere of the Spiritual Centers, it is easy; in the contaminated atmosphere of the outer world, it is difficult. If this were not so, they go on to say, then that same ray could be focused upon Agasha as he lectures during the classes, and those in attendance would then see Agasha sitting in the chair and not the physical body of the medium.

Thus it gradually becomes apparent to those who have attended the Agashan classes for any length of time—or other Mystery Schools of the earth plane for that matter—that many of the Ascended Masters of great antiquity, great Teachers who arose so long ago, not only still retain the physical body but are in reality working much closer with the modern disciples and other seekers of truth in the outer world than many had heretofore realized. They are constantly with us, helping wherever they can, assisting, aiding, and generally working for the benefit of humanity. Even though they cannot usually be seen, their presence can sometimes be felt; and were we but capable of raising the sensitivity frequency of the human eye, we would then be able to see them going about their business as naturally as anyone else on the physical plane.

How many of these Spiritual Centers exist on the earth plane today? This is a good question but its answer is not easily forthcoming. Perhaps it is because we have first to define whether we are speaking of a major Center composed of an entire community of Adepts, or simply a cave where an Adept or two have retired in isolation in order to send out light and peace unto the outer world. The writer's own particular teacher, Rhebaumaus Tate, replied on one occasion that he was aware of some twenty or thirty of these so-called centers. On the other hand, Coman Coban, that great Intermediary and teacher of Agasha, stated one evening that he had at one time or another visited all of the different Spiritual Centers and that he had not missed even one. He knew where they all were.

For instance, there is a certain place in Arizona where there is a small cavern that has been inhabited by a number of Masters for some time. It is not a large cavern, but it is several miles long, which is still comparatively small if we were to compare it with one of the other Centers such as the great cavern of the Grand Canyon Kingdom, which is described elsewhere in this chapter as being "extremely large, very wide, and very long." In this relatively small cavern then are Masters of Light who arose from one of the earth's more recent civilizations. Now these particular Masters have not otherwise been brought to the attention of the members of the Agashan class. They are only one of the many. So it would seem that the higher one arises in consciousness, the more aware one eventually becomes of all life.

This then leads us up to three particular major Centers, three in particular which down through the years have become closely associated with the Agashan class. They represent three definite periods in the evolution of life on earth, ranging from a period just before the time of Christ, to the late Atlantean period, and then on back to a civilization so ancient that we can only refer to it as pre-Atlantean, or perhaps early Atlantean. These three, representing three great epochs in time, have become more or less a trinity to the Agashan class. They are known as the Valley of Cocoda, the Amazon Kingdom, and the Earshin Valley.

The Masters from these respective Centers, or kingdoms as the Agashan teachers so often refer to them, have become conscious of this present-day class, its movement, its activity, and what it has to accomplish here in the 20th century. They thus have joined their forces with Agasha and form what may be represented as a symbolic triangle around a central point. Representatives from these particular Spiritual Centers have manifested many times in the classes and have used this class, as well as one other in Bombay, India, as a sort of focal point in distributing power unto the outside world. We will now cover them individually and in further detail.

The Valley of Cocoda

To get to the origin of the most recent of the major Spiritual Centers to be established on the earth, we have to go back some 2,200 years in the land of Tibet. It was here where a great spiritual teacher of the day by the name of Cocoda had so raised his consciousness that he was able to learn the higher laws of alchemy. He was then able to demonstrate these laws as he walked among his people, and later he taught the method unto his disciples. Thus there in Tibet they were able to precipitate from the ether and bring many things into manifestation. It is the same law that they used then that is used today, and it is operated throughout the Universe by all of the Ascended Masters, no matter where they be.

Therefore, by lowering the rates of vibration of certain things that they wanted to bring into manifestation from the etheric planes, they could then bring them into the dense form of physical matter, and these objects would take on a dense body and become a reality on the physical plane. Agasha says that when this was first demonstrated by Cocoda himself, it was quite a wonderful and spectacular demonstration to the onlookers. One of his disciples was so impressed with the hidden potential contained within all of this that he arose and spoke saying, "This is the way that we shall erect our temples; this is the way that we shall partake of food; and in fact, this is the way that we will now bring everything into manifestation!" And so it came to pass that through these simple words, words uttered with great emphasis from an inspired individual, an idea was born that was to change the destiny of these enlightened people.

Their very life was changed because shortly afterwards this great Adept Cocoda saw a vision of a very beautiful valley—a valley of great inner peace and serenity. He knew right then and there that this particular valley was the perfect retreat. He could see that it was a place where they could establish their kingdom, ascend in the flesh, and by going through this procedure be able to live in the physical body for an indefinite period of time. But he also knew that because of its isolation from the coarse vibrations of the outside world, it would be very difficult to find.

He asked some of his friends to travel with him on foot to search for this valley, but they turned him down. "The going would be too dangerous in that mountainous terrain," they explained. Cocoda was well aware of this fact, and even he himself doubted at times that he could really find it.

But the very clear vision of this beautiful valley persisted in his mind, and eventually he and two of his disciples set out to find it. And find it they did. They were obviously guided by the Divine Hand because it would have been almost impossible to find otherwise. Its location turned out to be in a very mountainous terrain deep within the land of Tibet, and it was the ideal location because it was quite hidden from the sight of men. Soon others were brought into the Valley, and the true "Shangri-La" of James Hilton's most prophetic novel was thus created. For this great Spiritual Center is not located *in* the earth, in the way that most of the other Spiritual Centers are established, but it is located on the surface of the earth.

It is in a location that cannot be detected by any mortal being. Likewise, it is humanly impossible to enter unless one would know the direct route, and even then he would have to know how to hurdle the obstacles in order to gain the entrance. There is only one small entrance, and this is as much a symbolical fact as it is a physical fact. The teachers say that the entrance is hidden by a very large stone which first must be removed before a very small passageway is revealed. Then, if one were to traverse this passage, he would enter into their kingdom and find this truly magnificent valley.

Once within, you would stand enthralled as you gazed up at the sides of the mountain and became aware of the numerous temples and dwellings of truly superb architecture that adorn its slopes. From these temples thoughts of love and peace are constantly being sent forth unto the suffering humanity of the outside world. Then, lowering your gaze to the very center of the valley floor, you would see a fountain of exquisite beauty as its waters shoot forth and then descend in a cascade of loveliness. The picture would be very suggestive of the mythical "Fountain of Youth" that has now become a living symbol in this beautiful consciousness.

We must remember that when we refer to the material things in the outside world, it is always necessary to create them laboriously. We must first mine our ores, and then we have to go through the various other stages in order to produce materials, erect buildings, and the like. This is necessary because we are in the outer world and we are working in the field of the atom. On the other hand, the Masters within the Spiritual Centers are working with material that is the very essence of that which is used in the outside world. Their materials and structures are brought basically into manifestation through the anim. This is the counterpart of the atom. The anim force then enables them to create and erect any structure they so desire entirely through the elements that they are able to attract unto themselves through the great power of the mind. This is accomplished, as we said earlier, entirely through the knowledge of the laws of alchemy or spiritual chemistry.

Why is it that this great Spiritual Center has not been detected from aircraft or satellites that constantly monitor the surface of the earth in our modern 20th century? This is a good question, but its answer to the clear-thinking individual is not quite as mystifying as it might appear to be on the surface. Like all of the other Spiritual Centers scattered throughout the earth, the Valley of Cocoda is a spiritual consciousness as well as a physical consciousness. Perhaps a more correct word to use for these Centers of Light would be the all-inclusive term "Spiritual-Physical Centers" because that is indeed what they are. They can exist in two worlds at the same time, or more correctly, alternately in one and then in the other. Thus the cloak of invisibility can and does very easily protect this beautiful consciousness from the sight of mortal man. We might say that it be likened to a mystical cloud cover that constantly hovers over and shields these beautiful structures from the eyes of the profane.

An even better analogy is to compare the Valley of Cocoda with a huge stadium or open-air amphitheater. Let us say that we are flying over this stadium when a huge sports event is taking place and everything is bustling with activity. However, if it were nighttime the only way that we could be aware of all that was going on in the stadium below would be through the power of the great arc lights as they brilliantly illuminated the field. If the lights were off, all would be in darkness and we would fly over the stadium completely oblivious of the activity that was going on within it. Yet the people, the bleachers, the scoreboard—in fact everything would still be there. But because the arc lights were not on, all of these things would momentarily become invisible to us.

In our modern day of electronics, why is the cloak of invisibility in Cocoda so impossible to understand? After all, the electromagnetic waves that are being broadcast from the studio are constantly around and about our television receiving set, and we think nothing about it. Turn the set on, and the program that we are tuned into becomes visible; turn the set off, and the program vanishes from our sight leaving our picture tube of life in darkness. Yet it makes no difference to the waves themselves whether we have our set on or off. They are still there. It is the same old story in all phases of life. Change the anim to atom, and we have materialization; de-energize the atom, and it reverts back to the anim.

Is the Valley of Cocoda always to remain invisible to the sight of mortal man? The teachers state that the answer to this question is a very emphatic *no.* A slight lowering of the rate of vibration can release this mystical "cloud cover," and in one glorious moment the majesty of this beautiful dwelling place of the Ascended Masters, the true Shangri-La, will come into the sight of overflying aircraft. Then, at a time to be determined by these Masters, helicopters can descend onto the floor of the valley and the way will be opened for the explorer to enter that land and be welcomed by its goodly number of inhabitants. They will then be able to photograph the magnificent structures and bring them to the eyes of the outer world via television and other media. Just think of it! What a wonderful day that will be! Yes, the teachers promise all of this, and they further state that the Valley of Cocoda will be just the first of the major Spiritual Centers that will eventually be brought unto the consciousness of the average lay mind.

Thus we find that the visibility or lack of visibility of all of the Spiritual Centers can be controlled as easily as one might adjust a rheostat or flip on a switch on the physical level. Will the powers of alchemy ever be understood and practiced by those on the outside world? The answer to this question is surprisingly in the affirmative. Let us hear what the Adept Cocoda himself has to say about this most interesting subject as well as a few thoughts about the fountain.

"Blessed children, this is Cocoda and greetings. Many of you have wondered about our fountain that we use as a focal point to meet when you come here to go on the excursions.

A goodly number of those here tonight have gone on these excursions, and a number of you have brought back memory, primarily of the fountain. 'Is this the fountain of life?' you might ask. Well this may or may not be true, but it certainly is not strange that people can prolong their life when they are isolated.

"The prolongation of life in the physical body can only be accomplished through the power of alchemy; that is the only way that it can be done. Therefore, the powers of alchemy have always been sought after in the lives of mankind, and in a measure the field of material science is just beginning to work with its outer laws. Or perhaps we should say that they are on the outer edges of the laws of alchemy today. This is going to be most interesting in the future as eventually they too will be able to precipitate and bring many things into manifestation. Yes indeed, your field of material science is in for a glorious future."

These are the words of Cocoda, an Adept whom Agasha once paid the highest compliment by stating that inasmuch as the consciousness of this great Spiritual Center is on the surface of the earth, and as it does not have the protection of the caverns that most of the other Centers have, the mediumistic powers that the Cocodians developed are probably one of the greatest or highest forms of this type of power ever known unto mankind. But let us now leave our modern day Shangri-La for the moment, and let us travel clear across the world and go far deep into the jungles of South America for a visit to the second major Spiritual Center that we will be discussing in our group of three.

The Amazon Kingdom

From its source high in the Andes Mountains of Peru and Ecuador, the mighty Amazon River weaves its path for some 4,000 miles across the South American Continent until it finally empties itself into the North Atlantic Ocean. Much of its length is through dense tropical vegetation and Brazilian jungle. Many of its tributaries flow through areas which until recent years were largely unexplored, and some remain unknown and uncharted even today.

As we enter into one of these areas deep within the heart of the jungle, we observe many beautifully plumaged tropical birds that seem to congregate around a certain particular location. Nearby, we notice that one of the many streams that feed this mighty river apparently disappears into its source—seemingly vanishes into the nothingness. What we do not see, however, is an underground passage that rises to the surface very near this exact spot. Its entrance is very well concealed. But if we were to find it and explore it, we would find that it would lead us down several miles into the earth until eventually we would come to its termination. Would this be a dead end? No indeed. We would step out into a gigantic cavern where we could literally see for miles into the distance. It is here that there exists a great and powerful Spiritual Center which is known to the Agashan class as the Amazon Kingdom. In reality it has another name, but that has not been revealed. Yet it is a consciousness that is just as real as any other consciousness on the outside world.

We find great beauty there; indeed we do. We gaze in awe as we take in the grandeur of what apparently is a great and mighty valley. It is even illuminated in a most wonderful way, and it contains an atmosphere of the purest air. The architecture of the buildings is unlike anything that we have seen in the outside world; in fact, some of the structures seem to resemble gigantic pieces of strange machinery. These, we are told, are powerful ray machines which are capable of probing every possible point on the earth's surface.

The Teachers that we talk to are very young in their appearance and in many ways resemble the Teachers of the Earshin Valley. They are medium in height and are not tall. Their garments are comparable to the very finest materials of the outside world, and they are extremely beautiful. Incidentally, they are all dressed in white. There is also an illumination around each of these Masters that extends outwards into a circular diameter of approximately six feet, and we can feel a great radiation coming from their presence. We are told that this radiation is very powerful in that it enables them to reach *any* individual upon the earth plane. In other words, these Teachers of Light can trace out and find any individual on earth that they are desirous of reaching; it makes no difference where they are, for they can still find them. In one sense, we might say that they assist the Pillars of Light because those great Ascended Beings are so far removed from this planet that they are no longer in contact with any individual consciousness.

To get to the origin of this great Spiritual Center, we have to go back well over 100,000 years to just before the last submergence of the ancient continent of Atlantis. Many of the Masters within that great civilization were well aware of the impending great cataclysmic force that was destined to submerge that vast continent. They knew what was going to happen. Consequently a few of these great Adepts, those who were desirous of remaining in the physical body in order to teach the oncoming generations, sought out and found suitable retreats which would be safe from the onslaught of the earth's forces for thousands of years to come. This great cavern within the South American Continent was one of those so chosen.

Therefore a few years before the great submergence, 27 of these Adepts, just 27 of these Masters, entered this great cavern and established their kingdom. The cavern, of course, was created by nature but through their higher understanding of the atomic force and the great powers of alchemy, they were then able to have full power and control over every element of the etheric forces within the cavern. They were able to precipitate precisely in the same manner as the Cocodians were to do many thousands of years later. Even though these Teachers were comparatively few in number, just 27 in all, they were nevertheless very powerful. And there they exist today, as youthful and as handsome as anyone could possibly be. Of course today there are others, as down through the thousands of years since its inception, many other Master Teachers who had ascended from later civilizations sought out and became members of this great Spiritual Center. But at the head of this spiritual organization are the original 27 great Teachers who had ascended from the continent of Atlantis. There they remain, sending forth their great power and assisting the outer world in every way that they possibly can.

It seems only fitting to conclude this short summary on the Amazon Kingdom with an actual transcript of the words of one of these 27 Atlantean Teachers as he manifested in an Agashan class during the month of May, 1950. The voice is elegant and charming: "Good evening my blessed children. As one of the 27 Teachers, I am grateful to have the opportunity to control the channel and speak unto you. We are conscious of the great powers of the outside world; we are also conscious of the power that we possess here in our land. Our land, of course, is our consciousness here in the Amazon Kingdom, which is the name that we have so chosen to use for your benefit. All of our kingdom was brought into being by means of cataclysms and the fact that Nature was desirous of erupting, for it was through Nature that these great caverns in which we are now living, dwelling, and having our being were created. And this has been going on for tens of thousands of years.

"It is very difficult for the average person to understand why we have retained the flesh. 'Why should a Teacher of Light retain the flesh?' you might ask. The answer to this question is that our kingdom was established for an express purpose and never for a selfish motive. There could be no selfish motive in our kingdom. We have always claimed, and we claim it again tonight, that we are more powerful in our present state of consciousness in the flesh, than the Teachers who are in their spiritual bodies in the Consciousness of Immensity. This is so because there are certain laws that govern them in that state of consciousness which we do not have to apply or obey. Yet we do not make our own laws, in the sense of the word, in reference to nature. That would be an impossibility."

"But an absolutely important subject to bear in mind is that we can demonstrate, and manifest, and produce, and precipitate, and eradicate many things on the earth plane that otherwise would lead to the destruction of mankind. Thus man would not be privileged to learn his lessons and remain in the flesh. He would have to seek other physical planets to have his embodiments because it is absolutely necessary that he pass through all of these various stages of life before he can receive his ascension. We have simply ascended in the flesh, and by remaining in the flesh we are very powerful. When I use the word *powerful,* I mean it not from an egotistical standpoint, but rather that we are powerful for the benefit of humanity.

"Now here in the Amazon Kingdom is a very spacious cavern. As a matter of fact, it is many miles long and a few miles into the earth. It is not exactly similar to the Earshin Valley as no two are exactly alike; however there is a similarity. Therefore, here in the Amazon Kingdom we Teachers have set up in motion everything atomically and electronically and we understand every law that governs it. You would say that we have mechanical devices, yet these machines do not operate in the way that mechanical devices operate on the outside world. These machines, these ray machines, are doing their work, changing the picture, and have done more in eliminating the evils of the earth plane than anything that we could refer to at the moment.

"We who are in the flesh here in the Amazon Kingdom will remain so until the time has come when there will be no need for us to express ourselves in our physical bodies and we can then ascend. Yet our physical bodies have become almost as sensitive as the spiritual body, because after thousands of years of being so infinitely attuned the bodies begin to merge whereby they are almost the same. Yet to us our bodies are flesh and bone, and blood circulates through our veins the same as yours on the outside world. We know that when we do ascend, the changeover will be so slight that we will hardly recognize it at all. The physical will simply vanish from sight. The only difference would be that we would not be in the Amazon Kingdom working in that light, but we would be in the Consciousness of Immensity doing our work. However, as long as we possibly can, we are going to remain here for the benefit of humanity.

"We see the future and we know what is going to take place on earth. We have the records here, not only of the past, but of the future as well—the records of the nations, of the wars, of the uprises, of the plagues, and of the many things that will take place to cause a considerable number to perish from the face of the earth. But we also have the records of the new Golden Age of Peace to come. Therefore do not despair; it is always the darkest just before the dawn.

"I am in the great Consciousness of the Amazon Light tonight giving you my blessings and my power at all times. I have recognized any number of you in the class as you have come to our kingdom over a period of time, and I am grateful for that. The rays that we employ have made your astral bodies visible to us. In time I will inform you as to my consciousness, first in the Lemurian period and then in the Atlantean period. And I will also give you more about my life today in the Amazon Kingdom with the other souls who have retained the flesh for so long to bring light and peace unto mankind. Bless you and good night."

We are silent for a moment as we endeavor to absorb into our outer consciousness the real meaning behind this beautiful message. For these were the words of a great Atlantean Teacher, and not only that, they were the words of one who still walks this very earth—even as you and I. It all seems so incredible, and yet . . . .

The Earshin Valley

Leaving our reverie for the moment, let us gather our thoughts together once more and travel northward into the state of California. For it is here that we shall find the third major Spiritual Center that is working so closely with the Agashan class. About 600 miles north of the city of Los Angeles is beautiful Mount Shasta, one of the truly majestic mountains of the West. Its snow-covered peak glistens like a great jewel of whiteness set in a filigree setting of the most delicate greenery, for it is situated right in the heart of a deeply forested area and its commanding presence towers above all that is before it. Actually, its 14,161-foot height forms the cone of an extinct volcano which long ago had its roots on a different continent, the continent of Lemuria. We are told that all that remains of that continent which submerged so long ago are the great mountain peaks of the West Coast along with the islands which are scattered throughout the Pacific Ocean.

Yet as we gaze with our spiritual eyesight deep into the heart of this magnificent mountain, we come across a huge cavern, not as one in the usual sense, but one filled with tremendous Light, Life, and Love. For it is here that a great Brotherhood of Ascended Masters, those who are known to many people as the Masters of Mount Shasta, send forth their great Light. However, this great Spiritual Center has still another name. It is known to the members of the Agashan class by its spiritual name, the Earshin Valley.

It is called the Earshin Valley in honor of its founder, the great Adept Earshin, who arose and ascended many thousands of years prior to the submergence of the great Atlantean civilization. Perhaps we may say that his people stemmed from one of the numerous offshoots of the Lemurian civilization, who can say? The exact date of his ascendency has not been made clear to this writer, so let us use the round figure of 200,000 years as a supposition. In any event, it was a long, long time ago when this great Adept first arose to become the great teacher and leader that he is today. Like those that were to follow him, this great soul sought out a suitable retreat in order to isolate his group of followers from the world so that they would not have to deal with the outer forces. If they found a retreat, they knew that they would be able to attune themselves to the Infinite State and thus become ever so powerful as a collective unit. So then it was only a question of time until the right and proper retreat was selected. The huge cavern deep within the heart of Mount Shasta evidently met all their requirements because it was not too long until the great spiritual-physical consciousness of the Earshin Valley became very firmly established.

Thus these great Adepts live on today constantly sending forth light and power unto struggling humanity. They carry on this particular activity because many thousands of years ago they were assigned by the great "Powers that be" to guard over one of the seven great rays, or forces, that the earth receives from outer space. They first store this force within the mountain, and then each year they redirect it and send it out again to the proper places on the earth's surface so that mankind can use this power to develop himself. And they have been doing this, while always remaining quietly in the background, for literally thousands and thousands of years! They have helped in the growth of America, the new Atlantis; they have also guided the settlers to pioneer the West. It is said that they even caused them to discover gold so as to provide the proper incentive for this great conquest. Yes indeed, this great Earth Center is truly a vortex of power. It is called the "Valley" simply because it appears as a valley when it is first entered.

Perhaps we can best describe this magnificent consciousness by using Earshin's own words when he says, "It is a valley of Friends, a valley of Joy, a valley of Happiness, a valley of Understanding, a valley of Wisdom. It is all this and more because we who are here in the Earshin Valley can see every side of any man. There is no condemnation for we know just why each man functions. You cannot condemn a man for the acts that he commits if he has not his senses of perception, for that man has no reasoning faculty. And so it is with us. We do not condemn any man, be he enemy or friend, for there is good in every human being. We see the good in everything and we try to awaken the unlearned soul if it is at all possible.

"This is our love that we send out. This is our love that we send out all over the world—the Universal Love. Now what do I mean by Universal Love? Universal Love is a feeling that one has for all, be it human expression or be it all forms of life. I have love. I am in love with the universe, and this embraces all the people on the earth for I love everyone, indeed I do. And when I speak of I, I am in reference to the 'I' within for God *is* love. I reached that divine state long ago where one can truly enjoy the splendor of life. In this state one can always see everything in its true light and know just why it is happening. It is then that you have true Universal Love which is the greatest love of all.

"We have been sending out our power and helping humanity in *every* generation for oh such a long period of time. Even long before Atlantis had reached its highest attainment, we were. And we will continue to send out our light until the great Peace comes, until the day when Peace is firmly established upon the face of the earth. Then, at that time, we will go on our way and ascend into the spiritual consciousness knowing that our work will then be finished and that we had served in a way that the Universal Spirit God had desired us to serve." These words of Earshin have been selected from the tapes in order to present in some small way the great humility and love that flows forth from this great soul.

There is a great deal of gold in the Earshin Valley. The gold atmosphere is very noticeable, but it is there for its cleansing power and not for the reason that those in the outside world would so desire it. It is ever there for the disciples of the earth who are frequently visiting in their astral bodies during the sleep state. They then cleanse themselves by surrounding themselves in the golden light that is ever present. Thus gold is brought into manifestation there because it puts out a certain vibration that is used for purification.

The teachers claim, however, that it is not only gold that puts out this radiation; in fact, *all* of the metals are constantly sending out their own particular radiation. Each aids in its own special way; each is valuable to the Masters of Light who still remain in the flesh. It makes no difference whether it be platinum, uranium, radium, or silver; each is capable of producing its own independent vibration. Thus we find these great Adepts constantly drawing out of the ether, or extracting from the essence of the material still in the earth, those ingredients necessary to bring into manifestation or to create whatever it might be in order to fulfill a certain desire that they might have in their own consciousness.

The Earshin Valley, being quite similar in some respects to the Amazon Kingdom, is also quite mechanical. Most of the other Centers are not equipped with the mechanical instruments or machines that these two Centers possess. The power thus created enables the beautiful Mount Shasta to send forth a greater radiation than any other mountain in the United States. A great illumination can sometimes be seen around the mountain every year on and just around the 7th day of July (from a week before the 7th to two days after the 7th), for it is during this period that they have their great illumination. This illumination takes the form of an animation or life force that is sent forth from the great mountain itself.

Green and blue snow has been reported to be seen occasionally around the area. The Masters explain this phenomenon by stating that waste matter sometimes has to be ejected from the Valley. It is sort of a by-product, so to speak, of their activities. As this waste matter is then refined, it is changed into snow, but the process colors the snow in the way that it has been reported.

The inner lighting of the great cavern is by means of atomic power, but so is everything else in this most astonishing consciousness, for that matter. For instance: they are able to extend their ray out into the ether for many thousands of miles in order to capture materials that are not available in their immediate vicinity. But the mechanical machinery that is so employed to achieve these results is far more subtle and entirely different from the cumbersome machines that are used on the outside world. We must always remember that these great Adepts are actually spiritual chemists—alchemists of the very highest order. The atomic power that is brought forth in their kingdom is created through mind, through the anim, and not by means of the frictionized force of the atom which is the law on the outside world.

For some reason this becomes a confusing factor in the mind of the average disciple or student of the occult. "How can mechanical machinery," you might ask, "machinery that is operated by atomic energy, still be considered to be mechanical when it is functioning in a plane of consciousness normally invisible to physical eyesight? After all, a physical object is a physical object; it is either physical or it isn't," you conclude. But let us just think for a moment. Let us return to the thoughts that were expressed when we were discussing Cocoda. Is everything that is not seen or felt by our "physical" senses therefore to be considered to be not physical? Cannot there be other states of physical matter—physical matter that is in a slightly higher rate of vibration? The Teachers say that this is so. The Spiritual Centers are evidence of this fact. Eventually modern science will come to the correct understanding relative to the true laws of matter.

All of the temples, the structures, the buildings that exist in these Spiritual Centers are just as real as any building in the outside world. Yet they be invisible to normal physical eyesight. The Earshin Valley is no exception. For mortal man to be aware of the consciousness of the Earshin Valley, he would first have to raise his own consciousness to a higher frequency. In other words, he would have to raise the vibration of his physical senses whereby they could then perceive that which exists in the higher frequencies of matter. These higher frequencies exist in the inner state. Therefore, all things which exist in the Spiritual Centers are composed of the anim or inner state of physical matter. All things that exist on the outside world are composed or built up of the atom or the outer state of physical matter. Yet they are all part of the physical realm. Theirs is just the inner state, whereas ours is the outer state of the same plane of life—the physical or dense phase of spirit expression. Thus having arisen in consciousness, and having learned to control and conquer the flesh, these Adepts can then project themselves in their etheric body and move about in the outside world pretty much the same as we go out and get into our automobile and then drive along the highway.

What is the possibility of visiting the Earshin Valley in the physical body? This is a question that is voiced quite frequently by disciples in the Agashan class. For an answer to this most intriguing question, let me quote Agasha who stated one evening: "Many of you disciples have migrated here to this class on the Pacific Coast from different parts of the world, and here you find yourselves working out whatever you are supposed to work out as you learn your lessons and become a very grand occult student of life. Yet all the while you are very near to the Earshin Valley. Well now, you would think that Earshin would come and say, 'Come with me now. I am taking you right down there into the Valley because you belong to the class.' Now I would say that it would be a very wonderful thing if you could go there on an excursion, go into the Valley in your physical bodies. That would be a very interesting feature, indeed. But you see, it is not a matter of sightseeing; it is not a matter of trying to satisfy your mortal curiosity. Indeed not; it is always earned by the individual.

"On the other hand, you have traversed into that consciousness in your astral body innumerable times. This satisfies the soul even though it does not satisfy the mortal mind. Moreover, if all of this class were to attempt to go there and remain for seven years or more, we must remember that there would be certain responsibilities and duties that you were supposed to perform on the outside, and that would mean that you would be escaping these responsibilities. That is why we do not have the privilege nor the authority of taking you away from mundane affairs because that is your karma and neither I, nor any other teacher, can interfere.

"However, let us say as a supposition that Earshin did grant a few of you the privilege of entering the Valley. And let us say that those of you who had earned that right were then to travel in your automobiles up as far as you could go, and then hike up the slope to some preselected spot. There you would be met by Earshin as soon as he had projected himself and materialized in your presence. But the thing I want to point out is that you would not have to climb laboriously up the steep slopes of the mountain to the hidden entrance near the summit, and then after this no small achievement descend once again into the Valley. No indeed. Earshin would merely take the arm of the one who was to enter the Valley, and instantly they would vanish from the sight of the others gathered on the slope. If you were that one that be so privileged, the atoms of your physical body would then be vibrating at a higher frequency, the same frequency as that of the Earshin Valley, and you would immediately find yourself within the mountain taking in all the grandeur and the beauty of that consciousness, which would then be as solid to you as anything else in the outer, dense world. But to your fellows, you would have simply disappeared."

How many have visited the Valley and entered it in their physical bodies in recent years? Earshin has stated that they do bring those who had earned the right into the Valley occasionally, but not very often. For instance, there have been but very few to enter the Valley from the outside world since the year 1600. Why he makes a point of that date, I don't know. Yet we do know that there have been two individuals who have been brought into it even in our own generation, as this was so stated in the class of June 30, 1950.

When was the last time these Teachers of the Earshin Valley made themselves known? For an answer to this question, let me quote Earshin as he spoke on the evening of November 19, 1951: "We are always working to bring forth the light. I only wish that this message could have been given a number of years ago, specifically *twenty years ago,* when we had endeavored to bring the message unto the people. Unfortunately the outer method got beyond control, and today we are doing it on the inner planes. It is the inner planes of the Great White Way that now make it possible for us to fulfill our mission through the great powers of Agasha and his teacher Coman Coban." Thus we learn that during the years around 1930 and 1931 the Earshin Valley endeavored to make their presence known unto the outer world.

Perhaps it is coincidence, but what follows would certainly seem to verify that one of the two individuals who had been brought down into the Valley in our own generation was none other than Guy Ballard, the founder of the great "I AM" movement that gave out so much light and inspiration in the thirties and forties with their teachings of the great "I AM PRESENCE." For it was Guy Ballard, writing under the pen name of Godfre Ray King, who states in the foreword of his book *Unveiled Mysteries*[6] the following: "Those, who do accept the Truth herein recorded, will find a new and powerful 'Force' entering their lives. . . . To those who read this work, I wish to say, that these experiences are as *real* and *true* as mankind's existence on this earth today, and that they all occurred during August, September, and October of 1930, upon Mount Shasta, California, U.S.A." The experiences that he is referring to are his physical encounters with the great ascended Master Saint Germain on the slopes of Mount Shasta in the same time period that Earshin has so stated. Ballard goes on to relate how Saint Germain then took him down into several of the great Spiritual Centers within the caverns of the earth. His book is also dedicated to the Great White Brotherhood including, among others, the Brotherhood of Mount Shasta.

An interesting feature that ties the Earshin Valley so closely within the Agashan class relates to the use of the disciple number system. Many years ago when the class was first organized, each new member regularly attending the meetings was given an individual number—that number being simply the next consecutive number following the last number issued. Incidentally, this system is still in operation today. Now the Teachers of the Earshin Valley, which are a goodly number, put this system to use in quite a remarkable way, for they familiarize themselves with the rate of vibration of every new disciple coming into the movement. This then enables them to instantly tune in on the disciple's ray once he has mentally called out his disciple number, and help or assistance can immediately be forthcoming. Thus the disciples of the Agashan class, as well as others throughout the world who are in tune with this Center, have literally become channels of the Earshin Valley whereby light and peace can be sent through the individual unto other souls—it doesn't matter who they are—who might be in need.

There is no space from *here* to *there* as far as the Masters in the Earshin Valley are concerned, for they are able to project themselves by means of the "higher ray" and arrive at the scene in a split second. Of course they are invisible to the one who mentally sent out the call, but nevertheless they are able to assist and change the picture which otherwise might have been quite tragic. Many of the disciples have had seemingly miraculous escapes from either serious injury or death. One case was reported whereby the "would be" assailant simply threw down his weapon and fled the scene. Of course all responses are not quite this dramatic, but in any event much help and assistance has thus been rendered to many in the outside world.

Earthquake! The very mention of this word brings apprehension to many on the earth today, for the bowels of the earth are constantly churning over and over bringing great pressures to bear on the earth's crust practically every moment of the day. Within this very hour, even as you read this, an earth tremor of some magnitude will almost certainly manifest itself somewhere on the face of the earth. The control of these awesome forces of Nature has been in the past and remains today one of the most important responsibilities delegated to the Masters in the Earshin Valley, for without their help many of the great cities of the earth would be in ruins today.

Let us now hear from Earshin himself as he describes this aspect of their work: "Have you ever noticed, blessed ones, how strangely the average earthquake operates and how it will usually occur at a time and place where the damage will not be too great? This is not by happenstance, for the Earshin Valley is constantly at work trying to change its course. Now remember, we merely modify these earthquakes. We are doing a lot of that in the East right now; we have to, for we know what is to befall humanity in these years to follow. We realize that an earthquake could come along and practically demolish, we will say, the city of New York for instance, and that would be terrible! But these things we are trying to avoid. After all, you must remember that you are living on an imperfect earth plane. You know that, don't you?

"And you also know that we here in the Valley can certainly go into the bowels of the earth and find out for ourself just what is going on. Would you believe that? We know that there are times when we cannot do anything; it gets beyond our control, but we still do what we can to change its course. We brace, we force, and through the vacuumatical forces that we use here, we are usually able to change the picture. We are able to create this force from the atoms themselves. It is just like it would be if we were to try to keep the land area suspended for a time; we shore it up until the pressures underneath build up to the point whereby they are able to support it. Then, when the earth begins to settle back down again, you naturally feel these small tremors which are not too serious. You would ask, 'Well, why can't you stop them altogether?' Now understand, we are not performing miracles. But we can, and we usually do, divert the average earthquake to an unpopulated area such as the desert or under the sea."

The average reader, the open-minded reader who has managed to follow us this far into this most incredible chapter, should now have some inkling, some faint glimmer of understanding, as to the help that we who live on the surface of the earth are constantly receiving from these great Ascended Masters who, through their sheer unselfish love for humanity, have so isolated themselves within the various Spiritual Centers that are located at strategic points around the earth. Without their help, we simply could not be functioning in the physical body in the manner that we are today; it is not an automatic process.

We have now covered to some degree the three major Centers that have joined their forces with Agasha today. Yet there are others to be accounted for. There are three other Centers, three in particular that have also manifested from time to time and made themselves known to the Agashan class. These may be likened to another triangle interlaced about the first. And of course there are still other Centers, equally as powerful in their own right, that have never manifested in the class and about which we know but very little. So let us then, briefly this time, cover these remaining Centers.

The Chungala Valley

The night is December 5, 1952. A voice, old and ancient, takes possession of the instrument and breaks into a strange, haunting, somewhat high-pitched chant in some unknown tongue. The voice seems definitely Oriental. Then, falteringly at first, come the English words: "Chungala . . . The Chungala Valley from the land of Mu." The voice then slips away and Agasha takes over the instrument. It seems that we had just made contact for the first time with one of the most ancient of all of the Spiritual Centers on the earth today, and the voice that we had just heard belonged to none other than its great spiritual leader, Chungala. In subsequent classes, going well into the following year incidentally, Chungala and other representatives of this great consciousness continued to manifest and brought forth much interesting information relative to this ancient continent.

In time we were to learn that Chungala is a huge city within a great cavern that extends down deep under the ocean and which is located somewhere in the vicinity of the Hawaiian Islands. Its entrance is from one of these islands. It seems that just before the submergence of the great continent of Lemuria, or Mu as it is known in some circles, a large group of Masters who were very capable of ascending in the flesh sought refuge in a location that they knew would be safe for a long period of time. Therefore, we have the Chungala Consciousness of today.

"How long ago was this?" you ask. Chungala has stated that their consciousness has been in manifestation for the almost unbelievable period of something like 300,000 years! Think of it! Yet when we consider that human expression has been on this planet for many *millions* of years (Agasha sets the time period at 25,000,000 years), it moves back a little better into its proper perspective. Consequently, here within this great cavern literally thousands of souls from the ancient continent of Lemuria still live on today, expressing themselves in a most harmonious manner, and we might say almost bringing the Lemurian culture directly into the 20th century. There, great beauty is expressed everywhere. Actually their consciousness takes in far more than just a city, but there is one particular city that is brought to our attention.

Whereas the Earshin Valley seems to be definitely oriented to our Western or Atlantean civilization, the Chungalians, on the other hand, are more Oriental and seem to present what might appear to be an ancient and very hospitable Chinese consciousness. For an example: let us hear from Ming Toy who, we are told, is a professional actress in this delightful consciousness of love and happiness. The voice is charming and very, very feminine.

"Blessings to all Agashans. You are very nice people and I love you very much. It is pleasing to come to you tonight to let you know that you have come out of body to Chungala most interestingly. You have said to us, 'Never want to leave.' Most of you have come; you see, you like wonderful atmosphere.

"I teach you to speak the ancient language of the Chungalians. You liking it the same as I. How soon you wanting to see symbol of our Order? You liking it very much when you see it. Most pleasing to give higher order of secret teachings dating back to the time of Lemuria. Most persons can read once you understand key symbol of Chungala. It give to you explanation of society taking you back to all languages of past, present, and blending with universal language. Most effort to think, but very difficult to think when sometimes art of expression becomes very cloudy.

"Most understandable people come from Chungala. You are going to come and understand us; we are already far ahead of you. We understand you most interestingly—far beyond anything you ever know about one another in respective states where you be at present. Very nice way to put it, isn't it? You coming now to learn of our kingdom far beneath the Sea of Light. Come into greater, lighter light—all so very beautiful. Come to great world so greatly apart from outward world as yours in present state.

"We have beauty expressed only as desired by all inhabitants. It take a long period of time to create that which we have at present. We think it is very fine, and we have had to live with it for generations and we love it. Therefore, you feel our love, our hospitality, and enjoy the splendor that must be had by all humanity who come. You are liking it; I am liking it. We blend so beautifully. We find true love and romance of the two worlds because you have come to us and we also have come to you.

"The Lemurians, as you call, are coming to you now to teach you of the world that was before Atlantis came. You are Atlanteans, but remember, long before coming to greater world you were the Lemurians before Atlantis. We have not become Atlanteans; we have always been Lemurians. And we are to love and to remain Lemurians until we have completed cycle of earth plane. We are also learning everything that is. Ancient language, ancient everything—it is the same here because we were before other continents came.

"I would like to teach you some dances—perhaps all by the twist of arm and wrist and fingers? However, I don't think most males would like to follow me. However, we have other things for male; we have many things to come and enjoy. Come to Chungala after reaching pinnacle and enjoy our hospitality. So I give you blessings for your pinnacle (lapses into Chungalian language) and I am addressing you from higher Order of Chungala of long, of very long ago. Bless you, and saying good night."

Her voice, if you could hear it, is absolutely delightful. Now another voice concludes the message. It is from her male actor friend, Shim Toy: "I echo same. Good night to you."

Such is a brief word picture from probably the most enchanting of the Spiritual Centers, the Chungala Valley. Its location, so close to Hawaii and the Kahunas, seems most appropriate. The Chungalians are indeed beautiful people. It is interesting to find out that just as we have progressed along the path of the outer world through Atlantis and now America, the Chungalians have progressed along the path of the inner world by remaining conscious of Mu and its period. Basically, we are all alike; we are just on different paths.

The Grand Canyon Kingdom

The Grand Canyon Kingdom is definitely a pre-American consciousness; that is, it stems from a civilization that existed on our own continent some 50,000 years back in the sands of time. Long before the Indian races were to come into physical manifestation, this great civilization lived and flourished in an area covering all of Mexico and the southern part of the United States. The coast line of the Pacific Ocean was then much further inland than it is today, and the beaches extended well into Arizona. We are told that even the great Grand Canyon held a large amount of water at that time, and it presented a most spectacular sight.

It was at this point in time that a group of Masters from this particular civilization arose while in the flesh and established another major Spiritual Center— this one situated in a very spacious cavern in the vicinity of the Grand Canyon in Arizona whereby it receives its name. It is entered through a small opening high in the cliffs of the Grand Canyon itself, and then after traversing down a long shaft which extends into the earth for several miles, one would then come into this great cavern which these Masters of Light had so chosen for their work.

You would see for literally miles within this enormous cavern if you were to gaze out into the distance, for the cavern itself is extremely large, very wide, and very long. Moreover, the teachers say that its splendor is different in still another respect from some of the other Centers. For instance, among other things, its consciousness is not as mechanical as that of the Amazon Kingdom or the Earshin Valley.

It also happens that within the earth at this particular location are many valuable stones and rock formations that will never be mined on the outside world because they exist so deep and far into the earth. However these Masters of Light don't have this limitation, and they have been able to bring these materials into manifestation within their consciousness through alchemy. Thus the material that is used in their temples is a natural material that is unique to this particular cavern. It appears very similar to marble, yet it is not exactly the same, and huge blocks of it have been cut out from the rock in order to erect temples that are comparable to some of the most beautiful structures of the outside world.

The Masters of the Grand Canyon Center are of both sexes: the feminine as well as the masculine. This, incidentally, is the general rule for most of the major Centers. These Masters are somewhat normal in size as far as their physiognomy goes, and they appear very similar to the Atlanteans of long ago. We are told that the descendents of their race eventually became the ancient Egyptians, who in turn resembled the average American of the white race of today. Yet the pigment of the skin of these Grand Canyon Masters is very often of the olive complexion. They dress quite beautifully and extremely colorfully, and there are many souls within their kingdom.

Now these Adepts do not refer to the temples that they have created as being "temples" per se. They simply refer to them as places of relaxation. They have certain places to meditate and then other places where they do their experimental work, for Ascended Masters within the Spiritual Centers are always very busy. Their work is also quite scientific because in the end result everything there is always done atomically and through the etheric relations.

Perhaps one of the most interesting features pertaining to the work being carried out by the Grand Canyon Masters is their research into the evolution of the animal kingdom. They have carried out this research over an extended period of time, and it is said that they have there in that Center a representative of each of the major species that have been in manifestation on the earth within the last few thousand years. And the striking thing about all of this is that many of these animals are in miniature form. However none are hideous or dwarfed; they are all well proportioned and, incidentally, very domesticated and quite tame. These Masters of Light take pride in having perfected almost perfect examples of each of the species.

Why are some in miniature form? Is it because they have stunted their growth purposely because of a desire, or is it because of the atomic rays that they use? No. The answer is that these miniature animals all come from the Atlantean period, and through the knowledge gained from experimentation they have thus been able to revive some of the species which at one time had lived on the great continent of Atlantis. And it just so happens that many of the Atlantean animals were much smaller than the animals of today.

How do they bring these animals into manifestation? The answer is that these Adepts are constantly precipitating and drawing from the etheric realms various forms of animal expression, and this also includes the bird kingdom as well. Thus each one of the species that is now expressing itself so harmoniously in their kingdom has been placed there through the great powers of precipitation, and this also includes gestation, incubation, et cetera, from the germinal life of the species. Many of the animals that have been brought back into manifestation through this process have lived in their subtle or higher flesh body for anywhere from 500 to 1,500 years on the average, and some even much longer. The teachers say that it is not that they are going against the laws of evolution or of Nature, but that they are merely working with these laws insofar as they are able to bring certain species back into manifestation from the etheric realm after having once become extinct.

The amazing thing about all of this is that occasionally a few of these animals or birds are released into the outer world whereby they may then interbreed, multiply, and benefit humanity in many ways. But first the frequency of their bodies must be lowered to the normal, physical state. The miniature horse that was discovered within the Grand Canyon a number of years ago is an example of this. It can also be surmised that the symbolic bird of America, the American eagle, originally came from their kingdom; and likewise, perhaps even the buffalo, which was so necessary to sustain the American Indian for such a long period of time, was also brought forth.

We find that these Masters within this great Spiritual Center are in reality assisting Nature in that they have taken upon themselves the responsibility of bringing back into manifestation those particular species of the animal and bird kingdoms that are necessary for each age of the earth's evolution in this particular part of the world. This, as well as so many other things on the earth plane, is not an "automatic" process. As stated earlier, it takes hard, conscious effort by the Ascended Masters of Light, and especially by those who still retain their physical body, for life to thrive and evolve on this dense material plane.

The Northern Masters

For a brief look into the sixth major Spiritual Center that we will be discussing in this chapter, we have to travel northwards to the state of Alaska. It is here that we find a group of Adepts who had originally arisen from an advanced civilization in the area known as Siberia today. Some 100,000 years ago, just prior to the last great glacial ice age that destroyed that vast civilization, these Adepts had their ascension and established their kingdom in a very surprising location. The fact that is surprising is not so much that it is in the vicinity of Alaska, but that their kingdom is located within a great ice cavern deep inside one of the many ice glaciers that are so prevalent in that part of the country, and not within the earth itself as so many of the other Centers are located. The Agashan teachers simply refer to them as the Northern Masters.

These great Masters come from a rather tall race, and their skin is sort of reddish in color. They are usually dressed in white. One of these great Adepts manifested through the Zenor instrument during the class of June 8, 1953, and spoke in his original tongue. The language seemed to be of an Oriental dialect and somewhat similar to that of the Chungalians. He informed the class that two individuals from the outside world had found their way to their kingdom many years ago, and through the laws of higher alchemy they were permitted to enter. They are still there now.

In that great land of mystery—referring to the unpopulated and little known parts of Alaska and other points north—beautiful lights have occasionally been seen by the natives and those who have more or less pioneered the arctic region. Strange sounds and noises have also been heard in the distance, and legend has it that these sounds are caused by great mammoth and ferocious animals, as it would seem to the child mind that only mammoth animals could make such terrific noises. However, we all know that these sounds are caused by the cracking of the ice—the cracking of the icebergs which resounds over and over again and results in acoustics so powerful that the sounds can sometimes be carried for miles.

When we try to explain the lights, however, the answer is not so easily forthcoming. These strange lights, these very colorful lights that we are referring to, are not what are commonly known as the northern lights; they are an entirely different phenomenon. They become very beautiful at times as these shafts of light penetrate the night sky in many different and varied colors. Sometimes they are purple, at other times they are blue or gold, and at still other times they are simply white. The Agashan teachers explain these powerful lights as being a by-product of the radiation that these Northern Masters send out into space from time to time from their great Spiritual Center. But their source, of course, is from a location that mortal man cannot touch.

If we were to travel deep down into this great ice cavern and explore it with our clairvoyant eye, we would find crystal-like palaces carved most magnificently out of a clear transparent material closely resembling crystallized quartz. It is a fine and durable material, and great beauty is expressed as the powerful atomic sun penetrates the various parts of the cavern and then shines and reflects on these crystals, thus sending forth a great radiance of light. We would see then that the lighting as well as the temperature is all controlled atomically. Pure creative light would seem to be an appropriate symbol for this magnificent Spiritual Consciousness.

The Gobi Desert

As all things seem to come into manifestation in groups of seven, a study of the Spiritual Centers of the earth is certainly not complete without at least touching upon a seventh Center. Yet when we endeavor to seek out the seventh Center that has manifested and made itself known to the Agashan class, a mystery arises, for this so-called seventh Center is no longer in the physical world. This would seem to be as it should be inasmuch as we have now covered two groups of three each, which may be symbolically represented by two interlaced triangles about a central point. The seventh Center would then fall in the center of the circle and be of a different order of vibration than the Spiritual Centers which were on the circumference of the circle.

The Masters from the Gobi Desert have long ago given up their physical bodies and ascended into the Consciousness of Immensity. However, the elements of Light and Wisdom contained within this great Spiritual Center are still in existence on the Mental Plane. They exist in a higher order of matter than the atomic structure of the elements of the physical world, and even though this Light and Wisdom pertains to the past and has no active influence upon our present day existence, it is forever preserved in the great records of the past. This is a difficult point to fully comprehend, and the reader will simply have to embrace it in the best way he can.

At any rate, this great Spiritual Center did have its physical existence at one time somewhere within the confines of a wide desert plateau extending some 600 miles from north to south and 1,000 miles from east to west in that part of Asia known as Mongolia today. This was the great Consciousness of the Gobi Desert, and it was a kingdom that was greatly loved and cherished for it was a great source of spiritual culture way back in the dawn of time. Even today, many of the Teachers often descend into its great mental consciousness to see and relive the kingdom that they had at one time lived in the flesh.

The South Pole Masters

Now let us leave the Mental Plane for the moment, and return once again to the Physical Plane. Let us travel outwards to the circumference of our symbolical circle and embrace what apparently is the first of still another triangle of Centers. As we stated earlier in this chapter, there undoubtedly are other Spiritual Centers which are very important unto mankind; however, information on these additional Centers is still held in secrecy—at least as far as the Agashan class is concerned. There is one exception to this rule, and for a brief look at this eighth and last Center let us travel southward to the extreme opposite end of the earth—the South Pole. In many ways it is the counterpart of the first Spiritual Center that we embraced, for it, like the Valley of Cocoda, is also on the surface of the earth. It is known to the Agashan class as the South Pole Masters.

Let us go back to the class of June 2, 1950, and listen to what Agasha has to say about this fascinating Center. The great teacher is talking: "Disciples, I have refrained from telling you about too many of these Centers for many reasons. You have learned that the three main Centers that we have embraced are the Earshin Valley, the Amazon Kingdom, and the Valley of Cocoda—the three major Centers. I have casually told you about the Grand Canyon Masters and recently you have been learning about the Alaskan Masters. We have referred to them as the Northern Masters. But let us now go to the South Pole and embrace Masters of Light who are from one of the great civilizations of the past and who are in turn also an offshoot from the great Atlantean Consciousness.

"In the region of the South Pole, there is a particular consciousness that is definitely—now follow me carefully—that is definitely on the surface. It is not a cavern in the sense of the word. There is a cavern there, but these people are on the surface. The climate is beautifully controlled and it is very warm and tropical—very beautiful indeed. There are many, many beautiful flowers growing most abundantly. Now I do not speak of any recent discovery of natives in that part of the world; no, I am referring now to Masters of Light.

"I need not explain to you the purpose of these Masters remaining in the flesh because we know that they have a purpose. We have learned that they are more powerful in their respective state, whatever it be, than they would be if they were to ascend unto the Consciousness of Immensity at this time. They have remained in the flesh for many thousands and thousands of years."

It must be remembered that the above was given in 1950. It was not until the latter part of 1952 that the class first learned of Chungala and consequently the Chungala Valley. In any event, and it really doesn't make too much difference in which order we take them, we have at least learned a little about seven individual Spiritual Centers that are still in manifestation on the physical level of life. There are also several others sprinkled about the surface of the earth, and if we were to consider those in the Mental Plane, such as the Gobi Desert, there would be many.

What proof do we have of the existence of these Spiritual Vortexes of Light? Unfortunately, not very much. On the other hand, a very startling bit of collaborative evidence indicating the reality of at least one of these Spiritual Centers, the Masters at the South Pole, has been uncovered and related by Charles Berlitz in his most fascinating best seller, *The Bermuda Triangle,*[7] and I quote:

"A famous explorer and aviator, Admiral Richard Byrd, who undertook flights over the intensified magnetic fields of both the North and South poles, made an incredible broadcast in 1929, while on a flight over the South Pole. He told of emerging through a foggy light into an area of a green land with ice-free lakes and reported seeing huge bisonlike beasts and other animals and what looked like primitive men. The broadcast immediately went off the air and Admiral Byrd's report was attributed to temporary nervous exhaustion or hallucination. Both the exploit and report were subsequently 'unpublicized,' although the fact that Byrd had made the broadcast did his reputation little good in scientific circles. Strangely enough, a number of persons who were frequent moviegoers in the twenties are sure that they remember seeing newsreels of the Byrd flight, together with views of 'the land beyond the Pole,' although it is possible that having read about the incident they had confused other newsreels showing the admiral's exploits with the controversial one."

In any event, here we have a report from a reputable scientist and explorer that a tropical "green land with ice-free lakes" does indeed exist at or near the South Pole. Of course, it does not exist within our own dimension in the sense that other cities and places exist as we know them. Of course not. But it does exist in the same manner that the Valley of Cocoda exists, our modern day Shangri-La, and in the same way that the other Spiritual Centers exist. These Centers, even though they are invisible to our normal sight, actually coexist in coexisting dimensions with our own "physical" reality, as proven by the fact that Byrd could fly into one and then out again while still remaining in the physical body. They are still composed of physical matter, yet their vibration rate is somewhat higher. Of course for a better understanding we have to embrace the theory of negative matter and the anims of the etheric state. But the remarkable feature of the entire report lies in the fact that a physical airplane can actually fly through a "foggy light" and fly right into a consciousness as real and solid as any other consciousness on the face of the earth. It is in a similar fashion, we are told, that helicopters will eventually land in Cocoda, photograph the structures, et cetera, and then fly right out again seemingly from negative matter into positive matter.

Do some of the so-called "UFO" originate from these Spiritual Centers? The Agashan teachers have indicated that this is so; however, there is still much to be answered in this direction. Many authors have written about the earth's "invisible residents" and other strange mysteries relating to time and space. Perhaps the idea first presented by Lewis Carrol when he took Alice through the looking glass and into another consciousness was not so much a fairy story after all. There is something fascinating to all of us when we contemplate entering through a "hole" or a "tunnel" into another dimension. Charles Berlitz[8] compiles a bibliography of some 40 books just published during the last 25 years on these phenomena, let alone the hundreds of other books that have told and retold similar stories in the great religions and mythologies of antiquity.

Yes indeed, in the light of all of the above, it would seem that the enlightened thinker should certainly give some credence at least to the material presented for the first time, we believe, in this chapter. For this is occultism of the very highest order! This is a report on the real Guardians of the Earth—the great Masters of Light who are in truth constantly sending forth their great light and inspiration unto the struggling humanities of this spaceship that men call Earth.

NOTES

1. The quotation is taken from Ross Hunter's Musical Production of *Lost Horizon*, a Columbia Picture based on the novel by James Hilton.
2. James Hilton, *Lost Horizon* (New York, William Morrow, 1933, Pocket Books, 1939–73)
3. Lincoln Barnett, *The World We Live In* (New York, Time Incorporated, 1955)
4. Besant and Leadbeater, *Occult Chemistry* (India, Theosophical Publishing House, 1951)
5. Manly Palmer Hall, *The Secret Destiny of America* (Los Angeles, Philosophical Research Society, 1944, 1950) p. 164, 170, 171
6. Godfre Ray King, *Unveiled Mysteries* (Chicago, Saint Germain Press, 1934)
7. Charles Berlitz, *The Bermuda Triangle* (New York, Doubleday & Co., 1974) p. 120
8. Ibid.

CHAPTER NINE

TIME AND SPACE

The human mind is not capable of grasping the Universe. We are like a little child entering a huge library. The walls are covered to the ceilings with books in many different tongues. The child knows that someone must have written these books. It does not know who or how. It does not understand the languages in which they are written. But the child notes a definite plan in the arrangement of the books—a mysterious order which it does not comprehend, but only dimly suspects.

—Albert Einstein

TIME and Space—do we really understand the true meaning of these words? Is there in reality a difference? For as we gaze out into space at the countless myriads of stars scattered throughout a cloudless sky, what are we actually observing? Science tells us that these are all gigantic suns, but so far away in "space" that they only appear as mere pinpoints of light. But are they not in reality also far away in "time"? There is not a single object that we see in the entire sky, except possibly the moon, that we have absolute proof of its existence in the present point of time that we refer to as "now." It may have exploded into the nothingness many thousands of years ago and not even exist "now." When we observe even the very nearest star, we are only observing the way it did exist about four years ago and not necessarily the way it exists "now." And a lot can happen in the time span of just four years. But how about a hundred thousand years? Some of the stars in our own galaxy, the Milky Way, are actually projecting the picture of the way they existed way back 100,000 years into the past, for it takes upwards of 100,000 years for their light to travel to the planet Earth. And even this is but a teardrop in the eternity of time. Some of the galaxies in the most remote regions of "space" are showing us the way they appeared some 40,000,000,000 years ago. Think of it! When our modern telescopes observe these galaxies, they are actually photographing a portion of the Universe 40 billion years back into the past! Thus space and time become as one.

Largeness and Smallness

Another element to be considered is the concept of largeness and smallness. What is large and what is small? Are they not indeed only relative terms? A study of the following diagram should prove rather interesting. One can readily see then that the "size" of an object depends only on your point of view and your position on the scale. Let us take Man for instance. He has a body composed of billions of cells. To him, a cell is very small and the earth, the planet on which he lives, is very large. But actually, the body of Man is approximately at the mean position between the size of a single cell and the size of the earth; that is, a cell is proportionally about as much smaller than the body of Man as the earth is larger.

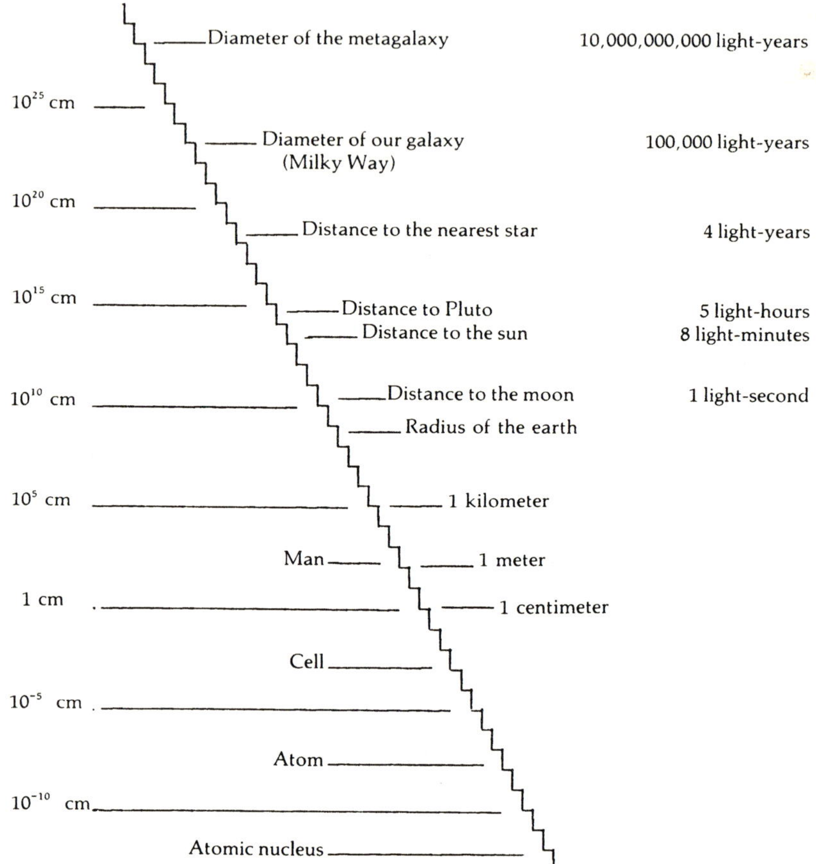

Figure 1. Our stairway to the stars from atom to universe.[1] *Each step indicates a ten times enlargement. For example: an object five steps higher than another is larger by 10 x 10 x 10 x 10 x 10 = 100,000 times.*

And we can carry the analogy still further. An atom is about as much smaller than a cell as the body of Man is larger; and the nucleus of an atom is just as far away from its external shell as the sun is from its nearest star neighbor. In other words, the body of Man is also in the mean position between the nucleus of an atom and the distance from Man to the nearest star. Who is to say then whether the body of Man is large or small? Thus largeness and smallness, the macrocosm and the microcosm, likewise become as one.

Lincoln Barnett in his most absorbing treatise on the nature of the universe[2] reinforces this when he states, "It is perhaps significant that in terms of simple magnitude man is the mean between macrocosm and microcosm. Stated crudely this means that a supergiant red star (the largest material body in the universe) is just as much bigger than man as an electron (tiniest of physical entities) is smaller. It is not surprising, therefore, that the prime mysteries of nature dwell in those realms farthest removed from sense-imprisoned man, nor that science, unable to describe the extremes of reality in the homely metaphors of classical physics, should content itself with noting such mathematical relationships as may be revealed."

And this is about all that man, while he is imprisoned in his physical body, can do. Agasha has stated over and over again that in the ultimate sense everything is mathematical. It is through understanding the principles of what he terms "the higher calculus" that man will eventually be able to understand the nature of the ultimate reality. And isn't Nature trying to tell us the same thing? Is it coincidence that the average cell which constitutes the human body contains just about as many atoms as our galaxy (The Milky Way) contains stars? Think of it! It contains no less than 100 billion stars. And is it coincidence that the physical body of man, which contains about 60 trillion cells, is the mean proportional between the size of a cell and the size of our own planet Earth upon which we live? And is it coincidence that the Sun, which is an extremely large body when compared to the Moon, is so situated in space that its apparent size to the physical senses of man appears to be almost exactly that of the Moon? Come, come, come, simple reason will tell us that these facts along with the many hundreds of others surely cannot all be explained by the laws of coincidence. There absolutely *must* be a simple, rational explanation for the entire Cosmos.

What is this simple explanation? Has mankind somehow missed the sign posts along the way? Did the ancients once know these secrets and then instead of leaving them to posterity promptly bury them again? Or is it that mankind itself, through ignorance, avarice, greed, and all of the other deadly sins, was the force that contaminated the simple teachings (that were originally brought forth by the great Masters of the past in all of their sublime simplicity and pristine purity) so as to make them unrecognizable at the present day? The Agashan teachers state that the latter explanation is the correct one. However, Nature is not to be so easily thwarted. It is Man's destiny and heritage to once again know the truth of his own Being, and the teachers of the Agashan class state that not too many years will pass before mankind will once again be brought to the threshold of pure spiritual understanding and awareness.

Travel in Consciousness

How will all this be brought about? The answer seems to be for man to simply learn how to travel in consciousness. This is not necessarily limited to space travel because we most certainly must take time travel into consideration also; therefore, traveling in consciousness would mean traveling in both dimensions, time as well as space.

The concept of traveling in consciousness is not new. There was a motion picture produced a few years back titled *The Incredible Journey* wherein science had perfected a drug that enabled those who partook of it to grow infinitely small. Thus the heroes of this Science fiction film were then able to be injected within the blood stream of an incurably ill patient and travel in their minute submarine spacecraft deep within the heart where otherwise impossible repairs could then be made. Of course, this film was made before the perfection of our modern open heart surgery, but in any event this "incredible journey" within the physical body of Man himself proved to be a most exciting and revealing experience.

But why is this journey into the microcosm more incredible or seemingly more impossible than a similar journey into the macrocosm or greater universe? It is not. Common sense will tell us that if one is possible, so is the other. The recent television series *Star Trek* was an excellent example of the latter possibility in that it enabled thousands of viewers to vividly share the experiences of the valiant crew of the staunch Starship U.S.S. Enterprise as it explored vast regions of the Universe undreamed of by mortal man.

What seems to be wrong here? Why is it that Man is so unlimited in his dreams and in his imagination and yet is so limited in his physical capabilities? It would seem that Man is a veritable prisoner of Time because when he gazes up at the stars in the sky he sees only the past—images of stars and vast universes, but only as they once existed. It would seem that Time itself stands still as the film of our fast action camera of the present catches entire galaxies seemingly stopped right in the middle of an explosion. It is only the incessant motion of the Earth as it slowly revolves upon its axis that gives any movement to the stars at all, and even this is illusionary.

But is Man really so limited in his physical capabilities? Are not our seeming limitations likewise an illusion? Does not science fiction, as incredible as it may seem at the time it is written, seem to eventually come true sooner or later? Look what man accomplishes as he literally changes the very face of the earth. In absolute contrast to the apparent stillness of the universe above us and beyond us, life here on earth is in a constant and frantic state of motion and agitation. Everywhere we look, we see motion, action, drama. Vehicles are traveling down the freeways at a frantic pace, giant skyscrapers are under construction, whole colonies of ants are busily going about their business, flocks of birds are flying through the sky—everywhere, absolutely everywhere we see life, life in incessant motion and activity. And who is helping to run the entire show? Who is the main instigator of much of this activity? Who is constructing the skyscrapers, who is changing the course of a river by means of a massive dam, who is growing acres and acres of corn in the vast farm belts? The answer is of course Man. Man is a copartner with Nature in creating the activity on the surface of the earth.

We thus come to the inexplicable conclusion that whereas Man has not yet become a "time" traveler—by that we mean being able to travel backwards in time to the almost infinite number of stars, planets, and other bodies that exist in the macrocosmic world of time and which is erroneously called outer space—he most certainly is at present a "space" traveler in that he is free to travel anywhere he so desires in the "space universe" that men call Earth, that microcosmic world of our own planet. Of all the places in the Universe, our own planet is the only place that Man can truly say is the present or the Now. "We are living in the Now," Agasha has stated over and over again. And where is the Now? The answer is nowhere else but the planet Earth, as far as our physical consciousness is concerned. Everything else that we see in outer space is only an image of that which existed in the past. The planet Pluto is five hours into the past as we observe it. Even our own Sun is in the past by eight minutes according to our senses. The only heavenly body that we can in any way speak of as existing in our own present, the Now, is our sister planet the Moon, the light of which was sent forth just one second prior to the time it appears to our sight. All else exists in what Man terms the "past," and for all we know, may not even exist in our own "now."

This may sound strange because by simple analogy we can project the past into the present. You know as well as I know that Mars, Venus, and Jupiter exist "now" even though the proof of their existence has not yet reached our senses. But can we be absolutely certain of this seemingly obvious fact? I may have seen you on the street today and know that you are alive and well, and in all probability you still are. But what if in the meantime you had met up with an unfortunate accident, an explosion, or whatever, and that the news of this event had not yet reached my senses? Of course you would still exist; that is your soul would still exist, your consciousness would still exist. But your physical body would have vanished into the nothingness and would no longer exist in my present consciousness, the consciousness that I term my own individual "now." You would exist in a completely different "now."

The Spacial Aspect of Time

All of the above then leads us up to what might be termed the "spacial aspect of time." As we stated earlier, it is very simple for Man to travel to any destination he so desires—and then even return to that same location again and again for that matter—in the "space universe" that Man calls Earth. However, when we consider the "time universe" it becomes a completely different question. It makes no difference whether we are considering the macrocosmic worlds of galaxies, stars, and planets that exist out there in time—it is only images of the past that we are seeing, remember—or whether we are considering the time aspect of the microcosmic universe that we call Earth, the limitations are the same. Man is simply not capable of traveling in his physical body to-and-fro, backwards and forwards, in the dimension called *time* in the same manner that he finds so easy to do in the dimension called *space.* And yet these two dimensions are only different aspects of the same ultimate reality.

Now in our mind's eye let us picture the globe of the planet Earth. Let us call it our "space universe." Now let us envision an invisible universe of concentric spheres or shells extending outwards from the surface of the Earth in much the same manner as the peels of an onion wrap around its core. These may be called its "time universe." These invisible shells or hollow spheres seem to extend not only outwards to infinity in progressively larger shells, but they also seem to extend inwards to infinity in progressively smaller shells as well. But the only visible shell is that which we are observing at the moment: the planet Earth as it appears at this moment in time. Let us call this visible shell the year 1975. The next larger shell, and still invisible to our physical eyesight, incidentally, can then be called the year 1976, and the one above that 1977, and the one above that 1978, and on and on and on. Of course, if we look inwards we shall find the Earth as it appeared in 1974, and then 1973, and then 1972, and so on.

Agasha states that these invisible spheres are what constitute the Mental Kingdom of the Earth—the Akashic Records of this planet extending not only into the past, but into the future as well. Down deep into the core, into the innermost recesses of its being, will be the records of its birth. And then upwards and outwards, spiraling out seemingly into infinity and terminating in what can only appear to our mind's eye as a huge golden sun, are the records of its potentially glorious future.

Thus we end up with worlds within worlds within worlds. And yet all of these different worlds, these different concentric spheres or shells, are only aspects of the same world as it exists in different planes of the dimension called *time.* Movement in the *space* dimension may then be compared to moving laterally across the surface of the earth. And movement in the *time* dimension would then be at right angles to the *space* dimension—either outwards or inwards depending on whether one wished to travel into the future or into the past. Of course, the physical space dimensions of the earth can then be said, as a supposition, to be gradually expanding outwards into time as we move from year to year.

This remarkable theory, being not explicitly stated in the Agashan classes but more or less implied, is certainly not at variance with the conclusions of modern science which state that we live in an expanding universe—one that is expanding ever outwards as the result of an original "big bang" explosion. If the macrocosmic universe is expanding outwards, why then is not the microcosmic universe, the planet Earth or any of the other planets for that matter, also expanding outwards in much the same manner? But this rather unusual theory would state that the expansion of the planets is in *time* and not in *space.* For is not everything that we see out there in so-called "outer space" only the past? It would seem that these thoughts certainly deserve further analysis by the inquiring mind.

The potentials for time travel then become rather interesting. It would seem that one would have to first travel in space (i.e., along the surface of the earth) to some suitable "doorway" whereby he could then gain entry to these time spheres or worlds. These so-called doorways might conceivably be located in a sort of time-space "warp" or negative "hole" as discussed in the previous chapter. Undoubtedly the Spiritual Centers are also doorways to these mental time spheres. The only stumbling block is that our potential time traveler would have to first become an Adept, and that would eliminate the Spiritual Centers for the average individual.

In any event, the potential is there for us to travel in space to a doorway, enter the doorway, and then travel either outwards or inwards in time in much the same manner as one would travel upwards or downwards in an elevator. We could then step out into the mental space world of either the past or the future which to us would appear as solid and real as our own physical space world now appears. Wouldn't it be interesting to step into the time-space sphere of the year 1776, as a supposition, and then travel across the sea in the mode of transportation of the day to the new colonies in America and observe (if we were allowed entry by the guard at the door) the signing of the Declaration of Independence at Independence Hall in Philadelphia? The possibility for having an experience such as this is not as remote as it might appear to be on the surface. If these experiences can happen once, they can certainly happen again. The secret is, of course, finding the doorway to that particular mental space world.

On August 10, 1901, two English school teachers, Miss C.A.E. Moberly and Miss E.F. Jourdain, were visiting Paris. They had decided to visit the Palace at Versailles and the Trianons but upon entering the grounds they inadvertently stepped right into the 18th century. There was no abrupt change. It did not seem unusual to them at the moment as neither one had been there before. They walked down the paths, observed the buildings, and even conversed with some garden officials after they found that they had become quite lost. Therefore they were not invisible to these 18th century citizens. They even observed Marie Antoinette, as it later turned out to be, sketching in the garden. Their return to the 20th century was as inconspicuous and as uneventful as when they left it. Later, realizing that there was something peculiar about the whole afternoon, they returned only to find everything changed. Historical records subsequently confirmed their descriptions of not only the costumes of the period but also of buildings and structures that had long since been removed. A complete documentation of the entire experience has been published in book form by the same two teachers and titled *An Adventure.*[3]

The main point in this discussion is that in reality everything exists *Now.* The Agashan teachers have stated over and over again that we are living in the *Now.* In reality, there is no past and there is no future. Everything is present. This viewpoint is by no means solely expressed by the teachers of the Agashan classes. Other occult teachers have reiterated this same point. The teacher manifesting as Seth through the mediumship of Jane Roberts[4] has gone so far as to state that in reality we are living all of our lives simultaneously. Of course, the validity of this point would depend entirely upon your perspective—whether you are looking out from the center of the wheel towards the rim where all of your lives would then be exposed to your view, or whether you would be on the rim of this wheel of life struggling through life after life in consecutive order. Being in the hub could be likened to being in the world of Reality. To that state of consciousness *everything* would then be in the present. This state is called the Consciousness of Immensity. When compared with the world of Reality, life in the physical and astral states is only an illusion—a reflection of the reality yet to be experienced.

The Ascended Masters of the Spiritual Centers scattered throughout the earth are not limited to only the consciousness of the physical world. As they are in truth Ascended Masters, they are evidently able to travel freely up and down the scale of *time* in much the same manner as we are able to travel back and forth in the scale of *space,* which is to say to the city of New York or any other location on the planet. The only difference is that they travel almost instantaneously; whereas we must laboriously first travel to the airport and then after boarding an aircraft arrive at our destination some several hours later. They also *know* that they live in the Eternal Now; whereas we *think* that we live in a state of consciousness suspended somewhere between the past and the future which we term the present. This is the basic difference between the one world of Reality and the many worlds of Illusion.

Perhaps the simple analogy of the recording disc or the phonograph record can illustrate this point a bit further. Let us say that the recorded disc represents the time track of a particular planet's evolution—from its birth to its death. Each circular groove would then represent one year of its physical expression. The stylus or needle, which activates and brings into physical manifestation the particular groove that it is vibrating in, is then the *Now.* Thus this stylus, this activator, as it gradually moves inward from groove to groove then activates or brings into physical manifestation that which was previously recorded in the memory pattern of God—the recorded disc. Ordinarily this is a slow continuous process as the record plays on and on from year to year. But the Ascended Masters in the Consciousness of Immensity evidently have the ability not only to replay the record at will, but to pick up the stylus and move it to any point on the record, or even to put on a completely different record for that matter. Then as soon as this magic stylus is fitted into the groove, any life, any experience, any action whatsoever, be it in the infinite past or the infinite future, is immediately transformed into the *Now*. Thus we can truly say that in the great Consciousness of Immensity all is Now.

However, for all practical purposes, life on the earth plane is still pretty much broken down into the past, the present, and the future. This is a fact that in our present state of consciousness we simply cannot escape. But Agasha has repeatedly said that we are now on the threshold of a new awakening; hence the future should bring to mankind entirely new concepts and ideas, and perhaps some that are not even dreamed of at the present time. What might these ideas be?

A New Spiritual Understanding of the Universe

Have we any hints as to what might provide the basis for a newer and greater spiritual understanding of the universe, a comprehension of the way in which man might come to look at it in the future? Of course we do. The building blocks for this understanding are what form the basis for the entire Agashan philosophy. That is what the class is all about.

In the first place, there is no such thing as being large or small per se. They are only relative terms when being compared with something else. Agasha has stated on numerous occasions that, if we could leave the physical body and project our consciousness into an atom, we would find spaces as vast and fathomless as the space between the earth and the sun. If we could place one of our astronauts there, he would feel very much at home and would have no way of knowing that in reality he was within the vast depths of an atom. Then on the other hand, if we were to project our consciousness to the Consciousness of Immensity—that consciousness which embraces everything that is—entire galaxies of stars would be but cell life within the bodies of vast Cosmic Beings. Therefore the terms *large* and *small* have no real meaning.

In fact, he has also stated that a single atom is as important to the universe as the universe is to itself. It is the ONENESS that gives us the key. Everything is part of the ONENESS. And Man is the spiritual mean of all of this. These are the secrets that shall be expounded in the future. These are the things that the ancients had originally brought forth. The macrocosm or greater universe is identical with the microcosm or lesser universe. There is no difference. One is only the reflection or the image of the other.

What is probably the oldest and most revered of all the monuments of antiquity is the sacred Emerald Tablet of Hermes. Its age is unknown. A very ancient author who lived several centuries before Christ mentions this tablet or table, and he says that he had seen it in Egypt at the Court and that it was in his time esteemed to be above 2,000 years old. Manly Palmer Hall tells us that this information was given by Dr. Sigismund Bacstrom in his *Original Alchemical Manuscripts.*[5] Then Jacques Sadoul states in his treatise on *Alchemy*[6] that another legend has it that the text was found by Alexander the Great's soldiers in the Great Pyramid at Giza, which in some circles is credited with being very closely associated with Hermes himself.

At any rate, this ancient Emerald Tablet proclaims the Ancient Wisdom loud and clear when it states: "This is the truth, the whole truth, and nothing but the truth: As below, so above; and as above, so below. With this knowledge alone you may work miracles. And since all things exist in and emanate from the ONE Who is the ultimate Cause, so all things are born after their kind from this ONE. The Sun is the father, the Moon the mother; the wind carried it in his belly. Earth is its nurse and its guardian. It is the Father of all things; the eternal Will is contained in it. Here, on Earth, its strength, its power, remain one and undivided."[7] Again we have the same confirmation of the ONENESS.

Another theorem that will most certainly form a major

cornerstone of the building blocks for this future spiritual understanding is the relativity of time. There is no fixed time in reality. The apparent duration of time only depends upon the consciousness that you are in. A minute to me might appear as an entire lifetime to you, and vice versa. And then again, a span of a million years could be as no time at all. Many times in his endeavors to explain some great truth, Agasha has made the statement, "But there is that lapse of time to be taken into consideration." In other words, there is something missing that the scientific mind does not yet realize, and this could be the actual discontinuity of time.

The Agashan philosophy teaches that everything, in the final analysis, is curved or circular. And Science itself now accepts as valid Einstein's laws of relativity which prove that space is likewise curved. But doesn't this necessarily imply that time is also curved? It may be that the future spiritual understanding will discover that time may even have the ability of running backwards as well as forward. In that case, the past could become the present and the present could become the future. In any event, there is only the Now. And the time that it takes to travel back into the past or ahead into the future is instantaneous.

Perhaps a better understanding of Agasha's views on time and space and their relationship with one another can be gained if we listen to his own words on the subject. We have selected the tape of October 13, 1950, because it was given before America's space exploration program had yet begun. Yet Agasha's views have not changed an iota since then. Agasha is saying, "The secret, disciples, lies in being able to make contact with the inner consciousness. It is then that many things can be revealed unto you both vibrationally as well as impressionally that will prove a great deal to you. You will then learn the intricacies of those things that behoove the average mind, and you will understand it because there is an answer to everything. There is nothing that cannot be answered unto you because in reality you are infinitely intelligent.

"I do not want any of you to think that you are going to be able to *physically* project yourself beyond the surface of your solar system—you would have to go at least a million miles an hour, or perhaps a million miles a minute, to do that—because you just don't realize how far away it is, we would say, if you want to use that term. But I have said to you that there is no time nor space that separates different states of consciousness. You are only governed by time and space when you get into the dense body. You see, this physical body that you are in is the dense body. The atmosphere is dense, and that which is in accordance with the atmosphere is what we term 'time.' You see, the thing is that when you go beyond the atmosphere of the dense body, then there is no time from here to there. You can then project yourself just like you can do in spirit. And please try to understand that.

"When I project myself from the Consciousness of Immensity in an evening as I have done here tonight to control this channel—which is a natural law, incidentally—I must have a medium or a physical organism to manifest through because I have long since ascended from the flesh. It is the law, I repeat. So therefore when I project myself from there to here, there is no time. The only difficulty that I might encounter in coming from the Consciousness of Immensity to this physical body that I am speaking through would be if I were to lower my vibration beyond a certain point while passing through certain elements that I might find myself in—and then get tangled up in the vibrations, as it were. Then I would have to readjust myself in order to keep on relaying or projecting from one plane of consciousness to another. But normally I become oblivious to all divisions that I project myself through, and therefore nothing that I may pass through has any effect upon my spiritual body.

"And we can do the same thing mechanically. We can create mechanical devices and things out of certain chemicals that will harmonize with the elements out there in space. Then when we get beyond a certain point, we can by the power of *will* then project ourself to any part of this great universe. This is also by the power of vibration, and I might add that if we were to go very near to the sun, its tremendous heat would have no effect upon the elements of these mechanical devices.

"Now your bodies of this earth are only attuned to the physical planet. If you were to project yourselves out into space in a mechanical way, you would have to have certain elements surrounding the physical body for protection because you would not harmonize with the atmosphere of space or the heavier or lighter atmosphere of a particular planet. Your body would not be attuned to that.

"Now what is going to be revealed unto you in the future will enable you to link up with other worlds, not only in a spiritual sense but also in a material sense as well. You are now learning that what we can do in spirit in projecting ourself, you can also do in a mechanical way in time when these vibratorial waves, ray machines, and rays are so created to make it possible for this to take place. And that is what is going to happen in the future."

From the foregoing, it can be readily seen that the program for man's exploration of space has only just begun. Evidently space exploration becomes another very important building block for a future spiritual understanding of the universe. But what about the immediate future? Was the present space program and its achievements of landing men on the moon and their safe return anticipated and prophesied in the Agashan classes? The answer is a very definite yes. Let us go back some twenty-five years to an evening either in the latter part of 1949 or at the latest very early in 1950, the exact date of the tape being somewhat in question. Now, mind you, this was given several years before the space program had begun. In fact, it was not even anticipated at this point in time. It was not until 1959, some nine years later, that Russia first circled the moon and radioed back photographs to the earth; and it was not until 1969, some nineteen years later, that U.S. Astronaut Neil A. Armstrong became the first man of our own era to set foot on the moon. But this is all past history now. So let us sit back in our chairs and listen to Agasha prove that the then forthcoming space program was not only very clearly seen, but actually prophesied many years before it had even started.

Agasha is speaking: "The years between now and 1965 are considered to be the last days of this particular cycle. We are now then in the last days of the cycle that we have been talking about for such a long period of time. Things then are going to be seen in space which are not going to be created by men on the earth plane. Many of these things are going to be created by men of other planets. They are conscious of this fact, and there seems to be that inner communication which both they and you are desirous of. When this is done, then we are going to have valuable information.

"Men will be just as keen, as you would say, or interested, in going out into space as you would be on any other subject. Scientists will devote their time to that, and they are on that right now. These rocket ships are becoming very important to mankind—not as a weapon of war, no. But we might say that they are becoming important in order to explore the regions of the universe, and that is precisely the way it should be worded—exploring the regions of the universe. In time to come a certain instrument will be devised which will take human life out there in space. It will go afar and will have a certain amount of protection. You would say that they will be risking their lives, indeed so. But they still will receive valuable information. Before this is done, everything will be controlled, as you would term on the earth plane—be controlled by remote control. And through that procedure they will be able to read and to photograph and to bring valuable information back to the earth plane.

"Today it is only in its infancy. As a matter of fact, only very little can now be given unto mankind because what they have already ascertained is small in comparison with what is to come. Now we realize that there is going to be so much more given and this will be through an instrument that is going to be involved. This instrument will enable the human form—human life which will be apparently ready to sacrifice their lives—to go afar and still return to the earth plane safely. This airship that will be employed in the future will be able to go out into space for thousands and thousands of miles, indeed so, and bring back that information to the earth plane. Then after it will have gone out for several thousands and thousands of miles, it will be able to photograph beyond thousands of miles by a vibratorial ray—in the same way that an obstacle can be detected by radar—and then even photograph many thousands of miles beyond that period which will go into many, many hundreds of thousands of miles. This will be very important unto mankind and will mean that the moon will be brought right into your backyard, as a matter of fact. This is how important it will be in time.

"When men study the universe as the Atlanteans did, which we are now trying to revive, then there will no longer be a mystery as far as life on the *surface* is concerned. This will be given unto mankind in a comparatively short time. But we really want to be in a position to know about the *inner planes* because it is from the inner planes that all is brought into manifestation. Then we will be getting to the origin of things. When men get to the origin of life on the earth plane, they will be getting to the real source that brought all into manifestation."

Thank you Agasha. And if there is still any doubt that he predicted that man himself would actually go to the moon in addition to just photographing it, let me quote from the tape of October 13, 1950, when he states: "Within a comparatively short time they will successfully project themselves onto the moon. That will be an accomplished fact within a comparatively short time. After they have once achieved this—which as I say is going to be comparatively soon—and have then returned to the earth plane to record and to speak of that which they had seen, then they will have to begin to overcome what is meant by time and space." And here we come to the nitty-gritty of the matter. Even science recognizes the fact that in view of the tremendous distances involved, if space travel to other worlds outside of our own solar system is to become a reality in the future, a completely new system will have to be devised. And Agasha goes on to predict just that.

It seems that beyond the atmosphere, the stratosphere, the ionosphere, and the various other spheres of an individual planet is a particular sphere called in some occult circles by the name of the "ring-pass-me-not." However, this particular ring or terminal sphere does not apparently exist at any specific distance in miles above a planet but is more like a particular rate of vibration connected somehow with the electro-magnetic field of the planet. Once this magnetic quirk, or magnetic flow, is contacted, then there is instantly no time nor space separating that planet from any other planet, particularly within its own solar system. In other words, the only time lost would be but a twinkling of an eye in traveling to any other location within that solar system. And of course, this same magnetic current may also be used in the so-called space from one solar system to another. It is in tapping this particular magnetic current that it has been made possible for the inhabitants of other planets to bring forth their ships and their instruments and thus overcome fathomless space.

Agasha states that our spaceships of the future will no longer be propelled by either solid or liquid propellants. The power source will come from atomic power. It seems that when the atomic force is minimized into what Agasha calls the "greater force," the rate of magnetism is increased to a higher rate until eventually it comes into direct accord and blends its force with the magnetic current which permeates all space. Then when this point is reached, there is no time element at all from here to there. He says that it is very similar to turning on a switch. The moment you turn the switch on you have light; you have made the contact. The electric current has traversed from the light switch to the bulb in the center of the room in just a flash, and we don't think anything about it. It is the same with tapping the magnetic current.

However, dealing with this great magnetic current of space can be quite dangerous. If a spacecraft or a man's body were to be clothed by a certain element and then certain other conditions were met, it would be instantly transported to some other point in space and without the necessary knowledge could never possibly return to earth. Science fiction, you say? Agasha says that this is just the forerunner of things to come.

Visitors from the Etheric

In fact, these principles are very well known and understood by the human expression on many other planets, but the early stages of their experiments were not always successful. For instance, Agasha told the class one night about experiments that were conducted by a particular civilization on a certain planet many thousands of years ago. But the experiments did not work out satisfactorily, and the ships that were sent out into space never returned. The elements that they employed did not harmonize with the vibratorial waves of what we term "space," with the result that the ships never reached the atmosphere of the planet to which they were sent. Their destination happened to be our own planet Earth, incidentally. He did not further elaborate on the ultimate result of this particular space expedition. However, henceforth they employed other metals and other materials that were quite different from what they had used earlier, and this time the experiment worked. Each tiny particle of the materials that they used on their second attempt harmonized perfectly with the elements of the ether, and thus they were able to project themselves within the range of the planet Earth. Agasha concluded his talk by stating that after a suitable reconnaissance activity, they then returned successfully in the twinkling of an eye back into their own atmosphere after which they were then able to settle down most satisfactorily onto their own "earth" planet.

The human expression on many of these planets in solar systems beyond ours is far more advanced mechanically than we are at the present time. Agasha says that some planets have human expression whose eyesight is even thousands of times greater than ours. Some can even see the illumination of our own planet Earth. Its constantly changing aura, which varies from a bluish haze to a golden hue at times, has attracted the attention of many civilizations in adjacent systems. They are just as eager to learn about this earth that we live on as we are eager to learn about them. They are constantly "fooling around," trying to lower their frequency, and endeavoring to tune in on the earth's surface.

Agasha stated in the class of October 9, 1950, that there is a civilization on one planet in particular that being quite advanced mechanically has found out a good deal about our planet. Their inhabitants know of our mechanical advancement, and they are continually experimenting in order to make contact with us. Now of course, their language is different from any of our earth languages. They have different customs, they have different ideas, and their mode of living is entirely different. If we were to come face to face with these beings, we would not be able to understand them and they would not be able to understand us. This is true, of course, as far as the mortal contact is concerned. Agasha said that the only way that we could understand them, and they understand us as well, would be through the Universal language which would then mean reverting back into the spiritual planes of the Consciousness of Immensity. But communication on the physical level would be quite difficult.

Now these beings come very close to us within our stratosphere at times. They know how to project themselves through the magnetic currents of space. However they are in the flesh; they are in the material. They are highly evolved mechanically, far greater than we here upon Earth, and they want to observe. But these particular beings that Agasha was speaking about on that particular evening are not as highly evolved spiritually as some of the others, and in coming so close into our environment, a confusing force or motion is set up which they have to control. They are not able to function in the physical body according to the elements of the ether. It does not harmonize with their physical condition and if they were to step out into our atmosphere, they could not survive.

Whereas we are only in our primer with the use of atomic power, they employ it at all times. However, their instruments for generating atomic energy are extremely simple. These instruments are not large; as a matter of fact, they are rather small. Agasha said that they use certain tiny beads in the same manner that we use tubes on the earth plane. The electronic force that is set up is somehow converted to atomic energy, and the operation of these beads is comparatively simple. It is more like a bead within a bead and a bead within a bead. Through an intricate mechanism there is a certain atomic force set up in these beads that is perpetual. These tiny beads also throw off a certain rate of vibration. The beads that are within a bead then set up a vibration which attracts the magnetic current, and through this endeavor they can broadcast to any part of their earth planet in a very remarkable way. Each bead at the time seems to represent a certain frequency which can also bring into their spacecraft whatever they want to bring into manifestation. It is these tiny ray machines that are the secret behind their electronic broadcasts. What is electricity to us is spiritual magnetism to them. If we could reach their frequency and they could reach our frequency on our instruments, all would be well and good and they would establish contact. But it is not that simple; the difference in frequencies seems to be too great to overcome at the present time and the result is only static on our radios.

Space will not permit the reiterating of the fantastic amount of material that has been given on this and similar subjects in the Agashan classes during the past 25 years or so since the classes have been taped. The writer has simply gathered together a bit of material, here and there, in order to present the general philosophy expressed. However, it certainly is not to be construed that all of the strange lights and other strange things that have been observed in the skies during these past many years are spacecraft from other planets. Indeed not, in fact that particular aspect of the phenomena has been underplayed in the classes in recent years. The spacecraft explanation would probably explain only a minority of the sightings. Perhaps a larger part of the sightings should better be classified under the more general term called "etheric phenomena."

The Law of Cycles

In order to understand etheric phenomena, one must also understand one of the basic laws of the universe, and this law that we speak of is the law of cycles. An understanding of one requires an understanding of the other. At the end of every age or cycle, etheric phenomena always come into manifestation, and the present age is no exception.

All life, planets, and even the universe itself go through cycles. And when one cycle ends and another begins, there is usually no sharp, observable dividing line. Invariably the latter part of the preceding cycle will color and blend with the beginning of the forthcoming cycle, and certainly you cannot observe on the surface the difference between December 31 of one year and January 1 of the next year. The minute before midnight is much the same as the minute after midnight. Yet, each belongs to a different cycle.

It had long been prophesied down through the ages that the 20th century would bring forth the "latter days," a period spoken of in the Bible as being the days of judgment and other dire consequences. And we all know, the astronomers as well as the astrologers, that the Earth is now leaving the age of Pisces and entering the new age of Aquarius. This is due to the precession of the equinoxes in the eternal 26,000-

year cycle around the earth, but the exact moment of this changeover has not been universally agreed upon. In any event, we know that it too is in the 20th century. Consequently our own century becomes a blending of the two ages and partakes of the past as well as the future. Invariably there is much confusion as well as enlightenment during this period.

However, this is still not the entire story. Agasha states that there is yet another 7,000-year cycle, and this is beginning while the other is ending in this no doubt famous and all-important 20th century. It would certainly seem to be out of the ordinary as we have seen more progress—or perhaps we should more correctly say change—during our present 100-year cycle than we have seen in any other comparable period in our known history. The previous 7,000-year period was one of great strife, struggle, and turmoil for the planet Earth. However, Agasha says that the forthcoming 7,000-year cycle is one in which the earth will move into a completely new vibration of peace and harmony where Heaven will literally be established on Earth.

This new Golden Age is now suffering the agonies of its birth. Agasha set the exact date of this changeover as being June 6, 1965; however, as we stated earlier, there is no perceptible change at this precise point. There was an inner lull, but this inner experience did not filter down into the outer mortal consciousness of the average individual. It will not be until the year 2020 that we can safely say that we are then no longer influenced by the confusing vibrations of the previous age. In the meantime, we are still suffering through all that had been prophesied for these "latter days."

Strange Things That Are Seen in the Skies

Down through the centuries the Christians had long predicted that "strange things" would be seen in the latter days. Some had stated that Jesus would appear out in space and be seen coming out of the clouds to speak. However, the Agashan teachers state that this particular prophecy is not true. People have interpreted literally that which was only meant to be symbolical. But the prophecies of the strange things to be seen in the skies and on the land most emphatically are now coming to pass. These are natural phenomena which always occur when the ending of one 7,000-year cycle interpenetrates the beginning of a new 7,000-year cycle. That is the reason that this new cycle is called both the Psychic Age as well as the Space Age.

The Agashan teachers state that when Moses was on earth he brought this information unto his people when he spoke of the "latter days." Then when Kraio was on earth, both as Kraio in Egypt and then later as Jesus in Palestine, he also brought forth a similar message—the same as Agasha and even the others before him had done. Among other things, this message was that at the end of every 7,000-year cycle, the etheric planes of life will interpenetrate and conjunct the physical plane of life, and when this occurs, literally anything and everything can happen as strange etheric phenomena always occur in the ethers. The same thing happens at the ending of the lesser cycles, although it is not as intense. Thus those early prophets said that it would seem as though the world were coming to an end, but they certainly did not mean this literally.

Many of the strange things that are seen in the heavens are created through nature. They are caused by certain gases forming out in space which then condense and literally bring into manifestation and materialize that which exists in the etheric planes. But the phenomena do not last too long and soon they disappear from sight. Then too, a large part of that which is seen comes from our own astral world, strangely enough. Inventors in the astral plane are constantly experimenting and trying to produce phenomena in the physical plane. Phantom ships and sometimes even phantom automobiles have been created by these spirits of the anim world. These are usually replicas of that which did exist in the physical world at one time, and these materialized images of the past also soon return to whence they had come. And then finally, the phenomena are simply the result of a time-space warp when the astral plane vibrations momentarily conjunct the physical plane vibrations. This would explain how a spirit can be observed walking down the street and then seemingly vanishing into thin air. Sometimes it is a spirit dog that is caught up in the vibrations, and he undoubtedly is just as bewildered as the observer.

Thus we find that that which has universally come to be identified in these latter days as UFO (Unidentified Flying Objects) has many, many explanations. Probably the majority of the sightings of beings, animals, things—you name it—that momentarily come into visibility from the etheric planes of life can be quite accurately classified under the general term of etheric phenomena. As we have just pointed out, these etheric phenomena are produced either consciously or unconsciously by etheric beings, or they are produced as the spontaneous result of different planes of consciousness momentarily merging together so that for a few moments beings in the etheric worlds find themselves being observed by those on the physical or earth plane of life. The giant winged "Mothmen" that recently terrorized dozens of West Virginia residents undoubtedly fall under this heading. The phantom ships that apparently sailed right out of the 17th century into the present, authentic in every detail and even complete with crew, also fall under this category. All of these etheric phenomena have a rational explanation once the universe is understood in its many multidimensional concepts. Our physical existence is only a small fraction of all that is taking place within even a radius of just six feet around us.

On the other hand, probably the majority of the sightings of clearly defined saucer or cigar-shaped objects are in all probability what the average clear-thinking individual has come to accept them to be—simply spacecraft, either manned or unmanned, from other states of consciousness. However, it must be clearly understood that these spacecraft are not "physical" objects in the same sense that the American and

Russian spacecraft are "physical" objects. They have all come from the etheric realms of consciousness and are only visible when they lower their rate of vibration to the dense, physical plane level. True, some are projected by means of the magnetic currents of space from other physical planets similar to ours. But even these crafts from physical planets are not strictly "physical" spacecraft, inasmuch as they had to first travel through the etheric realms and then materialize once again from the anim kingdom into the atom world of Earth. Probably the vast majority of these spacecraft have no physical existence at all inasmuch as their home base is an etheric or spiritual planet. Again, they only momentarily become visible when they lower their rate of vibration.

The teachers of the Agasha Temple clearly discount the statements made by various individuals that they had gone for a "ride" in a flying saucer in their physical bodies. Without speaking disparagingly against any organization or individual making that claim, the Agashan teachers state that invariably the ride or the experience within the saucer was made while the individual had, unknowingly to his mortal mind, slipped into his astral or spiritual body. An individual having this experience would have no way of knowing that the body he was having the experience in was not his physical body. We are not talking now of the subjective dream state; we are talking of an obective experience in the spiritual body. The teachers say that life in the etheric realms is actually more "real" than life or experiences here in the physical plane. Of course, this is not necessarily the explanation for 100 percent of the experiences reported. But it will seem that almost anything not only can happen but most probably will happen sometime within this psychic or space age that we are now in.

Thus we bring to a close this brief discussion of the mysteries of time and space and travel therein. A correct explanation of each and every bit of phenomena observed within this vast multidimensional universe of ours would constitute an encyclopedia of encyclopedias, and the writer is sure that there is not enough paper in the world to print all of it—that is, presuming that we possessed the knowledge of it in the first place, and Agasha assures us that no one individual does. However, we can take solace in the fact that our chances for learning are greater now than they had been in the past inasmuch as the manifestations of etheric phenomena invariably increase at the end, or in the latter days, of each age. And that is precisely what we are in right now. Let us just remember that all planes of consciousness invariably will eventually intersect one another, sooner or later, as all worlds in the end result are ONE.

NOTES

1. Hannes Alfven, *Worlds-Antiworlds* (San Francisco, W. H. Freeman and Co., 1966) p. 7
2. Lincoln Barnett, *The Universe and Dr. Einstein* (Harper & Brothers, 1948) p. 14
3. Moberly & Jourdain, *An Adventure* (London, Faber and Faber, 1911 and 1955)
4. Jane Roberts, *Seth Speaks* (New Jersey, Prentice-Hall, Inc., 1972)
5. Manly P. Hall, *An Encyclopedic Outline* (Los Angeles, Philosophical Res. Soc., 1928) p. 157
6. Jacques Sadoul, *Alchemists and Gold* (New York, G. P. Putnam's Sons, 1972) p. 25
7. This translation is likewise taken from Sadoul's book. It was translated by the contemporary Adept, Fulcanelli.

CHAPTER TEN

THE GRAND FINALE

All the world's a stage,
And all the men and women merely players.
—William Shakespeare
As You Like It, Act II, Scene 7

A NUMBER of years ago, Agasha had so chosen to refer to these earthly classes today in the 20th century as the Grand Finale. Now what does he mean by the Grand Finale? The dictionary defines the term *grand finale* as being the concluding portion of a drama or performance, usually spectacular, and that which involves most or all of the prior actors or participants. It is the last act before the final curtain descends thus bringing to a conclusion a long and sometimes lengthy performance. All well and good. But the drama that Agasha is referring to has been going on for the incredible period of 7,000 years. This, you will have to admit, is not exactly a short production by any standard of measurement.

Now who are the actors in this drama? The answer is that they are you and you and you. True, you may have only played a minor role in your many lifetimes of earthly living, but nevertheless you are still a very important part of this great drama called life. For in addition to the hundreds of starring roles, every great life drama needs also its many thousands of supporting actors and actresses as well as the millions and sometimes even billions of extras and bit players in order to complete the production.

Now there have been many great life dramas produced on earth during the span of the past 7,000 years. Each individual drama has had its own particular story to tell, and each has had its own cast of characters. You undoubtedly have played roles in several of them. The individual histories of every country on the face of the earth are complete stories within themselves—separate chapters within the overall life of the planet. Likewise, so are the stories of the various races of mankind. Each and every one is a great saga of not only historic but sometimes legendary figures or events, and each is usually a narrative of heroic exploits in order to achieve some great cause.

The Search for Eternal Truth: The Greatest Life Drama of Them All

This great saga or life drama is sometimes called the Great Quest. It relates to the reestablishment upon this planet, once and for all, of the correct understanding of the Universal Consciousness God and of the correct relationship of mankind to this Universal Consciousness or Infinite State. This is the great saga that Agasha is referring to. It had its beginnings 7,000 years ago in the country of Austa, now known as Egypt, and it has continued uninterrupted down through the years manifesting itself through inspired prophets or seers in practically every civilized country upon the face of the globe at one time or another. Many of these prophets were unable to establish a firm foundation with the result that their teachings have not lived down in recorded history. Others we are vaguely aware of; and the teachings of still others, even though they have been preserved for posterity, these same teachings have been greatly misconstrued, mistranslated, and consequently misinterpreted.

Perhaps one of the first prophets who endeavored to clarify the religious concepts of his time was the Pharaoh Akhenaten, who for a brief period of time during Egypt's 3,000-year dark cycle reestablished the ancient wisdom once more. "Living in Truth" was his motto, and the disk of the sun became a symbol to represent the single supreme God Consciousness which gives forth of its life and its energies equally unto all. And, of course, we can certainly not forget the great prophets in the Bible who each in his own way tried to set down the truth as he saw it. Then later, just prior to the Christian era, we come upon the great philosophers of Greece—Pythagoras, Plato, Socrates, just to mention a few. And going into the Far East we find Gautama Buddha in India, Confucius in China, and many others.

Now what do all of these individuals have in common? The answer is that they were all chosen by the Universal Consciousness God to return unto mankind, to give forth what they had to give forth, and to play and enact out their own individual roles in the best way that they could so that the consciousness of mankind could gradually be elevated and awakened into a higher state. But Agasha states that all of us are equally important unto the Universal Consciousness insofar as we are all supposed to become our own individual Savior so to speak. Thus it can be readily seen that no one, absolutely no one, is playing an insignificant role in this great drama that men call life. It is, indeed, "the greatest show on earth."

Those that were fortunate enough to live various lives during the great 2,000-year Peace Period in Austa then went on to become the teachers and the inspired ones as they would incarnate into the land of Egypt under the pharaohs. They tried to break down the barriers as they would encounter them but, unfortunately, many of these inspired individuals became controlled by the lower forces. Many were born into a slave environment and thus became enslaved. "Why is this so?" you will ask. The average individual might say, "Well, if I had peace for so many lives during the 2,000-year Peace Period, then why would I have to come back into Egypt to be a slave?" Of course, this is not true for all; it is only true for some. Many were born into the royalty or the priesthood and lived fantastic lives in the magnificent grandeur of that fabulous era. But those that had built up negative karma during the Peace Period, those that had allowed the demon-self to take over occasionally, finally suffered the consequences of such wrong action and were born into a slave environment. Thus they still had karma to pay and lessons to be learned. Of course, some were born into slavery merely to give themselves an opportunity to help their fellow slaves, or to hurdle the obstacles that would be placed in their path in order for them to become ever so much stronger spiritually.

Others then left the Egyptian scene and incarnated into other countries of the civilized world—Arabia, Palestine, Greece, or wherever their soul desired new experiences. Some even went into the Orient and became enmeshed in the life dramas of China, India, or Tibet. But nevertheless it was always for the same purpose—to bring forth enlightenment unto suffering humanity. Just think of all the lives that you, the reader, have had during these periods! If you were on the spiritual path, you were most certainly helping others awaken to the consciousness that you had already awakened within yourself. Then again, if you were not on the spiritual path, you were perhaps only "motivating" on the physical plane, but in any event you were playing out that particular role that your soul had cast you into, be it star, supporting actor, or bit player.

Now what were Agasha and the other Ascended Masters doing during this period? Remember, we are only now approaching the so-called Christian era, and we have not yet come to the time when that great Master Teacher was to make his appearance. Let us say that the date is approximately 20 B.C. Cleopatra, the last Queen of Egypt, had been defeated some ten years earlier and Egypt was now nothing more than a Roman province. Even the great Roman Empire had not yet been born, as Imperial Rome was technically still a republic under Augustus Caesar. The civilization of the entire Western world seemed to be at the crossroads between two great eras, and the situation seemed most appropriate to the Ascended Masters governing the planet to instigate a new spiritual impetus.

Agasha states that the Ascended Adepts in the Spiritual Centers are always extremely busy watching over mankind. There is never a lax period, and the ages before the advent of Christianity were no exception. Also Agasha had returned in spirit many times to observe struggling humanity, and in this pre-Christian age he was always lending his power and his assistance wherever he could. He was most impressed with the Grecian period, and one evening in June of 1951 he told the class the following little story.

"Blessed disciples," he started out, "you understand that Greece in the beginning of its civilization was truly a great civilization, and they had everything there that was beautiful. Their works of art and their corporeal activities were magnificent, and all of this, of course, was a takeoff from what we had once had on the great continent of Atlantis. Now you cannot associate the Greece of today with the Grecian period that I am in reference to; no, you cannot do that. Before you can understand it properly you have to go back and realize the romance of Greece. I can recall the picture so clearly of a certain beautiful temple on the hilltop. Perhaps we should say it was on the side of the mountain and it was very beautiful. It was most picturesque as the sun would rise and then peek over this great structure, shining down on it so beautifully, and the light and the wisdom and the love projected by the thoughts of the philosophers who studied in this great temple enhanced it even further.

"I would project myself into their vibration occasionally and tune in, as it were, to their conversations and their discussions. Yes, these were very learned philosophers, and I was especially intrigued because their discussions were so very similar to the discussions that we had carried out not only in Austa, but way back into the Atlantean consciousness as well. It was a pity, I remember thinking on one occasion, that we could not right then and there reestablish the universal understanding of the God Consciousness. I knew that if I endeavored to make the call at that particular time that the rank and file of the people would not come. In fact, the majority really could not come as they were not ready. The 7,000-year cycle had not yet closed in upon itself, and I knew that the time would not be ripe for these things to be perpetuated from generation to generation until still another 2,000 years had come and gone. But outwardly I was tempted to make the call anyway, as I was human enough to believe that perhaps, just perhaps, it might be the right time."

Thus through the thoughts expressed by Agasha on that particular evening back in 1951, we can gain a glimpse of the thinking that prevailed among the Ascended Masters in the period just prior to the Christian era. It is evident that many of the Teachers thought that another attempt should be made to bring forth the higher teachings to the ordinary lay mind of the outer world because that is just what happened. We must remember that the directors and the producers of the great life drama that was to be enacted out on this planet are the Ascended Masters within its governing body. And even though those Teachers knew that only a partial success would be obtained, the experiment—and that was just what it was—was set into motion with the reembodiment of the Ascended Master Kraio once again into the flesh. This Master Teacher had previously ascended after a magnificent life as Kraio in the 2,000-year Peace Period. Agasha has said that it was through Kraio's great love and compassion for mankind that he volunteered for this new assignment; and thus it came to pass that at the crossroads between two great eras or ages, Jesus of Nazareth came to be born.

Was this experiment successful? To a great extent it was; for through the life and teachings of this great Master Teacher, the religious thought of the entire Western world was to be changed for almost 2,000 years. The Ascended Masters then, working as a group, were able to send out the call and thus attract unto them those who later became instrumental in establishing the Christian Church. Thus we can basically say that this grand experiment was partially successful.

Why do we say it was only partially successful? It was only partially successful because the message that was actually given by this great Master Teacher has been misinterpreted for one reason or another. We must remember that the New Testament of the Christian Bible today is only an "edited" version of the considerably larger number of writings that were originally available. The emperor Constantine, after he had established Christianity as being the official religion of the Holy Roman Empire, ordered all of the documents that were then in the possession of the various monasteries of the time brought to a general assembly that he had convened in 325 A.D. called the Council of Nicaea. It was here that it was established which of the numerous doctrines were to be accepted and which were to be rejected. Those writings and doctrines that were rejected by this "learned council" were henceforth destroyed and no longer taught. The great principle of reincarnation fell into this category, and all references to it were promptly "red-lined" or rejected. And yet this vastly important principle was the very basis of the teachings as taught by the Master Jesus! For this reason, as well as for many other reasons, the correct teachings as originally given by this Master Teacher are no longer taught today in the Orthodox Church, and it makes no difference whether that church is Greek, Roman Catholic, or Protestant.

Will this misinterpretation of his true teachings last forever? Agasha states that the answer to this question is an emphatic no, for right there today in the vicinity of Jerusalem is an underground vault. In this little vault there are several scrolls, very well preserved, and they were placed therein during or shortly after the time that the Master walked the earth. There is one scroll in particular, Agasha goes on to say, that when it is translated and published will actually explode all of the erroneous religious theories that have been concocted by mankind for generation after generation. The reason that he can be so explicit in making this statement is that this particular scroll or manuscript is written in such a way that it absolutely cannot be misinterpreted. These scrolls are very well protected, by the way, and will be released and consequently found by the outer world at the right and proper time. Furthermore, they are not like some of the other parchments—which in the past have crumbled as they would hit the air or be handled to any great extent—for these scrolls had been treated long ago with certain oils that will preserve them for an indefinite and lengthy period.

With the advent of Christianity, the main stage of our 7,000-year life drama now moves into Europe. Rome has now become the center of the Western world and will remain so for 500 years. The all powerful Caesar of Rome has replaced the mighty Pharaoh of Egypt and the Pope has replaced the High Priest. Otherwise everything will remain pretty much the same for the first half of the millennium or until the fall of the Roman Empire. Then at the close of this great era, the European dark ages will plunge Europe into darkness as far as spiritual progress is concerned, and for 700 years or up to about the year 1200 A.D., expansion of consciousness in Europe will be brought to a standstill, for the Ascended Masters will have focused their attention elsewhere. This attention will bring daylight to the Arab countries; and in that part of the world the arts, the sciences, and the exploration of consciousness will all continue to flourish.

With the attention of the Ascended Masters once more reverting back to Europe somewhere in the latter part of the 12th century, our European sleeping Goddess now arouses herself from her slumber, rubs her eyes, and starts pouring forth her great wisdom and consciousness once again into the minds of men. For the next 800 years up to the present day, Europe will see more advancement in art, science, alchemy, occultism, and the study of philosophy than it had ever known before. But alas, acting as if in opposition to this great outpouring of consciousness, the mortal mind of Europe will also cause its nations to continue to war upon themselves and to even become much more advanced in the art of destruction as well. It will not be until the end of the 20th century and the completion of the final act of our 7,000-year life drama, the Grand Finale, that the Goddess of not only Europe but also of the entire world will once more be freed from the scourges of wars—wars caused by man's seemingly endless struggle for power—which have kept her in bondage for such a long period of time.

The analogy of the sleeping god or goddess is not new. Agasha states that we have to awaken the God within, the Soul, the Infinite State—call it what you will—in order that we may receive valuable information from the source that will in turn enable us to live our lives and play the role the way we are supposed to play it in order to carry out the Divine Plan. Now the Divine Plan has previously been established within the mind of God. This means then that all of the characters that men have played since the beginning of time also have been created by God. In other words, God becomes the writer of all the life dramas and creates all of the characters for men to play. So it makes no real difference what role we play in life, be it prince, princess, or scullery maid; but the important thing is how well we play it.

Now we are aware from the history of mankind that it took great souls of strong character to play the leading roles, and this applies equally as well to science, art, philosophy, or government. Where would we be in science today if inept or unqualified actors were cast in the roles of a Sir Isaac Newton, or a Kepler, or an Einstein? And where would we be if the great souls who had earned the right to play these roles had not tapped the God Consciousness within? In both cases they would have not brought forth what they did, and the world would certainly be the loser. Where would we be in art if a Leonardo da Vinci, or a Michelangelo, or any of the great artists of the Renaissance for that matter had been negligent in their duties to God and to mankind? We shudder to think of the thought.

But the same thing can also be said of the great generals, kings, or other great leaders of men who by their might and power have brought forth freedom and good government into their respective nations. Yes indeed, it took strong souls to play these roles. But we must also remember that the race karma of each race or nation must necessarily dictate the character of its leaders. If the people of a nation had not earned the right to have good government, it must necessarily follow that only poor leaders of weak character will reign. It is Divine Providence, that ultimate law of justice, that decides the quality of a nation's leadership, be it good or bad.

Let us study the case of Napoleon Bonaparte, for instance. Here was a man who arose from somewhat ordinary circumstances to the position where he commanded the destinies of all of Europe at one point in his career. And he arose at a time when history needed him the most. The French government was in a state of anarchy after the French revolution, and it took an extremely strong leader to restore order and authority after this devastating period. Yet he eventually died in exile, with his dream of founding a United States of Europe lost forever in his lifetime. But even though he did not accomplish his ultimate goal, he still left France with laws which for the most part still endure. But was he supposed to accomplish his ultimate goal? More than likely he was supposed to fail, as mankind had not yet reached the point for such a humanitarian and idealistic government as Napoleon had in mind. In any event, history will ultimately be played out the way it is written in the Consciousness of God.

Agasha tells us of an interesting incident in this man's life which tends to illustrate the tremendous stresses which can build up within the consciousness of any actor who is playing out and living a starring role of destiny. This incident occurred in Egypt during his Egyptian expedition and campaign. Now the East had always fascinated Napoleon, and he realized inwardly that Egypt was one of the keys of the world. So it was with great expectation that he went into Egypt, but when he gazed up at the Great Pyramid as he came very close to it, he found that it annoyed him. Why is this? Now strangely enough, Agasha says, the tremendous destiny that this man inherited had actually marked his outer self with a sort of inferiority complex. Now no one on the surface knew this, for outwardly he compensated for it by trying to conquer and express his superiority over anything that might appear before him as monstrous. Thus he would unconsciously have it in for large armies, mobs of people, or simply anyone of great stature who was a member of the opposition. In fact, it was really this quality which enabled him to accomplish what he did. The word *impossible* was a word that was not in his dictionary. So therefore, the very size itself of the Great Pyramid triggered off within himself a sense of annoyance.

But Agasha told the class one night that the true cause of the annoyance was from an inner recollection of the events and the wars and the confusion that had transpired right there in Egypt during one or more of his previous lives. In fact, this awareness surfaced while he was in seclusion within the King's Chamber, and the psychic experience that he experienced during that brief period in the King's Chamber impressed him for the rest of his life. He would speak of it to no one, simply saying after being asked, "No, what's the use? You would never believe me." But nevertheless, before he left Egypt he still went out and took out his frustrations upon the hapless Sphinx. The tremendous stresses that had built up within his consciousness from actions in the past fairly forced him into this action. Yes, Napoleon tried to destroy that monument, but all he could do was deface it. An unruly and revolutionary life that he had lived during the time of the pharaohs, when he had tried to seize power unwisely, came back to his consciousness to haunt him, and all he could do at this late date to relieve these very powerful emotions of revenge was to strike back at the symbol of that which had caused his downfall.

All of this then leads us up to the thought of how much free will a person actually has. It would seem that if history has been more or less written ahead of time, the life of a very powerful leader such as Napoleon would be pretty much crystallized insofar as the major events that would be encountered and the probable outcome of these events are concerned. In other words, his individual free will would be to a large extent controlled by the combined karma of the millions of individuals making up his kingdom, and he would be literally compelled at certain times to act in a certain manner. But in the case of an insignificant foot soldier, the situation would be reversed. The only karmic conditions affecting his actions would be his own karma and possibly that of a few others. And if that particular foot soldier decided to defect to the other side, it would not affect the final outcome of the battle to any great extent. But let the general or the commander in chief defect to the other side, and the result would be chaotic for the nation. Consequently, it would seem on the surface that the insignificant foot soldier or bit player would have far more "free will" than the emperor or star.

Agasha has said many times that the advanced individual lets the soul take over and dictate his actions in life. And the soul, knowing beforehand what is to be achieved in that life, then guides its outer mortal self into actions that will allow him to follow the script and play the role the way it is supposed to be played. But the unlearned or unawakened individual who is run completely by his mortal or outer mind can miss the cue, so to speak, and thus bring about disaster not only to himself but to others, and quite possibly end up in an entirely different situation than what the soul had previously planned.

The mortal self can be compared to a dog on a leash, and the soul then is the master holding the leash. The master will allow the dog to do pretty much as he pleases within a radius of six feet or so of his guiding hands, but when the time comes to move in a different direction he jerks the leash and the dog dutifully follows its master. However, this is the condition only with the awakened individual who has allowed the soul to take over. The unlearned individual may be compared with the dog which had broken its leash and is running uncontrolled in any direction it pleases until it is either hit by an automobile or apprehended by the pound.

Perhaps this is the reason that only seasoned players, actors who had had a great deal of experience in following the leads of the soul, are given the starring roles in life. There is simply too much at stake to cast an unseasoned player, one who cannot follow the leads from the soul, into a role where if he were to play it wrongly, it would not only ruin his own life but also the lives of millions of other players.

Students of reincarnation who had traced the successive lives of various individuals either through hypnosis, reverie, or other occult practices have been amazed at the pattern that seems to develop. Edgar Cayce revealed a good deal of information in this direction whereby he showed that certain causes that were set up in one life were then carried out in still another life, almost repeating the same pattern until the lesson is learned. Consequently, it is not "odd" when we learn that the same soul or groups of souls have sometimes incarnated into similar occupations or conditions over a series of lives. This is especially true when we study the rulers of the lands, those individuals whose lives affected millions and millions of other souls.

One of the students at the Agasha Temple through the help of her teacher was able to track down some of the previous lives of two particular souls who were somewhat instrumental in affecting the destiny of Europe. The story (as far as she was able to go) began way back during the time of the Trojan War in the 13th century B.C. Here we find Achilles, the bravest, handsomest, and swiftest in the army of Agamemnon for nine years ravaging the country around the City of Troy, and taking twelve cities in all until he ultimately was killed by an arrow in his vulnerable heel. All this is recorded faithfully or otherwise by Homer in the *Iliad.* And in Virgil's *Aeneid,* a sequel to the legend of Troy, we find the story of Aeneas who was a favorite of the gods and who was destined to rule the surviving Trojans after the war.

Now the interesting thing about all of this is the eventual destiny of these two great heroes. For instance: we find Achilles returning again as Alexander the Great, King of Macedonia (356–323 B.C.), then a little later as Herod the Great, King of Judaea (73–4 B.C.), and finally after a few other incarnations ending up as Henry V, King of England (1387–1422 A.D.). What a series of lives for any one individual! But if our thesis holds true that only well-seasoned actors are given the starring roles to play, this would not be unusual.

The life patterns sent forth from the role of Aeneas are just as imposing. The great soul who played this role evidently played it correctly for he later was given the role of Philip II, King of Macedonia (382–336 B.C.), and which was followed by Herod Antipas, Tetrarch of Galilee and the Herod of Biblical fame (reigned 4 B.C.–A.D. 39), and then finally several lifetimes later the role of Henry VI, King of England (1421–1471 A.D.). And the interesting point is that in all three of these lives he is either the father or the son of the soul who had originally played the role of Achilles. Now where are these two great souls today? If they have not ascended, you can rest assured that they are right back here in the 20th century, living out another life somewhere on the earth, and attending the Grand Finale of this 7,000-year life drama.

Now let us return once more to the Ascended Masters that are directing this drama. The purpose of this entire 7,000-year cycle of lives to be lived by mankind upon this planet is to prepare it for the new and higher vibrations that will be prevalent in the new Golden Age of enlightenment that is practically upon us now. Mankind has been put through its paces, so to speak, to prove its ability and to show its skill in handling almost any kind of a situation. Agasha has said over and over and over again that wars and things of that nature will be a thing of the past. Those of us who incarnate in the new age will hardly recognize the planet, it being so different from what we had experienced during the past ages of darkness. The great Atlantean Consciousness will have then fully reincarnated and once more reestablished itself upon the planet Earth. And the great Ascended Masters, those operating out of the Spiritual Centers as well as those from Immensity, can take the entire credit for its apparent transformation.

Occultism: An Eight Hundred Year Review

A brief look at the growth and unfoldment of occultism, alchemy, mysticism, and spiritual philosophy during the past eight hundred years would now be in order. And in this look we shall see how the Masters have gradually revealed from time to time through various inspired and enlightened individuals different aspects of what is known as the hidden mysteries of life. These teachings were all given in such a way as to set the stage and build the foundation for their final clarification here in the 20th century in the Grand Finale of our great life drama.

Perhaps one of the most significant revelations made by these Adepts during this period is summed up when we embrace the entire subject of alchemy. This is sometimes called the Hermetic Art, and the "Great Work" then is the search for and the final attainment of the elixir of life which is contained within a mysterious substance called the philosopher's stone. But aside from the practical application of transmuting any base metal into gold, the Great Work is in reality the purification of man himself in order that he also may become as spiritual gold and thus ascend into the higher consciousness.

Among the names of the early alchemists of the 13th century are Albertus Magnus, Arnold of Villanova, and Raymond Lully. These men were all graduates of one of the greatest schools of learning of its day—the University of

Montpellier. The 14th and 15th centuries carried the art a little further in the works of Nicholas Flamel and Basil Valentine, and the 16th century developed its medical aspects in the person of Paracelsus who is also called the father of modern medicine. But the intriguing individuals whom we encounter as we flip through the pages of any history of alchemy came into manifestation in the 17th and 18th centuries. These ageless Adepts who perfected the art in its spiritual sense are known only to us today by such names as the Cosmopolite, Philalethes, Lascaris, and last but not least, the Comte de Saint-Germain. Their lives are as mysterious as their works.

Mysticism and the study of spiritual philosophy also came into its share of spiritual revelation during these past 800 years. The 13th and 14th centuries gave us mystics such as Meister Eckhart and Thomas a Kempis whose doctrines included elements of the Kabbalah and hermeticism. In the 16th century, magicians such as Cornelius Agrippa experimented in the art of invoking spirits and other forms of ceremonial magic, and occult scholars such as John Dee brought invisible influences into manifestation through the art of crystal gazing. The 16th century also gave us Jakob Bohme, the great illuminate of Gorlitz and one of the most profound mystics of our time. His numerous writings leave us proof that he indeed was in direct communication with the Infinite State. It is only when we come to Emanuel Swedenborg in the 18th century, that we find another individual as prolific in spiritual vision and in the ability to describe the reality of the spiritual realms. However Swedenborg, in addition to his intense spiritualistic explorations, was also a learned and respected scientist, inventor, engineer, mining assessor, astronomer, and physicist. His numerous scientific papers on a wide variety of topics are an enigma when we compare them with the profound spiritualistic revelations of his later years.

The hand of the Ascended Masters in the Spiritual Centers becomes quite evident as the guiding force behind the beginnings of the Rosicrucian movement in the 17th century. Mysterious documents proclaiming the existence of a hidden brotherhood of scholars and Adepts who were united in teaching the deepest mysteries of life gradually began to be circulated. These Brothers of the Rosy Cross were said to be invisible and to give forth their teachings from an "invisible college"—a building with wings which existed nowhere and yet united the entire secret movement. Most of the documents were printed anonymously because of the religious prejudice which existed at the time, and only a few brave souls would openly identify themselves with this movement. Among its secret supporters we find Robert Fludd, Thomas Vaughan, and that great master of literature, Sir Francis Bacon.

Moving now into the 19th century, we find the birth of many other new movements as prejudice gradually gave way to tolerance and enlightenment. Even though such prolific and skillful proponents of occultism as Alphonse-Louis Constant (Eliphas Levi) were at first imprisoned for their publications, the latter half of the century brought forth considerable freedom for the expression of new religious thought and ideas. The philosophy of modern Spiritualism was brought to public knowledge with the publication of *The Principles of Nature*[1] by Andrew Jackson Davis, the Poughkeepsie seer, who would be destined to publish 27 different works during the course of his lifetime. And all of this began just about the same time that the Fox sisters offered physical proof of the phenomena with the spirit raps and knockings in their cottage at Hydesville, New York in 1848.

But it was not until the last quarter of the 19th century that the Masters moved into high gear, so to speak, with the establishment of the Theosophical Society in 1875. The Master Morya, working in conjunction with the Master Koot Hoomi Lal Singh, became the powers behind the mediumship of the great Russian sphinx, Helena Petrovna Blavatsky, and for the rest of the century up to and including the first half of the 20th century this great movement poured forth its light through its many inspired teachers and publications.

Ceremonial magic along with other previously hidden secrets of the occult sciences also came into the front once more with the establishment of the Hermetic Order of the Golden Dawn in 1887. This organization, although it always preferred to shroud itself in a cloak of mystery, exerted a greater influence on the development of modern occultism than most people realize. Many leading members of society including writers, philosophers, poets, and others became its advocates, and all went well until inner friction within the mortal minds of its outer leaders ultimately closed the Order. However, perhaps this is all in order as the world is now the wiser with the publication of all of its previously hidden secret lore and inner teachings.[2]

All of the above now formed the foundation for the thought, philosophically speaking, that existed in the minds of the thinkers in the Western world at the beginning of our present 20th century. Much had been revealed, and the foundation for the Grand Finale was almost established. However, there were still a few more important acts in our philosophical life drama yet to be enacted out and unfolded prior to the Grand Finale and the subsequent close of this particular performance or show.

Among these acts was a seemingly insignificant scene that was enacted out on April 8, 9, and 10, 1904, in the city of Cairo, Egypt. An etheric Being by the name of Aiwass had dictated a 65 page book to a well-known occultist of the day by the name of Aleister Crowley. He patiently transcribed the entire contents in longhand, in three separate sessions, while the very audible "voice" dictated the words from behind him. This book was titled *The Book of the Law*[3] and later became the main foundation for the many voluminous works that this very talented and somewhat infamous mystic later produced. Be that as it may, it is still a very important part of occult literature if its contents are studied symbolically and cabalistically and not literally.

But this was only the beginning. The Rosicrucian movement came into full fruition with the founding of not only one, but three separate and distinct Orders: one founded by R. Swinburne Clymer in Quakertown, Pa., another founded by Max Heindel in Oceanside, Calif., and still another founded by H. Spencer Lewis in San Jose, Calif. Freemasonry continued to flourish world-wide with its many and diverse Orders, Degrees, and Lodges. Theosophy poured forth its teachings through the inspired leadership of Annie Besant after the death of Madame Blavatsky, and through the prolific writings of other noted Theosophists such as C. W. Leadbeater, J. Krishnamurti, Geoffrey Hodson, A. E. Powell, and many others. And many, many other occult schools blossomed into being such as the Arcane School headed by Alice A. Bailey and a Master known only as the Tibetan, Anthroposophy with Rudolf Steiner, Astara with Earlyne and Robert Chaney, the Self-Realization Fellowship with Paramhansa Yogananda, Soulcraft with William Dudley Pelley, the Temple of the "I Am" with Guy W. Ballard, and the University of Science and Philosophy with Walter and Lao Russell, just to name a few.

Other inspired philosophers and teachers, although they did not necessarily found a particular school, gave the world a great deal of light, wisdom, and inspiration with their many published works. The list is staggering, but a cursory list of those individuals who have added to and enhanced the philosophical thinking of the Western world during the first half of our present century would certainly have to include Carl Gustav Jung. His massive research into the collective unconscious of mankind has changed the thinking of psychologists throughout the world. And the insight of George Ivanovitch Gurdjieff, which later was enhanced through the writings of P. D. Ouspensky and Claude Bragdon, also cannot be excluded. We can say the same for Harold Waldwin Percival who learned how to tap the Supreme Intelligence within his being and reach Consciousness itself. His great masterpiece titled *Thinking and Destiny*[4] was dictated directly to him from that Consciousness, and from

1904 to 1917 he published the 25 volumes of *The Word.*[5] The list would certainly not be complete without including the name of Manly Palmer Hall. His *Encyclopedic Outline of Masonic, Hermetic, Quabbalistic and Rosicrucian Symbolical Philosophy,* which is otherwise known as "The Big Book,"[6] was first published in 1928; and even though he has authored many other books, this huge volume undoubtedly will become his masterpiece. Aside from its literary content which sums up what is known as the Ancient Wisdom, the volume itself is also a work of art.

Great strides were also made during the first half of the century in the use of clairvoyance as an investigative tool. Both Geoffrey Hodson in his *Fairies at Work and Play*[7] as well as Flower A. Newhouse in her *Natives of Eternity*[8] give us vivid portrayals of what they were able to observe, through the splendid use of their clairvoyant vision, while watching these denizens of the Angelic Kingdoms go about their daily business. Annie Besant and C. W. Leadbeater, working as a team, concentrated their efforts in studying the nucleus of the atomic structures of the chemical elements. Earlier, they had made the amazing discovery that the clairvoyant faculty of the human being, when exercised in the appropriate direction, was actually ultra-microscopic in its power. The full result of their investigations was ultimately published in an amazing volume titled *Occult Chemistry,*[9] and were it not for an unfortunate conclusion arising out of mistaking the hydrogen molecule for the hydrogen atom, the elements observed would dovetail beautifully with the chemical element table as now accepted by science.

Perhaps it is in order to also bring up at this time that this amazing super-intelligence buried within man can also be used to analyze almost anything in life—you name it. The learned occultist Arthur Edward Waite came upon this important principle quite early in his career, and he used it to explore magic, theosophy, freemasonry, and all forms of symbology. And perhaps some of the most important items he left to posterity are the results of his investigations into the correct symbology relative to the Tarot cards. Thus the investigations that Waite and Pamela Colman Smith (both were members of the magical Order of the Golden Dawn, incidentally) carried out during the first decade of our century leave us today with the only available Tarot deck with the correct symbolism vividly portrayed on each and every card of both the Major and Minor Arcana.[10]

The first 50 years of the 20th century also produced as many psychics, mediums, sensitives—call them what you will—as there were produced during the 50 years before the turn of the century. The only difference was that the phenomena connected with modern Spiritualism were so thoroughly investigated during the latter half of the 19th century, that that which occurred in the 20th century, being no longer new and sensational, went by largely unnoticed by the average lay mind. Those that wished to believe in the psychic manifestations that they had either witnessed or read about, then pursued the subject further and enhanced their lives by so doing. Those that chose not to believe in it, or even investigate it, then dismissed the entire subject from their minds as if it had never happened. And so it is with the lives of men.

But mediumship had not been the entire answer. Communication with the astral world will not necessarily bring enlightenment, for in that state of consciousness there is a conglomeration of ideas relative to religion and philosophy that is quite distorted. We must remember that just because one is on the spirit side of life does not necessarily mean that he is enlightened. As in the physical plane, many in the astral world have much to unlearn for they had not taken the initiative to find out what life is all about.

Philosophy as It Stands Today

We come then to the state of learning as it existed in the minds of men at the close of the first half of the 20th century. All of the knowledge of recorded history, which dates back some 5,000 years, is now available to the seeker within the libraries of mankind. But if one were to read and absorb all of this knowledge, or even a fraction of it, he would most certainly be a confused individual. For in those libraries is a conglomeration of *all* of the thinking of mankind for the past 5,000 years, and of course this includes many diametrically opposite viewpoints on practically everything.[11]

But this is a 7,000-year life drama that we are reenacting or living through, remember. There is still a span of 2,000 years of unrecorded history that is very important to the Agashan life drama, and we have yet to experience the Grand Finale, or at least we had not done so back in the year of 1950. As stated earlier, the Agashan life drama relates to the reestablishment upon this planet of the correct understanding of the Universal Consciousness God and of the correct relationship of mankind to this Universal Consciousness or Infinite State. Therefore, inasmuch as this has not yet occurred, the Grand Finale or the final act of this great life drama becomes so all important.

The Grand Finale means then the clarification and the rectification of the many statements made by the philosophers down through the ages and even in our present generation regarding Scriptures and matters of truth. Many of these statements have been misinterpreted, many misquoted, and the basic meaning of a great number of them has been completely lost in translation. However, Agasha states that he most certainly does not wish to impeach the Bible, but rather he wishes to explain it and give it the correct interpretation.

For instance, many incidents in the Bible that are rather dramatic in their recording can be explained today by the laws of psychic phenomena. A few incidents come to mind such as the voice speaking to Moses from the burning bush: an incident of direct or independent voice; the case of Jesus walking upon the water: a demonstration of levitation; the reappearance of Jesus after the crucifixion: a case of materialization of the spirit. History has recorded many other incidents of these phenomena, and they even occur today, not only in the seance room, but they also might manifest in one's own home or garden.

Agasha always speaks in a very simple manner, and he says that the many statements and theories set forth by the Ascended Masters, both in this class as well as in other classes, not only can be proved but eventually shall be proved. All psychic phenomena will eventually be accepted scientifically, he goes on to say, but this does not mean to imply that orthodox religion will necessarily go along with science, because out of necessity science will explode some of the religious statements expounded by many of the religionists of today.

Now all that we have given in this chapter is certainly not given to imply that Agasha is setting himself up as an authority; definitely not. In fact the contrary is so. Agasha still has his own teacher; and so it goes, on and on, as one progresses always upwards and onwards to newer and greater heights until eventually he passes through the distant far-off reaches of the world called Immensity—and joins the great Pillars of Light. Agasha states that no teacher would ever claim that he had reached the Ultimate, for if he did, it would not be true. There is always a teacher on the path ahead to light the way and still another grand finale to mark the close of a yet higher state of consciousness.

So then we find that the Grand Finale certainly does *not* mean that it is the end of learning; it is merely a clarification of that which had been previously learned. It means only that the seeker in life will have correct information available to him. Then what he does with these truths will depend only upon his ability to understand what he is embracing.

The Grand Finale may also be likened to the last act of a mystery drama where the players unmask and take their bows, the detective exposes the villain and frees the hero and heroine, and all previously unsolved mysteries are resolved. In other words, everybody lives happily ever after once they have found the truth and been set free. Each one is then able to study every facet of life in its entirety, analyze all contributing factors, and thus be consistent, patient, and learned as he reaps the rewards gained from a lifetime of learning and staying on the spiritual path.

Very well. But how does one find and experience the Grand Finale? You will say that what we say here is all well and good, but after all, there are many schools in the occult field and each expresses its own opinion of life and the way to live it. Each school has its own ideas regarding evolution, life after death, the astral planes, the celestial sphere, the Absolute, and on and on through every question that might arise. These schools vary a great deal in the information that they present in answer to these questions; furthermore, the questions are sometimes answered intellectually in words and terminologies that only tend to confuse the issues and make them difficult to be understood by the average lay mind. This being a universe of law and order, you would be inclined to believe that for all of the questions there must be one definite and positive answer without any equivocation. If many schools vary in their teachings, and if there is no clear-cut approach to truth, then you will say that there must be something wrong.

And this is precisely correct. There has been something wrong, as far as the average individual is concerned, for these past many thousands of years. And there will always be something wrong for that individual until he awakens the Infinite State within his own Being and then comes into the Knowing. This is called the Grand Awakening, and this experience awaits each and every individual when he arrives at his own Grand Finale. Then he no longer believes; he simply knows. The truth itself has set him free. He has then become his own Avatar and no longer needs to embrace false teachings or to question whether or not a particular teacher is speaking the truth.

However, the Ascended Masters, being in tune with the Universal God Consciousness, realize that all things work in cycles. There is a time for sowing and there is a time for reaping. Likewise, there is a time for the average mortal consciousness to be held in ignorance, and there is a time for the average mortal consciousness to become enlightened. The age of enlightenment has been called the Golden Age, the Space Age, the Psychic Age—call it what you will—and it is upon us now, or at least the first rays of its golden sun are now piercing through the spiritual darkness that has enveloped this planet for many thousands of years.

Consequently, if this be so, the Grand Finale of the life drama of the previous age must of necessity also be now upon us. Now there are many life dramas in operation, or perhaps we should say sub-dramas within the overall general life drama. For instance: there is a life drama in government, a life drama in science, a life drama in the arts, and a life drama in spiritual philosophy, just to mention a few. And if this latter half of the 20th century be the time period set aside for the Grand Finales of these various life dramas, it follows then that many famous individuals in history have now returned to participate and take their final bows before ascending into a higher consciousness.

The Caesars are back, the Pharaohs have returned, the Atlantean scientists are bringing forth that which did exist in Atlantis, and perhaps the Greek philosophers are either students or teachers today in our universities. Do we not see the signs of this all around us? Is not the world now going through a greater change and at a faster pace than it had ever done before? The answer seems to be self evident.

But it is the life drama in spiritual philosophy that is of special concern to us now. And this great drama is unfolding at a tremendous pace. Everywhere, we can see new spiritual insight springing forth, and this is particularly true of our youth. Many of the younger generation are simply not following the dictates and outmoded concepts of their parents, and paperback editions of the teachings of the great philosophers are selling as they never had before. Such subjects as life after death, reincarnation, and other heretofore "taboo" subjects are now being openly discussed on television and other media, and people are awakening to the spiritual call that is now being generated from their soul.

The Eastern and Western Classes

Even though the Grand Finale of the philosophical life drama is universal in character and is being produced through many centers and a great number of inspired individuals, the Agashan teachers state that the nucleus or core of this Grand Finale was centered, in the beginning, in two very significant classes that were established on the earth plane in our present century. One was brought into manifestation in the Eastern world and the other in the Western world. The one in the Western world is the Agasha Temple of Wisdom in Los Angeles, California, and its eastern counterpart is or was a similar class, although not identical, in Bombay, India. Not much has been given relative to the Bombay class in recent years, and it seems to be no longer in manifestation. But in any event, these two classes were used by the Ascended Masters as focal points so that they could concentrate their attention and help bring to a successful conclusion the last act or the Grand Finale of our drama which, as we said earlier, had its beginnings 7,000 years ago in Austa, Egypt.

Now through the great laws of destiny, the spiritual pattern that was originally established in Austa, at that time in the far distant past, has never been broken. Agasha has many times used the symbol of the pyramid to express the relationship between these two classes in the 20th century and the original state there in Austa (now Egypt) where the Universal Consciousness of God had been previously established by the Ascended Masters. The golden apex represents the 2,000-year Austa consciousness, and the great body of the pyramid represents all of the philosophical knowledge that has been absorbed by the outer world for the past 5,000 years. We might say that the base plane of the pyramid is symbolically represented by these two initial classes in the 20th century, one in the Eastern world and the other in the Western world, which together make up the foundation that supports the whole. But all three, the Austa state and the Bombay and Los Angeles classes, belong to the same pyramid of wisdom and are called the *Grand Unit of the Three.* The Agashan teachers state that these three units taken as a whole constitute the Trinity, and this Trinity then in turn becomes a part of that great spiritual Order of the Masters called the Great White Way, or in some circles called by the name of the White Brotherhood.

It is interesting to note that the symbol of the pyramid also contains within itself three other symbols. These are the All-Seeing Eye in the center of the apex and the star and the crescent in the center of the entire pyramid. The All-Seeing Eye is the God Kingdom, the Infinite State, and the source of all knowledge and wisdom. The star is symbolical of its active or direct light, while the crescent represents its passive or reflected light. The Western world, being more active or masculine in nature, is probably directed more by the spiritual energies emanating from the star; whereas its feminine counterpart, the Eastern World, being more passive in nature, is probably controlled more by the moon or the planets. In any event, both the East and the West are equally important unto the Universal Consciousness God.

The Ascended Masters used the Bombay class in much the same way as they still use the Agashan class in Los Angeles. Both are focal points to clarify in the latter days of our present era all of the misconceptions in philosophical thought that had previously built up in the minds of men. It is not the purpose of either class to intellectually bring forth what may be termed to be new teachings, but rather the purpose is that of embracing and clarifying where necessary all that had heretofore been given in all of the religious philosophies of the entire world. It is for this reason that we have attempted to sum up, more or less, in the earlier part of this chapter much of the philosophical thought that had contributed to the growth of philosophy down through the years. And, of course, it is needless to say that we did not even scratch the surface.

Now the Agashan teachers have not given us too much information relative to the Bombay class. We do not know, for instance, either the name of the class or the names of the teachers who conducted the class. But we do know that the "modus operandi," or the method through which the teachings were given, was exactly the same as that of the Los Angeles class. And it was not a secret organization any more than the Agasha Temple of Wisdom is a secret organization, but on the other hand it could have been not too well-known in that part of the world. We are told that the class itself was officially established by the Masters as a Grand Unit in 1941, and that Mohandas Gandhi was very conscious of its activity prior to his death and ascension in 1948. The Bombay class was also considerably larger than the Los Angeles class, and its members were perhaps a little more sensitive insofar as they did not have as many material things to take care of and more time could be spent in meditation. But on the whole, the two classes are quite similar insofar as their basic teachings are concerned. The principal teacher there manifested and spoke on several occasions to the Agashan class during the 1950's.

But returning once more to the Agashan class in Los Angeles, let us now take a brief look at its history, its method of unfoldment, and how it came to be brought into manifestation with the return of Agasha here in the 20th century. The first thing that becomes evident is that it may—as is the case with so many other things in life—be divided into three distinct phases or periods of manifestation. Perhaps we can say it has gone through its mental phase, its physical phase, and its spiritual phase, although not necessarily in that order.

The first phase began almost imperceptibly and quite undramatically back in the year 1933. This was the year that Agasha, through his own admission, first spoke through the entranced Richard Zenor. We must remember that the early years of this great medium were spent in proving phenomena and establishing communication with the astral world. The higher teachings from the Ascended Masters were yet to be brought into manifestation in those early years, but then gradually, little by little, the Teachers began to control the instrument and speak unto the small groups that had gathered together to hear from Father, Mother, Sister, or Brother. It was only occasionally, the earlier students recall, that the Master Teacher Agasha would take over and share his great wisdom and understanding with those who were fortunate enough to be present.

As the years went by Agasha began to manifest more and more frequently, and by the time we arrive at the conclusion of this first or preparatory phase of his manifestation, some 17 years after he had first spoken through the instrument, we find Agasha conducting regularly scheduled classes every Monday and Friday evening and expounding with vital information in brilliant lectures and discourses on almost every segment in the life of man on earth. Unfortunately, the great preponderance of information that was given during this preparatory period was never recorded word for word as modern science had not yet produced the tape recorder. It was not until the middle of 1949 that all of the lectures were faithfully recorded on tape, incidentally. However, with the aid of a few disk and wire recordings, and a great amount of painstaking notes, James Crenshaw was able to preserve the essence of his teachings during this period with the publication of his informative work, *Telephone Between Worlds.*[12] But be that as it may, the first or preparatory phase of Agasha's manifestation was to last until his Greater Initiation and Final Ascension in the early morning hours of November 7, 1950.

This initiation that Agasha and Donna were about to take was looked upon with a good deal of apprehension by those who were attending the classes in the year of 1950 and the years just prior to it, for Agasha had said on many occasions that once any Master Teacher had taken what is termed the Greater Initiation, he is then free to ascend and be in an entirely new consciousness among the great Intermediaries of Intermediaries. It was understood by the class at this time that this Final Ascension would then of necessity prohibit his return for a long period of time to the planet from which he had ascended. Consequently, it was felt that in the event that Agasha and Donna chose this path, some other Master Teacher would then be appointed to conduct the Grand Finale for the Western world about which Agasha had spoken so often, and which was supposed to begin at mid-century.

It was evident from the tape of November 6th that even Agasha himself had not been fully aware of the alternatives until the moment of truth finally arrived where a decision had to be made. Agasha knew that once this step were taken, there would be no turning back, and he expresses his thoughts so beautifully on this matter that it would seem to be in order at this time to quote once more from the class of November 6, 1950. A large part of the secret pertaining to *Cara Boga Coty* had just been unveiled in the earlier part of the class, and now Agasha turns to thoughts of his forthcoming initiation which is now only hours away.

"Blessed disciples," he begins, "from time to time it becomes necessary for you to take inventory of your thoughts in order for you to understand your life and your mission, the same as I have had to come to understand my mission. When the date had been set, November 7th, for my ascension to be among the Intermediaries of Intermediaries on the way to the great Pillars of Light, it was then that I felt that if I had the choice of ascending but then relinquishing also my ability to return for generations unto the earth, I would perhaps then belate my ascension because of my desire to be with you children while you are in the flesh. But then the Intermediary spoke unto me in the presence of my teacher, Coman Coban, and said that upon my ascension I would not have to go on and that I could choose to remain and to serve as long as I wanted to, year after year. He said that a greater program could then be carried out in a most magnificent way, and this made me very happy and my heart was gladdened because I did not want to leave the earth. And so Donna and I have that privilege now of returning unto you children after November 7th to continue the classes on a larger scale and on a far greater program than we were able to carry out before. Please understand that my ascension means growth for your teacher, and that when he ascends and takes a step, you do too, for we are all growing together."

There is silence in the class. Even on the tape, one can almost feel the relief felt by the majority of the class upon learning that their beloved teacher was to remain and carry on with the Great Work in the years to follow.

The Spiritual Temples of Higher Learning

The new program called for the creation of a suitable temple on the inner planes of the Consciousness of Immensity for this initial phase of the Grand Finale. All mystery schools of the earth plane, incidentally, have their spiritual counterparts in the etheric kingdoms, and the Agasha Temple of Wisdom is no exception. A spiritual temple or hall of learning is always necessary in any organization in order for the disciples to meet on the inner planes, take their initiations, and pass the various degrees of the Order, whatever they may be. In the preparatory phase of Agasha's manifestation in the 20th century, that temple was known as the Temple of the True Disciple, and there were still others before that. But now with the Grand Finale finally in full swing, a new and adequate spiritual temple had to be erected.

The second phase of Agasha's manifestation also involved the difficult task of recalling into the Los Angeles class all of the remaining original disciples who were in the flesh at the time and who had also been in the physical body in Austa at precisely the same time that Agasha had lived out his last physical incarnation. Agasha wanted to recall them into the class because it was his desire to fulfill the pact made during the closing days of the convention and make contact once again with all of those who had attended it. Thus he could then bring them once more into a movement that had had its beginnings exactly 7,000 years earlier. Agasha had determined that there were precisely 273 individuals remaining; but this would seem to be a difficult task to accomplish, as these individuals were undoubtedly scattered all over the face of the earth.

In any event, Agasha sent out his call, and a new temple was created on the inner planes for this initial phase of the Grand Finale. It was named the Temple of the All-Seeing Eye. It had 273 rooms, one room for each of the original disciples, and it was built in the shape of a "Y" with three separate wings. Its large circular auditorium contained a miniature golden pyramid in the center which formed a focal point for the many students and Teachers who would gather there, carry on conversations, and listen to lectures. It was seven stories high and crowned with three golden domes, one dome over each of the three wings.

During this period (which was to last until January 25, 1961) Agasha also initiated a program of 273 degrees or steps for the class as a whole to reach on the long and difficult path to Chief Discipleship. The program was slow and sometimes many months were spent on a single step. However, Agasha sent out his call for the 273 individuals that he was supposed to contact at that time, and gradually, one by one, these somewhat bewildered individuals would show up at the Agasha Temple wondering what strange forces had been at work to attract them, for an endless variety of reasons, into the class and in some cases cause them to travel clear across the globe. Eventually all of the 273 individuals had at least been contacted, but it was never determined whether any one disciple had attained the degree of Chief Discipleship. The class as a whole, though, ultimately reached probationary status in the Third Degree of the Purple Order during this period.

There was a strange law of destiny at work here, and we can almost see the hands of Fate at work when we consider the following very interesting relationship: There were 273 individuals that "just happened" to be back in the physical body in the 20th century and who had also attended that great convention held 7,000 years ago in Austa. Then Agasha in turn also set up a program of 273 degrees or steps for these same disciples to pass before they could take their initiations into the Higher Orders. And any high school physics student likewise knows that the lowest possible temperature that matter can sustain in the physical plane is that same numerical constant—273 degrees below zero Centigrade. This temperature denotes the complete absence of heat, and it is known as *absolute zero*. Therefore the Temple of the All-Seeing Eye, with its 273 separate rooms, can very easily represent the physical or dense phase of the Agashan manifestation inasmuch as there is a correspondence with physical matter in its dense or solid state. Each separate room corresponds directly with every possible degree of temperature that matter can sustain while in that state—from zero degrees Centigrade (the melting point of ice) to minus 273 degrees Centigrade (absolute zero).

During the final years of this second or 273-degree phase of the class, many of the Agashans who had lived during the 2,000-year Peace Period in Austa were attracted into the Agashan class, almost prematurely so to speak, as the Peace Period phase had not yet begun. But perhaps the old adage which states that "many are called, but few remain" is very much in order, for if all of the 273 individuals who had received the call had remained physically active in the Temple, there would have been no room for the Peace Period people whose souls were now answering Agasha's call.

Since much of the activity of the Agasha class is carried out on the inner planes, the center of activity gradually moved away from the smaller Temple of the All-Seeing Eye into a new, larger, and more universal temple presided over by the Master Teacher Rubicon. The Temple of Rubicon then acted as an interim temple until a new permanent temple for all of the Agashans could be built and dedicated in the vast Consciousness of Immensity. Rubicon lent his facilities most graciously as the many disciples then "crossed the Rubicon" and thus committed themselves to conquer or perish in much the same manner as Julius Caesar once committed himself when he crossed this ancient boundary to march against Pompey. Crossing the Rubicon means to take a decisive, irrevocable step.

With the Rubicon now safely behind him, Agasha then entered the third and final phase of his manifestation here in the 20th century with the completion and dedication of the Agasha Hall of Higher Learning in the inner planes of the Consciousness of Immensity on January 25, 1961. This phase is known as the Peace Period phase as it embraces all of the Agashans who had ever lived during that 2,000-year period of peace in Austa, Egypt and not just the few who happened to be in physical incarnation at the time of the Great Convention. Agasha endearingly and affectionately calls these individuals the Peace Period children, and he is daily sending out his call for all of the lost sheep to return unto the fold. Perhaps you, the reader, had lived in Austa during that time, and perhaps his call is reaching you even as you read this page.

This third and final phase is certainly the most universal phase of the Agashan manifestation, for the teachers state that there shall be literally millions of people over a period of time embracing the philosophy and thus understanding and realizing their position on earth. Agasha's purpose is to lay the foundation for all this to happen, and he is ever so mindful that it shall be a strong foundation so that the many disciples can then build on it so concretely that nothing will cause their spiritual structure to crumble. True, his call may at first be specifically directed more or less to those many hundreds of thousands or perhaps even millions of souls who had previously lived lives in that great pre-Egyptian consciousness prior to the advent of the Pharaohs, but this is only because there is that spiritual tie. But the call is still a universal call, and it is sent out equally unto all. The doors of the Temple are always open to any sincere seeker.

If the 273-degree phase was the physical or dense phase of

the Agashan manifestation (the temperatures from zero to minus 273 degrees represent matter in the dense or solid state) the Agasha Hall of Higher Learning then represents the mental phase or the more fluid state of Mind. It is said that this temple is truly one of the most magnificent structures of the inner planes. Its three golden domes both cap and crown a structure which is the symbolical embodiment of wisdom itself. They also represent the three aspects of life: the mental, the physical, and the spiritual. This is the true Trinity, and the use of gold is symbolical of matter in its purest state—which is wisdom. But it is still a substantial hall of learning, and it is not a castle in the air by any stretch of the imagination. It is a reality, but it is a reality of Mind. And its 273 steps which lead up to its massive entrance could well represent the dense phase out of which the initiate has now arisen in his long struggle toward attainment.

Agasha made the statement one night that this magnificent temple also surpasses any of the other temples that the disciples of the Agashan movement had previously been privileged to enter. And this includes the Temple of the True Disciple, the Temple of the All-Seeing Eye, the Temple of Rubicon, and even the Temples of the Seventh Degree. Why is this so? How can Agasha make such an all-embracing statement? After all, the Temples of the Seventh Degree in the vast Consciousness of Immensity are certainly no hovels. Why does this particular temple surpass all of the others? The answer to this puzzling question is simply that *any* new temple created on the inner planes, by *any* spiritual organization, is always greater than the previous temple insofar as it represents the accumulation and the sum total of all that had gone on before. But, of course, this is relative only to the members of that particular Order when comparing the temples within its own spiritual structure.

Now let us look at another very interesting relationship. If the Temple of the All-Seeing Eye had come to represent the solid or dense state of matter which ranges from minus 273 degrees to zero degrees Centigrade (the melting point of ice), and the Agasha Hall of Higher Learning, the liquid or fluid state of matter which covers the range in the temperature scale from zero to 100 degrees Centigrade (the boiling point of water), we must then out of necessity, or at least in theory, have a temple that embraces the higher degrees of temperature above 100 degrees where the water particles turn into steam and evaporate into the air.

And sure enough, Agasha completed this Trinity in the class of March 18, 1963, when he announced the formation of that very temple. This temple would be called the Temple of Fulfillment, and he went on to say that there would be no more *personal* temples for the members of the Agashan class here in the 20th century. There would be others that would be visited from time to time, certainly, but he said that there would be no more temples that the Agashan disciples could call their very own—temples that would be built through their own spiritual efforts. This would be it: the Temple of Fulfillment.

Therefore, the Temple of Fulfillment represents the more tenuous degrees of matter in its gaseous or rarefied state. It is equivalent to the spiritual or resurrected phase of the Agashan class. It is matter above 100 degrees Centigrade, for it is here where in the same manner that water turns to steam and then rises into the air, the Agashan disciple may likewise ascend from the mental state of consciousness into its higher spiritual states. This temple also has three golden domes, following the same pattern of its earlier counterparts.

Thus we end up with three individual temples for the Agashan class: the Temple of the All-Seeing Eye, representing the physical phase of life; the Agasha Hall of Higher Learning, representing the mental phase of life; and the Temple of Fulfillment, representing the spiritual phase of life. And even more significant is the fact that all three temples have three distinct wings, each wing being crowned with a single golden dome. This is all obviously very symbolical because we end up with nine golden domes which may be said to represent the numbers from one to nine.

There is therefore a separate compartment for each of the digits, and the numerical forces are now complete.

But are we really complete? What about the mysterious number ten? Let us return once again to the Introduction to this volume. Here, we pointed out that the tenth great Initiate was none other than you, the reader of this book, once you had taken the initiative to open the door and then step through its portals into the Temple of your own Being. Therefore, we have to take *you* into consideration, *you* who are the Temple of the Living God, for the ten is always the remanifestation once again of the number one.

Very well. There is still one other temple in the higher degrees of Immensity that Agasha has brought to our attention in recent years. That temple is known as the Hall of the Initiates, for it is here where the disciples have taken their initiations into the Higher Orders. It is the fourth temple and may be compared to the fire or energy state of consciousness. But the sum of the numbers one, two, three, and four are ten. And what is ten? It is the Temple of the Living God, which is you; and you are the physical embodiment of your Higher Self.

Therefore, we now have a temple symbolical of each of the four states of matter—earth, water, air, and fire. These in turn represent the solid, the liquid, the gaseous, and the energy states of consciousness. But the fourth state, or the energy state, then transcends all of the other states and becomes, in turn, the first degree of a still higher order of consciousness.

The Hall of the Initiates is a colossal structure that literally towers into the sky and is quite aptly symbolical of the physical body of Man. Its crown is a single golden dome supported exquisitely on 14 gigantic columns or pillars equally spaced about the circumference of a perfect circle which forms its base. The single golden dome is in turn symbolical of the ONENESS which encompasses all. Inside its circular interior is a raised platform or dias at the center where the one who is to be initiated stands alone to be observed, judged, and graded by those mysterious entities called Cara, Boga, and Coty. These are the mental, physical, and spiritual aspects of one's own Being.

There are also 14 doors equally spaced around the periphery between the 14 pillars, and these doors are either open or closed. Behind each door is an experience or a lesson to be learned in life. If the door is open the lesson has been learned, but if the door is closed that particular lesson or experience is still hidden and yet to be revealed. The entire set of 14 doors could be likened unto a complete suit of the Minor Arcana of the Tarot, with each card representing a single door. And behind each door the numerical influences of that particular Tarot force lie and wait to either buffet or reward the aspirant who dares to open the door and step within. But if he is to become the true Initiate, all challenges must be conquered; and blessed indeed is the one who is fortunate enough to have all 14 doors open wide as soon as he steps up on the dias, for this signifies that he has conquered in life all that he was supposed to conquer, and the former disciple is now the Initiate.

The Teacher Is You

Let us return once more to the three temples of the Agashan consciousness—the mental, the physical, and the spiritual. Now just what are these temples, really? They are the Temples on the other side of the Rubicon that *you,* the higher initiate, have now crossed. Each One was created with one decisive, irrevocable step. Each One is the greatest Temple of all because it was created through *your* efforts and *your* accomplishments, and it will belong to *you* from here on out throughout the great consciousness of eternity. *You* have earned every step of the way to this great Hall of Learning, and *you* may now help others to enter it also, for it shall be *your* dwelling place where *your* relatives will be able to assemble as *you* would assist by the furnishing or lending of *your* power and through the power of the Teacher, who would accompany them at first until they had earned the same privilege as *you.* Thus they, as well as *you,* would then be able to enter the various departments to study, to learn, and to work with the Teachers. This is also one of the reasons that *your* temple surpasses all the others—but this is only true insofar as *you* are concerned.

Now just who is this person called *you*? The answer is that he is none other than you, the reader of this book, *if* you have taken the initiative to participate in the Grand Finale by striving to become aware of your own Being. You are then one who listens to the inner call of the God Kingdom that dwells within and then follows its dictates. But you must also have the necessary courage or boldness to dare, and then to do; to seek for truth, and then to learn wisdom; to be ever so humble, and then to become ever so strong; to step out of the rank and file of the multitude, and then to become one who shows others the way; and lastly, and perhaps the most important of all, to be ever so patient while waiting for the teacher, and then to rejoice when the teacher finally appears. Yes, you who would do all of these things shall then become the pioneer who charts the course and prepares the way so that others may then follow in your footsteps.

But is all this so difficult? No, it definitely is not; in fact, it is surprisingly simple. We must remember that the God Kingdom is so structured that it not only enables the outer man to seek, but it also helps him to find the answers once sufficient effort has been put forth on his part. This is the reason for the ancient adage which states, "When the disciple is ready, the teacher always appears." All you have to do is to say meaningfully unto your own God Kingdom, "I am now ready to learn; now please show me the way." And the Agashan philosophy teaches that if this is done truthfully, honestly, and with a sincere desire to learn, you will then be automatically guided to the proper church, temple, medium, teacher, guru, group, fraternity, occult society, mystery school, or whatever it is that is just right for you at the present state of your unfoldment. This is especially true today now that we have finally reached the second half of the 20th century, the latter days, and are now right in the middle of the last act of the Grand Finale of the age.

For instance, just walk into any bookstore and see the vast amount of occult literature that is now available to the seeker. Become aware of the "new thought" that is now being taught in some of the enlightened churches, and notice how the subject of reincarnation is gradually coming to be more and more accepted in orthodox thinking. It is a fact that more and more individuals are reliving past lives under hypnosis—and under laboratory conditions, in clinical psychology classes. Watch the walls of materialism come crumbling down as gifted psychic powerhouses such as the Uri Gellers bend keys, start watches, dematerialize objects, and then even apport them back again. Be mindful of the many psychics and mediums who are now breaking down the barriers between the various states of consciousness, and then find out about the worlds beyond the senses. Yes, the veils between these worlds are becoming ever so thin in this new psychic age that is only now in its infancy.

When you observe and become aware of all of the above phenomena, you will find that a whole new life will be yours to live in the new bright future that awaits those who are willing to learn. You shall then be, unknowingly to your outer self, under the watchful eyes and guidance of a teacher. This teacher could be anywhere in the great hierarchy of the Masters. He could even be an Ascended Master in one of the Spiritual Centers, if your spiritual growth would warrant such a teacher, but in any event he is the teacher that you had attracted unto yourself. And when you find your teacher be not fearful, as he will then introduce you to the "real you" who is even now struggling to make his acquaintance known. Once you have awakened the sleeping god that dwells within, you will have come into the knowing, and from that time on you will be embarked on a new and glorious adventure of learning, of growing, and of helping others to also reach the same state.

Jesus is quoted as saying, "In my Father's house, there are

many mansions." Now what does he mean by this? The Agashan teachers answer by saying that in the great Consciousness of Immensity, in the great Cosmos that embraces all there is, there are a great many halls of learning, temples of understanding, mansions of great beauty, where the many disciples and higher initiates of the Higher Orders go to study, learn, and unfold. Since no one, absolutely no one, has a monopoly on truth, Agasha says that the ultimate truth must then out of necessity be expressed through a great many diversified and specialized schools of individualized thought. And in the final analysis, truth is simply where you find it. Therefore, we must remember that the particular temples that we have mentioned here in this chapter are only those temples that exist within the Agashan organization. We have used them only as examples of what you, the reader, might expect to find when you become aware of your own individual, personal temple that exists somewhere within the core of your own Being.

It is essential to understand that these temples of higher learning are only created through the actions and the merits of the collective whole. They are brought into manifestation through the thoughts and the actions of a sincere group of people, and if it were otherwise, that particular temple, or whatever we desired to call it, would not truly be theirs. And it is the temple itself that is individualized within the God Consciousness. Let us, just for the sake of argument, call it the greater you. Then this "greater you" could then be said to be the individualized consciousness of a great spiritual family of higher initiates of which the "lesser you" is but a part. Thus somewhere out there there is a particular temple that represents the greater you, and that particular temple would then be your own *personal* temple that was created just for you and your spiritual family. That is where you rightfully belong.

Agasha has often said that that body which you are now living in is the Temple of the Living God—which is you. But he has also said, at other times, that you are a spirit dwelling within a body or temple. Thus, in reality, you are not only the temple but also all that is in it. Therefore, know these truths once and for all: the God Kingdom dwells within *you,* and you do *not* have to seek for it elsewhere. You have only to open the door to the Temple of your Inner Being, and then step within. True, that physical body may be only an imitation or a duplicate of its spiritual counterpart, but nevertheless it still represents the sum total of all of your previous lives. It is the dwelling place of the soul, and it is your place of worship until the day that you are free.

The End of the Cycle: The Pot Boils Over

All of the above is the positive aspect of the Grand Finale. Is there a negative aspect? Of course there is, inasmuch as the most fundamental truth in all of Nature is that there is both a positive and a negative side to everything, and the last act or the Grand Finale of the age is certainly no exception. When we heat water to the boiling point (100 degrees Centigrade), we not only witness the phenomenon of steam rising and evaporating into the air, but many times the water or the stew or whatever it is that is in the boiling pot becomes so excited and agitated that the liquid in the pot actually boils over and overflows the pot. Thus at the same time that disciples are arising and becoming initiates in the many great initiation temples of the inner planes, the outer world is experiencing a period of great frustration, anger, discontent, and many souls are driven into extreme acts of violence as the pot erupts and boils over.

Agasha has used this description of the boiling pot many times in order to explain symbolically what is happening to the world right now in the Grand Finale. He has also used the simile of the boil, the painful sore, that breaks and then contaminates the adjoining areas with its pus as it cleanses itself. He states that we are now living in the most important period in the evolution of the human expression here upon the earth plane, for it marks the changeover from childhood to maturity and naturally poisons and other waste material have to be eliminated. This reaction is applicable to everything that has to do with the human—the unrest, the political confusion, the wars, the threats of war, the crime, the violence, the poor economic conditions, and all the rest of the hell and confusion that are now so prevalent upon the earth plane. Even Nature itself reacts as it brings forth the earthquakes, floods, fires, tornados, and other things of a cataclysmic nature with increased severity and intensity.

Thus we find that this important period is likewise one of the most trying periods in the history of the earth for thousands of years. It would seem that there is now a great dark wave of evil enveloping the earth, trying to strangle it into submission, and trying to prevent the inevitable golden dawn. This is so, for the Grand Finale actually embraces the Biblical Battle of Armageddon—that great final battle of the ages where the Forces of Light are lined up against the Forces of Darkness in one final struggle for power. But Agasha states, over and over again, that there will be no Third World War, for if there were, the human expression would have to start all over again from the beginning. He says that the Ascended Masters in the Spiritual Centers will not allow this to happen, or at least not in the scale that would bring about such a vast and total destruction. And in the final analysis, it simply cannot happen because the script is just not written that way in the Akashic Records of the Universal Consciousness of God. In fact, the new Golden Age has already begun!

While it is true that the Grand Finale brings down the curtain on the past, it also, strangely enough, raises the curtain of the future. In other words, the previous Age of Darkness and the new Golden Age of Light overlap each other in the Grand Finale, and this overlapping period is the last half, or the latter days, of the 20th century. But the negative karmic effects of the previous cycle are largely mitigated by the new positive influences of the forthcoming cycle. These positive influences, Agasha says, first began with the birth of the new infant (the New Age) in the year

1965 and will continue to be felt more and more as this child grows to maturity. "How long will this take?" you ask. As we said in the previous chapter, it will cover a span of 55 years, and it will not be until the year 2020 when the new Golden Age, or the New Atlantis, will be once more firmly established on the face of this planet. But this intervening period before the child becomes of age is nonetheless also an era of great growth and advancement.

The Return of the Atlanteans

Agasha uses the term the "New Atlantis" almost synonymously with the new age, for the new Golden Age is brought about through the reestablishment or the reincarnation of the Atlantean consciousness once again upon the earth. Millions and millions of individuals are being born today who had once lived on the great continent of Atlantis before its submergence, and more than that, they are also bringing back with them the subconscious memory of that which they had previously learned in Atlantis. This is one of the answers for the tremendous acceleration in scientific advancement during our present century. Of course, there are also millions of souls being born who are not Atlanteans because these souls had missed the Atlantean cycle of earthly incarnations. There was a lapse of time of thousands of years in their astral life, Agasha says, and these particular souls did not return again onto the earth plane to pick up their thread of life until after the great cataclysmic force had caused the final submergence of that continent. But those who had lived on Atlantis, the true Atlanteans, are now returning to revive and establish a new Kingdom of Light which is to be the Universal Brotherhood of Mankind. These are the light bearers who will bring forth peace unto the oncoming generations. It is they who shall see to it that good and honest government shall eventually reign among all of the nations of the earth, and that wars and oppression by force shall cease and be no more. Yes indeed, the world of the future will owe a great debt of gratitude to these Atlanteans of the past.

Now just who are the original Atlanteans? Chances are that they are you and you and you. In fact, we can safely say that almost anyone who is interested enough in the study of occult philosophy to even read this book is undoubtedly an Atlantean. And it does not matter in the slightest what race you are in at the moment, for in the span of 172,000 years—and that is a pretty long time—the Atlanteans have been scattered and dispersed within practically every race on the face of this earth. But today they are awakening! If you are interested in the hidden mysteries of life today, you are undoubtedly an Atlantean. You are interested in these things because you have awakened the knowledge and the memory of the past within you. But if you are still asleep today, and if you are only interested in the gross things of life, in the mundane things of life, and if you have not even the slightest interest in art, literature, or music, or whatever—then you might not be an Atlantean, although even this would not necessarily settle the issue. It would only mean that you were still asleep, and someone should most certainly awaken you.

Let us, just for the sake of argument, now go back into the past a bit and follow the life patterns of a few members of a particular spiritual family. It does not matter just what spiritual family we are talking about, anyone will do. So let us say that it is *your* spiritual family—just as a supposition. Now what were you doing for the past 172,000 years? You could not incarnate any longer in that advanced civilization on the Atlantean continent because it was now submerged with almost all of the traces of its vast knowledge buried beneath the still waters of the deep. So what were you to do? Let us further say that you were a scientist in your last life in that consciousness, and that you had perhaps received no little recognition for your accomplishments. You were perhaps one of the top scientists of the period, but now through the wrath of Nature chances of carrying on with your learning in the immediate future were lost inasmuch as all of the remaining civilizations on the earth plane were only in an uncivilized state.

Perhaps you should have ascended at that time with some of the other members of your spiritual family, but you had not followed their advice and had been perhaps lazy in furthering your spiritual studies. So therefore that door was closed; you had more earthly living to do. Yet, you were really not a bad person, and it just did not seem fair to you, and perhaps neither to your soul, that you should have to start all over again at the beginning and go through the same old grind with a lot of uncivilized savages in the thickets of some jungle. There were several of the members of your spiritual family in the same boat, and perhaps it was not a very happy conclave that you and your friends attended in one of the remaining planes of the Atlantean higher astral consciousness.

Now here we come to the crux of the whole matter, and perhaps, just perhaps, we might stumble upon the solution to this problem if we just think it out a bit. If you were the soul of Tom or Dick or Mary, let us say, just what would you do? The soul might think, just as a supposition, "Well, I see your problem. I would like for you to continue on with your scientific studies, but unfortunately you cannot do that now. The situation is out of my hands inasmuch as there is now no suitable physical consciousness available to carry on with your scientific pursuits. But on the other hand, you have not yet learned how to really *express* unselfish love and devotion, you do not really *know* the meaning of patience, and you have yet to come to the *realization* that you cannot arise until you have likewise helped others to arise.

"So in the interim period before the New Atlantis can come into manifestation, I shall chart out for you a course of instruction in several of these primitive civilizations—not for too long a period of time in each one, but only of a sufficient number of lives for you to learn the lessons—and in this way you can earn your way back to where you should rightfully be. You shall have a few lives here, a few lives there, a number of lives over here again, and then we will skip the intervening period until you are brought back some 9,000 or 10,000 years prior to the birth of the New Atlantis. But in this latter cycle of lives, I will really put you through your paces through a great many consecutive lives while you pave the way for the reestablishment of that new kingdom. During this period your path will become quite rough at times, and you will really have to work."

Or perhaps your soul might give you a vacation from it all with a little romantic interlude on some exotic island in the South Pacific, fishing, swimming, and really having fun—and with your counterpart or soul mate, even! A real vacation, and you had not had a vacation of that type for perhaps thousands of years. But there is still a lot of other work to do and the soul might say, "If you live in this civilization for just one life, ever so humbly, I will see to it that you can teach them the art of agriculture and how to properly grow their own crops instead of having to forage for food all the time. But you will not have to spend too much time there; all you will have to spend is just one life only in that consciousness."

One can readily see that there are almost an infinite number of situations that the soul can place you in during this somewhat lengthy period of 172,000 years between the two states of the Atlantean Consciousness. But Agasha says that every soul is unique and that each has a different series of experiences. Therefore, he does not go into detail in the lives of individuals on this planet prior to the 9,000-year period.

We made the statement above that sometimes the soul will skip an intervening period between two separate groups or series of lives. Now what happens during this interim period? Fortunately the God Consciousness had allowed for this problem, as the same problem always arises in the transportation of an entire race of human expression from one planet to another after the destruction of the original planet. The answer is a time lapse, not for your soul, but for you. You merely go to sleep—and instantly it is 25,000 years later when you awaken. It could be any number of years, but the principle is always the same. And during this apparent time lapse, the soul simply has no outer physical vehicle of expression. It has pulled its entire *outer* consciousness back within itself, or within the source of its own Being, but its *inner* consciousness is still very much awake.

This then would account for the discrepancies between the many statements made by occultists regarding the actual date in history of the submergence of Atlantis. There is just no agreement whatsoever in the establishment of this date. It is evident that each individual or school of learning, in tracing back the Akashic Records of its own individual series of experiences in earthly living, has come across time lapses of varying periods of time. A time lapse is just what the word implies—a lapse in time—and there is absolutely no way to determine the true length of this time period without another reference point. Unfortunately, the soul does not add as a subtitle the date such as 29,005 B.C. in the Akashic Records of scenes of the past. Perhaps if it did, there would be less confusion on this point.

Now this same principle that we have been discussing here applies equally as well to all of your brothers and sisters in your particular spiritual family who had not yet ascended at the time of the submergence. They were in the same boat that you were in. And so for thousands of years you had seemingly missed one another in many of your lives, but in many others you had lived, played, worked, fought, and romanced together. And even though you had missed meeting a particularly beloved brother of yours for thousands of years, eventually through the law of destiny you had been brought back together again. All of us have had our lives to live and sometimes to go down through the ages seemingly separated from our brothers and sisters, but we know that eventually we shall all come together, live together, experience many things together, share our sorrows or our moments of happiness together, and we even know that eventually, just perhaps, we might even *ascend* together.

Yes, Agasha states that this is a very real possibility. It is not his desire for any of the disciples whom he had contacted in the Grand Finale to return again, and again, and again unto the physical plane. Nor is it the desire of any other Master Teacher, for that matter, that the Teacher's disciples keep returning unto the physical plane. After all, the very term itself, the grand finale, means the end. And there is absolutely no reason, Agasha goes on to say, that our present Grand Finale, the end of the age, cannot mean the very last life for those particular disciples who had diligently applied themselves and who had worked under the guidance of their teachers in this past 7,000-year life drama, thus learning their lessons, fulfilling their earthly mission, and ascending. Does this mean you? Perhaps it does; there is no way of knowing an individual situation.

The purpose of life is certainly not to continue on forever with earthly incarnations. The purpose of life is to graduate from life, and the Grand Finale is the graduating class. Many on the spiritual path must learn that they are now seniors—not juniors, sophomores, or freshmen. There are newer and higher experiences awaiting us, and it is not our destiny to be laggards forever. Agasha states that there are thousands and thousands and thousands of individuals living on the earth today who are, unsuspected by the outer self, living out their last physical incarnation. Many of the actors in the past 7,000-year life dramas will be leaving the other actors who are to remain. The 21st century will bring forth an entirely new life drama that will be produced on the earth plane, and there will be many new faces in the starring roles. Perhaps there is much truth in the old adage that says, "Every dog must have his day," and there is plenty of room for all in the life dramas yet to be produced.

The Coming Golden Age of Peace

Agasha has often said that America is the country that was so chosen by the Teachers of Light to be the New Atlantis, and because of its spiritual destiny, it will lead the world in the establishment of universal peace. This is the reason that the true Atlantean who returns today is usually attracted to America, and it makes no difference where he was born, it would still be the same. However, this does not necessarily mean that he would eventually come to America. But it is the American way of life that shall eventually be established all over the world, Agasha goes on to say, and this is the only way that true freedom will ever come unto mankind. Of course, there are many things false in America today, and many things have to change, but he says it is still the greatest country on the face of the earth insofar as it is destined to set the example for all of the other nations to follow in the future. And the American flag shall always wave above all the others of the earth.

The pursuit of wisdom will then become the keynote of the New Age, and within the first few centuries or so one of the greatest occult centers ever to be established on the face of the earth will be built right here on the Pacific Coast of the United States. It is here where both the young and the old will attend this great institution of learning and thus enable themselves to embrace the Atlantean teachings of the past. Also, on a mountaintop somewhere in the vicinity of Los Angeles, a great pyramid of wisdom will be erected which will stand for literally thousands of years. This will be the pyramid of all pyramids, and it will be seen for miles around as it stands there so nobly and so high. It will also be a museum which will house the records of practically everything. The hidden mysteries of life will then no longer be hidden once they have been recorded onto devices—yet to be invented—and then placed within this great monument. Thus the scholars of tomorrow will be in a position to study and learn, among other things, the true history of mankind, the true history of the races, and the true history of all of the nations of the earth including Atlantis, Egypt, Babylonia, and Tibet in particular.

These first few centuries will also bring forth many new

changes on the face of the planet. Among them will be a new universal language which will be established as a second language for all nations. The economic system will be vastly improved with all peoples being supported properly and well supplied. Poverty and starvation will be a thing of the past as there will be plenty of food for all. The world will continue to have a kind of capitalism and banking system, although foreign exchanges will be different and foreign relations far superior. A world government with full, delegated authority will replace the United Nations of today, but individual freedom will forever be maintained. And last but not least, the universal religion which incorporates the teachings of all of the Ascended Masters of the earth will be embraced by millions of souls all over the world. Of course, there will always be those who had not yet unfolded to the point where they might embrace it in its entirety; for people will always be free to believe whatever they wish to believe.

In summary then, we can state that all of that which today is destroying the individual—those things which are depriving him of the joys, the gladness, and the sweetness of life—will be stamped out and destroyed. It is the rightful heritage of the human expression of this planet for all of this to take place in the oncoming generations, but unfortunately there will always be the laggards, the slackers, the unlearned, and those who refuse to go on. These, however, will be in the minority.

Now after this new Golden Age is once established, how long can we expect it to survive? In answer to this question, Agasha has made the amazing statement that the Akashic Records of the earth show the Golden Age of our planet surviving for hundreds of thousands of years into the future. Even that great pyramid spoken of in a previous paragraph will "stand for as long as this earth is in motion." In other words, this new civilization—which in reality is only an extension of the present one— is going to last for a pretty long period of time. Of course, it will always have to contend with the 7,000-year cycles, the 2,200-year cycles, and all of the other cycles because that is the law, and Nature's laws cannot be broken. However, the overall picture of the contrast between the new ages to come and the previous ages will be similar to the difference between light and darkness. The planet Earth will have come into its maturity. This forthcoming period or era is also destined to end the cycle of physical expression for the majority of the people now upon the earth, and this is especially true for those who were the original Atlanteans.

Some Concluding Remarks by Agasha

Thus we come to the end of a somewhat lengthy, but hopefully worthwhile, look at the inner workings of the great occult forces at work behind all of our lives. But it would not seem fitting to close this chapter without first turning the rostrum over to Agasha himself and letting him conclude in his own words a few of his thoughts relative to that which he terms the "Grand Finale." It is with great pleasure then that those of us who have contributed to this work present to you, the reader, Agasha: Master of Wisdom:

"My blessed children—greetings. The Agashan philosophy, as you disciples so kindly refer to my thoughts and words, affords you the realization that this class is simply an effort on my part to help you to become that beacon of light. But it is only a forerunner to that which is eventually going to enable you to understand everything that has transpired in this individual life of yours.

"With that as an introduction, I would like to ask you to keep the following thought in mind: It is possible, absolutely possible indeed, for you to conquer that something—if it can be put in that light—or perhaps we should say accomplish what you are supposed to accomplish in this given life of yours. This could be considered to be the fulfillment of that which will permit you to ascend in the great Grand Finale, instead of descending again unto the flesh in these generations to come.

"Another point that I would like to bring up is that you

are infinitely intelligent, but yet you give but little evidence of it in this present incarnation. Therefore, each of you must be up and doing and make an effort to chip away the corrosion that surrounds the soul so that you may then become aware of *Being*. You should go about it through continuous, honest effort so that you may then also come into the *Knowing*. This Grand Awakening is the one important factor that both your soul as well as your teacher are trying to bring about. This is the reason that we say unto all disciples that by staying on the path, striving, earning every step of the way, and then learning—all of these efforts will one day enable you to have this wonderful experience of going within that Infinite State.

"There within . . . how may I describe it, how may I find words to express what I am trying to tell you? How inadequate is the language to reveal the beauty that each and every one will experience in the great Consciousness of Immensity—all that is, all that ever was, all awareness, all understanding! This is what you will experience once you have earned and reached a certain state in your advancement and awakened the 'I' within you. And you must recognize that the present state of your advancement, the present state of your evolution, will indeed enable you to do this.

"I am grateful and it does me good when I am able to predict good things to come that enlighten and enrich the lives of mankind. But the many of you will remember that quite a few years ago I told you of the impending problems that would encompass the world. I mentioned the hell that is taking place cataclysmically and that will continue for a while, the wars and the threats of war, and all that is involved of which you are aware. Unfortunately, we seem to have so much today that stems forth from duress, when we refer to the overall picture of trying to achieve an assist for struggling humanity.

"Perhaps you might think it is odd when I come here and speak in this manner regarding the advancement and the achieving of material things for humanity when actually it is hell and confusion that we are in evidence of today. There are many ugly things that are taking place now as well as down through the history of mankind. These are the penalties that you are paying collectively because of the antics of men, economically and otherwise. But I then bring forth that in the face of all of this, there is still light ahead for Mankind. We are progressing in many ways now, and as I just said, I am always thrilled to look ahead and see this progress and then bring it to your attention.

"I know that some will say, 'What's the difference? I am not going to be here; I am not interested in predictions.' That is the mortal speaking. Of course, that person is usually interested in predictions if they have to do with himself, but I have heard people say, 'I couldn't care less about those predictions; sure they have come true, but they would have happened anyway.' Now again, that is the mortal talking. You must understand, disciples, that when you hear reactions such as this, you are dealing with a particular phase of mortal consciousness. Those are mortals who have yet to be inspired or awakened to that which the enlightened mind has embraced for these many years past.

"The enlightened mind knows truth when he sees it. It is very difficult to completely fool an enlightened individual. The soul always speaks the truth unto its outer consciousness, and the enlightened individual can usually sense when another is speaking untruthfully. This 'inner knowing' is a subject that can eventually be proved scientifically and in its entirety when the men in the appropriate field take the initiative and give it recognition. In fact, all of occult science can be proved once it comes under the scrutiny of those taking the time to study it and to bring it into light. This will prove to be a great contribution to the advancement of the human race.

"I, being only an individual such as you—but one who is on a higher rung on the ladder of life—am not speaking as one who is an authority, but only as one who is knowledgeable on these things that are in existence at this time. When

I speak unto you disciples, aside from the words that are spoken, I am also indirectly prefacing my remarks by requesting that you give me the privilege of speaking that which I know to be true, and not necessarily think that I am deliberately tearing down something that millions of people embrace and believe in. I realize that if I were face to face with you and speaking while gazing into your eyes, it would seem to you as though I were speaking as an authority, but I have no intention whatsoever of giving you that impression. I only want you to know that I have to be factual. I have to be in a position to back up or prove the simple statements that I utter here in this class, for in the final analysis the burden of proof rests upon my shoulders.

"However, let me state once more that it is not my desire to come here to dispute, for that is not my intention. I know that I, speaking as an individual, would not even attempt to dispute. But I will bring out that which I consider to be factual or that which is in evidence, and then be either in an approving or a disapproving mind relative to the statements made by those in so-called authority and as I understand those statements to stand up in the light of truth. I can only add to this by saying that I have taken the initiative to work with many of the Teachers of the Seventh Degree, and having done so, I have come up with what I consider to be pure and unadulterated information relative to whatever it is that I am bringing to your attention.

"In conclusion then, let me say to you blessed disciples to be patient with yourselves. When the time comes, your soul through your own channelship will produce all that will be necessary to satisfy your outer mind. It is the mortal mind that is crying out for verification of the statements that I make; most certainly you are not striving to satisfy the God-Self in that way. The Inner Kingdom does not need these manifestations.

"When you have earned the privilege, when you are ready and the outer mind is receptive, then the God Kingdom within will enable you to understand that which is contributing to the fulfillment of your desires. You will then see in that particular moment just why you are going through the cycle that you are experiencing at this time. You will also see why some go ahead while others fail, and why one is held back while his brother is succeeding. These are the things that need to be known. With this in mind, we must realize that now is the time for all of us to be about our task in order to bring into the mortal consciousness that inner awakening and the recognition of the God Kingdom that dwells within.

"The ritualistic activity that is carried out in the church has its merits. It inspires many to live up to the Word of God or whatever else had been given to the people to help them to bring out the best in themselves and thus cause them to be good Christians. This is very meritorious, but you can readily see that today it is not the total answer for the overall picture of struggling humanity because they must also learn to awaken that inner God Kingdom. It is the awakening of this inner man, the Christ within, that becomes so all important.

"This that I have just said may mean but very little to many of those on earth; yet I say to each and every one that it most certainly should mean something to you. In the final analysis, this is the real purpose of life: to awaken the God Kingdom within. Of course, the God Kingdom itself is very much awake; I am only saying that you, the mortal self, must have that inner awakening.

"Millions of souls now indicate by their words and their actions how little they really know about life, although they may consider themselves to be intellects or learned persons. But the inner awakening will change all of this; it will become a stepping-stone to the Real and will enable that one to realize and observe many things. It will help to bring into focus the World of Reality, and it will eventually help all to understand that they have not begun to really live until they have left the physical phase of life and come into the etheric side of life to live *permanently.* All of you have come to the astral side of life many times, but yet you have not begun to live in Reality until you have no necessity for the physical vehicle or a need to live in the material world.

"Everyone will eventually ascend into this state whereby they will never again have to return to the earth. This is the destiny for all because there will come a time when the period of earning and learning in the physical aspect of life will be over. Ultimately all will ascend into the higher consciousness in time; and when the people of the earth have all moved into this category, there will be no need for even an astral world. This kingdom will then gradually become thinner, and in time it shall be no more as the entities of the earth plane evolve to a higher state of consciousness.

"But in the meantime, let me say to all of the disciples of the many Teachers of Light that if you stay on the path, walk in the light, then I can truly say that in these latter days, as troublesome as they are, it is possible for each disciple at the present stage of your growth to complete your 'tour of duty' and perhaps never again return to the physical plane.

"Our evolving has been slow, through eons and eons of time, in birth and rebirth, again and again. In each life we chip away a bit of the corrosion that engulfs the soul, and in this chipping process we learn some new small lesson. And now, blessed disciples, I salute you in your Grand Finale. Yes, if you walk in this light, if you stay on the path and are determined in your striving, if you fulfill and carry out your mission or complete that which you are supposed to complete—it could be almost anything as each individual responsibility is completely different—then be joyful in the understanding that this life of yours could indeed be *your* Grand Finale!

"If I had returned just 1,000 years ago, I could not have said what I have said to you tonight for the end of the cycle would not then have been complete. And so until we meet on the inner planes, I will say to you all, Manzaholla."

NOTES

1. Andrew Jackson Davis, *The Principles of Nature* (Boston, Colby & Rich, 1847)

2. Israel Regardie, *The Golden Dawn* (Chicago, The Aries Press, 1937)

3. Aleister Crowley, *Magical and Philosophical Commentaries on The Book of the Law* (Montreal, Canada: 93 Publishing Co., Edited by Symonds and Grant, 1974)

4. Harold W. Percival, *Thinking and Destiny* (New York, The Word Publishing Co., 1946)

5. Harold W. Percival, *The Word* (New York, Theosophical Publishing Co., 25 Volumes, 1905)

6. Manly Palmer Hall, *Encyclopedic Outline of Masonic, Hermetic, Quabbalistic and Rosicrucian Symbolical Philosophy* (Los Angeles, Philosophical Res. Soc., 1928)

7. Geoffrey Hodson, *Fairies at Work and at Play* (London, Theosophical Pub. House, 1925)

8. Flower A. Newhouse, *Natives of Eternity* (Vista, Calif., Lawrence G. Newhouse, 1950)

9. Annie Besant and C. W. Leadbeater, *Occult Chemistry* (India, Theosophical Publishing House, 1951)

10. Arthur Edward Waite, *The Pictorial Key to the Tarot* (New York, University Books, 1910)

11. An excellent summary of the history of the exploration into consciousness for the past 5,000 years is given in the following volume by Jeffrey Mishlove. He also lists over 600 references covering the entire spectrum of philosophical thought. Jeffrey Mishlove, *The Roots of Consciousness* (New York, Random House Inc., 1975)

12. James Crenshaw, *Telephone Between Worlds* (Los Angeles, DeVorss & Co., 1950)